"Barth Anderson's inventive viral emergency may be set in a speculative near-future of saints and cyborgs, but it has a persuasive real-world urgency. He nails the gritty essence of disease detection: frustration, exhaustion, obsession."

—Maryn McKenna, author of *Beating Back the Devil:*
On the Front Lines with the Disease Detectives
of the Epidemic Intelligence Service

THE
PATRON SAINT
OF PLAGUES

Barth Anderson

BANTAM SPECTRA

THE PATRON SAINT OF PLAGUES
A Bantam Spectra Book / April 2006

Published by Bantam Dell
A Division of Random House, Inc.
New York, New York

Book design by Helene Berinsky

Library of Congress Cataloging in Publication Data
Anderson, Barth.
The patron saint of plagues / Barth Anderson.
p. cm.
ISBN-13: 978-0-553-38358-4
ISBN-10: 0-553-38358-2
1. Center for Disease Control—Fiction. 2. Epidemics—Fiction.
3. Viruses—Fiction. 4. Virologists—Fiction.
5. Mexico City (Mexico)—Fiction. 6. Science fiction.
PS3601.N46 P37 2006
0604 2005059107

Printed in the United States of America
Published simultaneously in Canada

www.bantamdell.com

BVG 10 9 8 7 6 5 4 3 2 1

This book is dedicated to Jack Anderson and Robin Barringer, consummate travelers of Mexico and two fine fathers who left before anyone was ready for them to go; Greg Thompson and his unflagging friendship; and especially to Lisa Stuart. This book is your hard work as much as it is mine. I treasure you, my love.

ACKNOWLEDGMENTS

If it takes a village to raise a kid, then it takes a couple villages and a scattering of tribes to write a novel. I absolutely must acknowledge and thank:

- Clarion '98, an exceptional group of writers and critics.
- My two writers groups, who struggled through various iterations of this book: Karma Weasels (Paula Fleming, Manfred Gabriel, David J. Hoffman-Dachelet, Burke Kealey, Kelly McCullough, Lyda Morehouse) and the Ratbastards (Christopher Barzak, Alan DeNiro, and Kristin Livdahl).
- Also, James Patrick Kelly, who foresaw what the original short story might be, Mark Wicklund for Spanish language advice and careful editing, and Maureen McHugh for inspiration and friendship.
- Jesse Vogel and Kristopher O'Higgins of Scribe Agency. This book wouldn't have seen the light of day without them.
- My editor, Juliet Ulman, a wise, wise woman.
- Melissa Birch, Cindra Halm, Jim Handrigan, Jen Connell, Ian Handrigan, Rachael Hoffman-Dachelet, Midori Snyder, Jennette Turner, Amy and Hank Wicklund.
- All the members of my far-ranging blood, step-, and in-law families. You are legion, and naming each of you would take a book in itself. But I must especially thank Bonnie Anderson, who never stopped believing in me, and Isaiah, who snapped my life into focus.

I'd like to acknowledge the major sources of my research: *A Dancing Matrix* by Robin Marantz Henig (Vintage Books), *Immunology* by Ivan Roitt, Jonathan Brostoff, and David Male (Gower Medical Publishing), and *Holy Terrors: Latin American Women Perform* by Diana Taylor and Roselyn Constantino (Duke University Press). Problems with my book's various speculations should be traced to me, however, not these fine scholars.

THE
PATRON SAINT
OF PLAGUES

PROLOGUE

"*I HIJACKED a live remote to Puebla,*" said the voice behind the plastic pirate mask, its eye patch and gold teeth leering from the old-fashioned broadcast monitor. "*So assuming my link stays hot for the next sixty seconds, we'll go live to Sister Domenica at 8:00 P.M. sharp.*"

Adjusting the antenna on the ancient set that they had picked up on the street, the man said, "Good?"

"Good." Dolores grinned and shucked her bright yellow dress. "Pirate is still jabbering. We haven't missed her."

The man telescoped and untelescoped the antenna. He'd never seen such an old television, and the scientist in him wanted to examine it.

"*While the uplink heats up,*" Pirate said, "*let me remind you that Sister Domenica will be at the Basilica this Sunday the fifteenth at 1:00 P.M. delivering a sermon on the pending Reconquest of Texas.*"

"Where *is* Pirate?"

"Usually here in Ascensión," Dolores said. "But he moves around Mexico depending on where he can steal uplinks. The *servicio sagrado* has been after him for years. It looks like we have a few minutes. *Ven, macho.*"

When he returned to bed, Dolores, hair smelling of oranges, crushed herself against him. She was a small, broad-hipped prostitute who wore cosmetics to lighten her complexion, but beneath it, she was a dark *mestiza* woman. That's what had attracted him at the Italian restaurant where he'd found her smoking at the bar. She was like a butterfly under glass to him. "What's your native background, *chica*?" he'd asked. "Nahua, yes?"

Dolores tapped her cigarette. *Mestizos* didn't usually enjoy talking about their native roots, if they knew them at all. "Go to the euro zone, if you want a *blanca*."

"I don't want a white girl," he said, noting the shape of her nose. *Mestizo,* sure—most in Mexico were—but he took great pride in being able to identify Indian stock. "Is your family from the Central Highlands? Michoacán, maybe?"

"When you're good, you're good." She seemed offended but clearly didn't want him to slip away. Though nearly fifty, her admirer was well dressed and distractingly handsome. Dolores smiled but frowned with her eyes. "I grew up in Pátzcuaro."

A *mazahua,* probably. The man bought Dolores a drink and held her hand in both of his. She melted against him at the bar while he surreptitiously took her pulse, finding an athletic at-rest heart rate. *"Princesa,"* he said, looking her up and down, "you're the girl for me."

"OK. I'll be your girl tonight," Dolores whispered, "but I got to watch the nun while we do it. You can buy a cheap set on Reforma."

With a furtive show of fingers they haggled on a price. Then the man pressed his lips to hers.

Finally. It was happening. In his wonder, the man heard a redemptive chorus, like *Oedipus at Colonus*, a thunderous fleet of angels taking wing in triumph.

"We're on?" said Pirate, speaking to someone offscreen. *"Thank God for US garbage satellites!"*

Dolores felt so ripe and strong in his hands he couldn't stop examining her body. He ran his fingertips along her throat, delicately tracing across the lymph nodes below her jaw—not yet swollen. "Are you hot, *querida*?"

"Oh, very hot for your *pinga, papi*, I want—"

He grabbed her chin, hard. "Don't talk like that." Before he could stop himself, he had her throat.

Dolores didn't flinch, but her eyes were round over his clenching hand. "My fault, *papi*. My fault." She touched the crucifix hanging around his neck. "I can see you're a good Catholic."

He was grateful that she noticed and softened into his physician voice, releasing his grip. "Do you have a fever, *querida*?"

Dolores blinked her lashes and smiled. "No, I'm very clean, I promise."

"The link is hot!" Pirate said. *"Let's go live to Puebla, Mexico—just outside Ascensión—and the Convent of the Virgin of the Americas."*

Dolores broke away from him and stretched across the bed to turn up the volume.

The camera zoomed in close on a woman in her thirties, perhaps older. Her irises were ink-dark, and she had a big, horsy smile and barrettes holding back her hair. *"Hail Mary, full of grace, Virgin of Guadalupe. Blessed art thou among women of the Americas. Blessed be the fruit of thy womb, Jesus the Conquistador."*

The man went tense with rage. He was old enough that he remembered when Ascensión was still called Mexico City, back when Jesus was a shepherd not a conqueror. Before the dictator and his vicious political machine, the Holy Renaissance, came to power. The man's hand was again clenched in a fist, he noticed. He deliberately laid it flat on Dolores's thigh. "Who is that woman?"

Dolores watched the television with lustful eyes. "Sister Domenica. Pirate discovered her."

"Wipe our tears, Maria, and give us comfort and assistance. Bring us faith. Help us to believe." Sister Domenica opened her eyes, and said, *"Tonight, the woman in white came to me during vespers."*

Dolores crawled to the man over the bed. "That's what she calls the Virgin Mary. The woman in white. The Virgin tells her things, shows her the future. Domenica predicted the eruption of Popocatépetl last year and now everyone listens to her." She unbuttoned the man's pants and tugged them down. "She's ours. Our saint."

While Dolores kissed her way across his stomach, he stared into the nun's potent gaze. She seemed to peer right into this room.

Dolores reached over him for the condom-spray from the nightstand, contraband that she insisted on using. "A Mexican saint," said Dolores and spritzed his growing erection. She stroked him while the spray and the man hardened. "This nun is powerful. Look at her. It's in her eyes. God chose her for us."

"I'd just finished my prayers," Sister Domenica said, *"when the Virgin came out of the shadows in the chapel."*

Dolores swung a leg over his chest so they both faced the television. "She's a prophetess. Look at her. Ah. Ah. She's from Jesus Himself."

With those words, the man removed the tiny cross from around his neck, hooking it on the nightstand's drawer.

The nun tilted her chin and, speaking directly into the camera, said, *"The woman in white told me something that every Mexican should know."*

"Yes, Sister. Tell us." Dolores leaned back on her hands, arching her back as though offering her breasts to God, then slid herself onto the man with a sigh.

Without his crucifix, he felt overly aware of what was happening in the room, his every sense aflame. This prostitute was gasping, dying, a corpse astride his body. He let out a tortured groan.

The nun bowed her head over folded hands. *"Because she loves us and cares about us, she begged God to allow her to tell me—to tell you this message. To warn mothers who love their children—"*

The man clamped shut his eyes.

"Mexico," murmured Sister Domenica, *"is about to be tested."*

"Oh, God, that's good," said Dolores, grinding her hips with greater purpose now. Her body trembled hard and she shook her thick hair, filling the room with the smell of oranges and sweat.

"The woman in white told me that some will be strengthened by the test. But many, maybe millions, will be broken by it."

As though stirred by this thought, Dolores's patter stopped, her rhythm hitched. She leaned back, put a palm on his wide chest, and ground against him, as though grinding him and the prophecy into her. "Tested. Yeah. That's good."

Sister Domenica said, *"This test, my friends, will come to Mexico in the form of a devastating plague."*

The man gripped Dolores's wide hips. His body locked. He tried to open his eyes, tried to look at the television, but he shuddered hard.

How in the world could the nun know such a thing?

Groggy, he opened his eyes. The room had gone cool blue, Pirate's uplink snuffed to snow. He climbed out of bed and slipped his crucifix over his head, kissing it quickly. After moving Dolores's AZTECS, WE! jacket, he sat in the windowsill, and leaned his head of tight black curls against the window. The glass felt cold.

His room was on the uppermost floor, and from the window, he could see the volcanoes and mountains ringing the Valley of Mexico. All around him were the sparkling towers of La Alta, the gleaming spires that housed Ascensión's wealthiest. Hovering outside his window, the belly of a cloudboard read, *¡VIVA EL RENACIMIENTO!* "Long live the Renaissance!" A red-and-black swoop bus dove past his hotel window—probably taking rich *Altadores* down for a night of slumming in dusty, ground-level cantinas—below him, people jammed the wide sidewalks, while lanes glittered with bicycles. On La Reforma, the city's largest artery, a river of cars endlessly flowed in ten shimmering lanes of traffic.

The valley was only sixty kilometers across but it groaned under a teeming and burgeoning population, one-third the size of the United States.

In the hotel's narrow bed, Dolores moaned sleepily as she switched the channel and anxiously watched three men analyze the ramifications of another war with the US, which the dictator Emil Orbegón deemed inevitable now, as did the rival pope from Mexico, Cardinal de Veras. In the monitor's strobe of light, she scratched her chin.

The man noted her movement and crept slowly toward her. He could see pustules forming around her mouth in tiny, red eruptions—surprising as first shoots in spring. *Red flowers from my children,* he thought, eyes crinkling in wonder at Dolores. How hot was she now? Were her glands swelling yet? Was her abdomen distending?

Out of the corner of her eye, Dolores caught him staring at her. She rolled on her back to look at him, and said, "My arms really hurt, *papi.*"

That, he'd anticipated. He nodded as though she were a herald arriving on stage to deliver an aria of armies in motion, navies aweigh. "Just sleep, then, *princesa.*"

Dolores rolled over, scratching at her chin and lips.

He stood and stared out the hotel window at the gleaming chains of traffic in the night sky.

"Don't worry. I'm here," he whispered to the overwhelmed Valley of Mexico. "I'm here to save you."

PART
I

CHAPTER

vCaMV.

Mottled gold on green, like the shimmer of foil or the gleam on a sheen of motor oil, the plant looked unhealthy from stalk to leaves. Systemic cell death. Vein clearing and branding, which appeared as dark varicose veins shooting across withered leaves. Classic.

"This ain't happening," Stark said.

He scanned up the row, looking for more infected spinach plants. His grandfather's method of defense against vCaMV was to change up the varieties throughout the rows, planting no two plants of the same variety within ten feet of each other, which made for jagged, uneven growth and shaggy rows. Had the method broken down here? Stark could see the Bloomsdale spinaches, the Olympia, the Sailorman, de Wilde Savoy, and the Oklahoma Green, alternating through the rows. To outsiders, the seemingly haphazard plan looked like madness, but "gold mold," as the array of variants of cauliflower mosaic virus was commonly called, had never appeared here.

Adjusting his straw fedora to block the sun, Stark knelt and clipped a small leaf from the young spinach and slipped it into his field press.

"May 15," he said to the press, as it sighed nitrogen, enclosed the sample, and consulted with the NIA satellite.

A moment later, the field press confirmed the obvious. vCaMV was here, on this farm, the place he grew up.

He stood and looked across Nissevalle Valley. The greenhouses had been emptied of sprouts, and fields were planted and primed for summer storms and sun. For nearly two decades, farms from Alberta to Chihuahua had battled seasonal vCaMV outbreaks for meager yields. Gold mold was known to sweep through whole regions in a single season, like a slow-motion prairie fire. But it had never come to Nissevalle. This *quop* was poised for another very profitable year, and losing shares now would be a disaster. Spinach rippled with passes of May breeze, and so did the corn, low and fluttering. Field hands in hats like Stark's weaved through the young crops as tillers dogged behind, maneuvering through the tomatoes on preprogrammed weeding missions. The idyllic haze of Nissevalle Farm suddenly looked like so much rot.

"Jesus," he whispered. "It really here."

After eighteen years away from this farm, Henry David Stark was still getting himself apace with death's routine visits here. It was one thing to behold it in a hot zone, or an anonymous hospital, but another entirely to see death pass between the paddocks and hay barns of his childhood. Yesterday morning in the creamery, loud with lowing and meowing and the mechanical gasp of milkers, a heavy-headed cow swung her face away from bright headlights shooting suddenly through the dawn's fog and stepped backwards with a stomping hoof, catching a small kitten unawares. Stark had cried out, trying to scare the cat from danger. But blink. Gone. Then, last night in the goat barn, Stark watched as three kids, slick with blood, slid out of their nanny's body, but without so much as a kick, or even a breath. Stark was surprised how such small passings troubled him, after what he'd seen in, say, China's Borna outbreak. But he'd left the CDC's Special Pathogens Unit to take charge of its Surveillance and Response Central Command two years ago, in order to distance himself from death's rhythms. In bringing the Central Command (that is, himself) to the co-op farm last January, it was inevitable that he'd synchronize himself with death—yet again.

The biggest rhythm of all, however, was the one that pounded straight to the brink—the farm's end. It was always there, that deadly rhythm—hail, a tornado, financial ruin—but as a boy, he never listened to it. Standing over the dying spinach plant, Stark felt that countless days on a farm could never make it ordinary.

As he began thumbing information about the spinach's variety and location into the field press, a stylized, red asterisk appeared before his eyes, eclipsing the LED display and his fingertips.

Bad timing.

His impulse was to shout across the spinach field to his grandfather, who was just now returning from disking up the green manure field on his International. But the field hands would hear, and most of them had lost their own farms to vCaMV. Yelling that he'd found gold mold would be like shouting *fire* in a burn ward. Instead, he took off his hat and waved it over his head.

The red asterisk pulsed across his vision again. Congo's yellow fever, probably. Maybe the vaccination program's net hadn't been cast wide enough, and Queen Mum was alerting him to the need for more stockpiles. Stark glanced at the field hands working their way toward the spinach fields. On a *quop* farm like this one, everyone was judged by their work. It had always been that way, even from Stark's childhood, when he couldn't wait to get out of the Junior League gardens and show that he could work with the adults. Even with the CDC calling for him, Stark didn't like leaving the field so soon after entering it.

Grandfather pulled up on the International Harvester he called Methuselah. A tall man, sturdy as a two-by-four, Grandfather's skin was so dark he seemed made of wood—and thanks to the krono he'd received in his forties, he looked half his ninety-one years. "What's shaking?" he said over the blatting engine, hands resting on the steering wheel. His heavy work gloves looked absurd with such skinny wrists sticking out of them.

"Shaking?" Stark shouted back. He rarely understood his grandfather's anachronisms. Or at least, he pretended not to.

"Did you find something?" Grandfather asked from atop the Harvester, older, even, than the man driving it.

The tractor wafted an enticing smell toward Stark: cut cover, a green and nourishing smell. Grandfather's cover crops of choice were buckwheat and oats, and he'd just tilled a field of them into the dirt, where they would compost and enrich the soil. Grandfather also claimed it was a defense against gold mold. Strong soil. Strong plants. Fewer diseases.

"Look, I hate to leave," said Stark, smelling green buckwheat as his grandfather cut the engine. "We all just started, but I got to check in with Mum."

While the tractor gave a protracted cough as it tried to fall silent, a red asterisk lit before Stark's eyes again. Red (as opposed to blue or yellow) usually meant that the Queen Mum was simply alerting him to an emergency.

But when Stark blinked at this one to clear his vision, an URGENT was waiting for him. He'd be able to read it on the interface in his contact lens's receiver, but he wouldn't be able to save the message or respond to it. It was a one-time shot. Whoever sent this message was desperate and had formatted it so that Stark would receive it without having to use his "brain gear"—a high-ranking official in a major health organization in dire need of speaking with Stark directly. While his grandfather slid down from the tractor on slow, rickety knees, Stark read the message.

> *Sunday 15 May URGENT, Attention Dr. Henry Stark, the Ministry of*
> *Well-being of the Holy Renaissance is not negotiating this outbreak with*
> *momentous etiquette.*

The message would only be available for a few moments, but he took the time to reread that. Even after a third read, the sentence still made no sense to him.

Grandfather realized that Stark wasn't paying attention to him. "What? Bad news?"

Stark didn't answer.

> *Minister Alejandro bore into the kingdom two WHO virologists, but they are*
> *commencing on untrue discoveries. This dengue is not dengue. It is not*
> *allocated by small flying beasts. Please touch me as soon as possible. I am the*
> *unique man witnessing reality. Urgent. Dr. Pedro Muñoz.*

Stark pursed his lips, frustrated. The Central Command's surveillance and response software was falling apart, obviously. "Look, I got to check in."

"I know that," Grandfather said, slipping off his gloves.

Stark gave a little astonished laugh. "How you know?"

"You start blinking hard right after you get your bat signal," said Grandfather, gloves in one hand, the other resting on his hip. "Plus, it's the only time I actually see you look nervous about anything."

Stark smiled. He liked that, though he imagined it wasn't the Code Red that made him look nervous. "Something else you should know," said Stark.

"Oh?"

How to say it? Was it possible to break such news *gently*? This was a model farm in many ways, from its Land Reform cooperative structure to its success against vCaMV. In the corner of his eye, the infected plant fluttered like a green fire. Finally, he simply handed Grandfather the field press. "It all in here."

Grandfather took the press without opening it. "Why a doctor of your caliber, upon whom the whole world depends, elects to speak like a back-woods hick is beyond me. Whatever happened to the verb 'to be,' anyway?" he said in a sour voice.

"It clumsy."

"'It is all in here.' Say it."

"'It *is* all in here,'" Stark said in a grand English accent, slipping half-heartedly into their old banter. His eyes flitted to the field press. "I got to go."

He turned and ran up the gravel drive to the manor, feeling as though he'd activated the timer on a grenade and shoved it in his grandfather's hands.

Nissevalle Manor was a four-story mansion built with Land Reform earnings ten years ago, and it housed the fifty-three working members of the *quop*. The house stood on a small bluff overlooking the farm's barns and sheds, the quilt of five-acre private fields, and the much larger, hundred-acre coop-erative fields sprawling against the southern hill faces in this valley.

Stark ran up the dirt road from the spinach field and past the penetrat-ing stench of the poultry barn, then yanked open the back door. From the spiral staircase, he could smell the posture-straightening scent of bacon fry-ing. Dalia the Kitchen Czarina was feeding the early crew down in the din-ing hall after their shift, and as he ascended the spiral staircase to the fourth floor, Stark could hear a friendly argument about milk prices in the first-floor buyer's den, someone singing (badly) in a shower, the whine of the house pooch, an e-phone ringing on the second floor, the three Wheeler kids speaking in their imaginary language, a tractor's sudden bleat from the barn, laughter, chimes, a dripping faucet.

The cacophony of home.

Stark's fourth-floor room looked west over the members' private fields. An afterthought of a cubbyhole in the unfinished, pinewood hall, it was icy in winter, broiling in summer, and Stark knew the *quop* had given it to him because nobody else wanted it.

He didn't complain. As a CDC administrator, Stark didn't bring much to the daily workings of a farm. Sure, he was an intern, a weeder when he wasn't sampling for vCaMV, but if he'd stayed here for the last twenty years instead of accepting the Junior League's scholarship for college when he was eighteen, he would have been a coordinator with years of experience in the *quop* by now. His choice of rooms. A senior share at profit disbursement. But now he always had one foot planted in the outside world—in the Congo, or in the vast urban outbreaks that blossomed from Kazakhstan to Kirkuk. Stark knew that he was occupying a space that might better be filled by a farmer, so small as his room was, he was grateful that the *quop* was willing to house him at all.

Stark opened his bedroom door and swung his canvas bag onto the floor, ready to grab his brain gear, park his rump in the rocking chair, and contact the Command Center's satellite.

But he stopped short, hand still on the doorknob, as he realized that someone was standing in the middle of his room. Half in surprise, half in greeting, Stark said, "Hey."

The stranger lifted his face, lit with a sudden flash of alarm. It was Earl, the new arrival from Baltimore—a big, strapping fellow with forearms the size of bread loaves. As their eyes met, Stark was about to step backwards into the hall, but Earl seemed more frightened of Stark. "Oh. Hello," he said. "I—"

"What going on?" said Stark. "Why you in my room?"

"Pardon me, please," said Earl, his bush of black hair bobbing as he took a step toward Stark and the door. "I think I in the wrong room."

Stark snorted in mockery. Everyone knew that new arrivals like Earl stayed with the nonmember interns in the first-floor dorm. With gold mold still wiping out farms every summer, even experienced field hands were lucky to get a membership here. "I think you knew you ain't in the right room." Stark's eyes darted to his brain gear, still dangling like a rubber squid on his rocker. Then his eyes shifted to his desk, where all the discs and his memboard sat, just as he'd left them last night. His only valuables hadn't been touched or taken. "What you want in here?"

Earl looked honestly shocked and embarrassed. "Nothing. I promise. I—" He took a step toward Stark and the door.

Stark blocked his way. "Come on. What you doin here? You didn't steal nothing that I can—"

"No. Search me if you like." Earl raised his hands. "I ain't no thief."

"Then what you want?"

Earl's face colored. "I met a girl. She told me she lived up on the fourth floor. I thought this was—"

"You lie good," Stark said. "But you lyin." His fists clenched in anger—and fear, as he contemplated what this huge man could do to him if things got rough. "You looking for the head of Surveillance and Response, ain't you. You reporting to someone overseas?"

It wasn't long, but Earl paused and blinked, and Stark knew that he'd hit the mark. "No, this girl said—"

"Well, you found me," said Stark. He spread his hands and let them flop to his sides. "Now what? You obviously don't want to interfere with me, or hurt me, or you'd a done it already. Might as well tell me who you're with."

Earl sighed and apparently decided he was done with the act and done with Stark, shoving him aside with a hard sweep of his arm.

"Go downstairs and pack up," Stark shouted at Earl's back, following him to the stairwell and yelling after the man as he ran down the steps. "Gonna see to it you get kicked out! Tonight!"

Earl picked up speed, running downstairs, but then he stopped and stuck his head into the center of the spiral staircase, looking up at Stark. "You think that scares me? You think I some homeless farmer looking for a handout from your grampa?"

"You the one runnin."

Earl grinned wolfishly up at him, and said, "I ain't the first to get inside your room, Dr. Stark of the CDC." Then he started trotting down the stairs again, saying, "And I won't be the last."

Earl's words hit Stark like a pan in the face, and he backed down the hall to his bedroom as if a ghost had floated up the spiral stairs at him. Stark had known this day would come. He knew he would eventually bump into one of the spooks sent by God knows who to monitor his location, activity, field of research. Victoria told him—when he'd moved Surveillance and Response from the CDC headquarters in Atlanta—that the world's various intelligence services would have to come looking for him, just to know, just to have it on record where the head of Surveillance and Response was "secretly" located.

But even with that warning, even knowing that Earl would leave before Stark could explain to the *quop* that he was a spy, he still felt invaded, vulnerable. He slipped back into his room and shut the door, chest heaving in breathless fright. "When the last time you got accessed?" Stark said, turning to ask the memboard.

Its display lit and the first notes of Bach's third Brandenburg Concerto chimed. "Eleven-fifteen this morning," it told him.

So Earl had turned it on. "And when you last logged off?"

"Eleven-seventeen."

Ten minutes ago. Stark went to his desk and examined his memboard, but nothing had been opened. As far as Stark could tell, Earl had simply turned it on, looked, and turned it off. Not that it mattered, really, since Stark had nothing worth spying on. If Earl had been sent by a foreign power, all he could tell them was that Stark was working on a joint project between the CDC and the National Institutes of Agronomy and that Stark's grandfather was a hell of a farmer. Perhaps Stark's work on gold mold was of interest abroad, but he doubted it. Though nine years of continuous outbreaks made it a crippling problem, gold mold was a uniquely American phenomenon.

Stark walked over to his rocker, examined his brain gear—nothing missing. Nothing sabotaged that he could see.

His adrenaline still coursing, Stark reminded himself that he had far more important things to worry about than boys playing spy.

Then he walked to his door and slipped the little hook lock into its eye. For the first time in his life, as a boy or a grown man, Stark had locked the door of his *quop* room.

CHAPTER

STARK PICKED UP his brain gear, as most people in the house called his computer hardware, fidgeted with the tags, then stuck them to the skin over his right eyebrow, and slipped the goggles over his eyes. He sat down in his rocker and, when settled, uttered a single word. "Go."

A hundred kilometers above the Galapagos Islands, the CDC's Command Center satellite heard Stark's voice. His specs thrummed and the fiber-optic thread that encircled his contact lenses ignited to life. His optic nerve was tricked to the will of the AI on that satellite, and a screen seemed to appear against the bare north wall of Stark's room. SURVEILLANCE/RESPONSE CENTRAL COMMAND, it read. Below the seals of the CDC and World Health Organization, came the warning, PREPARE FOR G-SCAN.

Stark waited for the AI to identify him. The generic interface read Stark's genome and vanished, then Queen Mum intoned in her cool English accent, "Dr. Stark, were you able to read the urgent message from Mexico's Zapata Hospital?"

He took a deep breath. Getting connected like this caused a mild dopamine flush, which helped counter the last shudders of adrenaline from finding Earl in his room. "I read it," Stark said, "but it got mistranslated. Know why?"

There was a slight pause. With most of the CDC's funding coming from the European Union, the AI's Norwegian engineers had anticipated that a European epidemiologist would head the Central Command, so the AI's

English was British. After two years, the rinky-dink AI still had a hard time
with Stark's Mississippi River accent. "Multiple translations through various
postal AIs mangled it, to be sure," Queen Mum said. "It arrived via a
Namibian server. The message is gone, but the path it took to reach you is
still available."

"That doctor wanted me to contact him soon as possible."

"Not advisable."

"Yeah, I know."

Looking for the Urgent's path among his notes, Stark scanned the incoming reports, a collation of information from 158 WHO country offices,
190 Ministries of Health, 200 WHO Collaborating Centers, eighty sentinel
"Listening Posts," 190 disease control centers, and from various mednets
around the planet. This list was his "row to hoe," a filtered list of sites and
events over which he and the Queen Mum maintained a diligent watch:

- Health Impact of Earthquake in Sino-Jakarta
- Control and Surveillance of Communicable Disease among Texas
  Refugees
- Influenza. Cairo, Pan-Islamic Federation
- vCaMV. Monocropping farms, USA
- Dengue Fever. Ascensión, Holy Republic of Mexico
- Chagas Disease. Venezuela, Holy Republic of Mexico
- Cholera. Volgograd, Russo-Islamic DMZ
- HIV. Sino-Sydney
- Dengue Fever. Ascensión, Holy Republic of Mexico

"Queen Mum, why didn't you filter out the redundant Mexican report?"

"The reports are not identical," said Queen Mum, "and therefore not redundant."

"Who filed them?"

"One is the Urgent you read from Zapata Hospital in Ascensión, Mexico.
The other is from the Holy Renaissance's Central Command."

Helping Mexico with dengue was like helping Amsterdam with the clap.
His inclination was to pass this off to the Special Pathogens net, or even the
Tropical Disease Task Force. "Show me Mexico's Central Command report,
then."

15 May, '61, Zapata Hospital in Ascensión DF reports an outbreak of dengue fever. Twelve patients, three fatalities. All twelve patients reside in central, lower Ascensión. With the rainy season beginning, Mexico's Ministry of Health is taking steps to fumigate for Aedes aegypti. *Our own Special Pathogens Branch has been alerted to the outbreak. Dr. Miguel Cristóbal, National Institute's Central Command, Holy Republic of Mexico.*

Vanilla. Three deaths were considerable for dengue, but not catastrophic. "So who sent the Urgent, the one about the flying beasts?"

"Dr. Pedro Muñoz, Staff Epidemiologist, Zapata Hospital."

Stark swore. "A *staff* doctor figured out how to send me an Urgent?" He didn't have a copy of the message anymore, only a record that he'd been contacted, but the odd Urgent still thrummed in his thoughts:

Minister Alejandro bore into the kingdom two WHO virologists, but they are commencing on untrue discoveries.

This dengue is not dengue.

I am the unique man witnessing reality. Pedro Muñoz.

In retrospect, the message was obviously unauthorized—a scary gambit on this fellow Muñoz's part if Mexico's notorious *servicio sagrado* ever traced it to him. But Stark imagined he would do the same if he thought the powers-that-be were *commencing on untrue discoveries.* He couldn't help but admire Muñoz for it. "Which WHO physicians in Mexico on the dengue case?"

"Dr. Jacques Girard and Dr. Claire du Monde filed reports from Ascensión yesterday." She pronounced the names in pitch-perfect French, just as she had properly pronounced the Spanish name *Ascensión* with four, precise syllables.

Stark knew the names Girard and du Monde. *Good reputations. No problem there.* Muñoz mentioned Minister Alejandro in his Urgent. Diego Alejandro was a fellow student of Stark's in Oaxaca—a neighborhood *vato* who had gone on to become a beloved professor at Las Universidades Unidos de Oaxaca and a frequent volunteer in Mexico's emergency epidemic teams. Though Diego was the Minister of Health now, a bureaucrat in the murky church-state of Mexico's Holy Renaissance, perhaps he still had enough *vato* in him to tell Stark what was really happening in Ascensión. "Mum, find a private phone or message service for Minister Diego Alejandro, please."

"Finding the Minister of Health will require maneuvering around Mexico's satellite embargo on the US—a violation of international law."

"You the tool for the job, Mum. Go."

While a rectangle of sunlight slid across his bedroom floor, Queen Mum tried Stark's CDC override codes. All of them had been blocked, so Queen Mum tried an old medical hotline established before the rise of the Holy Renaissance some thirty years ago. The Mexican AIs that were enforcing the satellite embargo adjusted and severed her line. Mum did manage one connection to the Central Command in Mexico's National Institute of Health, but the Command's AI was so fast that Stark received the Holy Republic's entire embargo document (all forty-thousand words) before he could say *"Buenas tardes."*

Finally, Queen Mum found a path into Mexico through the World Health Organization's AI in Copenhagen linked to the Holy Republic of Quebec.

"I altered our code so that we appear to be a vaccine supply company," said Queen Mum. "This violates twelve paragraphs of the embargo."

"Go."

It took almost thirty minutes, but, finally, the eagle-and-snake seal of Mexico appeared before Stark's eyes and a deep, male voice spoke in his ear. *"Inteligentsia Artificial del Ministerio de Salud Publica, para servirle."*

Stark suddenly realized he would have to speak Spanish to pull this off. Interning in Oaxaca, Stark's Spanish had been quite good, but it had rusted over the last decade. His ability to lie smoothly to bureaucrats, however, hadn't. "Good evening, I'm Dr. Vincent Bergara with Viral Intercept International. I desire to speak at—pardon me—*with* Dr. Diego Alejandro of the—"

"The Minister is unavailable," said the buttery voice. "His office switchboard is completely occupied and he is currently attending a conference at Zapata Hospital."

Stark adjusted his goggles with curiosity. So Diego was personally handling this outbreak. Unusual. "What is the name of the conference he attends, please?"

"The Holy Renaissance's Emergency Conference on Dengue Outbreak, 2061."

Anticipating Stark's need, Queen Mum showed him several press releases and a document of the conference's agenda, along with a link to live multicoverage. Stark blinked at it.

Immediately he was given a grainy, badly lit shot of Mexico's Minister of Health. Silvering hair and sagging eyes, Diego hovered against Stark's pinewood walls. "Diego, *vato,* you belong at a poker table, not a press conference."

Stark tried to understand how he was seeing what he was seeing. He'd heard of Mexico's *ojo* reporters and their cybernetically implanted camera-eyes. But this looked like a run-of-the-mill netcast. Alejandro was standing in a hospital hallway fielding questions from two men before him, one with a microphone and one standing stiff, his blank, lidless eyes fixed on the Minister with catlike intensity. Shadows on the wall behind Diego suggested people crowding behind the camera, out of view. "How we viewing this? Through someone's eyes?"

"No. We are viewing this through the DVB camera of *Para Ustedes*, La Baja's Finest Net News, though *ojos* from other news media are present. *Para Ustedes* has been covering the outbreak in Zapata Hospital nonstop since 4:00 A.M., Ascensión time." La Baja was Ascensión's street level, and La Alta was the city balanced atop kilometer-high towers. Ascensión was so enormous it had become a schizophrenic city with two economies, two technologies, two distinct populations—a depressed, twentieth-century city below and a dynamic, wealthy, and futuristic marvel above.

Stark watched as the reporter with the microphone asked his question. "What do you say about the theory that Big Bonebreaker is *not* dengue fever?"

The stiff, round-eyed *ojo* glared at Diego throughout the other reporter's question.

"Not enough evidence to support that," said a woman offscreen.

The digital camera zoomed back and Stark recognized Dr. Elena Batista, a well-coiffed woman with an angry amount of mascara—Diego's longtime attack dog. "After the field teams brief the Minister, we'll understand the virus better," Batista said, "but we're certain that 'Big Bonebreaker' is a particularly deadly strain of dengue."

"Mum, reference. Big Bonebreaker?"

"It's a slang name for the disease coined by a dengue sufferer four hours ago. Wide usage across the entire Holy Renaissance is noted."

Of course Mexico would already have a nickname coined for this disease. Users on Mexico's advanced *pilone* net could culturally digest and spread slang fast as thought, so, nationwide, fads could burn and peak, from Tijuana to Caracas, in days. Mexico's *pilone* culture seemed like the be-witchments of a hellish machine to a backwoods American like Stark, but he'd witnessed Mexico make national changes in viral response in moments, too, changes that would have taken America months, even years. All thanks to the *pilone* net.

The robotlike *ojo* reporter looked almost menacing alongside Diego Alejandro's handsome, charming self. "Eight dead since this morning," said the *ojo*. "This virulence is unusual for a dengue outbreak, no, Minister?"

"Eight dead? Cristóbal told us three." Stark pounded the arms of his rocker with both fists. "Mum, I need updates *as they arrive!*"

"I've had no updates to give you, Doctor. All information on dengue has been classified by the Mexican Ministry of Health."

"They classified an outbreak?" Stark felt a growing heaviness in his chest. "The hell going on down there?"

The *ojo* was asking, "Do you believe this virus has mutated beyond the reach of dengue's traditional tetravalent vaccine, Dr. Batista?"

"I see Dr. Muñoz has been preaching to the press. *Again.*" Batista stabbed someone with a glance offscreen. "This is dengue—not Ebola or Marburg or skid-37. The tetravalent vaccine has been our chief weapon against the virus for decades. There is no need for alarm."

The *Para Ustedes* reporter with the mic turned away from Batista. "Comment, Dr. Muñoz?"

The frame of view edged to the right and revealed a tall, gangly man in need of a haircut standing behind the *ojo*. He looked like a kind fellow, with his long face and careful eyes. "Dr. Pedro Muñoz. The unique man witnessing reality," said Stark.

Without looking at Batista, Pedro Muñoz leaned toward the reporter with the microphone, and said, "Ask her about the chickens."

The reporter seemed surprised to have a question aimed at him. "Pardon me?"

Muñoz was quite tall and hunched his shoulders when he spoke. "Ask her, 'Have you looked at the chickens, and if so, how do you interpret them?'"

The reporter looked back and forth between Muñoz and Batista—one smiling kindly at him, the other glaring with hot eyes. Finally, he pointed the mic at Batista. "Comment on the chickens, Doctor?"

The reporter obviously didn't know what the significance of the chickens was. But Stark did. As soon as Muñoz mentioned them, he ordered Mum to bring up Ascensión's chicken report.

In the previous century, epidemiologists would place chicken coops on the outskirts of cities to monitor the spread of viruses like St. Louis encephalitis or Asian flu that affected both chickens and humans. Modern, sophisticated Central Commands, like the CDC's, WHO's, and Mexico's, collated data from millions of epidermal chips placed in the forearms of human volunteers throughout a given population. These chips, called "chickens," ran identification and quantitative assays of specific antibodies present in a given individual's blood. Because a body creates a specific T cell for each new virus it meets, an epidemic could be spotted before symptoms were ever exhibited, or before victims began to appear in hospitals. When they identified the popular presence of certain antibodies, these epidermal assays would alert the Central Command, and public health agents could identify the emerging disease from that information.

Stark scanned Ascensión's chicken report and saw that a vast but silent dengue epidemic was passing through town.

Batista answered the question patiently, though her eyes seemed to be cooking inside her head. "Dr. Muñoz is referring to the fact that Ascensión's line of sentinel volunteers, or 'chickens,' show a seroprevalence of 68 percent for IgG antidengue in the capital city."

To the reporter, Muñoz explained, "That means seven of ten people have already contracted Big Bonebreaker."

"Dr. Muñoz, please," said Batista. "It means the population of Ascensión is already *defeating* the virus."

With a nod of encouragement, Muñoz said, "Now ask about the vaccination program. Ask why it hasn't been mobilized as the staff epidemiologist recommended in his report."

"That *very* unofficial report," said Batista to Muñoz, "was concocted by a quack doctor without hot labs, without septic suits."

Muñoz patted the reporter on the back. "I'm the quack. M-U-Ñ-O-Z."

Stark laughed. He liked this guy already.

The stiff-backed *ojo* reporter took a step toward Batista, and said, "Couldn't the CDC's Central Command help with a vaccination program?"

Pedro Muñoz's eyes lifted with what looked like hope.

"We've contacted the CDC as a matter of courtesy, of course," Diego said. Then, to Stark's amazement, the Minister stole a page from the Holy

Renaissance's propaganda to make his point. "But we Anahuacs can handle this outbreak just fine on our own, and vaccination will soon be under way," he said, with a winning wink. "Now, let my assistants brief me before our field team arrives." Alejandro led Batista and two other doctors into the conference room.

Anahuacs. Diego used to laugh at people who bought that revisionist Mexican history from President for Life Emil Orbegón. "Diego deliberately deviating from the traditional outbreak script. He praying this normal dengue. Ain't like him."

Sound from the camera went dead. The netcast shifted over to a medical analyst; but Stark, wanting to see who was on the field team when they arrived, elected to keep his point of view with the stationary camera at the hospital. Though there was no audio, that camera, still uplinked and showing a hallway of doctors and reporters, might show the field team when it arrived, and Stark wanted to see who was on it. Meanwhile, he opened Muñoz's vita, and under the doctor's name and address, an e-phone was listed. "Can you get a phone line, Mum?"

"Quite easily done."

"Call the number listed here on Muñoz's résumé."

Queen Mum pronounced, "With the Minister of Health holding a conference at Zapata Hospital, a call to the staff epidemiologist could be construed as a serious breach of the Mexican embargo."

"Probably. But Mexico gonna break that embargo and call me before the day's over. Can't wait for that. Dial."

Stark watched on the netcast window, as far away in Ascensión, Pedro Muñoz looked down at his breast pocket. He removed an e-phone and cleared his throat. "¿Bueno?" The audio on the netcast feed had been shut off. Stark heard Muñoz through the e-phone line, a richer, more realistic connection.

"Buenas noches, Dr. Muñoz," said Stark. "Esto es Dr. Henry David Stark de los Estados Unidos. This is quite a show you're putting on for us."

Muñoz straightened as if a teacher were calling on him in class, then his eyes landed on the DVB camera. On-screen, it looked to Stark as if Muñoz had suddenly noticed him across a crowded room. For a moment, Muñoz looked like someone who'd had a heavy pack lifted from his back. But then he stiffened. "You shouldn't have called me. I'm in enough trouble as it is."

Stark was aghast as the line went dead, and on-screen, Muñoz folded up his phone, putting it back in his pocket. "Mum, redial! Quick!"

"Straightaway, Dr. Stark."

The phone rang. On-screen, Muñoz rolled his eyes and looked back at the camera. He shook his head.

"Let it ring, Mum!"

Muñoz looked about and finally pulled the phone out of his pocket again. "Dr. Stark, please, this conference is going to last all day and probably all night, and I—" He covered the phone with his other hand. On-screen, he looked like just another doctor in the crowded hallway. "This hospital is crawling with *servicio sagrado*. I can't be caught talking to you."

The hiss of fear he heard in Muñoz's voice snared Stark, stopped him. Mexico's secret police. Americans had heard rumors about the jungle camps located in undisclosed regions of Mexico's Honduras province, the terrifying spas where the "sick and abnormal" (dissidents) were "cured" (genetically reformed into model citizens) by the *servicio sagrado*. "I know it must be danger," stammered Stark. "I mean, dangerous. But please tell me what you know about this virus."

An intense look tightened the skin on Muñoz's face. He seemed to be reviewing his strategy for survival. "Can you get ahold of Ascensión's chicken report?"

"I have it right here," said Stark, blinking up the document.

"You do?" said Muñoz. He seemed surprised and tapped the zigzag brain surgery scar on his temple. "You aren't connected to the *pilone* net, are you?"

"No, it's fiber optics," muttered Stark, humiliated. "Cyber-goggles."

"Goggles. I see." Muñoz smiled. He looked like a grown-up encouraging a kid with his first two-wheeler. "Take a look at the chickens from a week ago, Dr. Stark."

Stark blinked through the document, pulling up the antibody numbers from May 8. He scanned the columns of various seroprevalences: a mild flu strain, high macrophage counts for what was no doubt a tainted water supply in La Baja, but no dengue antibodies. He blinked up the report from six days ago, then five days ago. It was the same thing, no dengue. Stark muttered in English, "Damn odd. No dengue antibodies five days ago?" It took four days for a body to create its specific immune response to dengue. With a current seroprevalence of sixty-eight percent, Stark should have seen a steady climb in dengue antibodies starting with this report at the latest. He pulled up the report from four days ago, and here the chickens began detecting dengue. Three days ago, antibodies to dengue started spiking, and by Saturday night, citywide seroprevalence for dengue had skyrocketed. "Only yesterday?" Stark read. "Sixty-eight percent of the population has dengue as of *yesterday*?"

Muñoz said, "And the Ministry of Health says mosquitoes did that."

Stark cleared his dry throat. "So four days ago—Wednesday—a virulent pathogen started spreading through the population of Ascensión. That's what you think?"

"I quarantined all of the dengue patients as soon as I got the fifth one at noon," said Muñoz. "Minister Alejandro got wind of the quarantine and before anyone even consulted me, I was taken off the Outbreak Task Force. I went from being the resident dengue authority to renegade crackpot."

Questions began flocking in his mind, but Stark couldn't take his eyes off the chicken report. "Dengue isn't this communicable. Is that why you say the virus mutates?"

Muñoz glanced at the doctors nearest him, presumably to see if anyone was eavesdropping. "My tests show a high mutation rate, yes."

Stark shook his head, though with these numbers, Muñoz had a legitimate theory. "It could be an emergent, too."

Muñoz made a scoffing noise at the back of his throat. "Emergent viruses *emerge,* Doctor. They don't fly in through the doors and windows."

"But that's what we could be seeing here. It's not like you're losing fifty people per day," said Stark. "Emergents almost always register on the chickens without anyone beyond the medical community even knowing it."

"But with a 35 percent mutation rate?" said Muñoz.

Muñoz had actually run tests while he hadn't, so Stark demurred. "Do you think it's a mutated form of dengue, or something else?"

"It *looks* like dengue."

"Do you have any—what's the word—facts? Truth? Proof. Do you have proof?"

"Yes," said Muñoz, "but the genome print of this virus is classified. I saw it. It's lean. The virus's shell looks like dengue-4, even under the DA scope, but its genome is half the length it should be."

"What? Classified," said Stark, playing dumb. "What do you mean it's classified? Who classified it?"

"The Ministry of Health," said Muñoz, risking a glance into the silent stationary camera through which Stark was watching him, and his voice was heavy with suppressed outrage. "The Ministry of Health."

"Diego did it?" Stark couldn't believe what he was hearing. "No, someone else must have—"

"Try to access my report. Try to access *any* record from this hospital from before noon today."

Stark gave Mum the order, but she hesitated. "We're disguised as a commercial server, Dr. Stark. Holy Renaissance authorities will certainly wonder why we're attempting to access a Mexican hospital's records, especially if they happen to be classified."

Queen Mum was a powerful tool, but Stark wished he could get someone to write a Lying Protocol for her. "One moment please, Doctor," said Stark. "Mum, contact Zapata Hospital and ask for information on bio-haz waste removal for Sunday May 15."

A moment later, Queen Mum presented Stark with an image of a signed Ministry of Health Quarantine of Information document, transposed over his room's ratty blue carpet. "'Quarantine of Information,'" scoffed Stark. And there, on the bottom of the form, was Diego Alejandro's florid signature. "Why quarantine records just hours into an outbreak? Any idea, Muñoz?"

"I'm not dumb enough to speculate on a phone line with an American." Muñoz showed the camera his back. His voice in the phone was urgent and demanding. "But what's the worst-case scenario for a dengue outbreak?"

Stark balked. He opened his mouth, then shut it, trying to follow Muñoz's line of thought. Finally, he rested his chin in his hand, thinking. He presumed he understood Muñoz's theory: One dengue serotype infects the body, and the immune system from then on recognizes that first dengue virus. But if one of the other three dengue serotypes infects the body, the immune system won't effectively recognize the virus because it's roughly 50 percent dissimilar from the first. Consequently, the second virus breeds unchecked. Victims suffer horribly: seizures, massive bleeding, then death.

Stark said, "Dengue hemorrhagic fever."

The young doctor looked over his shoulder into the camera for a moment, then turned away again. "A second dengue serotype would wipe this city out in bloody fashion."

"I don't understand. You think that's why Diego quarantined—?"

"The quarantine isn't the biggest issue right now, Dr. Stark. Look at the chickens. We're completely vulnerable to a widespread debilitating outbreak."

Professor Joaquin Delgado, Stark's mentor, would have said that Muñoz "hears hoofbeats in Central Park and thinks there must be zebras in New York." Without proof, his semilogical conclusions were absurd at best. "No wonder you were blackballed."

"I was blackballed because—"

"Yes?"

"I can't even say why, sir. I shouldn't say. The virus—our response is—" Muñoz fell silent. His back was still turned to the camera, and his narrow shoulders lowered. His head ducked almost out of view. "That, too, is classified."

Whether or not Muñoz's theory about hemorrhagic fever held water, the fact that Diego Alejandro had classified this outbreak indicated that the Ministry of Health believed that there was something unusual about this dengue. The simplest explanation, Stark deduced, was that someone in the Ministry was familiar with the pathogen and that Diego feared the early moments of the outbreak would show that. It was unusual, it had been mishandled in some way, and the Ministry was now hoping the outbreak would run its course and go away—something that Muñoz, at least, had warned them against.

That was just guesswork, but guesswork based on Stark's experience with reluctant governments who feared the appearance of botching a public-health crisis. He scratched the tag over his right eyebrow. "Is there a nanophagic analysis? Have genhunters been released yet?"

"I'm not on the Task Force anymore. I don't hear what the National Institute is doing, though I might hear about it at the conference today," said Muñoz. "Here's another question you should ask yourself, Dr. Stark. Why isn't there a vaccination program? They say it's almost mobilized, but I think they're delaying on purpose." Muñoz's voice suddenly sounded solemn, spooky.

"On purpose? They aren't vaccinating on purpose?" Stark almost rose from his chair. "What the hell are you talking about, Muñoz?"

Muñoz whispered. "I can't say any more. I'm in so much danger. That's all. The rest is up to you, sir."

Stark liked Muñoz and felt for him, an honest man trying to tell the truth in the midst of wild confusion. "You're right about one thing, Muñoz. This virus requires that your Ministry of Health vaccinate because Ascensión is now primed for a hemorrhagic fever outbreak. It's unlikely, but anyone might deduce from public medical information that it's a possibility. That's enough for me to take action. I can start rallying tetravalent vaccine stocks today," said Stark, noting that Queen Mum had already contacted WHO affiliates in the sub-Sahara for donations of dengue vaccine. "Meanwhile, I am a jury waiting to hear more than the weak case you've presented."

Muñoz seemed reenergized, the stoop in his posture less pronounced. "What do you need?"

"I need epidemiological data. Better, I'd love to see what Mexico's field teams say about that data. Can you get me their report when it becomes available?"

"I can't imagine how, but I'll try."

"Are you in serious danger at the moment?"

He sighed so deeply that Stark felt exhausted, too. "Yes," Muñoz said. "I'm surrounded by doctors from the *servicio sagrado* and they're the ones—" In that pause a well of fear opened, and Stark could tell that the young doctor had seen something terrible at the very bottom of it. "As long as I keep taking their punches in public, I think I'm safe. So that's my strategy for survival."

Stark gave Muñoz the clearance code to contact Queen Mum through the Quebec-Denmark link, then realized the *Para Ustedes* cameraman had returned to his post. Stark wanted to tell Muñoz to check in with him every couple of hours or so, just in case the Holy Renaissance tried to spirit him away, but he was distracted by the view on-screen. "Looks like the field team has arrived. Just take it easy, Pedro. Don't make any more enemies. Get some sleep and—"

But Muñoz had already hung up.

Twee audio crackled through the netcast line, and the view swung away from the hallway in front of the conference room. *Ojos* and reporters were crowding in front of the elevator doors.

On-screen, three women and two men were muscling their way out of the elevators. They had the drained, vacant look of a Special Pathogens team who didn't like where their research had led them, nor the direction it was headed. Two *ojos* were crowding the field team's leader with their zombie eyes and ramrod postures, but no one was talking. "Dr. Muñoz claims he's found thirty-five percent mutation, that this dengue passes from human to human," said one *ojo,* his voice surprisingly expressive for his robotic stance. "Is that what you found, Dr. Cristóbal?"

Cristóbal was a stoic man with a neat brush of a moustache, and, even on net-feed, he exuded clarity of mind and seriousness of purpose. But he brushed past the reporters and grimly stalked toward the conference room. He and his team disappeared inside and a moment later, a queue of doctors, including Pedro Muñoz, followed. Diego Alejandro and Elena Batista brought up the rear, with Batista shutting the doors behind them.

Stark blinked the coverage shut and sat for a moment, rocking in his chair without removing his goggles. A country on the brink of war, classifying information and thereby impeding the progress of its own scientists. Perhaps the pathogen was an experimental virus that was accidentally released—Mexico was famous for its viral therapy—and Diego didn't want the world to know it was his own Ministry's fault. Perhaps the Holy Renaissance wanted to downplay the outbreak to make sure the US knew Mexico wasn't to be tangled with, even in the middle of an outbreak. Perhaps there was a connection between Diego's quarantine and the spy in Stark's own room?

Stark scoffed at himself. *I just perhapsing myself to death.*

But there was little he could do, so far from Ascensión without blood samples or cryoslides of the virus. He could call Joaquin Delgado, his former teacher, but he wanted more information before bothering him. Stark supposed he could research dengue-4 now. Or brush up on the pathology of arboviruses. Or familiarize himself with recent nanophagic advances in regard to unfamiliar emergents.

Mainly he wondered if there was anyone besides Muñoz whom he could trust in Mexico, if even his old friend Diego Alejandro had compromised himself.

CHAPTER

THE MAN STOOD beneath the cavernous beauty of the Basilica's ceiling, his eyes drawing naturally along the gleaming, vaulted arches to the tattered, five-hundred-year-old cloak over the church's altar.

Shouldering his backpack, he folded his hands prayerfully. "It's a relief to see you, Blessed Virgin."

He half hoped that a booming voice would greet and repel him when he entered the Basilica of El Conquistador. A clap of thunder? Or could he be so bold as to hope for a welcome from Gabriel's trumpet? But the only sound that greeted him was the inane babble of tourists, as fifty rolling conveyer belts took chattering Euros and Japanese on a winding, back-and-forth path beneath the cloak.

The story of the cloak was well-known to any Mexican Catholic. Twelve years after the conquistador Hernando Cortés finished butchering the natives of this valley, the Virgin Mary had appeared to a Nahua *indígena* named Diego. Atop El Cerrito, the hill that now overlooked the Basilica, Mary soothed the Indian's fears saying, *"¿No estoy Yo aquí que soy tu Madre?"* Am I not here, I that am your Mother? Moved by his vision, Diego took a cloakful of roses as an offering to the church at the bottom of the hill (the site of the future Basilica). But when he arrived, the roses had vanished and branded on his cloak was the now famous image of the blue-robed Virgin, her skin and hair, native dark.

The Virgin of Guadalupe.

Now, he thought, Mexico has a prophetess to go with her Virgin and he wondered how rival pope Cardinal de Veras liked being upstaged by a nun. Cruddy, bootlegged *ojo* footage of the nun's old prophecies filled netcasts at night for the non*pilonistas*, and Sister Domenica spread her warnings. Her followers passed them mouth to ear, or *pilone* to *pilone*, until all of Mexico seemed to buzz with the word *plago*.

Her mention of a plague was sheer coincidence, the man told himself as he stared across the church at the tattered cloak and its faded image of the Indian Madonna. *Coincidences. Only coincidences, please*, he prayed. *No miracles*, Mamacita.

Hanging back, he watched and waited for a sign. On the broadcast two days ago, Pirate had said that the nun would be at the Basilica, delivering a Sunday sermon. Last night, the man hadn't been able get close enough to touch Domenica at the Church of Our Lady of Perpetual Sorrows, and he wasn't certain how many more chances he would receive before the city erupted in chaos.

He watched the local penitents filing in to the Basilica to find a confessor, looking into their pious faces and uplifted eyes, and dividing the crowd into *mestizo* and non*mestizo*, Indian and non-Indian. You. Not you. You. The population, here, was especially diverse, but most were *mestizo*. He knew that with his passage through the subway, market, and the Basilica, he had left behind a wake of infection, and imagined that he could watch it now, spreading, infiltrating. With every brush of skin on skin, his virus leapt like fire from match head to match head.

You. You.

Near him, a loud German couple, white as dead chickens, harangued at each other in their shearing language.

When the Spanish royalty came to their newly conquered land in the early sixteenth century, they were obsessed with *limpieza de sangre*. Purity of blood. Though they could not prevent interracial blending in Mexico, the Spanish literally charted the intermingling of races, giving them names like breeds of donkeys and mules: *mestizo, indigena, octaroon, mulato, lobo*. Portraits were even painted for the benefit of Old World dignitaries, cataloging the faces of the New.

You. Not you. You.

Standing in the rear of the church, feigning quiet contemplation beside the Germans, he noted the many lightning-strike scars on left temples: the brain of the Holy Renaissance. Other than the scar, they looked no different from anyone else—indeed, some obviously weren't even *mestizo*. But they were Connected, and they carried themselves differently, listening to and reading the barrage of information on the Holy Renaissance's central *pilone* net as it arrived in their minds' eyes, fast as sparking neurons, an Internet of flesh, blood, and slow cortical brain waves.

The German couple stepped forward, and, at that moment, a round-faced priest, in Holy Renaissance black-and-scarlet robes, edged himself into the man's peripheral vision. "Is this your first visit to the Basilica?"

He pretended not to hear.

The priest stepped into the man's line of sight. "Are you from Mexico, sir?"

"Yes," he said, annoyed. "Born and raised."

Eyes drifted over the older man's face. "And, yet, no *pilone*?"

The man took a step back and reminded himself that the priest had no reason to suspect him of anything. "No, I never got the surgery."

"That's what I find strange. I saw you standing here, a good-looking gentleman, so stately that I took you for a lawyer or a physician," the priest said. "It seemed strange to me that a man like you wouldn't have—"

The priest trailed off, and the man stared at him, hard, letting the silence stretch uncomfortably between them. "I can't afford it," he lied.

"Ah! My apologies. Are you a *bajadore,* then?"

He was asking if the man lived street level. "Yes," he lied again.

"I understand." The priest removed a card from a packet in his hand. "Take this, then."

The man took it, holding it at arm's length in order to read it clearly.

DIVINE INTERVENTION, PILONE IMPLANT SURGERY
AND WETWARE THERAPY, SLIDING SCALE FEES FOR
CITIZENS OF LA BAJA CIUDAD, *Ascensión DF*.

"The Holy Renaissance's hypereconomy can help anyone who's Connected. Not to mention the benefits of instant confession and guaranteed last rites. There are so many opportunities available to you after the surgery."

The man suddenly couldn't see the words printed upon the paper card. Blood seemed to wash across his vision, and, struggling to maintain his composure, he said, "I *have* heard that." He raised the card to his lips, as if considering, convinced that the pounding of his overburdened heart could be heard throughout the church.

They proselytize it. Priests push the Connection, here, in the Holy Basilica. I had no idea.

The German couple rolled back to where the man and the priest were standing, and, with his passable German, he understood the woman to say, "This is taking too long. Let's go and hear the nun at la Capilla now."

Ah. My sign. Gracias, Virgen de Guadalupe. *It's good to know that You are on my side,* the man prayed. He recovered himself and made sure that the edge of the card was damp as he lowered it from his mouth, then offered it to the priest. "I'm unable to receive the implants as my immune system rejects them."

"Oh, I see." The priest took the card gingerly, pursing his lips in irritation at its dampness. "You can't afford it *and* your immune system won't accept the *pilone.*" He wiped his fingertips on his satin robe. "That's an unbelievable tragedy, one that I've reported along with an image of you, sir," he said stiffly. "Conquer with Christ, *hijo.*"

The man frowned, trying to look stricken, or sad, or poor. Truly, though, he didn't care if the priest believed him or not. Beneath his brows, he was looking at the white line of the priest's *pilone* scar disappearing into his thinning hair, and thinking:

You.

Cerro de Tepeyac was a little mountain on the Valley of Mexico's floor overlooking the high Basilica. The steep hill, lush with gardens and green topiaries, drew a steady stream of people ascending to the chapel and the sacred site where Don Diego had seen the Virgin long ago.

The man climbed quickly in long steps, perspiring in the blaze of Mexico's sun, but slowed as he came upon three men with their shirts off who were whipping themselves as they walked, opening long creases of blood down their skinny backs. The man recoiled, stride faltering briefly before he found his feet. Black leather hood-masks hid their faces, the man knew, to keep them anonymous so their agony would not be equated with Christ's. The air around them was steely with the smell of sweat and blood.

At the summit, the flagellants' moans disappeared in the din of the murmuring crowd gathered before the hill's chapel. Standing in the rear, on the stairs, he couldn't see Sister Domenica. Most couldn't. The chapel's crowd was filled with *pilonistas,* the man surmised, accessing the chapel's node or Domenica's personal terminus, listening to her sermon via Connection and nodding to the words in their minds. Poorer people in the crowd, their temples unmarred by the lightning-strike incision, pushed toward the sound of Domenica's high soprano voice. The man moved with them.

Before the ornate sixteenth-century chapel, Sister Domenica stood like a common *indígena* woman in her dark blue serape and long, black braid. A number of nuns from the Order of Guadalupe were lined up nearby in pale blue mantles and white dresses, and between the crowd and Domenica were a cordon of young *machos.* Staring outward, statues of the nine archangels guarded the chapel, watchful eyes turned to the honking, thronging gridwork of La Baja Ciudad below and the pristine, sea-green towers of La Alta above.

"Orbegón calls Mexicans 'Anahuacs,' the First People of the Americas," the nun cried, her voice dripping with condescension. "But has Emil Orbegón allowed the Nahua Council or *any* Native Mexicans into his Majority Party?"

The shy woman from the Pirate's broadcast was gone. This was a hothead, a radical, not a soft-spoken nun.

"The Holy Mother told us about the eruption of Popo before it happened. She told us about the uprising in our Guatemala province. Her prophecy is unfinished. She begs you to believe Her, Mexico, when She warns that a greater lesson is coming.

"When this bloody plague arrives," Domenica said with both hands held high, palms outward, "a decision will be put before each one of you. Destroy or build. Fight Orbegón's wars or heal yourselves. Remember this when the dead are so many that they cannot be buried."

The man couldn't believe what he was hearing. Dissent to the Holy Renaissance? Did the loathsome little priest down in the Basilica know what the woman was saying on holy ground?

The nun shouted, "The great Marcos once said that Indians are those who remember. Well then, let's remember. Now. Together. Eight years ago Orbegón said the Aztec homeland, Aztlán, was in Arizona and New Mexico. So Orbegón went to war and took those two territories. Now his archaeologists claim that Aztlán was in Texas and Oklahoma too. In eight more years, he'll claim Aztlán was in Chicago, New York, Canada, Great Britain. Lies told to you by fascists who need your sons to fight their wars. Will your children follow marching orders while your own parents die of this unnatural disease at home? Will you bring war to the United States while Ascensión collapses?"

She couldn't know. She couldn't possibly know, but she knew. The man couldn't fathom how, but, by her words, Domenica knew what he'd introduced to Mexico just four days ago. Bloody plague? Unnatural disease? Somehow she understood that his fever was about to sink this city. The man had the distinct feeling that they were dueling—that he and the nun stood alone before the chapel—she with her back to the church, he with an archangel at either shoulder, the square between them shuffling with ghosts.

The frightened core of the crowd pressed forward and formed a line— students or poor *campesinos* from outside the city, and a cluster of wild-eyed men clutching to the scraps of their sanity—escapees of the *servicio sagrado*'s spas, the man imagined.

"Bless my baby!" a mother shouted. "Protect her from the plague!"

The man fell in line with the others, rolling up his sleeves, close enough now to see a zigzag scar disappearing into Domenica's thick hair as she reached for the infant. "Sister, touch me!" he cried out in a mix of fury and confusion. *She cannot know. She knows. She cannot know.* He wiped his nose on his palm, then extended his hand toward her, fingers spread.

The nun's head jerked toward him.

Her companion, a strapping young man with curly red hair, leaned toward her, whispering urgently. Domenica's eyelids fluttered, as if she were faint. She answered him, then he took the child from her arms, gazing down the line with a scowl—searching for someone who didn't belong.

The man stepped back from the line, willing himself to dissolve into the crowd's anonymity. *You saw nothing, you saw nothing,* he said silently.

Domenica stepped back from the line, too, turning to disappear into the little chapel, slipping farther from his grasp with each step.

You. *You.*

CHAPTER

4

"Two Code Reds in one day." Stark had just returned from dinner with the day crew after their shift. For dessert, they had delicious bananas, as many as they could eat—a rare treat that had arrived on a return truck from Chicago. "The hell happening now, Mum?"

The chatter of workers coming in from the fields floated up to Stark. Cool dusk had chilled the house, and after he slipped on his goggles, he shut his window against the night air, jerking his hand away before the sash could slam shut on his fingers.

"Dr. Stark," Queen Mum said, as the telephone icon for an incoming call seemed to stick against the windowpane where his vision had focused, "you have a message from Jerusalem."

Stark watched as his grandfather stopped in the yard below to gather a gaggle of tillers, shooing them into their shed for the night. Grandfather didn't look like a man whose life work was about to be devoured by gold mold. Perhaps he still hadn't looked at the field press. Stark turned away from the window, hoping that this was the Palestinian-Jewish Federation calling to pledge tetravalent vaccine for Mexico. "Hello, who calls, please?" he said in his passable Arabic-Yiddish argot. It was about all he knew beyond *Do you have a fever?* and *Urinate into this.*

An international AI spoke smooth English in his earplug. "I am routing an urgent call from the Pan-Islam Virological Institute in Islamabad."

Stark acknowledged the new link with a harrumph. PIVI hardly ever called the CDC's Central Command. In fact, some of its haughtier members felt superior to the Center for Disease Control, despite the fact that Stark often worked outbreaks with their best, Dr. Isabel Khushub. Stark hoped it was Isabel, calling him under the guise of professional consultation.

But a moment later, a pleasant, male voice said, *"Buenas tardes, Dr. Stark. ¿Puede oirme?"*

Stark had braced himself for Urdu, but the man was speaking Spanish. *"Sí, estoy aquí. ¿Quién es, por favor?"*

"Muy bien," said the man. "An artificial intelligence in Pakistan is to interpret and revive my voice for you at English."

"You're being translated back into Spanish, actually. And badly."

"Like you to me at the same once! But enough laughing. Dr. Stark, I do call to you from San Antonio, Mexican Texas."

"MexTexas? You're not my department and haven't been for eight years," Stark said. A San Antonio doctor should have been contacting Mexico's Central Command, not America's Centers for Disease Control—the city and the western half of Texas were under Mexican control now. "Mexico's National Institute is fully capable of—"

"I am not requiring our NIH, sir," said the man. "I am calling for *you,* Dr. Henry David Stark. You are sentient with the tragic event of dengue in Ascensión, I comply?"

Stark aimed his goggles at the dengue mortality statistics, an icon that he kept on his wrist like a watch. Ten dead at 7:43 P.M. Fifty-three confirmed cases. Bad numbers, especially for a young dengue outbreak, but still manageable. Mexico was obviously nervous about something other than mortality if they were calling a doctor behind enemy lines. "Who is this, please?"

"My identity is insubstantial," said the man, "but you may call me El Mono."

The Monkey? Here we go. It cloak-and-dagger time now, Stark thought. "Why are you calling, El Mono?"

The artificial intelligence rendered El Mono's voice in Spanish so succinct it sounded like either an act of extreme politeness or condescension. Whatever the case, it seemed to help the translation. "I have been allowed to invite you to the San Felipe de Mexico Federal Building here in San Antonio," El Mono said. "As you may have already calculated, this disease is not behaving like typical dengue fever. The Holy Renaissance requires your expertise. We would be distinguished if you came to Ascensión and consulted with our specialists."

"'We'? Who specifically authorized you to invite me?" Stark asked half-rhetorically, eager for an overdue conversation with Diego Alejandro.

"President Orbegón's most trusted advisor authorized me," said El Mono. "Chief of State Cazador."

Everyone in America knew Roberto Cazador, a name synonymous with the brutal bite that the Holy Renaissance had put on its opposition when Orbegón's religious movement–cum–political party, the Holy Renaissance, came to power eighteen years ago. Several thousand Mexicans had been "disappeared" in that power grab, and Chinese officials were constantly protesting the Holy Renaissance on behalf of the *Desaperecidos*—the disappeared. But perhaps even more ominous than those who vanished were the *Aperecidos*: individuals whose identities could not be traced to birth records or the federal school system—who simply "appeared" in new houses, new jobs, driving new cars. *Los Aperecidos* were well-mannered, devout, hardworking, and their coworkers and neighbors were expected to simply accept them into their communities and places of work without questioning who they were or where they'd come from. Roberto Cazador was credited with creating this new class of citizen in his spas dedicated to "faith realignment."

"Cazador certainly has the authority, I suppose. But let me ask you this. Why come to the enemy?" Stark said. "PIVI's pathologists are every bit as good as the CDC's. Isabel Khushub is probably the best pathologist in the world, and she's originally from Xalapa, Mexico."

"Dr. Khushub is on her passage from Islamabad as we verbalize. But, to clarify, we did not come to the foe," said El Mono, "we came to you, Dr. Stark."

The Holy Renaissance was bringing together the epidemiologist and pathologist who'd worked the famous Cairo outbreak. That much made sense. Isabel had written about that outbreak in her book, *The Mummy's Curse*, so obviously, Orbegón and Cazador wanted a high-profile team to calm the citizenry.

"Will you help us?"

On his wrist, the mortality icon flashed fourteen. "Of course I'll help."

"Good," said El Mono. "Your account has been credited for a military

cargo flight from Minneapolis to Houston in AmTexas. The flight departs at
6:30 A.M. tomorrow morning."

Stark glanced around his room in a moment of panic, but realized that
all of his clothes were folded in open suitcases on top of his dresser. Though
he hadn't actually entered a hot zone in more than two years, the need to
leave at a moment's notice was an ingrained habit from his days in the Special Pathogens Unit—he'd never completely unpacked upon returning to
the *quop*. "I'll make that flight."

"You will be met at Houston International by my attachés and driven
across the border to San Antonio. You must be here by 3:00 P.M. tomorrow.
If this intercourse between you and me becomes public, we will murder
your flight, and the concord will be discontinued."

"Um. I understand."

"Do you have initial suggestions for us before arriving in Ascensión?"

"I'm glad you asked. First of all, I want total access to *all* Mexican medical information from now on. Can you arrange that?"

"Visibly! We'll establish a live link between our National Institute and
your Central Command. The satellite embargo ends for you now."

"That's good," said Stark, "but I also need Mexico's sealed records on the
beginning of the outbreak. In order to help you, I'll need access to Zapata's
records from before noon this morning."

The silence from the other end of the line lasted so long Stark was about
to ask Mum if the line had been severed, when El Mono said, "How do you
know about the classification of those files, Dr. Stark?"

"I tried to access them and was denied."

"Hmm. You've taken an interest in this case already?"

Stark put on his irritated voice, hoping it would mask his fear for Pedro
Muñoz's safety. "The whole world has taken an interest, Mr. Monkey. The
whole world is watching Ascensión."

El Mono suddenly sounded congenial. "Zapata's earliest records are in
the process of being unsealed by the Minister of Health. You'll receive access
to them as soon as possible. You have access to everything after that, of
course."

"Of *course*," Stark said sarcastically, thoroughly disgusted with Diego
Alejandro. "Be sure that I do. Moving on, I've rallied"—Stark checked the
WHO icon on his other wrist, where Queen Mum kept a running tally of the
doses they'd gathered from around the planet—"two hundred thousand

doses of tetravalent vaccine, in addition to whatever Mexico has. But we need your country's omnivalent vaccines. How many doses has Mexico stockpiled?"

"Of omnivalents?" El Mono said. "Hardly any. Minister Alejandro has been hesitant to order their clonufacturing."

That made sense. Omnivalent vaccinia could modify its structure to attach itself to, theoretically, any virus's epitope, but it hadn't been thoroughly tested yet. An hour ago, Stark would have advised against what he was about to say. "I recommend getting all of your country's plants ready to produce several hundred thousand doses."

"Done. The Minister just gave the order and fifteen plants have started production," said El Mono. "The first round of fifty thousand should be ready in three days."

"Are you joking?"

"Welcome to Mexico, Dr. Stark," said El Mono. "Whole industries appear at the snapping fingers in Mexico."

Further enchantments from the pilone *network.* Stark's mind whirled, contemplating such power. The request had blinked from El Mono's wetwared synapses to Diego Alejandro's to the captains of Mexico's vaccine industry. Perhaps production had already been put in place and were poised, ready for clearance. Nonetheless, three days? When Stark entered the CDC, it took two months to complete production on a new vaccine. In the last century, years.

"Now the last I heard, Dr. Miguel Cristóbal was about to deliver his findings to the Minister of Health. I want that report, and all professional reactions to his work." Stark decided to ask for everything and see how far El Mono would let him go. "And I want the most recent genomic analysis of the virus, too, and all guesses on its pathology."

"Dr. Khushub will be examining pathology in flight from Pakistan. You'll have her report as soon as it's available."

"Good. Tell Bela—remind Dr. Khushub that all my epidemiological work is on hold until she tells me how this virus spreads. She knows that, and she'll swear at you for telling her what she already knows, but tell her anyway. What state is the epidemiological data in, anyway?"

"Field teams are still combing through the *centro histórico* in downtown Ascensión, where all the victims lived. We should have something for you tonight."

In that case, Stark couldn't do anything more. "Good. One last thing." Through the icons floating in his room, Stark located his library of discs and began thinking of titles he would like to take with him. He wanted to pack. He wanted to call down to his grandfather in the yard and arrange for a ride to Minneapolis. "Tell Minister Alejandro that I must speak with him immediately."

"I'll tell him." Then, the timbre of El Mono's voice dropped, and, he sounded, not like a secret agent, but a fan seeking an autograph. "I wanted very painfully to tell you that, as a physician myself, I am honored to work in even a small capacity with the Patron Saint of Plagues. Dr. Khushub called you that in her book, I believe?"

The change in this conversation's tone was so abrupt Stark didn't know if El Mono was being serious or sarcastic. "Yes. Um. Why, thank you. That's—thank you."

"Your handling of the smallpox outbreak remotely from the United States was inspired, sir," El Mono said. "I hope you're what you seem to be."

Then the line went dead and Stark was left contemplating that strange sign-off. *Another crappy translation,* Stark thought. Somewhere in the house, there was a crash of glass followed by ringing laughter. Systematically, he began clearing evidence of his conversation with El Mono from Queen Mum's interface, deleting call icons and copies of transcripts. He wondered what he would say to his old classmate when he finally met Diego face-to-face in Mexico. Diego Alejandro was no longer the friend he had once been, and the charges Stark planned to bring against Diego and his government would speak for themselves. Diego was now so much of a deterrent he was himself practically an aspect of the virus's pathology.

On the other hand, there *was* someone who might have something to say about Diego's "quarantine of information."

"Look, Mum, get me Joaquin Delgado's personal line," Stark said, standing, opening a lugall, and thumbing through his library.

"Connecting," said Mum.

Joaquin was the teacher who had encouraged Stark to enter epidemiology. A seething, arrogant talent in his youth, Joaquin had created the first nanophages, the half machine, half virus that had keyed on viruses like hunter-seeker missiles in a population's bloodstream or in the air over the city, and which forever altered the course of handling viral outbreaks. Now, late in life, the flaring burn of Joaquin's intellect was mellowing into coals, a quiet kingliness, with his own business and consulting firm. It suited him, and most of Europe wanted him, so he lived well in London. Stark was flattered that Joaquin had become his confidant over the years, so much so that when Stark was a CDC agent for Special Pathogens, it was his tradition to call Joaquin before jetting off to an outbreak, and several times, he had even managed to convince Joaquin to join him. Calling him now, he of course wanted to tell Joaquin about Diego, but he also simply wanted to swing in the hammock of that great mind before entering the battle.

When he answered his personal, Joaquin greeted Stark warmly. *"¿Qué va, compañero?"*

"Maestro," Stark said.

"Pues, I wondered when you would call me. Hold on. Something tells me this is going to be a long conversation. I want to find a place to sit and talk."

Joaquin's voice sounded strained to Stark. In English, he asked, "Everything all right?"

Joaquin sighed and Stark imagined the Spaniard wiping a hand across his brow. *"Ai.* I'm in Austria looking into a contract with Privatklinik Beobachtungen." A restaurant's clink and hum could be heard in the background.

Joaquin's business specialized in improving epidemiological services in private hospitals throughout Europe. Like watching a Thoroughbred pull a plow, in Stark's opinion, but they'd had that argument before. "A pretty good clinic, ain't it?"

"It's a death trap. My advice to you? Don't get sick in Vienna. *Bueno.* I've found a place to sit and talk." Joaquin sighed as he sat, and went visual. Stark didn't like how old he looked. Like Diego Alejandro, Joaquin was a handsome man who seemed built for old age, looking the part of distinguished gentleman. Unlike Diego, whose stately gray hair at forty-one made him look much older, Joaquin had always looked considerably younger than his years. But at fifty, Joaquin now looked it. "You're using your CDC interface," he said. "The connection is always better than your farm's cheap lines. So. Let's begin. You are calling about Mexico? Dengue, I take it?"

Joaquin was up to speed. "That right. What the last you heard?"

"Just what I saw on the mednets this morning. Eight dead, I saw." A waiter tried to get his attention, and Joaquin snapped at the person to be quiet and go away. "Sorry. That's highly unusual for dengue. Is the *Instituto Nacional* certain of that identification?"

"They ain't certain of nothing," said Stark. "Mortality at fourteen now, by the way. Not eight."

"*Ai, dios.*"

"It gets worse."

"Worse? Worse than fourteen dead in a dengue outbreak?"

"Diego Alejandro has turned *politico*. His Ministry of Health classified the outbreak."

Joaquin's face fell—almost literally. The skin under his eyes seemed to sag slightly, and his cheeks went gaunt as his mouth drooped open. "Who could have foreseen this?" Joaquin said finally. "Diego classified the outbreak?"

Diego Alejandro and Henry David Stark had been Joaquin's favorite and most successful students. If it had shocked and hurt Stark to learn of Diego's interference, then it was goring Joaquin's heart. Stark knew Joaquin well enough not to pull punches though. His teacher would rip into him if he sensed that Stark was withholding information. "Minister Alejandro has blocked the earliest data on the outbreak. They want me to consult with them."

"How do you know it was Diego who classified it?" Joaquin said, voice hardening. "Maybe the order came from higher up. Maybe *servicio sagrado* forced his hand."

"I saw his signature."

"But how much can one man in that bloody dictatorship do to—"

"I saw his signature, Joaquin."

Stark watched Joaquin, gave him the minutes he needed to digest this. He could see a bucket of ice chilling a bottle of champagne in the restaurant behind him. Finally, Joaquin's voice crushed flat, he said, "Quite right. Quite right, Henry David. This—this is such an insult. I don't mean that egotistically. I mean it medically. A blow to my very body."

"I know."

"*Ai, pues.* He was *always* one of us. I never imagined either of you becoming a foe like this."

That was an old idiom for Joaquin, his use of the word "foe": an antagonist of public health.

Despite the heavy moment, Stark was growing impatient. He still needed to find his grandfather and see if any farm trucks were departing with loads for Minneapolis tonight. "I glad you reading the mednets, Joaquin."

"Always. Every day."

"Give me your take, *por favor*?"

"It's an emergent, obviously."

"Does it sound familiar, Joaquin? Have you come across anything like it recently?"

Joaquin's brief pause was promising. Stark knew every gesture, every facial expression of Joaquin's, and right now his old teacher was putting a hand over his mouth, and his intense gaze lifted as if watching a balloon float upward—which meant a brainstorm.

"What? What you got for me?" said Stark.

"It's nothing but a hunch."

Before the smallpox outbreak in Cairo, Joaquin had advised Stark and Khushub to monitor the grave-robbing trade out of the newly discovered Ra-Imhotep site. "*Your* hunches are worth hard data. What you got?"

"Well, I must say, it reminds me of something I read on Ghana's Ministry of Textile boards last month."

Joaquin was the most voracious reader of mednets Stark knew. He was better than an AI for sifting through them, too, since AIs didn't carry with them twenty years of personal experience in handling viruses and outbreaks. "Ghana? What happened in Ghana?"

"Fascinating, actually." Joaquin's voice was still emotionless, perhaps wounded, but the fast gruffness with which he normally spoke had returned. "There's a pipeline of illegal fabric smugglers running between Ghana and Ascensión. Did you know that?"

"No." Stark laughed. "What? Contraband cotton?"

"Mexico is culling fields of the old US cotton cultivars, and their own indigenous ones, too, and replacing them all with new transgenic varieties whose patents the Holy Renaissance owns. Meanwhile, fabrics out of West Africa are cheaper for La Baja and out-state Mexican tailors. Read the Ghanaian Textile boards if you can. It's fascinating. The cotton—"

"Joaquin, I don't have time to hear about cotton. I barely got time for this conversation."

"Of course, of course. I'll summarize and Queen Mum can research it if it seems relevant. An emergent virus appeared in the workers' ranks of Ghana's cotton industry last month. The mutation rate was so high that it was impossible to isolate and identify the virus."

"Interesting. Have you heard that this virus's mutation rate is in double digits?"

"Is it? There may be a connection then."

"I didn't hear about the Ghana outbreak."

"You wouldn't have," said Joaquin. "Ghana's National Surveillance Unit released stock nanophages and ended the outbreak quickly, but their Health Department is still investigating what it was. Perhaps Mexico caught it from Ghana? I think a Dr. Kodzo was heading up the pathology team for the government, but I may have the name wrong. You may want to look into the backgrounds of the so-called dengue victims in Ascensión and see if any of them—especially poorer *bajadores*—have ties to the textile industry—clothing, printing, costuming, et cetera."

"We'll see. Right now, my working theory is that this dengue virus mutates too fast for stock nanophages, let alone custom-made ones," Stark said, though he tapped all of Joaquin's information into his memboard.

"Maybe Ghana caught it before it mutated," said Joaquin. "Maybe Mexico didn't."

It wasn't a great theory, but it made more sense than a dengue outbreak hitting fourteen deaths in a single day. "Thanks, Joaquin. I appreciate you taking the time."

"This means you'll be going to Mexico then?" said Joaquin.

"No, I'll stay here and consult from Wisconsin," Stark said. "There's a report due from an emergency dengue conference at Zapata Hospital, and I hope to review it."

"Who's at the conference?"

"Miguel, Elena, and a staff doctor named Muñoz, who's been on the case since the beginning," Stark said, "and Diego, too."

"Perhaps, you won't be too busy to call me in a few days. I'd like to hear if"—the slightest of hitches could be heard in Joaquin's voice—"my theory held water."

Stark said he would, even though they both knew that even Joaquin's wildest theories always held a little water, and signed off.

Down in the yard, he could hear his grandfather talking with Phil the Dairy King. Stark heard the words "truck" and "Minneapolis," and, though he was about to unleash Queen Mum on Joaquin's Ghana lead, he swept off his brain gear and leaned out the window, yelling, "What that? You hauling out?"

Grandfather looked up at him, shading his eyes from the blaring light of the goat barn. "Yes. The milk is cool and in the tank. Why?"

Stark clapped his hands. *Goddamn hallelujah!* "No reason. Hold up. I coming right down!"

CHAPTER

5

WITH GRANDFATHER at the wheel, the ride through the winding river valleys in the *quop's* beat-up milk tanker was heart-stopping. The old man decided that as long as Stark needed a ride to Minneapolis, he'd drive the pasteurized load in himself and sell it at the Urban Milk Alliance, an umbrella group for neighborhood *quops* and manors in the city. With distribution so poor these days, milk, especially pasteurized, was at a premium in cities.

Stark feared driving with his grandfather—the dour farmer was a daredevil on country roads—but he couldn't wait around for the produce trucks that left at dawn. So here he was, at the age of thirty-eight, in the same tanker that his grandfather had been driving when Stark was ten. Twenty-nine thousand pounds of milk in the tank made each upslope a suspenseful trudge and each downhill run a barreling, dashboard-gripping plunge. "Couldn't just take this load to *our* bottler, huh?" shouted Stark.

"UMA bottles it themselves, so we don't pay for glass."

"Where you learn to drive anyway?" Stark said, as his grandfather accelerated toward another hill.

"Costa Rica," shouted Grandfather over the gunning engine. "Pardon me. Tiquizia, now that the Mexicans own it. OK. Here comes another! Ready?"

"Gawd." After a grinding ascent, they reached the top and Stark's stomach rolled over on itself as they plummeted over the hillcrest. "Ever think about getting a skyboat?"

"Never!"

"Think about it."

Grandfather turned toward him, about to argue, then said, "Do you have to wear those in the truck?"

Stark looked at his grandfather, cybergoggles pushed up and bulging atop his head, brain tags stuck to his face. "Wear what in the truck?"

Grandfather swore at him quietly and downshifted into first in order to make it up the next hill, which would finally take them out of the hilliest stretch.

They had been in the tanker for almost thirty minutes, but neither of them had mentioned the spinach sample in the field press yet. Stark didn't know how to bring it up. Instead, he said, "You know that Earl? That new intern?"

"Sure I do. The one who left this morning?" Grandfather said. A light seemed to go on. "You had something to do with him taking off, didn't you?"

"Maybe."

The tanker's belching muffler sounded like it was about to abandon ship. "Was he a spy?" said Grandfather.

Stark sucked air in a gasp of surprise. His grandfather's deductions were positively spooky sometimes. "Makes you say that?"

"Well, I think he was from Mexico, not Baltimore like he told Jink," said Grandfather, leaning a hand against the shift as if that would help the whining tanker up the hill. He was chattier than usual, a little too eager to have this conversation, but Stark thought he understood why. Better this conversation than the obvious one. "In the field yesterday, I caught him tucking a crucifix under his shirt. It looked like a Holy Renaissance cross to me, you know, the shepherd's staff and sword? Not that I cared." Grandfather paused, and a mile went by. "Why would the Holy Renaissance take an interest in you?"

Stark felt like a pinned butterfly. He sat blinking, mouth dropped open, unable to confirm, deny, or obfuscate what his grandfather had just said. So he did the math. Earl had arrived on Thursday evening, three days before Zapata Hospital started receiving dengue patients. It didn't make sense that Earl been sent by Mexico. Unless, Stark thought, the Holy Renaissance knew about this outbreak sooner than Muñoz realized. The chicken reports had indicated that something virulent was passing through Ascensión, so,

conceivably, some Mexican scientists might have already known what the
virus was. Especially if it was theirs, in which case, maybe it made sense for
the Holy Renaissance to secretly investigate an American before inviting
him across the border.

Stark looked at the clock on the tanker's dash. Ten after four—which
meant it was really 11:30 or so (the clock hadn't worked right for eons). The
dengue conference should have let out by now, and he hoped that Muñoz
would contact him as soon as he could. Stark had a lot of questions for the
"unique man."

Another mile went by, and the tanker passed from wooded hills into me-
andering grasslands as it approached the Mississippi and the prairies of
Minnesota. "Come on. Fess up, kid," said Grandfather. "Are you going to
Mexico? Is that what this midnight run is about?"

Stark wished his grandfather would shut off his deductive mind for the
duration of the ride. But Stark couldn't lie to him. "I goin' to Mexico."

"You *are* going to Mexico."

"I *ammm* embarking for the Holy Republic of Mexico. They have a
dengue outbreak they want me to consult on."

"Well" —Grandfather sighed a weary breath— "I hope they aren't setting
you up."

The rumble of the tanker's engine filled the silence. Now that they'd
passed to the other side of the high bluffs overlooking the Mississippi River,
Stark saw the first abandoned farmlands burning with the gold mold that
surrounded the cluster of Land Reform Farms in southwest Wisconsin.
Even under the watery light of the moon, he could see the telltale ratty look
of the plants where viruses had found purchase years ago. As he watched
the terrain gradually change from the unglaciated, rolling hills to the flattened prairies, Stark debated whether or not to finally change the subject to
the spinach plant. But Grandfather's statement was still chewing on him.
"Setting me up how? What you mean?"

Grandfather lifted a skinny shoulder. "You tell me. Why are they bringing *you* there in the middle of *their* embargo?"

Stark could easily imagine why Pedro Muñoz and the Holy Renaissance
were both frightened enough to contact him. Bioweapon. He hadn't even allowed himself to entertain the thought until now, because it didn't really
matter if this dengue was natural or man-made—it had to be stopped. But
on the quiet road, speeding between ruined farm fields, breaking down this

situation with the help of his grandfather's sharp mind, he could allow himself to speculate. Perhaps even Muñoz thought it was an attack of some kind and that was part of what he couldn't say on the phone. *This dengue is not dengue.* It wasn't far-fetched. A core of prominent scientists at the National Institute of Agronomy still contended that the gold mold outbreaks were the result of a bioattack. Stark saw it as a convenient way to explain the complete collapse of US agriculture and subsequent crippling of her economy. But Stark understood the impulse to look in that direction. Viral warfare was silent, mysterious, and the mere thought of it could make a paranoiac of anyone. Even Stark.

He looked sidelong at his grandfather, and said, "You look at that field press yet?"

Grandfather's profile looked like a face from a coin. His lips tightened for a moment, then he said, "It was just one plant."

It never just one plant, Stark was about to say. But he kept his mouth shut and didn't prod his grandfather for once. In the wake of gold mold, the Land Reform Act had redistributed much of America's farmland from collapsing agribusiness to energetic *quops* like Nissevalle all over the country. So much depended on its being just one plant.

Stark filled the moment by flipping down his goggles and sticking his brain tags in place. "Go," Stark told his brain gear, and, once connected, he glanced down at the outbreak icon on his left wrist.

It looked like three digits for a moment, so he blinked and glanced back.

Three digits it was.

"What?" he said to his wrist.

112.
120.
127.

"Mum," whispered Stark. "What the hell happening in Ascensión?"

His grandfather took a long look at Stark, then faced the road.

"I've had nothing to relay, Doctor," said Queen Mum. "Reports are just now available. Are you in a proper, decision-making frame of mind?"

"Just show me what you got! Hurry!"

Grandfather slowly accelerated until the little tanker's engine started whining again.

Queen Mum avalanched a ton of recently written reports, their head-lines cascading over the nighttime prairie, each with the word "dengue" in it.

"Summarize, Mum."

Fifteen May, 2061 Ascensión, DF—President for Life Emil Orbegón of the
Holy Republic of Mexico declared Zapata Hospital a national disaster
Sunday night after fifteen doctors were found dead in the hospital's
conference room. Initial cause of death was diagnosed as an airborne version
of dengue hemorrhagic fever.

Stark felt like a boat taking on seawater. He scanned down the docu-ment, reading the names of the twenty-four doctors who had died.

Elena Batista was on the list.

Miguel Cristóbal.

And thirteen others, all of whose names and reputations Stark recog-nized. The best of Mexico's best.

Including Dr. Pedro Muñoz.

Stark heaved in a breath and read the last line of the press release. "An airborne version of dengue hemorrhagic fever." Stark thought, *No such thing.* He scanned the outbreak updates, grateful that this information had been declassified under Diego Alejandro's orders. One hundred and twenty-seven dead. These were shocking numbers even for a virulent disease like Ebola. For dengue, they were impossible.

Mexico needed help. Stark needed help. He had never heard of anything so virulent—and the doctors who'd died were the very heart of Mexico's chance at survival.

"Dr. Stark, you have a message waiting for you from Dr. Pedro Muñoz at Zapata—"

"Open it, open it!"

Mum had found a pathway into the Holy Renaissance through countries with a Romance language base. It made the translation of Muñoz's final words perfectly legible.

15 May URGENT Attention Dr. Henry David Stark. Dr. Stark, I stepped
away from the conference under the pretense of tending to a patient in order
to write you.

The field team has decided that "Big Bonebreaker," as the media calls this virus, is a fifth dengue serotype and have dubbed it D5 in all documents. They've also confirmed my findings that this serotype communicates human to human, without a mosquito vector. This discovery officially supports my work, and it might save me.

Miguel Cristóbal's field teams spoke openly to the conference about searching for patient zero and finding ample evidence of D5 appearing throughout La Baja in Ascensión. Of great interest, he spoke to us at length about several clinics in the Basilica neighborhood, charged with keeping the sex trade clean in La Baja, and how one of them may have handled D5 patients before Zapata saw its first this morning. My first patient arrived at 11:45 P.M. last night—we'll have to match her samples with the Zedillo clinic samples and see what we get—once the quarantine is lifted.

My suspicion is that you are coming to Ascensión. Hints were dropped, and signs point to an American. If you arrive, please contact me at Zapata so we can speak openly.

—P.M.

Stark blinked the letter away. He felt a plunging despair—

132, 133

—knowing that Muñoz was gone. He needed time to talk to someone who actually had experience with virulent bioweaponry, but there was no time. Stark blinked an open channel to the World Health Organization and issued a global alert, asking for any and all information on suspected dengue outbreaks or patients with symptoms similar to dengue, and recommending the suspension of all travel into and out of Mexico.

He immediately received alerts from AIs in reporting offices in Miami, New York, Los Angeles, Havana, and Manila that their hospitals had begun quarantining suspected D5 patients in the last two hours.

Damn, it got loose, thought Stark. With 133 already dead, the virus would span the globe by tomorrow night.

"Mum," said Stark, "can you get me a map of Ascensión's outbreaks? Someone in Mexico's NIH must have made one."

Immediately, Queen Mum flashed Stark a strategic map of Ascensión. *Good,* Stark thought, *El Mono got me access.* But as he feared, instead of one outbreak centering on Zapata Hospital and rippling outward, outbreaks were growing all over the city, depicted in red circles marked *hot zone,* and zones overlapped in such horrifying density that the center of Ascensión was a smear of red.

Stark felt his body slouch. It was already too far gone. The virus had already accomplished the only thing that viruses do.

Breed as fast as they can.

Stark stared at the reddened map of Ascensión in defeat. But he straightened in his seat as he noted that the various hot zones were actually highly localized. The viruses weren't spreading out of control—the opposite of what he expected. *Something strange about they pathology, something I can't see about the viruses from up here,* Stark thought, scanning the map. *They slower than they look maybe. Maybe I actually got time to rally a response before the next wave hits.*

"Mum, you in Mexico's NIH right now?"

"I'm accessing the NIH's Dengue Task Force data, if that's what you mean."

"Good. Do something illegal for me, would you?"

Grandfather pressed the gas pedal down even farther.

"My, won't that be a nice change of pace for you, Doctor?"

"Monitor any pathways and databases you can in NIH and see if you can find any reference to the word *bioweapon.*"

"After I spy on a foreign federal bureau, I presume you'll want me to violate Central Command protocol by erasing evidence of my investigation?"

"Don't make me explain the obvious. Now, omnivalents. Update me."

"Omnivalent vaccines are still in production. All existing stockpiles will be exhausted by morning."

Well, they finally got their vaccination program under way, Stark thought. "Any other messages for me?"

"No, Dr. Stark."

Isabel Khushub was still up to her chin in Pathology, then. Minister Diego Alejandro was no doubt up to his scalp in whatever panic the D5 crisis had awakened in the world's largest city. Stark desperately wished he could get information about the virus from before noon today.

Wait a minute. Stark forced himself to sit and think. Perhaps Joaquin had given him the earliest information about the virus available. Perhaps the age-old pattern of viruses leaping from Africa to the New World had been reversed, and the Ghanaians had been fighting D5 without knowing it.

"Mum, one more thing," Stark said. "I want you to contact a Dr. Kodzo in the Ghana Department of Health and scan all Ghanaian public health docs related to outbreaks in the cotton industry."

"There is a Dr. Imanuel Kodzo working for the GDH, and, yes, it appears that he's been working a yellow-fever outbreak in a remote village of the country," said Mum. "I just left him a message on his personal phone."

"What? He a health official. He got to have another way of getting hold of him."

Queen Mum lagged long, apparently parsing what Stark had just said. "Unfortunately, Dr. Kodzo doesn't have sat access of any kind—neither hookup, nor *pilone*," Mum said. "It could be several hours before he responds."

"Hours?" Stark shook his head, feeling like a new Special Pathogens agent on his first urban outbreak. Outside his window, the dark prairie sailed past and the moon raced alongside him. "Hours?"

PART
II

CHAPTER

6

SUNDAY, MAY 15. 9:08 P.M.

THIS WHIMSICAL COMPLEX of cells with its wobbling, oblong construction didn't resemble any other in the bloodstream. Though it was half virus, the complex passed unhindered through the body, because it was also half white blood cell. It was unique, a centaur trotting up Main Street.

Four days earlier, a different virus had entered the body and initiated a slow infection. Aware that something had infiltrated its precious system, the body slicked moisture upon its skin and elevated its temperature, while mounting a more complicated response to the virus. A killer T cell investigated the viral infection and learned the identity of the virus.

Dengue. You don't belong here, the T cell decided. *Previous generations of mine have killed you.*

The T cell then replicated itself and spread through the body like a healing epidemic, attacking and killing the virus wherever it had found purchase in the body. Once the virus was subdued, these antibodies remained in the bloodstream, vigilant for another dengue infection.

After four days, a brother strain to the first virus entered the bloodstream. The dengue killer T cell, seeing what appeared to be a familiar foe, attached itself to the new virus before it could do any damage. The brother virus, however, was not dengue, at least not dengue as this T cell knew it, nor as previous generations had ever seen it. Though it tried, the antibody couldn't kill the virus. It could manage only an awkward grasp on the invader, so that now white cell and virus clutched one another. They rolled as a single mass through the blood's flow, a whimsical marriage of enemies in a battle fought to a draw.

Or so it seemed to other agents of the immune system. Noting that the T cell had done its duty in arresting a foreign body, a voracious macrophage cell with grasping tentacles approached the immune complex, preparing to eat whatever polluting molecule the antibody had disabled.

But the macrophage ignored the danger posed by this new virus, hand-cuffed as it was to the antibody like a violent criminal to the body's own cop. As the macrophage attached itself to the immune complex, the virus ambushed it. Hundreds of times smaller than the macrophage, the virus pierced its cell wall, stripping back the outer sheath, and dumping the macrophage's contents into the bloodstream. The new virus then found the macrophage's DNA and unzipped it, pulling the strands apart like a pair of legs, inserting its own code into the cell and replicating itself. Worse, it sorted through the macrophage's DNA and gleaned the body's unique, iden-tifying protein, the code that designated the body's own cells as integrally *belonging* to this body, and adopted that code like a clever disguise.

Offspring from the new virus's infection scattered into the blood's flow of traffic. They attacked with swift purpose, plunging themselves first into lung cells.

The body coughed and coughed again. The man thought something was wrong but merely asked a colleague to hand him a glass of water.

The body mounted a new response. It poured young T cells into the bloodstream to identify the mysterious invader, clone themselves, and begin another bodywide attack on the child viruses. Infections throughout the lungs and esophagus cried to the antibodies, begging to be investigated. But when T cells swarmed over the infected site, searching for traces of the in-vader, the virus presented the appropriate code of identification, designat-ing itself as belonging.

The man convulsed.

The immune system, recognizing that the T cells had failed their mis-sion, spiked a fever in a vain attempt to burn and kill the new virus and its children. The viral cells, however, could survive a higher temperature than the body. A red-pink rash prickled across the skin of the man's throat.

The virus wreaked havoc, feeding and breeding at the body's expense. It rolled back the walls of infected lung cells. It unsheathed esophagus cells and dumped their innards into the bloodstream.

The man coughed again, spraying the air with infected sputum. He covered his mouth with a handkerchief, saw dots of red when he lifted the cloth from his lips.

Layers of tissue lining the man's lungs and throat were dissolving and the body expelled them through the mouth and nose, through the ears and eyes and rapidly forming sores on the skin. The same thing was happening in the stomach, the intestines, the urethra, as the virus destroyed cells throughout the body.

The mouth tried to speak. *"Ave Virgen de Guadalupe,"* was all it said before the coughing became too wet, drowning the voice.

Around him, the man's colleagues crumpled to the ground. The man used his *pilone* hookup to link with the Holy Renaissance's net. > *From Dr. Miguel Cristóbal: Quarantine Zapata Hospital's second floor. Code Blue Klaxon, now! A hemorrhagic fever. Perhaps airborne.*<

The man fell to his knees, frontal lobe suffusing with blood, dead before his head hit the floor.

He was the last person of fifteen to die.

CHAPTER

7

THE CONFERENCE ROOM stank with released bowels, vomit, coppery blood—the smell of sudden death. Every instinct in him commanded him to flee. But he had stayed to watch the doctors—versed like Bible students on the symptoms of hemorrhagic fever—as they looked about the room in panic, as breath became short, as the cramping and seizures began, and their body temperatures soared. No more computer models running on his home AI. No more hellish nightmares, dark musings in his diary, nor empty confessions.

The war was under way.

A moment earlier, Miguel Cristóbal, whom the man admired deeply, had told the group that he had given the order to quarantine Zapata Hospital and Ascensión via *pilone*. Miguel, moustache standing out like a smudge of shoe polish on his pale skin, then looked right at the man who stood guarding the door in hospital scrubs. Recognition. Confusion. Betrayal. Then Miguel clutched his head and folded up into a ball, slacks and suit coat staining wet.

The man closed his eyes in respect for his longtime colleague, then slipped the aerosol can in his backpack. He zipped it up and stepped out of the conference room, shutting the door behind him.

The elevator chimed, and the man, all alone in the hallway, threw himself at the conference-room door in fright. To hide his face, he cupped his hands around his face and pressed his forehead against the glass of the door's window.

"Get away from there! Are you crazy?" came a voice from the elevator.

Three orderlies in *Racalitos,* disposable biohazard suits and helmets were standing in the air lock with what looked like a giant white doorframe. An ALHEPA air lock, the man noted, the new generation of biohazard-grade air filter. "Didn't you get the Code Red?" an orderly shouted. "It's airborne! Are you insane? Get away from the door!"

The man had just enough time to slip a surgical mask over his face. Then he picked up his backpack and inched away. "I'm sorry. I heard the quarantine alarm and I wanted to—"

"Shut up and get out of our way," the orderly muttered. "We have to get this up fast before it spreads. If it hasn't already." The orderly looked through the conference room's window and shook his skullcapped head in slow disbelief. "Holy Mother of God." Behind the plastic mask his eyes were round and damp.

Balling one hand into a fist, the man watched him look into the room. Was the worker simply frightened by the bloody scene? Or did those eyes see past the man's white lab coat, surgical mask, and gentex gloves to the larger horror at work? Backpack clutched to his stomach, the man felt as if he were standing with a bloody knife in his hands.

The orderly blinked away his fear and turned back to the ALHEPA air lock. "Come on, come on," he kept chanting as he and the other two fitted the particle arrester over the conference-room door.

"Can I help?" the man asked.

"You'll need a blood draw to make sure you're clean." The frame sighed as it sealed itself to the wall around the door's frame and hummed to life. "Marcos, take this guy up to the biolab on seven. Dr. Cristóbal just certified it. You'll be one of the first patients," he said to the man. "Congratulations."

"Come on," Marcos said, walking to the elevator. "We should use the stairs to keep the lifts free, but I think you qualify as an emergency. Let's go."

When they reached seven, the elevator doors opened on an entire floor that had been turned into a hot lab. The man figured it had probably been an old surgery unit, which would have been easily made into a series of sterile fields with low-pressure atmospheres. Hospital staffers and paramedics were already queuing for bloodwork, according to standard outbreak protocol.

Marcos led the man deep into the hot lab. This was no longer a unit for sick people, but a place to cull the immune from the doomed.

They were about to pass through an ALHEPA filter fitted across an office door when Marcos stopped, and said, "Cover your mouth and close your eyes."

The man did as he was told, placing a hand over his eyes. Marcos picked up a spritz bottle, the kind used for misting ferns. He sprayed the man down until he had a fine sheen of moisture all over his head, lab coat, and pants. "What's this?" the man asked, smelling that it was a contact antiviral, probably cytolise-9. Useless.

"It's routine, don't worry," Marcos said, leading him through the doorway. On the other side, two nurses sat at a desk in front of a line of *medicos*—one was interviewing, the other leaned casually on the corner of the desk, swinging her leg. Both wore baggy biohazard suits.

Marcos scooted past the line of doctors and ambulance drivers, and said to the interviewing nurse, "This guy was down on two."

All chatting in the queue stopped. Both nurses looked up. The stately older woman being interviewed didn't look at the man, but she leaned away from him. "Take Dr. Carpintero," the interviewing nurse said, nodding at her. "I'll get this guy."

Marcos said to the man, "Have a seat."

The others in line watched the man with the backpack warily as he pulled the chair out and sat. Everyone noted where his hand touched the back of the chair.

The nurse pulled out paper and pen.

Funny to see paper, thought the man.

Marcos apparently thought so, too. He gave her a quizzical look.

"The *pilone* is down, OK?" she said. "Can *you* remember anything without your Connection?"

The man was grateful that he happened to be seated for that exchange. *The* pilone *is down?* He tried to clear his throat, but it had gone dry as ash.

Already?

After he'd gathered himself, he asked as calmly as he could, "Has there been a netcrash?"

"They hope to prevent one," the nurse said. "They're advising that no one Connect tonight." She didn't look at him as she shuffled through her papers, which she handled awkwardly, as though unfamiliar with their shape. She began reading in a well-rehearsed drone, "Where were you at the time of the quarantine announcement?"

The Holy Renaissance's greatest strength was its *pilone* network, and he'd presumed it would take days of geometrically increasing mortality rates before the network crashed, if it happened at all. "Name?"

He blurted out his cousin's name. "Andres Villanova."

"Position."

"Orderly. Volunteer."

"Which is it?"

"Um. Volunteer."

The nurse cleared her throat. "Where were you?"

"Will I need a blood test?"

"Of course."

Clasping right hand over left wrist, the man felt with his fingertips for the case he had taped there this morning, the syringe inside loaded with a lethal dose of bumped-up palitoxin. The viruses were both loose. If they weren't here already, WHO and the CDC would descend on this hospital like paratroopers soon.

And now, the blood test. This happened so fast, so incredibly fast.

The nurse seemed to be interpreting his silence as emotion. "*Señor,* where were you please?" she asked, softer this time.

He decided that if he had to speak, then the closer to the truth, the better. "I was down there. On the second floor. I accompanied Cristóbal's—Dr. Cristóbal's field team into the hospital."

She looked up at him tenderly, showing him her sadness for just a breath. Apparently everyone knew that the entire Dengue Task Force was dead. "Were you gloved and masked?"

"And skullcapped. Yes, luckily." That's how Cristóbal and the others had missed identifying him through the course of the Conference.

She continued reading. "Have you touched anyone, eaten anything, used the bathroom? Have you changed your gloves and/or mask and if so, did you dispose of them according to proper hospital biohazard protocol?"

He gave all the correct answers, of course.

"Well, you're probably going to be all right," said the nurse, clearly not believing her own words. "Sign this. Here's a pen. Put the pen in that sharps box when you're done. Then roll up your sleeve." She pulled out a syringe and uncapped it.

He signed the piece of paper and disposed of the pen in the red box next to him marked by a cartoon of a needle. Then he rolled up his right sleeve.

The nurse stopped him and pointed to his other shoulder. "Left arm."

That arm had the palitoxin-syringe case taped to it. He stammered, "What?"

"I said I need your left arm."

He looked at his wrist and the case taped there seemed to bulge like a gun holster. "What happened to infrared? Can't you take a blood test with infrared?"

"Whatever you say, *Doctor.*" She looked bored with him and held up her needle. "Look, sharps are Ministry of Health protocol. So is the left arm. Been this way all weekend. Now let's go."

"That arm is hurt."

If the nurse had gum, she would have snapped it. To make her point she blinked once, very slowly at the man.

The man had a point to make, too. He batted his eyelashes at the nurse and let his brows knit for the slimmest of heartbeats. "I just gave blood, miss." As if embarrassed, he whispered, "It hurts."

She looked away from him quickly as if he had shined a light in her eyes. She sighed, relenting, and pointed the needle at his right arm. "You must have been a beautiful little boy."

He smiled at her with his eyes and rolled up his right sleeve, but he felt little accomplishment in his victory. He was still getting a blood draw. If the hospital was testing blood with a nanophage-based assay, which was *de rigueur* in state-of-the-art hospitals, the nurse would be intrigued, to say the least, by the eight octillian dengue-5 cells broiling in his blood. If she was using ELISA, however, an assay that examined white blood cells to see if the immune system was fighting an infection, he might slide past unnoticed.

The nurse pressed her needle to his skin, and he distantly wondered if he would be sticking himself again in a moment. She slid it in neatly, no blubbering around the vein, and quickly filled the syringe with blood. Then she carried it over to a pheresis machine and plugged the syringe into a capsule dock.

He wanted to ask which it was—ELISA or nanophages. Both assays would use the same hardware these days, he figured. Surely Miguel Cristóbal would have brought nanophage-based assays to Zapata Hospital the minute he realized that this dengue wasn't being spread by mosquitoes.

The woman had her back to him as she set the correct centrifugal speed. Reaching up the sleeve of his lab coat, he carefully peeled the syringe case from his left wrist and held it out of sight beneath the desk. He could stick himself fast—it wouldn't matter where—and drop the plunger. The doctors here would piece the whole thing together from his blood draw, his suicide, and later, his autopsy.

The machine chugged to a stop. The man held his breath. He watched the nurse. She was just staring at the machine.

She is staring longer than necessary, he thought. He opened the case. *She's amazed, no, she's aghast. Eight octillian? She's in shock. I would turn and scream if I saw that number.* The man had his syringe in hand when the nurse finally shook her head.

"*Dios,* I'm sitting here waiting for the report to come by *pilone.*" She rapped her helmet with two hollow knocks then typed in a request for a readout. "What a moron."

The man swallowed hard as she turned back to him with the printout in her hand. "ELISA says you're clean." The nurse sighed in relief. People in line behind him sighed, too. "Good. Take this piece of paper, it's the only indication you have that you don't have the disease."

"Mother of God." He crossed himself with his free hand. "Is that piece of paper official?"

"The pheresis notarized it in the corner."

He took the paper. "It says I have dengue-5."

"Don't worry. You just have the antibodies for dengue," she said. "Everybody in Mexico has those right now, but your count is unusually low. Your guardian angels are taking care of you."

Looking at the notarized paper, his ticket, the man grew giddy with astonishment.

He was about to raise his hand, wave good-bye, then realized he had slipped the syringe back in the case— which was still in his hand. As his eyes flicked up from the case, he saw hers look down at it, frowning. "Spectacles," he said.

She batted her eyes at him. "I'm sure they make you look very distinguished. *Vaya con dios, papi.*"

The man slipped the case into his breast pocket and left the hot lab, the virus filter seeming to suck at him as he passed through its archway.

He was about to fold up his clean bill of health when a man in the waiting room wearing a pressure mask and back-tank stepped up to him and plucked the paper out of his hand. "You're clean, I hear. An orderly?"

"No, *señor,* a volunteer."

"I'm Dr. Reynaldo Cruz. I need help," he said, handing the paper back. Inside the helmet, Dr. Cruz looked harried but excited. "I need to set up another quarantine area, one that can house patients with impaired immune systems. Care to help me?"

Cruz strode purposefully to a back stairwell. The man followed as if drawn by invisible ropes, unable to make sense of what was supposed to happen now. According to his version of the outbreak script, written weeks ago, he wasn't supposed to have slipped past the blood draw.

"If you're clean, you're practically on staff now. Me? I needed eight years of medical school." Cruz's voice echoed in the stairwell. They descended to a landing outside the fifth floor, the entrance marked by a badge scanner.

The man stopped on the stairs and stared at the scan module, its laser eye gleaming like a viper's.

Cruz pulled out his badge and waved it before the eye. The door didn't open.

"It senses two of us." Head bowed, Cruz took a step back to give the man access.

But he didn't have a badge, and no lies came to him.

"It wants your badge, friend," Dr. Cruz said, swinging his arm casually, pointing at the scanner.

The man's eyes darted between Cruz's hand and the scanner's red laser. He imagined he saw electricity flicking between the scanning module and the hand, tasting Cruz's fingers like a tongue.

Dr. Cruz said something to the man, asked him why he wouldn't have a badge. Why *wouldn't* an orderly have a badge? Shouldn't he? Even as a volunteer, shouldn't he? What was the right answer?

Flick, flick, went the tongue of electricity. He couldn't answer. The red laser seemed to turn from Dr. Cruz and flick at the man with knowing distaste.

During those long months in his hot lab, when doubt, guilt, and shame wracked him with migraines, he had sent himself away to a place where the thought of suicide was like morphine to him. His mind would release himself to a clean room with long white draperies undulating in a breeze. There was no piercing self-hatred, no cruel morals in that beautiful room. Just death. And relief.

He took a deep breath, relishing that peaceful place, then realized that something had changed. The laser's red tongue was still flicking, but Dr. Reynaldo Cruz was not standing next to him anymore. Somehow, he was lying at the bottom of the stairs, at the next landing. The harness holding his tanks was twisted around his torso, and his neck and head lay at bad angles to his body.

Who put you down there, Dr. Cruz? The man floated over the steps, down to the crumpled body. A ringing sound was in his ears, like a fading, sustained note. *High D major, to be correct,* he thought. He remembered now that the clang of the tanks striking the cement stairs had rung that stunning note.

He crouched and carefully removed Dr. Cruz's helmet, pressing his fingers into the tender skin over the man's carotid. The neck might have been broken, he thought, and the fluttery pulse, the clammy, white face, the trickle of blood from the ears spoke of extreme shock.

"How brittle," the man whispered, moved. "How brief."

Doors were opening in the stairwell below. Sirens and screaming filtered up the stairs. A mass of people was tromping up the steps.

He stood. As if in a dream, his eyes drifted to the ID badge clipped to the doctor's belt.

He rubbed his forehead hard and pressed his fingers into a spot just above the bridge of his nose. He was being tested. How far would he go?

He wasn't supposed to have slipped past the blood assay. He hadn't anticipated facing the question of how to escape the hospital once he infected it. He was supposed to have been checkmated already by doctors using rapid *pilone* communication. *Why are they still using ELISA to identify this virus? Why didn't Miguel identify me before he died?*

The crowd ascended the staircase toward him.

The man bent down and read the badge. DR. REYNALDO CRUZ, EPIDEMI-OLOGY, ZAPATA HOSPITAL, ASCENSIÓN DF. Reynaldo's DNA chip gleamed silver at the center of the eagle-and-snake seal of Mexico. He flipped the badge over to see the picture. Dr. Cruz looked serious and pensive. But Cruz was taller and darker than he, and looked younger in the photograph. It wasn't a very good match.

He placed a hand against his chest, pressing it flat against the crucifix where it hung beneath hospital scrubs, and shut his eyes. *Why haven't You stopped me?* It was all he could think to pray. Then he unfastened the badge and clipped it to his own belt. The voices and footsteps were just below him now on the next lower landing. He turned and ran back up to the seventh floor, where there was no scanning module. As he opened the door, he could hear someone below shout, "I bet he fell! He's not breathing!"

The man shut the door behind him and tried to control his panting. He crossed through the surgical unit, walking fast, and reached the elevators without anyone stopping him.

When he reached the main floor, the man readjusted the filter over his mouth and walked briskly through the lobby, staring through the glass at three fat army trucks descending into the hospital's courtyard on turbulent air cushions. Angry gawkers standing across the street in the Square of Saint John were pushed back even farther by a line of police wearing gensafe gloves and old-fashioned biowarfare masks. It was building into something nasty, the man could tell. He wouldn't get out that way.

To his right, a woman in scrubs and clamp mask shoved open a swinging door and shouted from what must have been the emergency room beyond, herding patients through the open air lock into the lobby. The patients wore surgical scrubs and Zapata ID badges—*medicos* all. His viruses were feeding on hospital staff now. The woman shouted back into the emergency room, "No, we're done, 'Nardo. The American-British Clinic is taking our incoming! Everyone up to seven!"

The ABC? he thought with contempt. *They can't be serious.* Someone was coordinating from afar. A Mexican outbreak coordinator wouldn't make the ABC a fallback clinic, antiquated as it was. He guessed that WHO and the CDC were involved now, which meant Mexico's public-health system was helpless. Ascensión was about to teeter and fall.

Three officers in full antiviral uniform passed through the corridor of particle-arresting air locks and entered the hospital. Through the plate-glass window, the man could see soldiers outside setting up a riot line.

An officer with captain's bars on his septic uniform turned suddenly and caught the man staring at him. He strode forward, not letting him look away. "Doctor, may I see your ID badge please?"

The man unclipped it from his lab coat and handed it to the captain. "I'm Dr. Reynaldo Cruz, Epidemiology."

"No moon suit, Doctor?"

"I'd love one. I just came down from the lab on seven," he said, trying hard to believe what he was saying. "I'm clean."

The captain ran the badge under his memboard. After a moment, he said, "Reynaldo Cruz? Yes, I see you're clean, but I have you listed as a recent casualty."

"That is—well—I don't know what to say. I'm not dead, as you can see."

After scanning the memboard's screen, the captain's eyes fixed on his. "I have it that you were to attend the Dengue Task Force's conference. Did you?"

"I did. At first. Then I left. I mean, I was called away. Patients. One patient, a woman. She—"

"So you were in the room? You were with them before they all died?"

The man wished he could stop stammering. "Yes. Yes, I was. One minute we were all arguing about Dr. Cristóbal's findings. I was called away to consult—on the dengue patients we received this afternoon. When I returned, I—they were—they were dead. All dead. Some orderlies were putting up an ALHEPA lock."

"They air-locked the room?" The captain nodded and straightened. "Good. That's what I wanted to know."

The man's shoulders lowered in relief. He looked at the lobby's front door. Soldiers were guarding it. There had to be another way out. The emergency room perhaps. He took a step toward its swinging doors, but the captain pressed his hand against the man's chest.

"Another moment, please. If you were invited to the Minister's conference," the captain said, "then you're an expert, and I feared we just lost the best of our best." His efficient tone was gone, and his voice ached with appeal. "Please give me your assessment of the new outbreak, Doctor."

"It's a virulent airborne hemorrhagic fever," he replied, stunned at himself for saying it out loud.

"That's what Central Command reported before it went down. What makes you think hemorrhagic fever?"

His blood raced. It was as if some lunatic part of him itched to spill all his secrets. He found himself ready to tell the captain how he had bought the dengue cells from the Virological Institute in Jakarta, how he cloned them, designing the second, airborne virus, DEN-6, to finish off all the people who had been infected by and survived DEN-5. Instead, he said, "I could tell from the dead bodies, how they died, that this was some kind of hemorrhagic fever—the massive bleeding from every orifice. It's a rapid killer. Must be a megavirus, breeding at a couple octillian per day." That was a little too close to the truth—he wished he could suck the words back into his mouth. "It attacks much faster than—than any hemorrhagic fever I've seen before. If I were you, I'd get all my troops into the same gear that you have on."

The captain seemed impressed, but cautious. His eyes dropped down to the memboard for a moment, then he looked back at the man with suspicion. "You were a colleague of Pedro Muñoz. You signed the petition against Minister Alejandro's handling of the dengue outbreak."

"That's right. I signed that petition." The man perspired and stammered so badly he felt certain the captain would arrest him. He could feel a betrayal of blood surging into his cheeks, so furious that his ears felt hot. "But what does that matter when people are dying like—?"

The captain raised his hand. The elevator doors had opened and a doctor in a biohazard suit emerged. This man's suit made the captain's look like a small-town Mardi Gras costume. The doctor's cuff and collar locks were thick white manacles and the dense plastic fabric creaked like leather as he moved. Pressure made the suit's upper body puffy. Encased in a plastic hood and face mask, the doctor's voice sounded as if it were coming from behind a pillow. "Captain Berenguer?"

"Dr. Simon? Why are you here? Why aren't you coordinating the hot lab?"

"I had to talk to you in person," said Dr. Simon. "The *pilone* wetware is crashing in infected patients as soon as they try to access the net for last rites. People are dying by the score up there." He nodded by way of acknowledging the man and sighed heavily, his breath rushing as if through a long tube. "It's airborne, Captain. We can't contain it within Zapata. There's no way. A flood of DHF victims is about to hit this city."

The captain kept an eye on the man as he said, "What's DHF?"

"Dengue hemorrhagic fever," said the man and Dr. Simon together.

"Dengue isn't an airborne virus," said Simon, "not naturally."

"Virulence?" the man asked, feeling absurd playing the role of consulting epidemiologist on an outbreak he instigated.

"It's the worst I've ever seen. Worse than anything I've ever heard of," answered Simon. "It's breeding and spreading so fast that it's killing patients while we examine them. This site is a complete disaster."

"I'll send my lieutenants and the hospital administration up for a consultation on how to proceed. My orders are to secure this site, so I want a plan of immediate action. We have two hours before new pathology teams arrive from Oaxaca and Monterrey. It may be a day or two before anyone from WHO can get here. You," the captain said to the man. He jerked a thumb at his own chest. *"Ven, Doctor."*

Berenguer turned and walked outside.

Outside. He just walked out of a quarantined building. The man helplessly followed the captain through the hallway of particle arresters leading out of the hospital's lobby, feeling as though he were walking on the bottom of the ocean. He had coordinated outbreaks in regions of the globe where cultural traditions required survivors to kiss the body of a loved one, even if that person had died of skid-37. But this was first world. The captain's behavior seemed willfully ignorant. *Does Berenguer think these ALHEPA filters are arresting the virus? This is madness! Why doesn't he have doctors and soldiers guarding this door?*

Captain Berenguer walked to a truck and stood against its fender. He barked orders at his lieutenants as they strode into the hospital with the newly suited hospital administration. Berenguer waited until the group had entered the hospital, then said, *"Esto hospital esta chingado.* Securing this site is the wrong strategy, isn't it, Dr. Cruz?"

"Yes, it is." If he really were the epidemiologist working this outbreak, he knew what his own advice would be. He decided to give it rather than risk the captain suspecting that he was a moron, or worse, that he was withholding something. "That little biolab on seven won't do any good now. If the virus killed that many people that fast, anyone who isn't naturally immune is as good as dead. That whole hospital is a morgue."

Berenguer seemed to shrug off a nagging fear, then said, "My orders are to save doctors who might be able to help us." He looked at the man with deference, humility. "Your blood was clean?"

Dios mio. Those are his orders? This isn't WHO or CDC in charge. Something evil is working this outbreak. His heart beat so hard he felt it might punch through his chest. "Yes, sir. I have a paper. I'm certified."

"Then I'm taking you to the perimeter clinic where you can do the Holy Renaissance some good." He stared at the man's badge and then said, "What's your node? So I can contact you when the net is up again."

"I am not Connected, Captain."

For the first time, Berenguer looked at him with open distrust. It obviously didn't make sense to the captain that a doctor wouldn't also be Connected. "You disagree with President Orbegón politically, *señor.*"

"Captain, I am a doctor—"

"I just want to know exactly what I'm bringing into the Holy Renaissance's inner sanctum," said Berenguer with a wry smile, crossing his arms over his massive chest.

Unbelievable. Now *he's concerned about me.* "Captain, we have more important matters to—"

"Just answer me. Why did you sign Muñoz's letter? Why aren't you Connected?" said Berenguer as though reasoning with a hysterical person. "Simple questions, aren't they?"

The human rights groups that the man belonged to as a young man when Mexico City was still called Mexico City had cataloged instances of torture and abuse on the part of the Holy Renaissance. Not everyone had to have the Connection; the Renaissance didn't care about ranchers or shopkeepers or street musicians. But prominent officials who refused to undergo the wetware therapy told of the fear tactics, the all-night interrogations into religious affiliation, evenings of beatings and "simple questions" to root out leftists, academics, and even "confused Catholics" who still remained loyal to the Vatican's pope. That was over twenty years ago. But the desire to probe and break obviously still lingered in career officers like Berenguer. He was everything the man hated about the Holy Renaissance, from its sanctimonious top down to its rotten bottom of thuggery. He wanted to rip off this bastard's helmet and kiss him on the mouth.

Instead, he met the captain's eyes and lied as smoothly as he could. "I'm not Connected because I'm a Jew."

Berenguer's face lit up and he let out a loud laugh. "Well, that's a relief. I thought you were going to tell me you were an atheist!" His eyes darkened back into their fierce military scowl. *"¡Mira! ¡Hidalgo!"* The captain shouted to a jeep driver who had just lowered his craft next to Berenguer's truck, emptying a trio of suited Holy Renaissance officials in their crisp black-and-red uniforms. "Take Dr. Cruz here to Clinica Primera. Tell Dr. Menendez I have cleared him and vouch for him personally."

"Yes, sir!" shouted Hidalgo over the scream of his engines. "Hop in, Doctor!"

Priests, the man figured as he passed the officials circling around to the other side of the jeep. He resisted the urge to follow and touch them.

He was reminded of what these men and men like them had done to Mexico, to the Church, to the miracle of the *pilone,* and he was glad that he hadn't played his endgame with the syringe. There was so much more to do—and Lieutenant Hidalgo would escort him straight into the Holy Renaissance's quarantine system, behind their line of pawns.

He climbed into the back, and as the jeep lifted and pivoted toward the nearest La Alta tower, a mad little tickle scurried in his throat. He began to laugh. Hidalgo turned around and looked at him. "Are you all right, Doctor?"

He had tears in his eyes he was laughing so hard. "I'm losing it a little, that's all." He caught his breath and sighed. "Boy, am I losing it."

CHAPTER

THE MASTER SERGEANT locked the cargo down in the center of the hold then did the same for the civilian in his seat, securing his harness and locking him against the forward bulkhead as if he were just another crate of parts shipping to Houston. He gave a thumbs-up accompanied by questioning eyebrows. His passenger, wearing face tags and goggles that matted back his hay-straw hair, sank back in his seat and nodded.

The four lieutenants couldn't hide their glee. Already strapped into their harnesses, they swapped eager little smiles, clearly hoping the civilian, who'd refused a jump seat with the pilots, would puke on takeoff.

The cargo plane taxied into position, engines whining, and the big-bellied plane with wide wings began its long rumbling surge down the runway, all six passengers pressed back into their seats. The airframe shook, then the plane's four engines screamed in full throat.

A breath later, the plane was up, its wheels lifted and locked below, while the civilian calmly murmured to his faraway AI.

One lieutenant shrugged to the others, disappointed, then settled into his harness as comfortably as he could, shutting his eyes for the long ride to Texas.

Stark didn't have an iron constitution, but he did have experience: All Special Pathogens agents found themselves on a cargo plane eventually. Stark's first ride had been fourteen years ago, and the pilot of that plane had refused to bring it to a stop after a nighttime touchdown. Honolulu was lawless back then, and separatists of the indigenous *na 'oiwi* movement were famous for hijacking planes as they unloaded, so Stark and two other doctors were forced to deplane with a crate of malaria vaccine while the C-130 continued rolling. They had dragged their crate into the shadows of the old Honolulu International, listening to rifle fire in the distance, then watched the cargo plane rev back up to takeoff speed and bank away over the island.

Compared to that ride, this, Stark's fifth, was luxury's lap.

He wanted to sleep, but there was too much to do. The midnight milk run with his grandfather had been exhausting, as was the bureaucracy at Fort 3M in Minneapolis, early this morning. Not because the Holy Renaissance's phony orders to carry a CDC doctor to Houston caused him any delays, but because a corporal at the gate tried commandeering the milk truck until Grandfather showed him that the transmission was held up with a web of baling wire. At which point, the night officer arrived. He didn't want the truck but rather its contents, and started bidding on the load of milk in Grandfather's tanker. He couldn't match the Urban Milk Alliance's fixed price with the *quop*—but he had something better. Gas. Grandfather sold for just under the Urban Milk Alliance's price per pound, a full tank, and his grandson's speedy clearance into the base.

"Too tired to drive home now," Grandfather said, poking his head out the driver's seat window to talk to Stark standing on the blacktop. When he was tired, like this, he looked ancient. "I'll see if I can beg a bed at the Methodists' camp tonight. I mean this morning. Call me at the farm tomorrow—I mean today—so I know you got to Houston OK."

"I do that."

"You will do that."

"I *will* do that," Stark had said, by way of saying good-bye, and dragged his lugalls through Fort 3M's open gate.

Leaning out the milk truck window, his grandfather called after him, "And don't jump into the middle of anything and bullshit your way out, like you usually do!"

Now, several hours later, he was slouched in his harness on a C-130 murmuring orders to Queen Mum, answering e from the World Health Organization's DEN-5 and DEN-6 coordinator, and logging clearance codes for medical flights to land in quarantined Ascensión International—all as if he were sitting in Wisconsin, voicing frustration to his CDC colleagues that he hadn't been invited to help Mexico's Central Command.

The C-130's hum lulled the other passengers to sleep almost immediately, but Stark kept working. While he begged for volunteers from the Chinese Institute of Epidemiology (in whose good graces he'd stood ever since the Borna outbreak), Queen Mum flashed Stark a strategic map of Ascensión. To his relief, perimeter clinics—where the infected could be quarantined and survivors treated—ringed twelve distinct hot zones, any one of which could have taxed the country's public-health resources. One hot zone centered on the north of the city at La Villa de Guadalupe where the National Basilica sat, another circled the airport, and perimeters had been formed around various neighborhoods where the viruses had found purchase. But most importantly, rings within rings of clinics surrounded Zapata Hospital, the National Square, and the rest of Ascensión's *centro histórico*, where the outbreaks had been thickest.

Queen Mum, her voice perfectly audible over the whine of the C-130, informed him, "The Ministry of Health reports that a door-to-door vaccination program began this morning." Her voice became jolly. "Nothing like locking the barn door after the cattle have run away, yes, Dr. Stark?"

He pulled up the Ministry of Health's vaccination report. They were using dengue tetravalents, which theoretically would slow the advance of the disease, but no one of authority in Mexico believed it was a cure. Mexico's omnivalent vaccine, which Stark was eager to see employed, would apparently have to wait. After a Zapata Hospital courier service literally delivered Big Bonebreaker to the plant last night, antiviral cleaning crews were busy scrubbing down the lone production facility in Ascensión. Omnivalents would be unavailable for three to four more days—an eternity in this rapid outbreak.

Stark peered at the map, which appeared plastered against the scuffed and dingy wall of the cargo hold, a splash of light from the sole window near Stark washing out part of southern Ascensión. He counted the largest routes out of the city. "They got those highways blocked?"

Mum opened a new screen. Live *ojo* coverage showed bumper-to-bumper gridlock on an arid mountain highway. In a wash of horror and relief, Stark watched as *servicio sagrado* troops in antiviral "moon suits" patrolled alongside the cars, rifles raised, while frightened people within looked out at the troops. "All major routes out of the city are blocked," Mum said, "and evacuees from the city are being quarantined in their autos until physicians can attend to them."

Got to hand it to fascists, Stark thought, nauseated by the looks of terror he'd seen in the dim faces behind windshields. *They know how to lock down during an outbreak.* He blinked the highway footage away, figuring that most of those people would perish in their cars.

Stark flicked his wrist, glancing down at the mortality number there—203. Clearly, mortality wasn't being updated—there had to be three times that many dead—which meant data was still being collected on the ground. "Update me on reports of dengue-5 and dengue-6 outside Mexico, Mum," Stark said, opening his hand.

On his palm, Mum flashed the figures: Caracas 7; Havana 22; Los Angeles 8; Manila 3; New York City 8; Miami 11; Raleigh, North Carolina 1. Big Bonebreaker, which had turned out to be an effective term to describe the hemorrhagic fever caused by dengue-5 and dengue-6 acting in tandem, wasn't finding purchase anywhere else. Obviously, dengue-6, the airborne virus, wasn't as communicable as it first appeared. Besides, four days of dengue-5 coursing through Ascensión's collective bloodstream had rendered that city vulnerable to Big Bonebreaker's hemorrhagic syndrome. But these were questions of pathology, not epidemiology, and he had to trust that Isabel Khushub would answer them by the time Stark got to Mexico.

Queen Mum said, "Dr. Kodzo in Ghana is calling for you, Dr. Stark."

Stark closed his hand and blinked at the icon. "Stark here. Dr. Kodzo?"

"Yes, hello, good evening, Dr. Stark. It's a distinct pleasure. My apologies for not getting back to you sooner."

Eight hours of coordinating the global response to Ascensión's outbreak was burning away Stark's patience. He hoped Mum could translate a softer tone, because he didn't have it. "I gonna need immediate responses from you from now on, Doctor. You'll need to get sat access. Talk to the WHO office in Accra as soon as we finished here. Now," Stark tugged down his shirt, feeling as if he were finally getting somewhere. "You heard about the outbreak in Mexico?"

Kodzo's voice lowered into a chastised flatness. "I have. It sounds very bad, Doctor."

"Dr. Joaquin Delgado advised me about a dengue outbreak you all had among your cotton workers in Ghana."

"Yes. Yes. A dengue outbreak three weeks ago." It obviously rattled Dr. Kodzo that such prominent doctors had been paying attention to him. "I coordinated it myself. Yes."

"I don't have time to read your reports. Can you summarize for me?"

It would have been quicker for Stark to read Kodzo's work, as the doctor was all too eager to explain how an unusually rainy season along with a faulty fumigation program had combined to create a window of breeding opportunity for *Aedes aegypti,* dengue's mosquito vector. "There were nearly twenty cases reported in area hospitals," said Kodzo. "Very embarrassing for our Department of Public Health. We pride ourselves on keeping an endemic virus like dengue under control."

"Mortality?"

"No deaths. All the cotton workers who contracted dengue are back in the fields, to my knowledge."

"And which serotype did you encounter?"

"We had great success building nanophages against dengue-4."

Ghana had clearly identified the virus correctly and, consequently, mortality was typical. "Doctor, within the next two hours, send me a schematic for the hunter you built. I need to see what therapeutic genes you used in your nanophages. Also, do you have any epidemiological data on your dengue patients' backgrounds?"

"Nanophagic genomics, we have. The other? I don't know," Kodzo said, bristling at Stark's bluntness. "I don't see how that will help you, at any rate."

"Delgado speculated a connection between the underground cotton trade between your country and Mexico. I want to see if your dengue and Mexico's are related."

"An exciting theory. I'll see what I have for you."

"This outbreak is moving fast, Doctor. As soon as possible, please." Stark signed off asking Queen Mum to give Kodzo all the necessary codes for fastest access to the Central Command.

Stark placed a call to Joaquin Delgado, left a message when he didn't get an answer, then realized he had hit the first natural stopping place since he'd accepted this job from El Mono. Though he was jacked on bad army coffee, Stark could feel his shoulder muscles unclenching. The outbreak was a logistical nightmare, to be sure, but Ascensión was now following his outbreak script, and he had a line on Ghana's epidemiology, too. His mind was eased, immersed again in the familiar world of Special Pathogens. It filled the empty corners of him, and comforted Stark so deeply that when he sighed and eased back in his seat, his back cracked in relief and he fell asleep.

He woke to Queen Mum whispering in his ear. "Dr. Stark? I can tell by your vitals that you're sleeping, but I have something you might want to see before you land."

Stark shook himself awake and aimed his goggles out of the cargo plane's lone portal. The plane was flying over the detritus of Houston's outer rings, as if the city's skyline had crashed on the coast and scattered garbage in all directions. He hadn't wanted to sleep so long, but he was grateful for the chance to recharge. "What you got?"

"Preliminary epidemiological data from Mexico's Ministry of Health, courtesy of Minister Diego Alejandro."

The name cleared Stark's mind like a shot of adrenaline. "Oh, really? Give me a look, Mum." Stark blinked at the report and saw it was over three hundred pages long, but it covered the first thirty-six hours of the outbreak. Stark immediately thumbed through to the Zapata Hospital material, but as expected, nothing earlier than noon on May 15, the crucial day of the outbreak, and no data from Pedro Muñoz. "Bastard."

"Two things, Dr. Stark. I have a call waiting from Dr. Kodzo. And I took the liberty of assessing some of the Ministry of Health's epidemiological report."

"Dr. Kodzo?" said Stark, as he pulled up Queen Mum's assessment and glanced at the mortality number—455. "What do you have for me?"

"Hello, Dr. Stark," said Kodzo. "I have a sat phone now. The WHO office was very helpful in giving me instructions how—"

"Get to the point, Doctor. I about to land."

"Did you—er—I see—were you able to read the nanophagic genomic analysis?"

Stark glanced at that icon. "No, but glad to have it. Thank you."

"Excellent. I also have a report, here, from an epidemiologist hired by the Federated Cotton Workers Union. The link that Delgado suggested does exist."

"Really?" said Stark. "Explain."

"The black market in Ghana was accused of transporting Ghanaian cotton into Mexico and bringing an *Aedes aegypti* vector back from Mexico, which they claim took residence in unused irrigation systems here, thus endangering the lives of our workers. The Union's epidemiological data seems to support this, as our vector appears to be New World, not Old."

The Ghana dengue was serotype dengue-4. Before the outbreak made it clear that the Ascensión virus wasn't dengue, Mexican doctors thought it was dengue-4. Mortality and pathology, however, were obviously very different. Besides, dengue was constantly crossing back and forth across the Atlantic, so while Kodzo's wasn't the flashing red "aha" that Stark was looking for, still, it was something to go on. He thanked Kodzo, blinked the line shut, then immediately began inhaling the Ghanaian report.

"Joaquin Delgado for you, Dr. Stark," Mum said.

Stark's head snapped up as if Joaquin had entered the cargo hold. *"Maestro."* He reacted so suddenly that the officers in their harnesses jerked their heads toward him in confusion. "Hello!"

"¿Qué va, compañero?" Joaquin had gone visual and was sitting with his back against a yellow-tiled wall, his voice echoing. "Did you find a connection between Mexico and Ghana?"

"Where you at?" Stark said with a laugh. "A bathroom?"

"A health club. I came to a gymnasium. To relax," Joaquin said. His face looked haggard, and he seemed exhausted. "The work here is so tedious. Completely, utterly, bone-numbingly tedious." His eyes searched the air for a moment, listening. "What's that god-awful noise, Enrique?"

"Pasteurizer," Stark said quickly. "I out in the dairy." He might have been brilliant, but the cosmopolitan Delgado wouldn't know that a pasteurizer was virtually silent compared to a C-130. For once, Stark was grateful that he couldn't go visual with his Central Command interface. "Listen, I been in contact with Dr. Kodzo," Stark said, "and, you right, it looks like a match at first, but the two dengues don't seem that similar to me."

"So it was a complete dead end?" Joaquin said skeptically.

"Well, I gonna go ahead and send Mexico the specifications on Dr. Kodzo's nanophages—at least it's something. But more and more, I thinkin bioweapon." Stark paused, deliberately derailing his own train of thought. He didn't want to talk about pathology, Ghana, nanophages, or bioweapons right now. He didn't want to theorize, or postulate, or wrangle over minutiae. He yearned for Delgado's actual help, not his theories. "Shit, Joaquin," Stark said, "what you doin in Vienna?"

Joaquin's voice softened, sounding defensive. "I told you, I'm fishing for a contract here so that I—"

"No," Stark said, hoping he didn't sound too desperate. "I mean, the *hell* you doin in Vienna?"

"I have responsibilities here, Enrique," Joaquin said. But his eyes grew bright. He couldn't hide it from Stark: the old man was eager, thirsty to be asked this very question. "I can't leave. My work is here."

"Your work ain't in Vienna. It in Mexico." If Stark could get Joaquin to go to Ascensión, he decided, then he'd confide in his old friend that he was already on his way. "You belong at this outbreak—*this* outbreak—and you know it."

"What do you mean by that? I 'belong' there?"

"Because it the biggest, Joaquin, and you the best."

Joaquin chuckled. "*You're* the best, *compañero*. Why aren't *you* there?"

"Mexico ain't inviting me. Won't neither, and I doubt I'd go if they asked. Holy Renaissance got an embargo on my country—but it's a clear shot for you."

"Fly to Ascensión and *help* the Holy Renaissance? Help Emil Orbegón?" Joaquin said, with a tartness that bordered on hostility. "I don't think so, young man."

"People, Joaquin, they just people. Hundreds of em dyin, too."

The Spaniard leaned his back against the yellow tiles, and a wave of emotion hit him, so strong, so visible on his tortured face, that Stark was sorry he'd played to Joaquin's compassion.

Joaquin pressed the heels of his hands against his eyes by way of drying them, gathered himself, and said, "Have you heard from Diego yet? Have you heard why he classified the outbreak?"

"No. Not a word," Stark said. "It like he vanished."

"Emergent pathogens. A hateful fascist state. The betrayal of a *compañero*." Joaquin's eyes burned with tired anger as he stared into his phone at Stark. "This one is such a big fight, Enrique, and I thought I was out of Special Pathogens work. You just can't ask me to—"

"We could work it together, like Guangzhou. You know we make a great team. You on the ground," Stark said, knowing he'd crossed the line into pleading, "me up here—coordinating the CDC response. Mexico needs you, *maestro*."

Joaquin's heavy emotion passed, and with Stark's words, his face hardened in a cold, appreciative smile. "You make that Herculean work sound fun, Doctor."

"Think about it," said Stark. "Your Viennese colleagues might *expect* you to go."

"All right. All right, Enrique," said Joaquin, a releasing in his voice, astounded by his own words, it seemed, and by this turn of events. "I'll talk to my people here. Let's talk later today and I'll tell you my decision. *Pues*. I'm going to sign off, someone's coming. Don't give up on Ghana's cotton fields too soon. I still say there's something there."

Stark gave a hurried good-bye before Joaquin disappeared; then he turned his attention back to the Ghanaian report. He found it difficult to concentrate, though; his thoughts were humming with the hope of having Joaquin Delgado's vast experience at his disposal.

While skimming it, Stark said to Mum, "You assimilated the Mexican epi data, Mum?"

"Correct, Doctor."

"What did you find?"

"I found incidences of an unexplained malady at a poverty clinic in northern Ascensión. Dr. Miguel Cristóbal flagged it, and I thought you might find it interesting as well."

Stark glanced out the window and saw the plane's shadow snaking across the ground below. They would be landing any moment. "Sounds promising. And?"

"A Dr. Sierra reported to the Holy Renaissance that he was dealing with several incidents of a mysterious digestive problem combined with mouth pustules and wanted advice."

He had cued Mum to respond to words like "unexplained," "mysterious," and "anomalous" when assessing epidemiological data. But it didn't always work. "Digestive tract, eh? Great, Mum. Keep that flagged. I'm going to finish this Ghana report and meanwhile, I want you to send the genomics on Ghana's nanophage to Bela and tell her it may be a tool we can use, may not. I'll check in again as soon as I can, Mum."

Stark scanned through the rest of the cotton Union report, but found nothing that would indicate that Ghana's dengue was anything other than garden-variety dengue. The epidemiologist even went so far as to include a chicken report, showing the population of the cotton-growing region and its communal response to dengue's appearance among them. Mexico's virus had entrenched in 68 percent of Ascensión. Ghana's dengue, less than 2 percent. Stark blinked the report shut, filed the icon, and began peeling off his face tags. Perhaps he was being foolhardy, dismissing a theory of Joaquin's so quickly. But he could return to the material and sift through it more thoroughly once he was in Ascensión.

Stark swept off his goggles and watched the suburbs stream beneath his window as he packed his brain gear. With Mexico and Texas knuckle-locked at the border, less than a hundred miles away, the Houston burbs were now a repository for refugees and itinerant Texans. In the clustering subdivisions below, refugee encampments sprawled like insane street fairs. Corrugated metal shacks surrounded gutted buses and people thronged in cul-de-sacs turned free clinics.

The C-130 swung around and Stark could see Houston International now. He pulled the leather bag holding his brain gear close. West of the airport, Stark could see distant columns of smoke where American and Mexican missile drones vied for position along the Guadalupe River.

A moment later, the plane was bumping down the runway in Houston, taxiing toward the airport. It stopped long before it got there, and Stark could see loaders filing up to the C-130, ready to remove its contents. That's when he looked down at one of the crates and realized he'd been shipped to Houston with parts for war drones.

Climbing down the ladder from the cargo hold, Stark frowned beneath Houston's crushing humidity. Though only midmorning, the tarmac felt like a griddle as he shouldered his luggage and walked with the four lieutenants toward the airport. To do so, they had to run a gauntlet of young peddlers with net bags of plump grapefruits and marionettes of President Orbegón with cartoon, bandito moustaches, jigging on strings to attract buyers.

"No, thanks," Stark growled, muscling past the vendors. Five other boys immediately swung in front of him, hoisting fruit and toys in his face. "No, *thanks,* I said, now let me—"

Suddenly, two of the boys cried out in pain and jumped back from Stark, rubbing their elbows and scowling. The mob of young vendors parted and Stark could see a lit cigarette bouncing on the tarmac before a girl of ten or so, who was smiling a sweet but arch smile for such a young face. "For two hundred dollars," she said in a deep Southern accent. It sounded like, "*Yew* c'n mike the dictitor day-ance." Her Orbegón puppet bounced and capered madly.

The boys slid away from her and followed the lieutenants toward the sliding doors of the airport, leaving Stark to walk with the imp.

"Come on, Yankee, you can spare it." She matched his stride. "You got a place to stay in Houston?"

"Ain't staying in Houston," said Stark, and immediately regretted it. He was now in a conversation.

"US Army, ain't you? Hey, hey, what do you say? Lend a buck to the USA?" she said, quoting a popular tune from the Border War. Midair, President for Life Orbegón knelt and held a hand out to Stark.

Stark figured what the hell. Two hundred was a cheap meal for him. In the drained Houston economy, it was probably a day's work. He fished out two crumpled C-notes from his front pocket and handed them to the girl. "Keep the puppet."

"Thanks, Yank. Want me to carry your bags or something?"

Stark looked up and grimaced at the oppressive Texas sun. Still a hundred yards from the airport and the back of his shirt was already damp. "Why not?" Stark handed her his lugall but kept the case with his brain gear.

The puppet seller handled the bag awkwardly but Stark didn't offer to take it back. She swung the strap across her slim shoulders, almost toppling, and led the way, reaching into her breast pocket for a cigarette, lighting it with a rusty flame lighter. "Need a ride somewhere?"

Stark's public health reflex kicked. "A kid your age? Shouldn't smoke. Causes all kinds of nasty—"

"Don't worry. I don't really smoke," said the girl, inhaling deeply and grinning wickedly. The lighter clacked shut. "Anyway, don't hang around the airport too long. Tempers high today."

Fifty feet from the airport, Stark could feel cool air gasping from the entrance's sliding doors. "Whose tempers?"

"Everybody's. Federals approved the draft."

"That's got folks riled? Why?"

"Guess you *ain't* US Army." She gave him an annoyed glance. "We got a last-minute land grab going on between here and Austin. Militias jockeying for position before the US Blues bring in their draftees." She drew at her cigarette. "There were two shootouts yesterday in the food court."

Stark followed his guide into Houston International, and the cool air was a relief, even though the place smelled terrible.

The airport was more market than terminal, with stalls of food vendors packing the central concourse. Wet sides of beef hung from tent crossbeams, swinging over pint baskets of shrimp and red filets of marlin on ice. Card tables held pyramids of oranges and lemons, and racks of motherboards were displayed under a sign reading THE CHAIRMAN'S. As soon as vendors saw the passengers, the hawking started.

"I got *man*darins! *Tex*as satsuma manda-*rinos*!"

"Gulf shrimp! Right off the boat! Gulf shrimp!"

"Meow!" shouted a woman with whiskered, whole catfish. "Meow!"

"Sammy Houston Original! Mama bottled it herself! Home brew *heeere*!"

If any vendors got too close to Stark, the puppet seller waved them back with the lit end of her cigarette. "See? Kid my size has to have a weapon. Anyway, where you meeting your ride, Yank?"

Stark realized he had been given no clue, no secret phrase with which to find El Mono's emissaries. He glanced at the nearest vendors, the Asian shrimp boaters. Would the Mexicans be in disguise? Perhaps they would prefer posing as the Hispanic leather workers. Stark scanned the crowd of ratty-haired, Caucasian women selling ganja buds as thick as their dreds, the pale-eyed cattlemen, Hmong cowboys at their tobacco stall, the Afro-Cubans in big-pocketed *guayabera* shirts, the Jewish men in *yamulkas*, prayer shawls, and snakeskin boots, and all the rival uniforms—Republic of Texas, US Army, the West Texas Confederacy—brushing against one another between vendor stalls. Holy Renaissance officers would stand out like Thoroughbreds in this mishmash. Stark sucked his teeth. "I'm not sure where to meet my ride."

"I'll take you down to the old baggage claim," said the girl. "Some folks still think airbuses stow luggage."

They pushed their way through the market and Stark was glad to have his guide. She moved like a wedge in front of him, the cherry of her cigarette clearing their way with shouts of surprise and pain.

She came to a stop when she found a dense crowd that wouldn't part for her. It was a ring of officers cheering beneath a netmonitor. Stark squinted at the face shown there and realized it was the bespectacled President of Mexico, Emil Orbegón, addressing his people on the outbreak. "Wait, miss. Wait a minute!"

"They been showing that all morning," the girl said, bored.

Stark edged forward so he could read the subtitles through the broadcast's blurry reception. "What he say?"

The girl made a dismissive gesture with her cigarette, like *listen if you want,* then took a drag. "Blaming us for something in the capital."

Trying to ignore the war whoops of the officers, Stark read the words scrawling below Orbegón's chin and cravat, tied in a perfect Cancún knot.

"*. . . not a heroic act of war, but a cowardly act of bioterrorism. Two genetically engineered viruses have been released upon the civilians in our great capital. One is meant to weaken us, the second is meant to kill.*"

For Mexico's sake, Stark hoped Diego Alejandro didn't write that awful description of dengue hemorrhagic fever.

"*Now, whether these diseases were designed in the United States, Great Britain, France, or Germany,*" Orbegón said, "*I promise you, mexicanistas, I will bring the culprits to justice. I promise, too, that I will repair the pilone network as soon as humanly possible, so that you may communicate with your priests and churches. But while I slave for you, promise me that you will cooperate with our Ministry of Health. Promise me that you will wear the gloves and masks being distributed in your neighborhoods, and promise that you will lay down your arms against the police attempting to protect you.*"

Stark started as if splashed with water. "The hell?"

"They rioting in the streets down there," grinned a young man with straight white teeth. He nudged Stark like they were watching a sporting event. "Their 'sacred service' killed a couple hundred so far! Rioters think the Holy Renaissance released the viruses, but don't you hope *we* infected em? Ho, man, what a hoot and a half if the ol' U.S. of A. pulled this off!"

Stark backed out of the cluster of officers and found the girl again. Mum had said nothing about rioting. Widespread civic violence would make his rings of hot labs and perimeter clinics virtually useless. He made a note to himself to find out why Mum hadn't reported this. "Let's go, kid," said Stark, turning away from Orbegón. "I can hear the rest later."

As they walked down a flight of stationary escalators, Stark saw two Hispanic-looking men on the floor below. Both wore the stiff-brimmed hats and brown uniforms of Texas Rangers. The five-pointed stars on their chests shone like little mirrors. The taller of the two carried a sign that read, HENRY DAVID ESTARQUE.

Stark smirked at the disguise. It was a good choice. Stark had heard from officers back in Minneapolis that the Rangers were loose and powerful cannons, allying themselves somewhere between the Republic of Texas and the old state Railroad Commission. The United States was trying desperately to form an alliance between Texas splinter groups, bringing in drafted soldiers to serve alongside Railroad Men and Texas Republicans. But the Rangers refused to sign off on the Fed's stated willingness to use nukes on Texas soil, so the Rangers remained fiercely independent. Three US soldiers, waiting for transport on the lower level, stole fearful looks at the two Rangers.

"I'm Dr. Stark," Stark called to them from the escalator.

The girl shushed him violently. "You crazy? They Rangers, man!"

Stark said, "Don't worry. I know them."

"You do, huh?" the girl said with a flat, wary voice.

"Henry David? From Wisconsin?" said the shorter of the two Rangers, strolling forward to greet him at the base of the escalators. "My pleasure. I Sergeant Weitzel. This here Lieutenant Valesquez." He took Stark's hand as Stark stepped onto the ground floor.

The girl kept her eyes on the Rangers' stars as the three men shook hands.

"I ready," said Stark. "You guys got a car nearby?"

"Right outside," said Weitzel.

Lieutenant Valesquez, a tall, glowering man with a bad complexion, said nothing, but he matched distrustful stares with the puppet seller.

"Where y'all goin?" said the girl as she walked alongside Stark, refusing to relinquish his lugall.

They passed through the sliding-door exit and back into the blast furnace of Houston midday heat.

Valesquez raised his finger as if he were drawing a gun and pointed to a glossy black sedan in the airport's roundabout. "None of your business."

"You Rangers goin to *Bastrop*?"

Stark didn't understand the tension that suddenly straightened the spines of the two agents.

"Maybe." Sergeant Weitzel tilted his head back and forth, making the brim of his hat seesaw. "Maybe not."

"Gonna put the bite on the PAT once and for all, ain't you?" said the girl.

Sergeant Weitzel remained military stoic but tilted that hat brim side to side again. "No, ma'am, we're not."

Valesquez waited by the passenger door and Weitzel fumbled for his keys. A good detail for the American disguise, Stark thought, having a "car" that needed "keys."

While Weitzel opened the driver's side, and lanky Valesquez folded himself into the sedan, the girl put a hand on Stark's arm and whispered, "They ain't Rangers."

Stark was impressed. "No?"

"Aw, man. You knew that already."

"Relax. These guys aren't going to hurt me."

"Maybe. But don't let them take you through Bastrop."

Stark leaned toward her. "Bastrop dangerous?"

"That town belongs to the People's Army. These guys think they cute in their Ranger stars, but they in a world of crap if they bump into the PAT."

Stark opened the back door and slipped his brain gear inside, then he took his lugall from the girl. After he stashed it, he reached into his pocket. "Thanks, miss. Look. Take another C. Don't tell no one you saw me, OK?"

"You all right. I hope you know what you doin, though." She kissed the bill. *"Adios, amigo."*

Stark saluted the girl and crawled into the car.

Weitzel started the engine and pulled out of the loading zone, veering between a truckload of watermelons and a big, Caucasian family waiting to cross the street, all holding hands.

"Reminds me of a joke," said Weitzel. He maneuvered the car into the exit queue. "Why did the Anglo cross the road?"

Valesquez chuckled like an indulgent father. "Why?"

"He saw a *peso* on the other side."

Weitzel and Valesquez laughed together, a little too long and a little too loud.

Stark figured he was missing nuances and ignored the slur. Enough Americans had told Mexican jokes over the years to draw several decades of return fire. "So," said Stark. "We going to Bastrop?"

The laughter dried into a sober silence. Valesquez showed Stark his profile. "As a matter of fact, yes," he said. The older man was obviously a native Spanish speaker with his crisp accent. "It is the only corridor into *Tejas* that is not patrolled by the Blues."

As they approached the exit's checkpoint, Stark buckled his safety belt. The car smelled like leather and gun oil. Weitzel flashed the airport's security bot a laser ID and Stark fussed with his seat belt. He didn't want to think about the staggering number of battalions, squadrons of jets, missile drones, and satellites focused on the border he was about to cross. Calming his rising anxiety, Stark forced himself to think about the outbreak, the riots. He had the urge to wrestle into his brain gear and find out more about the rioting. "You guys hooked up?"

"Of course," Valesquez replied like he was waiting for the question. He tapped his temple where Stark could see the faint white end of a scar disappearing into his hairline. "But the network is down temporarily."

"I know. But you must have heard something about the riots in Ascensión."

The car swerved hard from the airport's boulevard. A moment later they were jockeying in four lanes of traffic on a crowded three-lane highway. Once he was in his lane, Weitzel looked at Valesquez. Valesquez looked over the back seat at Stark. "What have *you* heard?"

"I heard about a hundred were killed."

"We've lost a lot more than that," said Valesquez in a slow, dark voice.

"Were these riots citywide? Were they near the hot zones?" Stark asked.

Valesquez adjusted his tie. Cancún knot. "I am not at liberty to say."

"The riots, they affecting the quarantine?"

"I told you, I am not at liberty to say, Dr. Stark."

"Screw liberty. Don't you *care*?" Stark snorted in disbelief. Then he reconsidered. Perhaps the cloaks and daggers had already been donned and drawn. Perhaps the Holy Renaissance was deliberately keeping these officers in the dark to protect them. Stark was making a sincere observation when he said, "Maybe you guys don't even know who I am."

Weitzel looked like he was gnawing an angry bone as he drove. "*¿Piensa que estamos idiotas?*"

"Don't worry. We know you." Valesquez held up the little placard, HENRY DAVID ESTARQUE, and gave it to Stark.

Weitzel managed a smile. "You comin' to save poor old Mexico, that it, *yanqui*?" The smile turned leering and sarcastic as he met Stark's eye in the rearview mirror. "'Maybe you don't know who I am.' *Chinga,* you *gringos* still think you own the world." The car accelerated as Weitzel grew angrier with every word he spoke. "You all so damn vain, you make me sick. You *still* think you're better than us. Even after we carve you up like a roast and eat—"

"Sergeant." Valesquez touched Weitzel's thigh, and the car decelerated. Valesquez then looked over his shoulder at Stark and lowered his eyes in apology.

Stark folded his hands in his lap and looked down. "Got a joke for you guys."

Weitzel raised his eyes to the rearview mirror again, and Valesquez seemed relieved to have the mood lightened. "Let's hear it."

Stark said, "Why did the two Mexicans sneak across the river?"

Both men turned to scowl at Stark. Valesquez sneered with incredulous anger.

"Don't know that one?" asked Stark, pasting on a good-natured smile.

Both men stiffened and glared at the crowded traffic on the highway. By their reaction, they were Texans, and while it might have been years since Americans told "wetback" jokes, the sting of them remained.

"I'll repeat it, nice and slow," said Stark, baiting them with a condescending voice. "'Why—did the *Mexicans*—cross the *river*?'"

The furious silence in the sedan ticked like a bomb.

"Give up?" Stark said. He leaned forward so that they both could see him with peripheral vision. "To bring a doctor back home because their people were dying by the hundreds, maybe thousands." He looked back and forth between the two officers until their smoldering eyes cooled. "Get it?"

Weitzel turned back to the road and hunched over the steering wheel, choking it. Valesquez didn't smile, but a shadow of a dimple appeared in his acne-scarred cheek. "Good one." His eyebrows flashed upward. "Let's see if you are the concerned doctor you say you are. Credentials, please."

Stark wondered why they hadn't asked for his ID at the airport, but as he passed his card over to Valesquez, he realized it made sense. Now, if they discovered his identification was invalid, they could kill him. Especially after his snide little joke.

Valesquez fed the card into his memboard. Stark presumed he was processing his CDC identification number. After a moment, Valesquez returned it. "Henry David Stark, you're clear to travel with us. And by the way," he said, "El Mono sends his regards."

CHAPTER

9

WEITZEL MANEUVERED the black sedan through chaotic traffic exiting Houston on the Old Telephone Road, then joined a convoy of twenty Railroad Commission jeeps roaring west toward the Mexican border. After several miles of following their dust, he saluted the convoy, mumbling, *"Chíngate,"* then left the highway at Rosenberg. A sign at the city limits informed them that the Railroad Commission controlled this town. The Commission's seal was plastered over a garbage can and hung on the signpost. Below it was scrawled *"Blues Go Home"* in English, which was crossed out and rescrawled in Spanish.

"We're switching vehicles here," Valesquez told Stark. "We need something faster to cross the border."

Steering the sedan away from the military's point of control at the edge of town, Weitzel took them into an abandoned strip mall, where a dim PAWN AMERICA sign flashed like failing synapses on the edge of the parking lot. Weitzel drove straight into the mall through the gutted Walmart.

"Get your things," said Valesquez, leaving the sedan.

"We're over here," said Weitzel. He pointed to a tarp obviously covering a *barco* beneath a ceiling sign that read HOUSEWARES.

Stark had seen pictures of *barcos del cielo*, skyboats, the newest toys courtesy of Pemex-Lockheed International Corp, but he had never traveled in one. They were a favorite of the *mundo*-wealthy *clase de prima* living in the Sierra Madre Mountains of central Mexico, too rich to deal with mountain roads and hairpin turns. Only the upper crust in American cities like New York and Miami could afford a skyboat's fuel consumption.

Weitzel flicked back the tarp, revealing a black-hulled monstrosity that looked like a fat, 1940s gangster car with clipped, falconlike wings. *"Abra, barco."*

The doors slid aside and Stark tossed his packs into the backseat. Once the other two were strapped into their seats, Stark said, "How long to San Antonio in one of these?"

Weitzel slipped into the driver's seat.

"Thirty or forty minutes," said Valesquez, "once we're airborne."

Weitzel steered the skyboat out of the mall on a purring cushion of air that blew the garbage out of the Walmart. Once in the parking lot, he told the skyboat to fly—*"Vuele, barco"*—and the air cushion moaned its increase beneath them. Soon they were soaring fifty feet above the road, racing west.

Just a few minutes outside of Rosenberg, however, Weitzel swore. *"Mierda."* His voice was quiet and urgent.

"¿Qué hondo?" muttered Valesquez. What's up?

Stark straightened, straining to catch their hurried Spanish.

"Tenemos amigos," said Weitzel, jerking his thumb over his shoulder. *"Tres barcos del cielo detrás de nosotros."* We have friends. Three skyboats behind us.

"¿Quién es?" asked Valesquez, looking back and seeing nothing.

"Tienen los faros del Ejército Mexicano." They have Mexican Army beacons.

Stark looked over his shoulder but saw nothing out of the rear window, just the rapidly retreating town of Rosenberg clouded by the *barco*'s heat exhaust.

Valesquez tapped a screen awake on his dashboard console. "Are you strapped in, Dr. Estarque? Good." He swore and dropped a lever, then told Weitzel to head all out for the border. "Don't worry about their drones, Sergeant. Rosa got us good code. We'll sail through."

"Who's back there?" Stark buckled himself with every strap he could find. He heard a deep, rocketing noise, looked out the rear window, and saw two vapor trails fire out from the back of the *barco*. "Why you firing? Didn't you just say they Mexican Army?"

Weitzel said, "Mexican Army wouldn't use their own beacons this side of—"

Suddenly, fire flashed and burst against the driver's door.

"What the hell?" screamed Stark.

The explosion sent the skyboat into a fast plunge. At fifty feet, there wasn't much room to plunge. Weitzel dropped the landing air cushion and the *barco* caromed off of it, and up into the sky. Stark gagged as his stomach surged to the back of his throat. Weitzel dropped landing gear, but not before another explosion had rocked them from below, jarring Stark's bones.

"*Bajo, bajo, Sargento,*" growled Valesquez, his thin body forced back into his seat.

The skyboat lurched toward the abandoned highway again and this time it skated neatly atop the air cushion below. But as the cushion diminished, a sickening, boat-vibrating scrape began. Something bad was happening to the landing gear.

When the *barco* came to a stop, the silence that followed was brief, the whine of three landing skyboats soon split the air. The vehicles Stark saw through his window bore Mexico's traditional emblem, the eagle-eating-rattlesnake, but the men within appeared Anglo.

Stark looked at his two escorts in the front seat. He assumed they were armed and hoped they were prudent. "When does my flight leave from San Antonio?"

Men wearing uniforms that Stark didn't recognize poured out of the three skyboats. They aimed rifles at Stark, Weitzel, and Valesquez.

"Three," Valesquez said without turning his head, "but I don't think you're going to make it, Doctor."

The thought of missing that flight made Stark want to vomit. He felt as if he were racing against a slowly exploding bomb. If he didn't make the flight to Ascensión, the explosion of this outbreak would keep expanding, keep burning up everything in its path until it immolated North America. "No. Promise me right now," Stark shouted, "that you won't do anything to make me miss that flight!"

"Get out of the vehicle," a voice came from behind the *barco*. "Hands over your head! If you have weapons, throw them out first!"

"*Bueno.* But remember, Stark, it's black letter that we came to get you," Valesquez hissed.

"The hell that? Black letter? What that mean?"

"Just relax and let me do all the talking!"

Valesquez and Weitzel opened their doors. Stark opened his and immediately found three guns jutting in his face. "I American!" Stark shouted.

At the sight of gun barrels, he rolled his eyes away from them in terror, and said, "Centers for Disease Control! CDC! I a doctor!"

Valesquez glared at Stark, then shut his eyes in anger.

"On the ground! Now!"

Valesquez and Weitzel struggled down to their knees, then onto their bellies.

A man walked alongside the prone Mexicans. His voice was high, almost cracking with stress. "Ho. Lee. Crap! Texas Rangers. The hell Texas *Rangers* doing this far south in Free Texas?"

A pair of muddy black boots stepped up next to Stark's face, the boots of a very big man. "They ain't Rangers, Luther."

"They got stars on. They got the hats." Luther sounded like he didn't want to consider who the "Rangers" really might be.

"Look under they hats, boss," said the big man.

Luther, a hard little man built like a crowbar, bent down and knocked off Valesquez's starch-brimmed Ranger hat. It rolled away like a hubcap. A white, zigzagging scar, stretched from Valesquez's temple into his thin hairline.

"He hooked up," breathed Luther.

"I thought so," said the big man.

"*¿Quién están, amigos?*" said Luther with a bad accent, shouting down at the two Mexican officers.

In the silence, turkey buzzards screamed overhead.

"Nobody got nothing to say," said Luther.

"Maybe they want us to turn them over to the real Rangers, huh?" said the big man.

"Yeah, you right, Kevin. Texas Rangers would love to see a couple Holy Rollers wearing they precious hats and stars. We can arrange that pronto!"

Stark heard Valesquez rolling onto his back. "We are from the Holy Renaissance but this is a humanitarian mission. There is a typhoid fever outbreak outside San Antonio and that man is Dr. Henry David Stark from the CDC."

The men inspecting the captured *barco* stopped what they were doing. They looked at Valesquez with a mixture of fear and excitement.

"Holy crap," Luther said. "Mexican officials, huh? Kevin, check the American. See if that hunts."

The muddy boots stepped closer to Stark. "I got a gun pointed at your head. You got a card or something?"

Stark reached into his breast pocket with thumb and forefinger and tossed his card's envelope at Kevin's boots.

"Dr. Henry David Stark," read Kevin. "Central Command Chief Coordinator and Special Pathogens Consultant. Centers for Disease Control."

Luther waved at his men to keep searching the *barco*. "America still got a CDC, huh? All right," Luther said. "Get up, Doctor. Sorry to treat you so rough."

As Stark stood, Kevin grabbed Stark's black-leather brain-gear bag. On instinct, Stark lunged for it.

Kevin kept him at gun's length.

Stark hadn't been apart from his brain gear in nearly two years. "What are you doing? I need that!"

Kevin grinned at him. "Don't fret, Doctor. I keep it safe for you."

Stark shouted, "Who the hell you guys, anyway?"

Luther said, "We the People's Army of Texas. *East* Texas," he said as if this should evoke something different for Stark than "West."

Stark could feel himself turning red. "Why didn't you announce yourselves before firing?"

Kevin's face hardened. Beneath his beard, his lips barely moved. "We fired when the Mexicans fired on *us*."

Luther strolled from behind the skyboat, watching the Mexicans as he spoke. "I ain't sure what to do about this. Holy Roller attachés. This real hot, Kev."

"Forget about the attachés for a minute," said Stark, raising his eyes from the black bag in Kevin's hand to glare at Luther. "What about me?"

Kevin and Luther looked at Stark as if he had just appeared on the highway. "What about you?" said Luther.

"How the US gonna feel when they find out you kidnapped an American?"

"We didn't kidnap you. We *saved* you," said the giant Kevin, making Luther laugh. "Don't worry, we'll get you back to Houston."

"I don't want to go to *Houston*!" Stark said, on the verge of hysteria. "I have to get to San Antonio."

A big idea seemed to light up in Kevin's eyes. "We could ransom these boys to just about any interested faction. Hell, even the Choctaw Separatists up in Oklahoma might pay decent for em if—"

"Hell with the Choctaw," spit Luther. "The Choctaw callin themselves

Anahuacs now. Callin their land Aztlán. They *want* the Holy Rollers to take Texas."

"Just sayin," Kevin continued with patience, "maybe we should think *bigger* than Texas factions."

Luther's eyes widened in suspense. He clearly couldn't imagine anything bigger than Texas. "What you mean, Kev?"

"Maybe we go straight to the Holy Renaissance." Kevin looked west, squinting under the high sun as if he could see Emil Orbegón standing over there.

"Prisoner exchange? Yeah, a couple attachés ought to be worth about every PAT prisoner in Mexican Texas." Luther nodded. "OK. Let's take em home and talk this over with the Chairman. At least we got one fine Mexican skyboat out of the deal." Luther rested his hand on the *barco's* roof.

Stark felt as though he could hear a plane engine revving in far away San Antonio. "You *can't* take this skyboat. You *can't* delay this mission."

Luther seemed amused by Stark, blue eyes twinkling below black eyebrows. "And why not?"

Stark tried to remember the lie Valesquez had told. "Because I have to consult with the Mexican physicians regarding—the typhoid fever outbreak." Stark felt absurd saying it. There hadn't been a typhoid outbreak in Texas in centuries. "If I don't get to San Antonio, the disease will spread all over Texas. And to stop it," said Stark, pointing at the brain gear bag in Kevin's hand, "I need my computer so I can connect to the CDC. And I need *this* skyboat. And I need *those* two men to drive me. Let's let this whole thing just go by as a misunderstanding, OK?"

Two men who had been searching the damaged skyboat shut its doors and hood. "Skyboat in good shape, but ain't nothing here 'cept a couple handguns, Luther."

Luther seemed to have a long conversation of looks with his troops. Finally, he nodded. "Let's take them all back to Bastrop and we'll contact Mexican Texas."

"You ain't listening!" Stark shouted. "I have to get to San Antonio in less than five hours."

Luther pointed to the Mexican officials. "Kevin, you take them. I'll take Dr. Mile-a-Minute in my boat."

Luther put his hand on Stark's shoulder and steered him toward another skyboat. "Can I at least have my bag back please?" Stark pleaded.

"Why? What you got here?"

"My computer," Stark said. "I need it to communicate with the CDC."

"I'll keep it safe for you." Luther guided him gently but firmly into his skyboat. "I promise."

After Kevin took Valesquez and Weitzel away in his skyboat, Luther led Stark inside the People's Army of Texas "retainment facility," as Luther called it. The heat was smothering in the makeshift jail, originally the Bastrop Opera House. The large, dark theater evoked "gymnasium" more than "opera" or "jail," but Stark wasn't about to criticize.

A good-looking young man with red-blond curls sat playing solitaire at a desk near three giant chain-link "cells," locked by padlocks. The young man's rifle leaned against the wall by the farthest cage.

Stark's eyes hadn't adjusted from stepping out of the sunlight, but he could make out a silhouette in the middle cell, either a woman or another young man seated on a chair, elbows resting on knees.

Luther said, "Howell, this here Dr. Henry David Stark, a doctor of dermatology."

Howell stood and fumbled for the keys in his pocket, turning to the empty cell on his right.

"No, no," Luther said, grabbing the kid's arm. "Say hello to him, Howell. He our guest."

Stark nodded in greeting to Howell. "Epidemiology, actually, not dermatology."

Unimpressed, the kid slouched back into his chair and looked at the third card off his deck, curls bouncing before his eyes.

"We gonna head up to comm with a couple Pee-Oh-Double-Youse," said Luther, taking off his shirt and gun holster. He slipped them over the back of a chair and pulled out a clean shirt from the desk drawer, shrugging it over his wiry frame. "We'll come back within the hour, Dr. Stark."

Kevin had taken Valesquez and Weitzel to the People's Army communication center, presumably to arrange a swap or ransom with the Mexican Army. If they really could arrange a prisoner exchange that quickly, and presuming they would let Stark go, he would have less than an hour and a half to get to San Antonio once Luther returned. Stark said, "Come back soon."

Luther peered into the one occupied cell. "You feed her today, Howell?"

"Not yet."

"Good," Luther said. Then he whispered something in Spanish that Stark couldn't hear. The person within, an androgynous woman in black jeans, black boots, and a dirty denim jacket, folded her arms and didn't respond. With his eyes on the jailed woman, Luther said, "You look after Dr. Stark now, Howell, and give him anything he needs. So long, Doc. Lemonade in the icebox."

Luther left and the skyboats screamed away. The quiet they left behind was suffocating.

Howell looked up from his game of solitaire, gathered the cards into a pile, then offered the deck to Stark. "Rummy?"

Stark shrugged and took the deck. His game was poker but he sat down across from the boy. "How about some of that lemonade? It like a steam room in here."

"I drank it all," said Howell. "I get you a water."

Shuffling the deck, Stark glanced into the occupied cell. The woman leaned her long frame forward, illuminated by bounce-light from the Opera House's open door. Stark stopped shuffling and stared at what he saw. Her ratty black hair was pushed back from her brow, revealing a hairline that had been shaved back several inches from her face. Unnatural wrinkles distorted her exposed scalp and temples, as if thick twine coiled just below the skin. She looked briefly at Stark, then away, and Stark realized who, *what* she was. Her eyes shone in the dark but the gleam wasn't happiness. It was an augmented optic nerve and silicon lens, which turned that organ into another brain, or rather, a computer. Or so Joaquin had once told Stark. She was a *sabihonda* as the Mexicans called them. A cyborg.

Stark stared through the chain links at this captured specimen. She represented something so new that she shattered what most Americans conceived of as "future," representing a new superpower, a new kind of labor force, and an economy so lush that people would surgically alter their optic nerves and frontal lobes to take part in it. Her head twitched as she sat in her cell, looking at things that only she could see. She was speaking, too, but Stark couldn't hear what she was saying.

Howell returned with two antique plastic soda bottles filled with water, set one down in front of Stark, and then sat at the table. Stark dealt seven cards each. After the kid took the first hand, Stark felt the rhythm of the game gradually relieving his anxiety. Howell dealt another, after tallying the score.

"You said your name is Henry David Stark," came the woman's voice from her dark cell. She had a Mexican accent and her voice was groggy.

Stark and Howell looked up from their hands. They stared at the *sabi-honda* as if she might rip the chain links out of the concrete. Perhaps she was even capable of it, for all Stark knew. "Right. I Henry David Stark."

"Virologist? CDC? Atlanta? Yes?"

"Epidemiologist. *Epidemiologist.*"

The woman sighed as if annoyed with Stark, or maybe it was exhaustion. "What the hell are you doing *here*?"

Stark arranged the cards in his hand. "You tell me."

"I guess I'd better," she said, hands flat on her thighs. She took a deep breath as though preparing for a scary dive. Staring somewhere far away, her head twitched. She was whispering in a raspy, clipped voice. Stark could barely make out the words. "And. Toward. Jaunt. *Y. Mesa. O.* And. *Pero.* But."

Howell watched her for a moment, muttering, "That gives me the creeps." He picked up the jack of spades. "Goddamn sobby-honda."

"*Musica.* Oval. *Otro.*"

Rodriguez's aphasia, Stark thought, looking at her over his cards. It was a common side effect of early brain wetware recipients, and one of the main reasons Americans had wanted nothing to do with *pilones* or wetware when the technology first emerged. The wetware formed lesions on the language centers of the brain, scrambling wordbits while uplinking. This woman's aphasia was different than Rodriguez's, though: She was stringing together nonsense in two languages.

"*Ella. Llena. Lo. O.* And. Which. Ponder. *Brujo . . .*"

Stark briefly wondered if anyone had written a paper on this condition yet, then examined the discard pile.

"Oatmeal. Boatman. *Boleta.* Busflight into Houston. Arrived safely. Weitzel reports in. Valesquez confirms. *Mierda.* Timing is right. These cowboy *gananes* got big lucky." Her voice sounded weak, and when she spoke, she rested her head against the back wall of the makeshift cell, as if her words sapped all her energy. "*Animales. Timbales.* Valleys. Assisted in the dramatic discoveries made at the Borna outbreak with Dr. Joaquin Delgado."

When the *sabihonda* spoke Joaquin's name, she might as well have touched a cavity in Stark's teeth. He folded his cards with a snap.

"Keep playing," said the kid, sounding like a jaded old man. "She does that just to rattle us."

Stark looked down at his cards again. He picked up the seven that Howell discarded. "It works."

"Dios." The woman said, "Roberto wants you to make a flight in less than two hours."

Stark glanced at Howell, wondering if he would consider which *Roberto* she was referring to—Mexico's Chief of State—but the boy was deciding whether to pick up the whole discard pile or not.

"Rondo. Average. Detriment. *Aleman.* Cup."

"Knock that off," Howell shouted at the woman. "You won't get nothin to eat if you keep that up!"

Stark grimaced. "You starving her?"

"Got to. She needs carbos to run her *pilone,"* said Howell, still making eyes at the discard pile. He said *pilone* like pea-loan.

"Who she anyways?" asked Stark. "How'd she wind up in your jail?"

Howell picked up the whole discard pile and began rearranging his hand. "Kevin caught her outside Houston, near the old Jet Propulsion Lab. Messin with our satellites, probably. I think she must be someone important. The antiaircraft drones stopped shooting at us once we locked her up here."

The *sabihonda* knew his drivers by name. She knew of Joaquin. She referred to Chief of State Cazador as "Roberto." This woman was not only hooked up, she was seriously *connected.* "What will you do with her?"

"Trade her, probably." The crowd of cards in his hand distracted Howell. "Our Chairman tryin to figure out what she doin in the old JPL. Wants to increase her value. Is it my turn?"

The *sabihonda* was looking at Stark again, not up at the ceiling anymore, and the strange litany of nonsense had ceased. "Hey," said the *sabihonda.* She scooted her wooden chair up to the chain links. "Hey, Stark."

The kid looked over his shoulder at the rifle.

Stark didn't want to look at her shiny pupils, so he concentrated on the straight he was building. "What?"

In Spanish, she said, "You lied to Luther about the typhoid outbreak."

Either Howell knew Spanish or he heard the name of his leader. The kid looked at Stark over his big hand of cards.

Stark smirked, but in Spanish, he asked who said so. *"¿Quién diga esa?"*

"Diga Luther," she told him.

Stark shook his head, trying to look annoyed, but he wondered how the hell the *sabihonda* could know about that typhoid-fever lie.

"Don't get riled," said Howell. "She just wants to get us fighting."

The *sabihonda* stared urgently at Stark until he finally relented and looked at her. In Spanish she said, "Luther is checking up on your story. He's scanning the CDC's current caseload and he's determining that no Special Pathogens agents are assigned to San Antonio."

Stark felt his cheeks tingle, and suddenly the jail felt even hotter.

Howell looked at the woman. "What she saying to you?"

"Ahorita," the *sabihonda* said in rapid Spanish, "he is figuring out that there is no reported typhoid fever outbreak anywhere in Texas."

Howell turned and threw his bottle of water at the woman. It splashed against the chain links and sprayed the floor. "Never should have given you that spaghetti, bitch!"

Stark's eyes felt hot. His shoulders shivered with fear. Maybe the *sabihonda* was trying to create a distraction, but mentioning typhoid fever had convinced Stark it was time to flee the Opera House, or he'd never get to San Antonio. "Kid." Stark trembled so hard he had to hold his cards in both hands. "Listen, I want to explain something to you."

Howell kept his eyes on the *sabihonda*. "You shouldn't listen to her, man. She been usin her hook-up to play us for days. That why we don't feed her."

The woman pressed her long, half-shaved face against the chain links of the cell, hissing like a cat.

"Both of you, shut up," said Stark, unnerved by the *sabihonda*. "Kid, I got to go. I got to get out of here. You got a skyboat or anything I can use?"

Howell looked anxiously at Stark. "What you talking about? I can't let you go."

"I know." Stark nodded reasonably. "But you have to."

"I oughta just kill her right now, the way she lies and lies."

"With your little balls, *muchacho*?" the *sabihonda* said. "I don't think so."

Stark pointed a finger at the woman. "Shut up, lady. Kid, look at me. You don't owe me nothing, but I need you to help me get to San Antonio."

"Help you?" Howell laughed, his eyes blazing bright beneath the curls. "Why?"

"Because of the outbreak in Ascensión."

Howell tossed his head back in surprise. "Ascensión?" He said it so it rhymed with *attention*. "Oh, I get it. You heading there 'cause of that Big Bonebreaker?"

"Right. If I don't get to San Antonio in the next couple hours, I'll miss my flight. And if I miss that flight, I don't think those people have a prayer."

The kid's sweet face transformed as anger burned through him. His close-set eyes and narrow chin made him look like a ferret. "Hey, you know, we at war with Mexico. Maybe the rest of America don't think so, but we been at war nearly my whole life," Howell said, and his voice broke in indignation. "Whose side you on anyway?"

Stark said, "Medicine don't got 'sides.'"

Howell said, flat and mad, "War sure does."

Stark didn't want to look at it or even tell himself he knew it was there, but from the corner of his eye, he could see the gun holster bulging under Luther's plaid shirt beside the desk. "You know how many people have died since the outbreak started? A couple hundred, probably."

Howell fanned his cards and began rearranging his hand. "And they say God don't bless America no more."

"The disease won't stop at the Guadalupe River and turn around. It'll spread through Texas, too, kid."

"Shut up about all that," Howell said. He pointed to the table. "Sit down and play cards, for chrissakes."

"Luther won't come back for you, Estarque," said the *sabihonda,* still speaking in Spanish. "He's going to call here in a couple minutes and tell Howell to lock you up."

Stark looked at the phone. It sat on the desk like a bomb with a burning fuse. He felt like his blood was broiling. "I have to get out of here, kid."

"You shut up, lady!" Howell said, jumping out of his chair. "Mister, she got Kevin and Luther at each other's throats yesterday, and they like brothers. She a damn rattler, I tell you what." He spun and kicked the chain-link wall of her cell.

As Howell turned away, Stark darted for the desk and the holster on Luther's chair.

Howell turned back and realized why the doctor was fumbling with Luther's shirt. The kid froze and Stark snatched away the shirt, digging at the stiff leather strap of the gun's holster.

Howell looked like a bug scurrying in bright light. He started for the card table, as if for cover, then he took three scrambling steps backwards and scooped up his rifle without looking at it.

Stark drew the gun, a weighty revolver with a boost on the barrel that felt like an anchor in his hands. He had just wanted to scare the kid with it. But with Howell armed too, now, panic took control of Stark's body.

Stark and Howell lifted their guns at the same moment and fired.

But both safeties were on.

"Dang it!" shouted Howell.

Stark and Howell struggled with their safeties, barrels still pointed at each other. "Goddamnit. Goddamnit," muttered Stark.

The *sabihonda* shoved her chair straight backwards, and looked back and forth between the blundering men.

The kid fired first and his shot went into the wall behind Stark, spraying plaster and dust over his back. Stark flinched and fired, and he wished, instead, that he'd held the revolver in the kid's face, telling the frightened boy to drop his rifle in the loudest, deepest, daddiest voice he could muster.

But Stark didn't think of that. He thought of the plane leaving San Antonio in just a few hours, the climbing mortality count in Ascensión, and the riots. Stark fired, and the boost made it recoil hard, flying out of his hand, hitting him in the mouth. Stark and the kid fell backwards.

"*¡Ai, mamacita!*" The *sabihonda* jumped up and pressed herself against the chain links of her cell.

For a moment Stark couldn't tell what had just happened. He shivered uncontrollably with excitement and fright. Touching his mouth, Stark looked at the blood on his fingertips, then he scooted across the floor to Howell and looked at the boy's wound. The bullet had gone straight through the kid's throat. Stark's eyes filled; he shook his head in bitter disbelief.

"Christ, I can't believe you!" the *sabihonda* shouted. "Don't you know how to hold a gun?"

Stark splayed his fingers and combed them straight back through his hair. "Man, oh man." He touched his fingertips to his bruised and cut lip, then looked at the revolver. "I—I didn't think that—" He savagely kicked the gun away as if it were a rat clawing at him.

"*Oye,*" the *sabihonda* said. "*Oye,* Stark. Get Howell's keys." She pointed at the dead man.

Stark looked back and forth from the gun to Howell to the rifle and back again. Stark couldn't clear his thoughts, couldn't stop looking from kid to gun to rifle, kid to gun to rifle, as if his brain were whirling on a nauseating merry-go-round.

"OK. You got to get a grip," the *sabihonda* said, shifting to English. She snapped her fingers at Stark as if he were a distracted dog. "OK? You listening? *Oye.* You and me want the same thing. Get Howell's keys and let me out," she said, speaking each word slowly and succinctly, grabbing his eyes with her own metallic gaze.

His thoughts spun round Howell's unplayed rummy hand, as if he and Stark could somehow just back up, start over, and finish the game.

"Estarque, all I need is something to eat. As soon as I get some food, I'll get you to San Antonio, I promise."

San Antonio. She right. Three o'clock. San Antonio. Stark took a breath and quelled his rising nausea, then reached into Howell's pocket. "Sorry, kid. I'm really sorry."

Through the carousel of his thoughts, Stark remembered some other words.

She got Kevin and Luther at each other's throats.

Stark stared up at the *sabihonda,* as she watched him with eagerness in her disfigured face. He wanted to trust her but she was so alien that he shivered when he looked at her. "What your name?"

She said, "Rosangelica."

It was hard to get the accent right. "Rose—Rosan—?"

"Rosangelica. Emphasis on the *hell.*" She stuck her hand through the wide chain links, offering to shake. "Rosangelica Catalina de San Clemente."

Her extended hand was like a tentacle in Stark's eyes. He didn't want to touch it. *She a damn rattler.* "What were you doing at the JPL, Rosangelica?"

Just then, the phone on Luther's desk buzzed.

Stark listened to the buzz as if it were a reminder.

Rosangelica gave him a look that said, *See? That's Luther. I told you the truth.*

With no choices left, Stark dug in the boy's pocket until he found the key chain, then he put it in the *sabihonda's* waiting hand.

CHAPTER

10

AS SOON AS the cell door rattled open, the *sabihonda* grabbed her grimy jacket and sprinted for the jail's exit.

The kid had been right about her all along, Stark figured. She had no intention of getting him to San Antonio. The desk phone was still buzzing but he couldn't look away from the bullet hole in the kid's throat.

A moment later Rosangelica appeared at the door, holding a loaf of homemade bread and a bowl of what looked like leftover spaghetti noodles. Her straight black hair was pulled back in a ponytail and she stared pointedly at the phone. "Answer it."

Stark looked at her in fear. "Me?"

"You think they'll talk to *me*?" She pointed at the phone with her fork. "Answer it. *¡Ahorita!*"

Stark put his hand on the receiver and gathered a long, catching breath. Then he picked up the phone and listened.

"Hello?" came Luther's voice.

"It me. Stark."

"Dr. Stark? Where Howell at?"

Stark looked helplessly at the *sabihonda* and shook his head slowly.

Luther's voice was an insectlike buzz from the receiver. "Hello? You okay, Doc?"

"Just hot," said Stark, resting a hand on his sizzling brow and looking down at the dead boy on the Opera House floor. "Howell went to get us some lemonade."

"Well, I'll wait. I got to tell him something."

Stark's brain shut off. He couldn't think of anything else to satisfy Luther so he gently hit DISCONNECT and set the receiver down on the desk.

Rosangelica watched him, incredulous, fork looped with noodles held before her face. "No. You didn't just hang up on Luther."

"Yes!" he shouted. In a seizure of anger, he swiped phone, weapons, specs, pictures, and *barco* diagrams off the desk with both arms. He swore a long line of profanities and kicked the desk as hard as he could, knocking it into the jail's stone wall. "I hung up, I hung up, I hung up, I hung up!"

The *sabihonda* nodded. "All right. Get it out of your system," she said reasonably, slurping noodles as if his reaction was to be expected.

Stark ran to the door and stood there looking out at the long barren street stretching toward the Colorado River. War drones buzzed over the flat, western horizon beyond—Stark could see the air boiling in the distance. He could have said that Howell went to take a cold bath. That he wasn't feeling well. That he was outside with some visitors. He could think of a thousand lies now that he was off the phone. Stark rubbed his neck. The day was so hot that the sky felt yellow. He imagined Luther and the giant Kevin speeding toward the Opera House. "How long till they get here? Do you know that?"

"That's what I'm going to find out, but I need to eat first," Rosangelica said, casually tearing into a slice of bread and tapping her forehead with an index finger. "Carbos."

Stark stood in the doorway and watched her eat in the dark jail. String seemed to jump beneath the skin of her temple making her look like a bogey from a childhood dream.

The *sabihonda* glanced down at Howell's body and spoke around a mouthful of bread. "You saved me, you know that? Princess *Organismo Cibernetico* in my ivory tower, and all that? *¿Estás un caballero* in shining armor, *sabes?*"

Stark turned away and stared at the war drones' heat devils shimmering.

"Tell me something," said the *sabihonda*, pausing over her leftover spaghetti. "Tell me the truth, and I'll get you to San Antonio."

Stark leaned against the doorway and looked back at her. "What?"

"The Ascensión outbreak. Tell me your diagnosis." She set the bowl of noodles in her lap, giving him her full, spooky attention. "Naturally emergent virus or bioterrorism?"

Who *was* this creature? Of course a person with her capabilities would know about the mystery of the new virus. But what was she doing in a jail cell on the wrong side of the front, if she had such incredible access even after the *pilone* net had crashed? "I don't see how it could be natural, though I just guessing."

"Who could have designed it? Americans? Euros?" she asked. "Assuming it's not natural, of course."

Stark wasn't ready to begin such speculations until he got to the capital. "How about if you tell me your title first."

"Title? My 'title'?" She grinned. "I'm the last line of defense," Rosangelica said, chewing. "I decide whether to let you into Mexico or not. That's my title."

"What you doin in Free Texas?"

The cyborg laughed, and Stark didn't like the way her face wrinkled when she did. "I was monitoring Valesquez and Weitzel from this cell."

The *sabihonda* was being evasive. "You were monitoring *me*," Stark said.

"Don't get excited about it. I monitor everything." She chewed and chewed. "Now I have to decide if you're friend or foe."

Stark figured that Rosangelica was a major piece on this chessboard, so big that war drones stopped shelling the PAT when they took her prisoner. He decided to tell her his wildest guess about dengue-5 and dengue-6. "I think America or the Euros wrote the wetcode on those viruses. I don't know who else would have motive for such a complex assault," said Stark. "But if I make a more irresponsible guess than that, then you shouldn't believe that I a real scientist."

Rosangelica thought about that, tearing into the spaghetti with a plastic fork, tails of noodles lashing as they vanished between her lips, then she sized him up with a nod. *"Bueno,"* she said. "Howell used a skycycle every morning when he went to Austin. Kawasaki's new plasma injection. Who knows how these *gananes* got it," said Rosangelica. She wiped the corners of her mouth with the back of her hand. "That'll hold me till we can get some frijoles and good tortillas in San Antonio, but *mama,* I could eat a ton more." She sealed the top on the plastic bowl of noodles, then shoved it, the bread, and the bottles of water into what must have been Howell's backpack. She froze, then looked at Stark, looking through him. "*Tipo.* Jeep. *Chililolco.* That's it. The Chairman just gave the order. Luther and Kevin are on their way!"

She slid past Stark through the jail door.

Stark looked back at the body inside, then it occurred to him. Kevin still had his brain gear. "Wait! They have my equipment!"

The *sabihonda* stood in a blast of sunlight at the corner of the Opera House. "What equipment?"

"Kevin has my goggles and brain tags. I use them to connect to the CDC's satellite. It has all my information from Zapata Hospital and Muñoz. I can't stop the outbreak without it. I in the middle of consulting with Ghana on—"

"Stupid *gringo,*" she said. The skin around her subcutaneous wiring rolled in protest against the laugh lines by her eyes. "Your AI is just a calculator compared to me. I'm *pues-humano.* You got a password or a prefix or something for the *i.a.,* right?" She used the Spanish construction for *inteligentsia artificial.*

"Of course."

"I can access it." Rosangelica shrugged. "Let's go. I'll drive."

He looked at the sky over Bastrop. No sign of the People's Army yet. Could he be in touch with Joaquin through her? More importantly, did he want a Holy Renaissance *pues-humano* spy accessing Queen Mum?

The skycycle was parked in the rectangular shadow of the little jail. The bike was a sleek thing with a long nose, a high shield, and wings that angled back like a swoop jet's. It sat two, and two helmets were locked in place. The *sabihonda* started fumbling with the sheaf of keys on Howell's chain. Stark watched her select key after key, poking each into the ignition. "This is crazy." She put down the keys and stood still. *"De.* From. *Haber. Ruto.* Scrum. Envelope. *Piel.* Love. Torque. *Andar."* She stared skyward for a moment as if listening to a faraway voice, smiling. Then she rattled through the keys and selected one, holding it up like a prize fish. The key unlocked the first helmet, which she handed to Stark.

"What did you do? How did you find the right key?"

"I melted the PAT's defenses around their jail security server. These are cowboys, not coders." She unlocked a helmet for herself. "They had the jail rekeyed last month after Howell lost his set, and they kept all the info on net in case he did it again. And number 22-31 is the ignition." She held up that key as evidence. "Hop on, Stark. San Antonio's waiting for you."

Stark slipped a helmet on as three distant fly-sized specks appeared in the sky behind them.

"C'mon!" Rosangelica's voice buzzed in the helmet mic.

He climbed on the cycle, strapped himself in, and it shot forward, down the street and into the sky. Acceleration forced Rosangelica against his chest and crotch. It surprised him how squeamish he felt to have a "posthuman" between his thighs.

"It's going to be close," said Rosangelica. She took the skycycle up about twenty feet and opened up the throttle, using its velocity for speed instead of altitude.

Even with three skyboats behind him, and a Holy Renaissance wetwared spy between his legs, Stark was relieved to feel mile after mile of Texas blur below the cycle. As long as he didn't think about Howell and their unfinished game of rummy, the sick sensation he had back in the Opera House was replaced by adrenaline. "They faster than us?"

"No. But their weapons are."

"They gonna try to kill us?" asked Stark. "Because—because of what I did?"

"Probably. Though I'm worth more alive than dead. We'll see what the Chairman told them to do in a second."

Your AI is just a calculator compared to me, Rosangelica said. Nonetheless, she certainly was calculating. She knew exactly what needed to be done as soon as Stark shot Howell—the jail-cell keys, the food, the cycle, the cycle's keys. A woman like her could have left almost anytime she wanted. *Our Chairman tryin to figure out what she doin in the old JPL,* the kid had said. Stark imagined that whatever Rosangelica was doing in Houston, it was major.

I'm the last line of defense.

A wild squawking blasted inside his helmet and Rosangelica almost lost control of the bike as she involuntarily brought a hand up to her head. "What the hell is—"

"Land that skycycle right now," Luther's voice echoed in Stark's helmet, "and we won't land it for you."

Stark craned his head to look behind them and the fly-sized specks had become wasps. "Luther right behind us!"

"They've been trying to get a missile lock on us for the past twenty kilometers," said Rosangelica. "I can't shrug off their scopeware much longer."

Luther sounded bitter and frayed. "Which one of you killed Howell? Gonna knock you out of the sky if you don't land that bike!"

Rosangelica said, "The drones on the border aren't afraid to cross into Texas territory. I *know* you know that, Luther."

"I see. The savvy Honda killed Howell," said Luther. "Dr. Stark, maybe this don't matter to you, but that woman stole military secrets about a key US satellite. She a thief sent to the JPL by Orbegón himself. She'll use you to get across the border, then it's *adios, muchacho.* Don't trust her if you value your life."

Stark figured Luther might well be right about Rosangelica. "Who I gonna trust, Luther? You?"

"No, I expect you can't. This conversation over." He sounded resigned and tired. "Got something just for you here, *sabihonda. Vaya con carne.*"

Luther's squelching override snapped silent.

"*Chinga,*" swore Rosangelica. "A code-seeker. Melt-through. Gonna eat this *valemadre* cycle's defense."

Stark looked back and could see the white trail of an approaching missile. "Can you do anything?"

"Get up close to me," she said and reached back, pulling him tight against her. She grabbed his right hand and put it on the throttle with her hand over it. "You are going to take the controls, Stark. I'm—"

"No!"

"—going to hack my way into the missile's geo-sat—yes, you have to, Stark!"

"I can't drive this—"

"Too late. It's done."

The cycle swooped and dove as Rosangelica lifted her hands. Stark grabbed the handlebars, cyborg cradled in his arms, the land below veering up into his face.

"Hold the nose up, idiot! Thumb lever! There you go," Rosangelica said, "and keep the throttle open till I say."

The skycycle felt like a heavy sea animal that wanted to dive deep and fast. Stark looked over his shoulder and the cycle jerked with his movement.

"*¡Cálmate!*" Rosangelica screamed.

Stark gripped the bars. "What you doing?"

Her voice hissed in that eerie, clipped tone again. "Couch. *Epazote*. Zipper. *Papagallo*. Pump."

Stark had to resist every nerve in his body telling him to turn around and see how close the missile was. He looked over Rosangelica's shoulder at the controls and found a circular screen marked 5-KILO RANGE. He flicked a toggle and an arrow labeled PATSEEKER-#3, the missile, was bearing down on the center of the screen. "Um. Rosangelica?"

"*Noviembre*. Cutlet. There!" she shouted.

Suddenly there was a blinding streak before the skycycle, a shrieking flash of light and vapor. Stark gripped the handlebars and lowered his head as a concussion hit them from behind, lifting the back of the skycycle. He pressed the thumb lever all the way forward to keep the cycle's nose level. A moment later, three huge explosions sounded behind them.

Then quiet. Nothing but the purr of the cycle.

Stark looked down at the screen and saw the PATSEEKER was gone. He was about to ask Rosangelica what happened, but then he realized they were racing westward along the track of four diminishing vapor trails that had sailed in from the west. The border. Mexican Texas.

Stark looked west and could see a flock of small jets or gliders hanging in the distance like gleaming hawks circling on a thermal.

War drones.

They'd stopped shelling Bastrop when the PAT took Rosangelica captive, Howell had told him. Now, Stark realized, they had just let those missiles fly at her command.

Who was this woman?

Rosangelica's voice sounded in his ear. "Close call, eh, Estarque?" She was laughing. "Don't worry. Those missile drones weren't coded for us. We weren't in any danger." She turned her head slightly to the right. "I'll take over. Let go of the handlebars."

As the skycycle shot westward toward the Guadalupe River, Stark released his grip and leaned back a bit. He looked over his shoulder, but couldn't see the pursuing PAT *barcos*—just smoke hanging in the air.

Silence carried them for a while, as the clay prairie of central Texas gave way to hillier, greener ground, and derelict farm fields that still bloomed yellow with gold mold. This terrain had not fully recovered from the Border War seven years ago, but young cottonwoods grew from the trunks of the old, and little wildflowers broke red in yawning craters. Soon they saw the Guadalupe River, a narrow, shallow trickle over dry land, hardly enough to separate these two immense militaries. The cycle tore over the scorched earth on the west bank of the river.

"Dormouse. *Dormir.* Adore. Fleck." Stark wondered what she was really doing as she pronounced her absurd spells. "A Dulce jet just landed in San Antonio," Rosangelica said. "There's an escort waiting for you on the other side of the river. They'll follow us and make sure we get to San Antonio safely."

"We? You and me?" said Stark. "Thanks for your help, but 'we' ain't going to San Antonio together."

They zoomed past the little green dell that was once the city of San Marcos, thick green vines crawling over urban wreckage. The skycycle raced over its military *punto de control,* protected by war drones hanging in the air.

"Without your—what did you call it—your brain gear? Your computer?" she said as if helping him work out a math problem. "You'll need me. The outbreak just reached a critical stage. Death toll is nearly two thousand now."

The number was so absurd, it made Stark angry. *Two thousand? Already?* She had to be lying. He hadn't heard a reliable mortality figure since last night, but with such virulence, the virus would have crossed the US by now. Stark wished he could see Rosangelica's face. She had to be lying to him in order to get to San Antonio. "Impossible. Two thousand? Impossible."

"Not all of those deaths are from the outbreak," Rosangelica said, speaking in a monotone as if summarizing from an article. "*Los destitutos* are rioting."

Finally, Stark spoke. "Who that? ¿*Los destitutos?*"

"The lowest class in Mexico. The state-sanctioned Minority Party represents them, saying they haven't really seen the benefits of the Holy Renaissance's expansion yet." By her tone, Stark got the impression Rosangelica didn't really care what *los destitutos* thought of the Holy Renaissance. Keeping her hands on the handlebars, she pointed her index fingers to another swarm of war drones hovering over three landed *barcos* in a long-abandoned farm field. "See that? Your escort. Just like I said."

She banked the cycle toward the skyboats and the war drones parted for her, dispersing toward San Marcos. "Who's the officer in charge?" asked Stark.

"Why?" asked Rosangelica.

"Because I ain't getting off this cycle unless you tell me."

"El Mono. At least, that's the name he gave you."

Satellites couldn't have told her that, he thought, with a sinking sag in his stomach. Which meant that the mortality number Rosangelica claimed might be accurate. As if Stark's preparations and perimeters were nothing, the outbreak's next wave had hit.

"I'm going to have to cross-check everything you've told me, *sabihonda.*"

"I hope you do," said Rosangelica, circling the cycle once over the convoy of *barcos,* then speeding off toward San Antonio as they took wing behind her. "I want you to figure out for yourself that you can't do this without me."

CHAPTER

11

SITTING IN A CYLINDER of pale light cutting through darkness, two middle-aged men in red-and-black three-piece suits were playing backgammon, rattling dice in leather-bound cups and swearing softly after a throw. Cigarettes, symbols of superlative opulence in Stark's America, burned silver threads into the light, and now and then, one of the men blew smoke into the shadows.

Stark couldn't decide why these two men were on the Dulce. Clearly, they were associates of the *sabihonda,* who'd ushered them aboard without so much as an introduction to Stark, but beyond that he couldn't decide if they were travelers, spies, subordinates, or what. The plane went up, the lights went down, and out came the cigarettes and backgammon board.

In a second wide shaft of light, Rosangelica sat between the jet's wings in a horseshoe-shaped chair, stretching her long legs beneath a table of empty plates and glasses. She had exchanged her dirty denim jacket and jeans for her version of the traditional Holy Renaissance uniform: long, black-wool skirt, black leather duster with red lining, *ranchera* boots. Her hair was combed straight, brushed back from her disfigured face, and she sat staring at the ceiling. Stark could hear her clipped, aphasic chant as she accessed satellites. "*Hacer.* Asiago. Stock. Citation. *Llave.*" She was collating hospital information. He hoped.

Stark sat in a third splash of light at the rear of the coach. In front of him was a squat, thick glass brimming with sweet-as-candy whiskey—his favorite indication that he'd left outback farming and entered the sumptuous excesses of the Holy Renaissance. Near his table of memboards glowing with hospital reports and epidemiological data was a wet bar loaded with as much booze as his heart desired, and right now, his heart desired quite a bit.

He pressed the tumbler to his cut lip and stared at the nearest memboard without reading it. A lifetime of jetting into cholera and yellow-fever outbreaks couldn't have prepared him for this. On Friday, twenty-eight hundred people had put on shirts and worried about their hair and drunk some coffee. Today, they were gone. And each one of them had suffered bone-cracking seizures and lymph nodes bulging the size of apples. Bleeding, horrible bleeding. It was almost too much for Stark to read, and he'd read plenty of hemorrhagic-fever accounts. One nurse reported speaking to a patient who she assumed had survived the disease. During the interview, the patient seemed overcome with emotion, and as he wiped his eyes, he came away with a smear of blood on the back of his hand. A moment later he was convulsing.

To make matters worse, violence had claimed several hundred in the riots of Ascensión's National Square. Three hundred thousand people, furious at their government's handling of the outbreak, had poured into the National Square, one of the most widely infected regions of the city, in what seemed part communal outrage, and part coordinated insurgency. Either way, the very definition of nothing to lose.

In the peaceful hum of the Dulce jet, a tumbler of ice and whiskey in hand, Stark had, at last, hours to read and read and read. Rosangelica had offered to sift through the information for him, but Stark wanted it all to himself. He finally had full accounts of the outbreak written by doctors, not to mention the epidemiological report written by the late-great Miguel Cristóbal, and the genomic analysis of dengues five and six written by Isabel Khushub, Stark's ace. Stark needed the ritual digestion of data to feel a certain amount of control and connection to this tidal wave, but after two hours of drinking and reading, he realized that all the information would really do him no good.

The viruses were unstoppable. Wherever they found purchase, dengue-5 and dengue-6 seemed to be killing with bloody abandon, especially where public-health standards were weak. Big Bonebreaker hadn't spread far and wide, but it was killing the poorest regions of Mexico, wiping out the seasonal Indian refugee camps that cropped up at the end of the coffee harvest in the Guatemalan and Honduras provinces. Nonetheless, class wasn't the deciding factor: The lone case in North Carolina was a white Anglo-Saxon professor, after all, and reports from the overburdened American British Clinic reported deaths of several African and European businessmen. The viruses had spread rampantly in Ascensión, but hardly at all overseas. One neighborhood in La Baja had been left untouched, while an adjacent *barrio* was crushed with one hundred percent mortality.

It was too much. He was accustomed to dragging populations back from this headlong plunge. He wasn't a mop-up man. He wasn't a corpse-hauler. And at the moment, he couldn't picture a path out of the outbreak.

Stark reached for the sat phone Rosangelica had given him, and, across the Dulce's coach, they met each other's eyes. Immediately, her gaze darted back to the ceiling, and out flew her aphasic poetry.

Stark watched her, phone in hand. He wasn't fooled. She would be listening to his conversation.

Slam. One of the backgammon players brought his dice cup down hard. "Got you now, boss," he said.

Let her listen, he decided. He needed a reprieve after two hours of this research, after everything that had happened to him this day. He tapped in Nissevalle Cooperative's main line and let the phone ring seventeen times before someone answered.

"'Lo?"

It was Cretin. His real name was Ben, but he was the hardest-drinking man at Nissevalle, so he'd earned himself a more descriptive tag. "Cretin, this Henry David."

"Oh, hey. Where you at, brother?"

"Timbuktu."

"Again? Thought you just got back from there."

It sounded like there was a party in the kitchen. Lots of laughter and hilarious yelling. Stark checked the time on one of his memboards. *Starting the festivities pretty early. It only six-thirty.* "Can I talk to Grandfather? He there, Cretin?"

"Sure, sure. We just eating some frozen blueberries in the kitchen, actually. Hold up, I get him."

Frozen blueberries? Stark wondered. *Someone celebrating something.*

"Well, hello, kid," came Grandfather's voice. He sounded rested, happy. "Where are you?"

Grandfather had looked so tired and old when Stark left him—it was soothing to hear him sound so good. He took a sip of whiskey, and said, "In the sky. Somewhere over Mexico."

"Made it there no problem, then?"

Stark had no idea how to answer that question. He stared into his own silence wondering what he would say, when the only thing that came to mind was an unplayed hand of rummy.

"Hello?"

"Yeah. No problem. Got to San Antonio, anyway."

"You sound weird, kid. What's wrong?"

If Grandfather didn't stop asking questions that he couldn't answer, Stark feared he might crack apart right there on the phone. All he wanted was to hear something normal. Something about the new farm interns or the bickering between the day crews and the irrigation teams. Something normal.

Sip.

Grandfather seemed to hear the weight on his grandson's end of the line. "Ask me about the spinach, then."

"Jesus. The spinach?" Stark didn't think he could bear such a conversation. Not now. "No. I don't want—"

"It died."

Of course it did, thought Stark. *Gold mold fast as hell. And thorough.* "The whole field, then?"

"No, just the plants of that variety. By sundown, it was all withered. Amazing. Probably already in an advanced state."

"The hell you say," Stark scoffed. "*All* your spinach should be gone."

"I had some bad seed, came from an unknown source. I tracked it back to the purchase and realized it came from a warehouse, not a seed-saver, like I thought. Could have come from anywhere."

Stark took a deep pull on his whiskey and set the glass down on the table. He couldn't stop analyzing diseases no matter which way he turned. "The seed? You think the seed saved you?"

"Well, I told you my method when you first came home with this project, but you dismissed me out of hand like I was some dumb farmer," Grandfather said. "Gold mold eats the old genetically modified varieties. That's my theory. So I don't use them. This seed came from a seller that I've wondered about for years, and those are the ones that got hit. I didn't do anything special. Gold mold just overate its food supply."

Stark found himself about to contradict, about to say the very same thing he said last winter when Grandfather spoke to him of the theory that ten years of vCaMV research couldn't prove, that there was no common DNA in all genetically modified crops that would entice the same virus, even an array of viruses like the variants of Cauliflower Mosaic Virus.

But Stark didn't want to argue about this. Somehow, Grandfather's strategy worked and that warranted breaking out the frozen berries, for sure. By planting different varieties every six feet, gold mold couldn't find purchase in a heterogeneous crop.

It was targeted. It was specific about *something,* but who knew what?

Didn't matter to the farmer, but it mattered to the epidemiologist, who looked back at his memboard, wondering if the Holy Renaissance's data was collated well enough for him to dig in deep. "OK. Thanks for that. Look, I just wanted to make sure you got home all right. Better run."

"Just as well. Cretin's about to tap the spring brew. You stay in touch, then."

He clicked off the phone. "Rosangelica?"

"What did you just figure out?" she asked. She'd been staring at him, as if waiting for him to ask a question.

"Nothing. But I need to get data on a patient in North Carolina. The lone Big Bonebreaker case there. Can you get that for me?"

"Don't insult me. Of course I can," Rosangelica said. "What do you want to know?"

Stark stood, walked over to her splash of light and sat in a chair beside her. "Just tell me who he was?"

"His name?"

"No, his life. Tell me about *him.*" He pointed to his memboard. "Here. Give it to me here when you got it."

"Elm. Heinous. *Galeria. Joven.* Flytrap. Academic from Raleigh, it looks like," she said. She was looking at Stark but not looking at Stark, as if she were sleepwalking. He didn't like the effect.

Stark looked away and took a nice long pull on his drink. Waiting. The netmonitor encased in the wall near Stark was bright with pictures of the Ascensión street war, with gunfire bursting in darkness, and young *machos* wearing gas masks waving rifles in the camera. Stark ignored it, looking out his window and down at the skin of clouds stretching over the Sierra Madres far below.

But Mexican media was difficult to ignore. Seven overlapping windows on-screen expanded and contracted, shuffled backwards and forwards, and the audio constantly shifted to the foremost screen as the producers showed what they wanted their viewers to see. It simulated, Rosangelica had explained, the sensation of "*mundo*-interactivity," what it was like to have the *pilone* hookup.

The main screen showed a live *ojo* feed of a firefight on La Reforma Avenue. Gunboats gave air cover above burning barricades, as mobs cresting in the thousands pushed toward the National Square. Other screens flashed more images of fighting. A Holy Renaissance squad in black fired into a crowd of brick throwers. "Holy Renaissance officials painted a bleak picture of the insurgents," said the commentary accompanying this window. Another window popped up inside this one and showed Mexico's Chief of State Roberto Cazador, the official who had hired Stark. "They, in essence, express a clear political joining with the radical nun and her proinsurgent agenda," said the portly Chief of State, reading from handheld notes. "Rather than help the sick, they elect to take advantage of this disaster politically."

Stark looked at Rosangelica but she was still far away in a trance of satellites. Instead of bothering her, he thumbed his memboard, pulling up the genomic analyses of the two viruses again from Isabel Khushub.

AGTTGTTAGT CTGTGTGGAC CGACAAGGAC
AGTTCCAAAT CGGAAGCTTG CTTAACACAG . . .

Stark needed to know a little of everything to be a good field epidemiologist—virology and statistics in particular, but bacteriology, languages, and politics helped. Genomics, however, was his weak study. Stark wished he could have Queen Mum run the codon analysis program that Joaquin had written long ago for Stark's benefit.

Though he had little hope of gleaning anything useful, Stark opened the full genomes. He couldn't gather much from them, but he could see one thing: no natural redundancies. As Muñoz had said, there was no so-called junk DNA. The structures of the new dengue viruses were delicate and far more fragile than natural dengue, twin demons made of crystal. He also saw how the viruses could be mistaken for natural dengue at first, even second glance. Had he not known to look for the absence of junk DNA, Stark would have assumed they were dengue-2 and dengue-4. They were intentionally designed to elicit debate, so that virologists, pathologists, and field epidemiologists would argue over the viruses' structure and behavior, giving the swift killer a few more precious hours to spread.

The viruses were weapons, and not just an amateur bioweapon like anthrax or smallpox. Whoever designed them knew all the shortcuts that public-health officials might take in a frightening outbreak. Someone intended to exploit harried doctors who would rely on skimped genomes and initial symptoms for diagnosis. Whoever had let slip these twin dogs of war knew that the ensuing debate would center on vectors and spraying for mosquitoes, because that was the logical response to a dengue outbreak. This wasn't merely an attack on Mexico. It was an attack on modern medicine.

Rosangelica turned to Stark, and said from her chair, "*Almena.* Punditry. *Rejas.* Primp. I got something interesting," she said. "Sullivan was one of me, Stark."

"What?" he said, blinking at her.

"Your *gringo* in North Carolina," she said, excited. "Read."

Stark pressed the cool glass to his swollen lip, where the gun had hit him, and read from his memboard.

Madison Frank Sullivan. Marine biologist who had worked for an oil company out of New Delhi before the Sino-Indian War. The poor fellow had just returned from Ascensión via Havana, and the attending physician who wrote the report figured that's where he must have contracted the disease—Havana.

"Sufferer of Rodriguez's aphasia," the physician noted in his report. The same disorder as Rosangelica's.

When he was young, apparently, Sullivan was an international, looking to work for any oil cartel who would hire him. "Ten years ago," the physician wrote, "Sullivan traveled to Ascensión, seeking to take part in the illegal petrol market, and was one of the first non-Mexicans to get the Connection."

Stark looked at the *sabihonda,* whose eyes were focused on him, really seeing him. "He had the *pilone,*" she said. "So did his fellows at the University of International Harmony. And the Euros who contracted Big Bonebreaker in Paris? Also *pilonistas.* In North Carolina and in Paris, both sets of researchers had built networks and most of the users went down with Big Bonebreaker. Those networks crashed just like ours did."

Stark pounced on the Ministry of Health's collated data to see if there was a pattern, sifting through hundreds of reports as fast he could, using twin searchers combing out references to the word *pilone*.

But many of the poorest victims were Native Mexicans who didn't even have homes, let alone a Connection. After an hour of reading, Stark sat back, exhausted.

"Anything?" Rosangelica said.

"No. Hard to believe there ain't a pattern."

He turned to her and found the *sabihonda* staring at him. Not her vacant, metallic stare, but a scrutinizing and angry distrust in her face. "You looked at the genome, too?"

Stark frowned at her. "Yes."

She said, "You didn't find a pattern?"

"No." Stark suddenly read her tone as accusatory. "What? Did you find one?"

Rosangelica's hard stare drilled through him. "Did I make a mistake about you, Dr. Stark? Are you what you seem to be?"

Stark pivoted in his chair to face her. "The hell you talking about?"

"*Hacer.* Addling. Shuck. *Dormitorio.* Primary Big Bonebreaker hospital, the university, just closed. It redlined," she said. "Secondary is fine for the moment."

Stark was offended, wanted to ask what she meant by her comment, why she would suddenly question him. But he turned his attention to the ship of Ascensión that was suddenly listing again in the water. He rubbed his tired eyes. "What's the first secondary hospital in line?"

"*San José Nacional.* It's across town in southern Ascensión."

"It'll hit capacity within the next twenty-four hours," said Stark, looking out the window.

Rosangelica nodded. "That's what the hospital's own report says, too." When Stark didn't respond, she said, "Do you want to hear more bad news or some good news?"

The jet faintly vibrated in a calm, meditative hum—he looked back at Rosangelica, unable to discern if anything she said to him was a veiled barb, a lie, or the truth, and wished he had his brain gear and the ever-clunky Queen Mum. "Bad news first."

"The national union of nurses and health care workers is demanding that the military turn over its stockpile of omnivalent vaccines."

"A military stockpile? Do we have one?" Stark frowned at her.

"We do, but those stockpiles are for troops in *Tejas*."

"I doubt that's my call to make, but send my recommendation to meet the union's demand."

The *sabihonda* swore. "Typical leftist knee-jerk—"

"What else?" Stark said loudly over her muttering. "That can't be all the bad news."

"It may be, for now. Nanophages that were built upon your Ghana design were dusted over the hot zones an hour ago. No report on efficacy yet, obviously." Rosangelica took a big bite of tortilla and, with a full mouth, said, "That brings you to the good news. We finally have pathology reports."

That *was* good news but he didn't like Rosangelica using the first-person plural. "They from Dr. Khushub?"

"Khushub and Ahwaz," Rosangelica read. "Sounds like a Muslim comedy act."

"They are. Give it to me."

She tossed him the memboard with the prelims. Stark thumbed through Isabel's report, looking for signs of discrimination in the 150 patients whose bloodwork she had analyzed, but he couldn't spot anything that Bela hadn't already fingered. All of the patients whose records she studied were *capitalinos* from various neighborhoods in downtown Ascensión: *la zona rosa* and *el centro histórico,* mainly. They ran the spectrum of occupations from priests to photographers to musicians. Various ages. Some Euros and transplanted Americans, even. Some were *pilonistas,* some weren't.

Just as Stark had determined: no pattern. The only thing they had in common was they all tested positive for both dengue-5 and dengue-6 and had died from massive hemorrhaging.

Pedro Muñoz's assertion that virologists all toyed with the idea of creating the "perfect virus" had Stark trying to guess what sort of bioweapon this really was. In the abstract, it made sense to wetcode two dengue serotypes—one to prime the population, the next to wipe it out fast—but there were easier ways to do it.

Maybe the attacker ain't really concerned with killing lots of people. Maybe that just a by-product of another aim altogether. If that was true, then maybe this wasn't a strictly military maneuver, or an act of terrorism, at all.

Stark stood and walked to the wet bar for a refill, following that thought for a drink. Attacking innocents was chaotic and unstrategic. Not exactly the profile of a military attack. A random bomb in a market would kill everyone within a certain radius, but this wasn't like that, either. Some people seemingly within Big Bonebreaker's radius survived: UnConnected Mexicans had died of Big Bonebreaker, as had Euros and other non-Mexicans. Stark uncapped the whiskey and poured himself a tall one, dropping ice in after the liquor.

Stark was an epidemiologist, a numbers man, but he figured he had to start thinking like a sleuth, because this was proving to be a nuanced and well-plotted homicide. Stark had the murder weapon: two strains of stripped-down dengue, and he assumed that Isabel Khushub or Jarum Ahwaz would eventually find a fingerprint on them, a genetic marker of some kind that would lead them to a specific lab or corporation. But for Stark, despite the fact that he had nearly three thousand bodies, the question was: Who is the killer after?

Stark looked out the window. The *pilone,* perhaps, figured in, but he couldn't see how at the moment, and so did an as-yet-unknown factor of being Mexican, since the disease raged here, but guttered everywhere else on the planet. But what could it be? Mexico was one of the most heterogeneous populations in the world. With no immediate plan for this outbreak visible— something that had never happened to him as an epidemiologist—Stark now felt like the absurd squire Sancho at the end of the great Mexican opera *El Quijote,* trying to find his way in the mad knight's upside-down world of distorted mirrors and no exits.

In the far pool of light, Stark could see the jagged *pilone* scars on the temples of the backgammon players. The cyborg sat stuffing her gaunt face with tortillas, whispering her nonsensical satellite language, her silver stare glinting in the overhead light. The screen before Stark flashed images of a skytank covering troops along the Guadalupe River.

The dice fell. The player, a gun bulging beneath his jacket, counted out his move in deliberate taps. Triumphant, he doubled up his opponent.

"*Uva.* This. Rejuvenate. On," said the cyborg.

CHAPTER

12

THOUGH MARCELA couldn't see any windows from inside the hot lab, she could tell the sun was close to setting by the noises from the clinic's dormitory. It felt much later than that to her. Before entering the lab, she heard the evening netcasts, twittering along as if it were just another news day come to a close in the mighty capital. Now she sat at the bloodwork station, analyzing draws from the two newest patients, knowing there was no quitting time.

Beneath her level-five Racal-plus suit, Marcela wore maroon scrubs and a gold bracelet that her boyfriend had given her. Around her neck she wore a rosary, which she'd worn for weeks, running fingertips over the reassuring beads. The priest who heard her confession over *pilone* had asked her to wear it and remember where love came from.

She wished she could Connect now and gather some strength from a priest. But hospital directives were clear—accessing the net was fatal.

Marcela sighed and smacked her dry lips. They itched. She put her eye to the digitally amplified microscope where she saw an enhanced image of robust white blood cell complexes wrinkling like raisins. She replaced this cryo sample with the other. Ditto. These slides from the two new patients showed the initial cellular damage associated with dual dengues five and six infections. She wished she could touch the rosary.

Marcela had cheated on her boyfriend. That's why the priest told her to wear her rosary. Several weeks ago, Marcela had a giddy fling on a night out

that began with a pal, Jita, who worked the emergency room. Jita had decided she wanted to see the clubs of La Alta Ciudad and since Marcela had
just been paid, she decided to join her. They stood outside the hospital
atrium convincing others to come with them and eventually roped two
women and two men, all from pediatrics, into chipping in on the fare for a
bus "upstairs." They hailed a little swoop and Marcela sat across the aisle
from one of the pediatrics nurses, a pretty *italiano*-looking man named
Patricio, who kept looking at her out of the corner of his eye while Jita chattered about a bar fight she got in the last time she went up to La Alta.

Marcela rarely made the trip up to that wealthier world. It was too
trendy, too intimidating, and she could rarely afford it. When Patricio struck
up a conversation with her, however, she decided to leave her hesitation on
the earth below. Those eyes of his, she kept thinking, as the enormous wall
of a La Alta tower loomed over the riders. *Que hermosos esos.*

They found a café named Suavé Maria, which opened onto the dock
where the *pesero* driver in his custom swoop bus had dropped them. Suavé
Maria blared with *pavonear,* a slow, syncopated music designed for sexy hips
and rolling shoulders. The *pavonear* playing here, however, had been
stripped of a hard beat. No percussion. No bass. Very flat. The café's chic
clientele tapped their full tumblers, nodded as if to an irresistible rhythm,
and the dance floor bobbed like a single body. Patricio swayed in his tight,
black pants, eager to dance. "This is some *altadoro* bullshit," he said, looking
out at the beatless dance floor.

They were about to leave and find a better dance spot, when a passing
cocktail waitress saw their skeptical faces. She stopped long enough to tap
her *pilone* scar and say, "Suavé Maria."

Feeling foolish, Marcela and the others accessed the café's node and immediately their *pilones* piped thundering drums into their heads. The jaded
waitress went to the bar and rolled her eyes at the bartender. Marcela read
her lips: *"Bajadores."*

Marcela grabbed Patricio's wrist and pulled him onto the dance floor.
The beat shook out their skeletons and they danced hard and long, drinking
a steady flow of expensive tequila and *pavonear.* She felt different in Suavé
Maria. Sexier. At the hospital, Holy Renaissance work monitors appraised
her as steady, honest, and (the worst) "punctual." But in the charged atmos-
phere of Suavé Maria, Marcela felt so much more than timely.

She loved dancing with Patricio, a Euro-looking man, not a *mestizo* like her boyfriend. Other women, rich *Altadoras* draped at the hem of the dance floor, watched him move with thirsty eyes; when that man danced, he was all hips, a toreador displaying his body just for Marcela. He was built, this man, especially in the lower body, like a hardy steed. Somehow his masculinity made Marcela feel powerful. *Macha,* Jita called it. A woman who deserved many lovers.

"You got a girlfriend, *hombre*?" Marcela asked Patricio between songs.

He smiled—a sweet, choirboy smile. "No. No girlfriend."

Perspiration beaded on the black feather of a moustache when he smiled. She wanted to kiss the sweat from his mouth. "You want one?"

Patricio's pretty smile turned salacious. "I'm not that kind of a boy."

Marcela's eyes dimmed in disappointment. "What kind?"

"The boyfriend kind."

Another seductive beat poured into Marcela's brain. Patricio set his feet wide apart and ground his hips into the rhythm. He raised his fists over his head and his shirt lifted. Marcela could see skin and a faint feather of black hair beneath his navel. She closed her eyes and danced closer. She couldn't access a confessor without leaving the café's node and the intoxicating beat. *Hail Mary, full of grace,* she prayed lamely, putting her hands on Patricio's bare stomach, *blessed art thou among women. Blessed is the fruit of thy loins . . . ¡Ai, que hombre!*

"What are you laughing about?" Patricio asked her.

She shook her head, watching his stomach muscles go.

Jita and the others from the hospital disappeared. The whole night dissolved into Patricio. His dance. His embrace. His lap on the swoop bus when they went back "downstairs" (going down was cheaper than going up—Patricio picked up the fare himself). His apartment in the well-lawned suburb of Cuoyocán was neat and spare. His bed was wide. His thighs, sturdy. The taste of his skin sparkled, and so fair in color compared to her own man's.

In the bloodwork lab, the head doctor on duty said through his helmet of clear plastic, "What's the verdict, Marcela?"

Marcela didn't look up from her scope. She licked her dry lips. "About what you'd expect."

This doctor was a pillar. With peripheral vision, she saw him clasp his hands, a gesture of resolution, or maybe it was a prayer. Reynaldo Cruz was the doctor's name. That morning she watched him move from bed to bed like a holy man, tending to patients as if they were his kin. Cruz had arrived this morning bringing food for the two-hundred-patient field clinic. He was tall, in his late forties, light-skinned, and his hair had tight, dark curls. He reminded her of Patricio.

Because of their incredible workload, with no help in sight, Marcela had leaned on Dr. Cruz immediately. When he heard bad news, he would purse his Cupid's bow lips and shrug it off with an ease that almost frightened Marcela. Around one in the afternoon, the first of the other two nurses, Juana, had come down with fever and pustules. Juana didn't want to admit to herself that she had Big Bonebreaker. Cruz listened to her describe her symptoms—nodding, pursing—then told Juana to work as long as she could. She was in a moon suit, he reasoned, so she would not spread anything. About an hour and a half later, the other nurse, Andres, complained of feverlike symptoms. By that time, Juana had been strapped down in a bed, waiting for the painful "bone-breaking" convulsions to start. Cruz asked Andres if he wanted to continue working, but Andres could not answer. His lonely stare said more than words anyway. Cruz helped him to a bed, and Marcela handled the bloodwork, grateful that Cruz was willing to sit with Andres and Juana.

Now, Dr. Cruz unclasped his hands and leaned on the counter next to the DA-scope. "Do you want to try isolating the virus? We just got the new nanophages from the NI."

She shook her head and pushed her chair back from the DA-scope. There was no point. The cryo samples of Juana's and Andres' blood had confirmed the worst. The clinic had been compromised.

Cruz stepped behind Marcela and rested both hands on her shoulders.

She shivered. Marcela laughed at herself. Was it possible she could be aroused in the middle of this horror? He squeezed her shoulders and she closed her eyes.

That night after Suavé Maria, Marcela had kept her wits well enough not to make love to Patricio. There was caressing, hungry kissing, and a loud, mutual release, but he never entered her. A small comfort, yes, but she clutched that scrap like a crucifix when she confessed via *pilone* on the subway home from Cuoyocán.

>Basilica Confession, Central Node<

>Forgive me, Father, for I have sinned,< she said, hoping she didn't draw a strict priest. A man with a guitar case sitting next to her was

confessing, too. They rocked with the subway car's jostlings and crossed themselves in unison.

The priest who answered her was Father Gregorio. Marcela wondered if the Holy Renaissance deliberately funneled penitents to the same confessor. She always drew Father Gregorio. >Unknown Confessor. How long has it been since your last confession?<

>Twenty-four hours, Father Gregorio.<

>*Ai,* Marcela. So much for your anonymity. *Bueno.* Let's hear it. Friday morning you were cleansed. Friday *night* comes along and, boom, out the window. What happened?<

>I accuse myself of having carnal relations with a man, *padre.*<

>Please tell me he was your boyfriend. Do you love this man?<

>I only met him yesterday. I *could* love him. But no. No.<

>So you meet this guy at a bar, you go home together, you make love to him . . . <

Marcela played her ace. >We did *not* make love.<

>Marcela,< Father Gregorio cajoled. >You know how many thieves and murderers I have waiting to confess real sins to me? Let's cut the crap. You shouldn't treat the man you love like this.<

>I know. I don't deserve a good man like Martín.<

>And is this a way to treat your Blessed Savior? Hmm? Is Jesus a laundromat to you, or what? You think He died on the cross so that you can bring Him your sins like loads of dirty shirts?<

>Unknown confessor laughs,< her *pilone* provided for the priest. In the real world, her laugh came out like a snort. The man with the guitar looked sidelong at her.

>Good. I could already tell you're sorry so I wanted to hear you laugh. Now then, talk to your boyfriend. Yes? Forgiveness will be yours if you tell him what happened.<

>Oh, please, I can't do that. Give me a different penance, Father.<

>You'll hurt him, is that it? You just can't bear to hurt that poor, sweet boy?<

>Father, ask me to do anything else. Martín is a strong man, and I rely on his strength so much. Don't make me a better person by weakening him.<

>Hey. That's pretty good. All right. Here's what you do. Ready? Thirteen Hail Marys every day for the next thirteen weeks.<

Marcela put both hands over her mouth. >Wow.<

>Keep a rosary with you at all times to remind you what love is. All right? And this Sunday go to your church and pray to the Virgin. You'll get through this, Marcela, because you have a good heart. *Ego te absolvo.*<

Sitting at her microscope, Marcela shivered a third time. She looked at Cruz, and then away. Then her eyes widened and her heart collapsed, as she grasped that attraction was not the cause of her trembling.

She could taste blood. She didn't have chapped lips, after all. Her lips were bleeding. A pustule was forming, like the pustules Juana had.

No, Dios mío, no.

"What's wrong?" said Cruz. He was looking at her face in the reflection of a stainless-steel cabinet door.

She stood and he caught her when her legs wouldn't hold her weight.

Dr. Cruz held her against his chest. "What is it, Marcela? You have something on your—" His eyes lifted from her mouth to her eyes. "You're shivering badly."

The nervousness in Cruz's voice made her want to flee the clinic in fright. "Oh no," she said and began to cry.

He held her elbows and led her away from the microscope and blood-work station. "Come on. Come with me."

He was going to lead her to the locker room. When the other two nurses went into the locker room with Cruz, they came out as patients. "No. Oh, I don't want to go with you. This can't be. How could it get through my moon suit?"

Reynaldo Cruz was gentle, but he insisted. "Shh. Marcela, it doesn't matter. Forget about that." This field clinic had been a bathhouse just a week ago. He led her out of the bloodwork lab and into the locker room.

"Forget it?" she shrieked. She stood gaping into the large communal shower where a great pile of clothing mounded, alongside rows of shoes. Her voice echoed against the yellow tiles. "But I was so careful!"

He shut the door to the locker room. "Think about the other patients, Marcela. Quiet, please." He sat her on the wooden bench and stood next to her.

"I think it was the food from Clinica Primera. It had to be. We all ate it."

"I tested it myself," said Dr. Cruz. "I ate it too."

Marcela was shivering harder now. The symptoms of this infection were coming on just as fast as Juana's and Andres'. She could feel her temperature spiking in a vain attempt to kill the viruses. The hemorrhaging was next. "It helps to have a theory, even if it won't save me."

"Then let me tell you my theory," Cruz said in a prayerful voice. He took her hand. "No one who is infected survives. It's too fast and strong. Too perfect."

She was feeling colder and colder. At times, the floor of the locker room felt unstable, as if it might lurch up and hit her. "I know that."

"As *medicos,* the only thing we can do is keep the infected together." Cruz held her hand for a long time. Then he said, "Marcela?"

She kept her eyes on his thick blue gloves. She didn't want him saying her name in that tone of voice.

"You have to take off the moon suit now, my friend."

Someone else would wear her suit now, that is, if they could disinfect it. She let Cruz unfasten the air locks at her wrist and on the collar of the helmet. They hissed as the pressure in the suit matched the pressure in the clinic. Her ears popped with the change. Dr. Cruz helped her take the helmet off, then she was breathing fresh, contaminated air. She felt light-headed, but that was the fever, she knew. Cruz took her helmet and placed it on the wooden bench.

She shimmied out of the suit and stood in the center of the locker room in just her maroon scrubs and rosary. "I'm cold," Marcela said, shivering. She could barely speak through her chattering teeth. "I'm so cold."

"I know." Cruz led her out of the locker room and into the infirmary, where he found a vacant cot for her.

The patients lying nearby in their own cots silently watched them enter the room. The illusion that anyone would leave this clinic alive had been shattered hours ago when the nursing staff began to trickle into the infirmary.

As she lay down, Marcela noticed an old man standing behind Dr. Cruz, even though all the patients were supposed to be strapped in. Red-eyed, with sores on his mouth, he stood leaning on a wooden crutch. He tried to speak to Cruz, but when he opened his mouth, he emitted a froglike rasp. A three-legged dog licked an open sore on the man's leg. She could see something like another appendage emerging from the man's back like a wing. The light around him was cold and bright.

"Doctor," she told Cruz, "I'm falling apart."

Cruz helped Marcela into a cot and piled blankets on top of her. She began to sweat as soon as she was lying down. From her cot, she could see the netmonitor sitting atop an old dresser. On-screen was a shot of Sister Domenica, no longer in the "pirate ship," the hidden broadcast studio that she and Pirate had been using for the last two days. She was sitting in a library now and seemed to be meditating, her face a kind oval in the dark.

Marcela said to the image of Domenica, "I cheated on my boyfriend."

Cruz pulled a chair next to her. "How's that?"

"I spent the night with another man about two months ago," said Marcela. "I never told my boyfriend. Martín is gone. They both are gone probably. It hasn't been thirteen weeks. I can't talk to a priest now because the *pilone*—I can't—I'm going to die without—"

"Because the *pilone* what?" said Dr. Cruz.

Marcela looked at Cruz curiously. She couldn't see his *pilone* scar because of his helmet. But surely he had one, a doctor of his stature. "The network crashed, *señor,* so I can't confess," she said, angry that he made her say it.

Cruz looked around the room at the other patients, then back at Marcela. "That is a terrible dilemma."

"Look!" hissed a woman next to Marcela and pointed at the monitor. "The Plague Saint has opened her eyes!"

For the first time, Marcela saw something other than kindness and strength in Dr. Reynaldo Cruz. His lip curled and his eyes lifted to the screen with nothing short of hatred. "So? Who cares about her? So what?" His voice was so filled with contempt that Marcela stared at him, wondering if she was still hallucinating.

"She's been waiting all day for the Virgin to complete her prophecy," said the woman. "Watch!"

Jaw muscles clenched, Cruz mouthed something and shook his head.

Those who were able sat up in their cots and watched the image of Domenica.

Pirate appeared on-screen and handed the nun a glass of water. Her face had gone from serene to terrified.

"She always gets really, really scared when the Virgin is near her!" someone shouted.

Sister Domenica refused the water. Her eyes kept darting to the left, as if she didn't dare look over her left shoulder. Behind her was nothing but shelves of books and the darkness of the library.

"The vg nodes in?" asked Pirate in *pilone* slang.

"He always asks that," clucked an old woman. "Of course the Virgin of Guadalupe is here, Pirate! Just look at that poor girl!" The woman crossed herself.

Domenica managed to rally her confidence and finally looked over her left shoulder. She gave a little cry of surprise.

"She's there!" cried a young man, though his voice was wet and weak.

On-screen, Pirate asked, "What's the Virgin doing?"

"I think she's listing names," said Domenica.

"What a crock!" yelled a young man from the far end of the dormitory.

Her face was turned from the camera, and Domenica's voice was a plea of gratitude. "Thank you, *mamacita*. Thank you. You are so good to me. Thank you."

Everyone in the room, including Cruz and Marcela, watched the monitor.

Just then, the nun clapped her hands over her ears and her face strained with terror. "What is it? *Mamacita*, what is it? Why are you screaming?" Pirate pulled the camera's frame out as if he could reveal to Mexico what Domenica was hearing and seeing. Domenica stared into a dark corner of the library behind her, hands over her ears, shoulders hunched. There was nothing in the corner but shelves jammed with books. Finally, Domenica looked back into the camera. Her face was wet with tears, but serene. "All right. All right," she said, facing the camera.

Several patients, unable to cross themselves because their hands were tied down, began uttering the prayer to the Virgin of Guadalupe.

In a quiet voice, Domenica said, "The woman in white says that there is an intelligence behind Big Bonebreaker, but it isn't the Holy Renaissance. And it isn't the United States. A single scientist, working alone, created this unnatural plague. He's Hitler and Cortés reborn in one body, an infiltrator, and we're defenseless against him."

No one in the room was watching Cruz except Marcela. She saw him stand in slow motion, like an old man rising on bad knees. The muscle on his wide chin quivered.

"Cortés?" the cynical young man shouted. "The disease was engineered by a backwoods thug looking for easy gold? Is that it? This is so *stupid*, people!"

Everyone shushed him and trained ears to the monitors.

"The Virgin," Domenica was saying, "said this scientist means to bring down the Holy Renaissance and Mexico, and he will do it. Because President Orbegón chose to pretend that Big Bonebreaker was a normal disease, this Cortés will succeed. Because Orbegón sees his own *indígena* citizens as expendable, this Satan will spread the virus. This is the test that the Holy Mother warned us about. And this is the end of her prophecy."

"Domenica is whipping *los destitutos* into a frenzy," said the woman strapped down next to Marcela. "She's turning the Minority against the Majority."

"We'll never reunite Aztlán now," an old man cried. "The *reconquista* is doomed."

"You people piss me off so much. What a bunch of stupid crap!"

Heat devils seemed to waver before Dr. Cruz. Marcela peered through them, trying to get a clear glimpse of him. *I tested it myself,* he had said of the food he'd brought from Clinica Primera. How strange, that look of triumph on his face had seemed. Marcela could just make out his profile under the moon suit's helmet as he stared in awe at the monitor. His pale face and tight dark curls. A Euro. A Spaniard, she thought.

"Hitler?" Marcela heard Cruz whispering to himself. "Hitler?" Behind him, the man with the crutch and the wounded dog at his side drew closer. Again, he tried to say something to Cruz, pointing at him, but nothing cogent came, just the awful croaking. *Allí está,* the crippled man seemed to say.

It's him.

Distantly Marcela was aware that her stomach was distending, that her breath was rattling and phlegmy. Her chill was gone, replaced by a burning heat. Marcela now felt like a buoy on a river of lava. They said it was fast.

"It's you," she said to Cruz.

His helmet remained still, but Cruz's head whipped in her direction. She could only see one of his eyes. It was wild and round, and he snapped at her like a cornered animal, "What's that? What did you say to me?"

Nausea rocked her. Marcela shut her eyes tight, and said, "You're the Cortés."

From the pile of bedding at the foot of her cot, Cruz picked up a pillow. He ignored the other patients, who were staring at him now with curiosity and concern, as he came to stand beside the head of Marcela's cot.

The Plague Saint called him Hitler. Satan. Marcela prayed to San Miguel to protect her, and she prayed to the sacred heart of Santa Maria to forgive her for helping to unbalance the world with her unforgiven sin.

The burning lava flowed and flowed and flowed.

The man could swear the nun had said his name. He took a step toward the netmonitor to hear better, but she did not repeat it. She used other names that distracted him—Hitler? Cortés?—but the penetrating way the nun looked at him with that wide-eyed amphibian stare, he was sure he'd heard his name.

"It's you," said the young, infected nurse.

He turned away from the monitor and found Marcela glaring at him, just as the nun had. The man wondered if the nurse had heard Domenica say his name too. "What's that?" he said to Marcela, clearing his throat and trying to sound calm. A moment ago, everything had been airtight. "What did you say to me?"

The nurse screwed her eyes shut as though she were trapped on a diving swoop jet and didn't want to witness her plummet. "You're the Cortés."

He felt like a tower struck by lightning. He felt like little needles were poking him in the cheeks. Things were falling down. The nurse had no reason to say what she said. The nun had no way to know what she knew. Below his whirling anger, he knew that he ought to ignore Marcela, that it was time to abandon his façade as a medical worker but he couldn't control his rational mind's need to make sense of this.

"*¡Tu chingado* Hitler!" The nurse's fever was cresting and she was about to start hemorrhaging. He could tell by the size of her stomach. "No, you're worse! You're worse! Hear me, Archangel Michael! Save me in this desperate hour from the devil Reynaldo Cruz! Oh Sacred Heart of Jesus! Grant the grace that I ask! Pour your—"

The man saw that he had a pillow in his hands. He didn't remember picking it up, but it felt good to hold. It felt good to fit it over Marcela's face—so satisfying to silence her ridiculous plea. "No. No, grant the grace that *I* ask," he whispered, completing Marcela's prayer to the Sacred Heart. It felt like a good cough to be able to say that prayer aloud, to hold the nurse's face under this pillow. "Pour your blessings and mercies over *me*."

The nurse began to convulse beneath the pillow. The man struggled to keep his grip on her and saliva shot through his teeth, hitting his face shield.

"So that I may be worthy of your divine Sacred Heart," the man whispered, "for *I* am acting in your cause, in the cause of nature and God. Please give *me* a sign that you understand."

He couldn't feel wetness through his gloves, but he could sense moisture in the pillow, so he lifted his hands and gave out a little cry of surprise. The pillow was soaked through with blood from her hemorrhaging. He backed away from Marcela's bed. His hands trembled so hard that he had to make tight fists in an effort to control them. He stood in the central aisle, staring at Marcela's cot as if her corpse might decide to lurch to its feet and call him Hitler again.

Down the row of cots, those who were able sat up and watched him. They'd heard and seen everything. Their swollen lymphs and sores gleamed wet in the dark, and their terrified faces flickered in fire.

Fire?

The man turned and looked at the other end of the infirmary and saw leaping flames through the clinic's thick, airtight windows. Outside, a riot was in full gallop, with skytrucks and cloud-boards hovering overhead. The avenue was jammed with people, some trying to leave the city in cars loaded down with boxes and suitcases. A group of young men ran past the sealed windows. Soldiers chased them with charged stunsticks.

"It's all falling down," he said in wonder, watching searchlights cut pretty arcs over the sea-green towers of La Alta.

"Nurse Marcela was right," a teenage boy said. "You're the one Domenica was prophesying about!"

In a bed near him, a haggard cadaver of a woman folded her hands, and said, "Hear me, Santa Domenica, protectress of the infected. The devil is here. Bring him to justice before almighty God!"

Two men argued whether they should leave the clinic or not. "We'll infect the city even worse if we go. Besides I'm strapped down!"

"The *pilone* is dead. Someone, find a telephone. Tell the world who that man is!"

The man turned and walked to the front door of the clinic. He unsnapped the wrist and neck airlocks on his suit, then removed his helmet. He returned the stare of each patient, all of whom looked at him with their

haunted, hating eyes as he shrugged out of the suit and stepped from its leggings. He scrubbed his palms over his face as if wiping himself clean of the
nun's accusations.

"He's not afraid of the disease!" cried the old woman, interrupting her
prayer to Domenica.

"No. He's immune."

The boy's voice was shrill with horror. "Why? Why would you do this,
señor?"

The man turned to the door and opened the air lock on the ALHEPA.
The bedlam of riot boomed into the old bathhouse. The patients flinched in
their beds as the din hit them. Sirens. Shrieking *barcos*. The searing hiss of
rapid-fire plasma-injected guns. A Saint John's Procession of fifteen masked
flagellants shuffled past the field clinic's window, whipping themselves as
they staggered by.

The man raised his hand to his mouth, kissed his fingertips, and blew
the kiss into the clinic. "I'm sorry. Good-bye. I'm sorry."

Then he stepped outside and opened the outer air lock's memboard. A
line of army ground trucks rolled toward the clinic; rioters in gas masks fled
in every direction. No one even looked at what he was doing. On the door's
memscreen appeared options for levels of containment. The man chose
CONDEMNED.

ASCENSIÓN IS UNDER MARTIAL LAW! RETURN TO YOUR HOMES! a cloud-
screen over the clinic read. A low haze, which veiled the bulbed crowns of
La Alta, flickered orange with fires and explosions.

Down the avenue, sprawling crowds had encamped at the base of
Chapultepec Hill. High above, he could see the marble castle that surveyed
the city. Emperor Maximilian Hapsburg had built the castle two hundred
years ago. Beside it now loomed Torre Cuauhtémoc, the castle of a greater
king than Hapsburg had ever been. Torre Cuauhtémoc, whose base sat in
Chapultepec Park, had become Orbegón's tower dubbed "The Majority
Cloister," a quarantined stronghold that protected the Holy Renaissance
from the outbreak. Shrill bullhorn voices of the Minority Party's armed radical wing, *Los Hijos de Marcos,* screamed at the troops massing around Torre
Cuauhtémoc. A command van hovered over the square in front of the
Cloister's main gate. The crowd of thousands sounded poised on the edge of
mass fury, and it seemed ready to vent its emotion on the Holy Renaissance
troops.

He stood on the granite steps of the clinic. The avenue before him was clogged with flagellants. At the avenue's other end, Holy Renaissance jeeps and trucks came to a halt. The man watched, dazed, as the crazed, bloody parade swarmed the olive green ground trucks.

"Move or you'll be shot!" a rodent-faced lieutenant shouted over the top of his jeep's windshield.

The man stepped back until he felt the clinic's air lock at his heels.

A bare-chested old man with sagging pectorals threw his head back and shouted the *Ave* to the Virgin of Guadalupe at the lieutenant.

"La Baja is under martial law," the lieutenant shouted. "Get out of the way. Now!" Another set of sirens howled from down the avenue, from Ascensión's main square. The lieutenant put his hands over his ears, listening to his headset, then shouted at his driver, "Tell the rear guard to back up!" He turned and screamed at the truck behind him. "Reverse! Revolutionaries are burning the banks and cathedral!" Farther down the avenue, the man could hear gears shifting in diesel trucks.

Somehow the revolutionaries had warning, the man thought. *Somehow, they knew to attack when the* pilone *went down.*

The answer set his teeth grinding. *Domenica.*

She troubled him. Somehow, she knew what he was doing. She knew about the outbreak before it started. She began this prophecy of hers two days before Zapata Hospital was quarantined. She began it a day before Diego Alejandro had ordered a field team to investigate the dengue outbreak. In fact, she began it the very moment that he himself began the epidemic by infecting Dolores. And Domenica had been there, too, on the old television set, as if Dolores herself had summoned the nun. She had. She had. She had conjured the nun. Dolores *insisted* the Plague Saint be onscreen while they made love. It didn't make sense but it had happened. He felt his mind fluttering over these mad thoughts like a bird looking for a place to perch.

Before him, the convoy began lurching into reverse. The sound of gunfire and screaming skyboats ripped across the city. The man followed the ground convoy toward the other riots in the National Square, the *zócalo*. The man thought, *A force of some kind looked into the future and told her what it saw.*

In the streets, the infection was spreading not only as a virus, but as something worse, something human. Fires tongued the walls of old buildings. Kids smashed windows. A circle of rioters separated a Holy Renaissance soldier from his unit and shredded his moon suit, spitting and urinating on him once he was exposed.

The man stopped near the exposed soldier and bowed his head. He prayed as he had prayed to Mother Mary his whole life. *Santa Maria? Are you here? Are you with me? You have given a sign to the nun. Would you do me the great favor of telling me what you want from me?*

Ten young men, none of them wearing masks or gloves, overturned a police ground car. But before they could remove the driver and his screaming passengers, a red-and-black hover van descended over the street from high above, the shepherd's staff symbol of the Holy Renaissance printed on the underbelly of its hull. A loudspeaker voice said, "Disperse immediately!"

Whose side are you on, Holy Mother? The man prayed.

A young *indígena* boy aimed a *Sangre de Cristo* rifle at the hull over his head and squeezed the trigger. A spurt of bullets hit the van and ricocheted back into the street, scattering the rioters.

The man watched while he prayed. *Aren't I acting out God's natural will, Santa Maria?*

He could not understand why she'd oppose him. The city of Ascensión was ungodly, unnatural. It was unnatural in Montezuma's day, with so many living on Lake Texcoco that the Aztecs began filling it in to make more room for their growing numbers. And now. Now natural diseases could do nothing—dengue, smallpox, cholera—all too weak to leap past the walls of human defense even in such a large, vulnerable city. Pollution and violent crime were ineffectual. War. Nothing could stop this city from growing in its unnatural numbers, expanding at a rate equivalent to adding another city every year into this poor little valley. Earthquakes. Volcanoes. Mudslides. Nothing stemmed the human infection here. By the time the Holy Renaissance came along, admonishing its people to "Be Fruitful and Multiply in the Cause of God," the city had been forced to thrust upward. It balanced populations atop quake-proof towers. It domesticated its people, leashing them with wetware and implants. The man said to the flashing haze overhead, "Am I not God's response to the profane fascism of the Holy Renaissance? Am I not a natural response, *Virgen*?"

The man continued walking up La Reforma, through the death throes of Mexico's capital. *The Virgin is against me,* he thought. *The Virgin is against nature.* He could see the *zócalo* ahead and hear the thunderous rioting. *I am nature and God is against me.*

When the man finally reached the *zócalo*, he stood at the intersection of La Reforma Avenue and the National Square, watching a full-fledged revolt. Thousands upon thousands seethed in the great space before the cathedral and the old National Palace. Their voices banked off the old Viennese-style buildings in deafening clamor, while a squad of Holy Renaissance elite soldiers stood before the high double doors of the cathedral. The lieutenant's small platoon had formed a barrier of vehicles before the Banco Real. Overhead, a cloud-board floated: CEASE AND DESIST!

"I thought I was acting in God's cause," he said softly, explaining himself to the ancient cathedral across the great expanse of flagstones. The Ascensión National Square was the largest city square on the planet, so it dizzied the eye to behold so many people here. The crowd roiled toward the glass banks one moment, met the resistance of troops, then sloshed toward the cathedral a moment later. Makeshift Vatican and Minority Party flags swooped over their heads.

"I thought I was one with God."

The man heard bubbling, just loud enough to catch his attention. Musical water. He looked down at his feet and saw a bubble of blood pulsing up between the cobblestones.

Pressed between colonial edifices and Holy Renaissance glass-and-steel bank towers, an arm of the riot coiled out from the main crowd and stretched toward the banks. Troops fired from the bank lobby and several people fell.

One of the trucks in the cordon lurched forward as the driver shifted into first and knocked four people down. They scrambled away as it plowed forward.

At the man's feet, blood continued to shoot like a slim ribbon from the earth. The bubbling became a beat, as bright, red blood seeped in rills through the pavement.

Through a bullhorn, a panicked voice screamed from the cathedral, "Captain! These people are all infected!"

Amazed, he watched blood spread over the volcanic rock of the paving stones like a silk sheet. He bent down and touched his finger to the little fountain, tasted it. It was real. It was there.

"This is me insane," he thought, examining the blood on his fingertip, and yet he could not discount the possibility that this was a vision. He had just asked for a sign, after all. He stood up, still staring down at the blood.

The crowd rushed the Holy Renaissance troops guarding the cathedral. Wave after wave of protesters fell until the crowd poured into the church. The bullhorn screeched, "We need septic troops, Captain! Now!"

The man turned back to the embattled cathedral and folded his hands again. "Madness or divinity, I am ready for you."

In the burning church, gunshots thudded. Black smoke wreathed the cathedral's bell tower and twin spires, curling into a mysterious gesture.

He held his breath, waiting, praying.

The curtain of smoke over the old church parted and twisted like a hand in benediction.

Here comes my sign.

The smoke unveiled two skyboats circling over the *zócalo*. Jets of lit gas blasted down into the crowd. The man stood still as thousands of people fanned out through the square. A large woman knocked him down, and he covered his head as a stampede trampled over him. Explosions rattled the ground and his body, and a missile hit the intersection where the man had been standing. Cobblestones, chunks of new pavement, and several people fell on top of him. The concrete under his head quivered.

Bodies choked the square when he regained consciousness. Long shadows of morning stretched over the *zócalo's* carnage and the ancient cathedral was a gutted heap behind a teetering façade. Sirens screamed over riots elsewhere in La Baja.

Moon-suited teams stacked bodies, dead and dying alike, next to ambulances limned with a Red Crescent, Pan-Islam's international rescue mission. The man tried to push himself up but his hand was broken, so he fell forward hitting his shoulder on the pavement.

In susurrant, sliding steps, nearly fifty flagellants in black-leather masks entered the wide *zócalo*. Haunting in their masks, with zippers up the front of their blank, black faces, they raised their elbows high to deliver blows upon their own backs, sweaty chests thrust forward. A man in a tattered priest's cowl of Holy Renaissance red and black stepped to the front of the procession, holding a cross like a torch. Vampirically pale and wild-eyed, he stood among the snapping whips and pointed into the smoking cathedral, screaming a mad mix of Spanish and Latin. *"Virus y veneno! Virus y veneno."*

The man understood him.

"Poison and poison and poison."

When the mad chanting stopped, the man leaned on his elbow and crawled up to his feet. He called out in Latin, "I am poison, too! I confess it! I am the virus!"

The vampire priest gaped, then pulled up his cowl. He lifted his hand and made a cross in the air. *"Ego te absolvo!"*

The man cried out in Spanish. "Are you my sign from the Blessed Virgin?"

The priest nodded fervently. "Yes! We are!"

A child, or maybe it was a young lady with a flutelike voice, sang the *Ave Maria* as the procession began winding out of the square. *They must be real,* he thought. *They must be.*

The cross-bearer held out his leather strap and called across the bodies, "It's your time. Come with us."

PART

III

CHAPTER

EYES SHUT TIGHT, Domenica prayed on the floor of the abandoned library, sitting on a red seat cushion. Pirate sat atop the oak reference desk about five feet away, behind the camera trained on Domenica's face. They were alone in this little library, and the keening of sirens swirled outside like hurricane winds.

Domenica felt hot and trapped. She opened her eyes and looked at her old friend, wondering if he was warm, too. The muzzle of the gas mask the Khazak relief worker had given him was tapping against his chest as he nodded toward sleep.

Domenica and Pirate had found this place after waiting in vain for a visitation at the "pirate ship." Pirate's netcast studio was located on the eighth floor of the Bad Water Commons, an old hotel turned commune near the heart of what was now the hot zone. The little culture surrounding Domenica, which started budding and growing a year ago with Pirate alone, had lately been growing rapidly into an entourage. By the time Big Bonebreaker came stomping into town, she was constantly surrounded by dissident seminary students, Minority Party activists, *Hijos de Marcos* insurgents, and cast-off nuns loyal to the Vatican. Waiting for the final chapter of the prophecy in the Bad Water Commons, with all the people around her, was the wrong strategy. The Virgin simply didn't come, no matter how hard Domenica prayed.

Meanwhile, offgrid street-*ojos* were contacting Pirate, telling him to get

Domenica out of the Commons; they said that as soon as the barricade around the *centro histórico* hot zone was complete, kill teams in antiviral suits would be sweeping the ancient neighborhood for holdouts. Flagellants and other pilgrims kept interrupting their netcasts, too, hoping to receive a blessing from the Patron Saint of Plagues, as they called Domenica. After the fifth interruption, she had gone downstairs and found the lobby of the Commons crammed with clamp-masked penitents—she decided then and there that it was time to leave the hot zone.

With nothing but a sat camera and a link-blinder, she and Pirate had vacated the studio, despite warnings from overhead cloud-boards telling *capitalinos* to stay inside behind locked doors. The chaotic streets teemed with Renaissance convoys, Ascensión city patrols, street fighters with red bandanas over their faces, and looters running with whatever they could find (netmonitors, clothing, shovels, pew cushions). But they couldn't find an exit: Every street that Domenica and Pirate took was barricaded with military checkpoints, hurricane fences, or twenty-foot-high portable walls.

Pirate figured the way out—as always. He led Domenica through a ransacked jewelry store, downstairs, and through a catacomb of connected basements, splashing through puddles formed by the ancient subterranean tides of the old lake bed on which the city was built.

Hello, Lake Texcoco, thought Domenica. *You'll never let us forget you, eh?*

When they finally found stairs leading up, they had emerged here, inside a firehouse turned library just a block outside the barricaded hot zone.

From the basement stairs, Domenica had stared into the library's calm emptiness and silent stacks of books. The musty scent of moldering paper smelled exotic, surreal. "What if the plague is here and killed everyone already, Pirate?"

"Then we're in trouble."

A thorough search of the big, one-room building revealed open soda bottles abandoned on tables, high heels parked or forgotten beneath desks, coffee-cup handles aimed at the front door, and sweaters draped over the backs of chairs. A netmonitor was on and tuned to the Holy Renaissance's emergency channels. No bodies, no blood anywhere in the library. Whatever sad, oldtime paper-book fanatics had been here had wisely fled when given the chance. Pirate shut the windows, spraying them down with a black-plastic sealant that he'd brought with him, and dug the word PLAGUE into the library's front door with a screwdriver.

After three hours of prayer, Domenica felt safe. The library, solemn as a sepulchre, reminded her of the Order of Guadalupe's meditation rooms.

If only it weren't so hot in here.

As she retied her braid, Domenica swallowed in a mouth dry with fear. She was thirsty, too. Both were dengue-5 symptoms, she knew. She tightened the seal of her clamp mask and adjusted her gloves. It didn't feel like fever. This felt hotter. Dizzying. She couldn't control the oven of her thoughts as her eyes skittered over the spines of book titles.

Behind her, Domenica heard a footstep.

Had someone snuck past the six-foot bookcase she and Pirate had slid in front of the basement door? Domenica kept her head stone still. Her eyes darted to the left, the direction from which she'd heard the footstep.

"Pirate," she whispered.

Pirate's upper body bobbed slowly with the breath of sleep, and air shushed through his rubber mask's filter.

Domenica cocked her head without turning around, listening to the noises behind her. Another step. Fabric brushed the ground. "Pirate!" she whispered again. *She's here. She's finally come!*

From the corner of her eye, she could see Pirate rousing himself and checking the camera's uplink, nodding.

Good. We're still hot. Domenica rallied her nerve and turned to look behind her.

The library was dark. Against the wall, someone had stacked towers of magazines from pre*pilone* days. In front of those stacks was a scuffed and scratched oak bench, half-hidden in shadow. The woman in white sat there, hands flat on her thighs, lively brown eyes staring at Domenica.

Domenica willed herself not to greet the woman. She had made big displays of happiness and joy when these visitations began a year ago, only to have the woman vanish, leaving Domenica with an inconsolable cavity of loss and a piercing headache. Domenica turned back to Pirate, relieved and terrified that she'd actually seen the virgin this time.

Pirate stiffened as he seemed to note Domenica's posture. "The vg nodes in?" he asked. *The Virgin of Guadalupe has arrived?*

Domenica hissed, "Yes."

"Is she speaking to you now?" Pirate asked.

Domenica turned an ear. She could hear the woman in white listing Nahuatl Indian names behind her. Domenica's grandmother had used the old tongue too, only when talking to fellow scholars of ancient Mexico, but often enough that Domenica recognized the language when she heard it. She nodded to Pirate with a single urgent ducking of her head, worried that even this subtle movement might frighten away the woman in white.

Pirate accessed the audio uplink with a tap on the camera. His movements suddenly seemed far away, as if he were outside the library. The room felt heavy, trembling.

Her list finished, the woman in white fidgeted behind Domenica, shifting sandals soled with tire treads. She wanted Domenica to look at her, the nun imagined, but Domenica would not do so until invited. Any misstep in the woman's mysterious protocol could end the visit.

"Little lamb," came the Virgin's deep, melodic voice. "Such a lovely little lamb, I'd know you anywhere by the smell of your brow and hair. Do you believe me?"

Domenica's heart urged her to look at the woman, but she kept her eyes trained somewhere between Pirate and the woman, gazing off into the corridors of books. "You're so kind to me. Thank you, *mamacita*."

Yearning filled the woman's voice. "I would do anything for you. Anything. That's a mother's curse. You'll never be a *mamacita,* so you'll never experience this great love I feel for you."

Domenica never deflected her praise or called herself unworthy as the sisters in the Order of Guadalupe had urged her to do. If she ever demurred, the Virgin departed and the headache came, so Domenica had learned not to question or doubt, but to accept the marvel of the woman in white.

"Look at me, lamb, let me see that beautiful face."

Domenica pivoted on her rump and commanded herself to look the Virgin in the eye. The woman was small and elderly, with a deeply wrinkled face, and heavyset like the matronly women of Domenica's own family. She wore a white gauze dress that fell to her thick ankles, with a whiter neckline and short sleeves that showed her upper arms. The dress was perfect, uncreased, and made her skin look almost black. The woman's eyes twinkled as if Domenica were an adorable three-year-old and the sight of her filled the Virgin with delight.

Domenica knew that from a certain point of view the quaint construction of her mind was being flicked aside during these visitations. Oh, but to feel the glory of the woman in white, no matter who or what she was. No crass, grumbling human deserved this blessing, let alone Domenica with all her shortcomings. The woman in white adored Domenica, though Domenica didn't understand why. Domenica shushed herself. *Accept it. She has accepted you. Accept it.*

Her emotions a torrent of awe and gratitude, love and confusion, Domenica began crying. She couldn't help it.

Pirate stood and handed Domenica a box of tissues from the reference desk. "Tell me if you need anything, Domenica."

Domenica dabbed her nose and looked at him quickly, long enough to say *I'm fine* with her eyes.

"Listen," said the Virgin.

Domenica looked back, the woman's dress—a fire of white in the shadows.

"Listen, I said."

Domenica bowed her head.

"I have something to tell you." The charming mama face fell, and the Virgin's voice became weighty. "There is something—in here with me. It isn't—" she looked about suspiciously at the dark library, "one of us."

Domenica had learned months ago not to question or request clarification. Either the woman would explain herself further without prompting or Domenica would simply be left to interpret the message on her own, though paraphrasing helped. Domenica said, "It isn't one of you."

"No, lamb, he isn't one of . . . *us*." The woman in white stood, still looking about as if she'd heard something frightening in the library. She lifted her left hand, and Domenica could see she was holding a white egg. The Virgin held it as if she meant to toss it to Domenica, then cupped her right hand over the egg. "I have been doing some research. I haven't understood everything. But now I see—there's someone in here that doesn't belong." Then the Virgin began listing names again in her clucking, throaty Nahuatl.

"Are you all right?" Pirate asked Domenica.

Domenica whispered without looking at him, "The prophecy is starting."

The woman in white squatted and the fabric of her dress stretched between her knees. She placed the egg in front of her on the ground and she looked at Domenica. She struggled to her knees and knelt in front of the egg. "A second conquest—trickery—Hitler and Cortés reborn, dressed as an Aztec ancestor. But he isn't one of us and now—he's in here with me." The woman in white whispered, "But listen: I have a fighter—for every foe."

Domenica was about to paraphrase when the woman in white opened her mouth wide, making a little smacking noise. A hiss came from her throat. Her eyes flashed white as the irises rolled upward into her head and she screamed, "Get it out! Get it out! Get it out! Get it out!"

The Virgin stood and began trembling. She quivered hard as if someone were shaking her from behind. She spread her hands and her eyes darted from side to side. "Stop. Don't touch. Don't put that in your mouth. Take your medicine," she said, as though surrounded by mischievous children. "Don't shake hands. Chew with your mouth closed. Wash your face! Don't kiss that man! He doesn't belong! Stop that, all of you! I said get away from each other!"

Terrified, Domenica kept her head bowed, watching from beneath her brows.

The Virgin's eyes went haywire with anger, and her voice carved through the room. "Diseases of the conqueror, I know them all, but not this one. I'll burn everything in my path. I'll kill the Spaniard this time. Don't let him in my cell. I'm rallying my forces and I'll destroy the city to kill the invader. To kill what was hatched in my own land, I'd kill my own children, kill myself. Do you believe me? Say if you do!"

"I believe you!"

The Virgin raised one hand. Domenica could see a spray of age spots on her wrist. The woman in white held this pose for a long time, eyes closed as if calming herself. Then she bent over to pick up the egg. She said, "I'm using all my forces to keep the disease away from you, Chana."

Domenica straightened as though cuffed under the chin. She felt her throat constrict around that name. "Mama?"

"And this is the last time that I will come to you."

Her heart seemed to press against the back of her throat. "No!" Domenica said, her voice a croak. *Why did she call me that?* Domenica shook her head so frantically that hair threaded free from her braid. "No, *mamacita,* Mexico needs you!"

The egg vanished. The woman in white straightened her dress and sat down on the bench. Suddenly, the room was filled with smells of the High Sierras, the most comforting smells of home for Domenica: sage, horses, dry grass, hay. Sturdy Catholics formed the tight farming community in which Domenica was born and raised, mountain *campesinos* who hated the sinful capital, who went to church with or without the admonitions of the Holy

Renaissance. It calmed Domenica to smell stewed meat in a fragrant *guisado*. Fried cactus. The smoky-chocolate smell of mesquite and the warm aroma of corn tortillas.

Domenica frowned and pressed her fingertips into her shut eyes. *Wait. What is this?* she thought. *I wasn't raised on a farm. I was raised in Mexico City. What is this?*

Mesquite smoke. The grassy whiff of manure.

The woman in white shook her head as if to keep Domenica from fussing. "You are yourself, Chana. Don't be deceived by the lies of false priests. Have I ever guided you in the wrong direction? *¿No yo estoy aqui que—?*"

Domenica folded her hands and beseeched the Virgin, *"¡No te vayas, mamá, no te vayas! ¡Te faltaremos—!"*

"¡—soy que tu Madre por siglos y siglos, Chanacita?"

Domenica didn't care about assurances, nor did she care about the consequences of questioning the Virgin. She couldn't stand it that the woman in white was calling her by the wrong name before abandoning her forever. Domenica shouted, "Why are you calling me that, mama?"

"Shh, Chana, shh. I am right here. I am right here."

That corner of the library fell in to total blackness. Domenica looked over her shoulder at Pirate, wondering why he had doused the candles, but she could see that they burned with long, straight flames. Domenica whipped her head back to the wooden bench.

The woman in white was gone.

A tight, pinching sensation over the bridge of her nose seemed to drive straight into Domenica's skull. "Oh no." She covered her forehead with her palm as a shaft of pain shot through her head. Domenica fell forward. "Why?"

Pirate was immediately at her side. "Domenica! What is it? What's wrong?"

The swoon of pain disoriented her. She opened her eyes and winced, unable to remember where she was in the astounding pain.

"Are you hot? Are you thirsty?" demanded Pirate, holding her shoulders in his big grip.

"Yes."

His voice became more urgent. "Domenica! Look at me! Are your limbs sore?"

"I don't have Big Bonebreaker, Pirate," said Domenica annoyed, fatigued. "It's the headache I get when I ask too many questions."

Pirate made a pillow with the seat cushion and urged her to lie down. Domenica lifted her hand to show him he was crowding her and he backed off. She peered at the camera, her lids like oyster shells closing over the dark pearls of her eyes. The camera was still aimed at her, and the uplink light was red. She wondered how many people could watch her in the midst of this outbreak.

"Mexicanistas," she said to the camera, "I have the promised message from the Virgin. It is her last message. She says she will not come again to me."

Domenica translated the images that the woman in white had given her, delivering them as prophecy. The virus was made by a Spaniard and more deaths were coming. If everyone obeyed the doctors, stayed clean and careful, they might live. If not, the Spaniard's virus would find them.

Then she collapsed, her head sinking against the cushion with a sigh of relief. Pirate snuffed out the link on his way to the bathroom to get Domenica a compress.

While she waited for him, arm thrown over her eyes, Domenica could hear the netmonitor across the library, tuned to the Holy Renaissance's emergency channel. The incessant noise of it was infuriating, but without the Connection, netcasts were the only means of getting news. Domenica listened to the running commentary on the outbreak, and in the avalanche of the netcast chatter, one name leapt out, almost like a *pilone* data packet filling Domenica's VisionField.

She heard the name again. Domenica leaned on one elbow and looked at the netmonitor.

Chana.

"Could it be that Mexico's hot new prophetess is really just a sham artist posing as a nun?"

Domenica crawled to a sitting position and frowned at the netmonitor.

"If you're living outside Ascensión, vote by touching the appropriate box on your screen. We'll have the poll results right after this."

The screen went to a Ministry of Health message about mixing bleach and water. Another screen tumbled forward and split down the middle. The split screen showed Domenica's own wide smile on one half, a *Jesuchristo el conquistador* pin on the collar of her Order's uniform. On the other half was the once-popular actress Chana Chenalho. The eleven-year-old picture, bleached hair cut razor short, a grimace of fury and mockery on her face, was the famous shot of her arrest after her *coatl* protest.

"Mary Mother of God," said Domenica, covering her face with her hand. "What in the world is happening to me?"

Pirate emerged from the bathroom with a soaked bandana folded into a square. He stopped and looked at the netmonitor as he passed. "What is this?"

The emergency channels were running old footage of Chana Chenalho's famous street performance, the one at the wrecked construction site of the first La Alta tower, the performance that had landed the actress "in spa" eleven years ago. "They're telling people that I'm Chana Chenalho."

"The protester?" said Pirate, handing Domenica the compress. "Why?"

On-screen, Chana Chenalho was wearing her piggishly fat Madame Stephanie Orbegón costume and chattering in the First Lady's *gringa* accent and clueless mix of Spanish and English. Behind the actress were the ruins of the first tower, toppled in the earthquake that had unearthed the foundation of the forgotten Temple of Xipe Totec. "I can't wait! Shopping malls a *kilometro* above Ascensión! *¡Que puro!*" Chana-as-Madame-Orbegón said, thrusting out her great foam chest into the camera. Then she turned and shouted at the workers milling in the construction site. "*¡Ándale, muchachos!* I have a ten-thirty brunch! Let's get this tower up!"

Construction workers stopped and shaded their eyes, smiling in Chana's direction.

"*Vámanos,* OK? Back to work! Emil outlawed unions two years ago!"

Pirate laughed. "I remember that. I was in orbit, working the satellite relays for Cancún Control when she did this. The *servicio sagrado* got called in to arrest her because the censors couldn't shut her down. Her popularity and approval were too high for them to override without risking a revolt. S.S. had to arrest her right in the middle of a hot uplink." He shook his head in appreciation and handed Domenica the cold bandana. "She sure knew how to work the media."

Domenica pressed the compress to her face and stared at the netmonitor through the haze of her headache. She felt like that bent tower, that razed Aztec temple. "The Holy Renaissance is smearing me."

Pirate nodded toward the screen. "You're in good company."

On-screen, she could see block rectangles of the Aztec temple's foundation thrusting through the concrete base of the modern tower. Vertical girders splayed like broken fingers overhead. At the center of the destruction was the two-ton marble head of a feathered serpent, a *coatl,* pushed up by the earthquake from where Cortés's soldiers had buried it, archaeologists later determined, in 1519. And the actress ranted. Her fat foam legs, pinched into teeny boots, scissored across the demolished construction site. "I can't wait until everyone in Mexico gets the Connection!" Chana was saying. "Then you watch, we'll all get rich, rich, rich on La Bolsa's hypereconomy. Even *las indígenas*! That's what Emil says, OK? No *pobres* anymore. And I can't wait to see *what* Emil does to the poor old *Estados Unidos* then!"

Domenica listened to this with the cold compress warming itself against her hot eyes. The headache wouldn't go away, not until she slept it off. But she was too angry and shocked for sleep.

Am I not here, little Chana, the woman in white had said, *I that am your Mother forever and ever?*

Eyes closed again, she could hear Pirate shutting down the camera, packing it up. "We can't stay here much longer. *Servicio sagrado* is everywhere," he said. "What about going back to the hot zone?"

"Sounds like a death sentence," she groaned. Domenica opened her eyes and looked at the netmonitor.

A new frame flipped forward and showed a Holy Renaissance psychologist, wearing the now customary black-and-red antiviral suit of a government official. It was a wide-angle shot, showing the psychologist in a garden with an eagle topiary behind him. An interviewer, also wearing a moon suit, sat beside him on a deck chair. Domenica had the distinct feeling that she had once been in that garden. "She was a hard case," the doctor was saying. Domenica couldn't see his face through his helmet shield. "Chana Chenalho came through in the end and signed a loyalty oath to the Renaissance after her seven-month spa, but it was a hard seven months."

"Praise God," the interviewer cooed in her helmet. *"¡Que puro!"*

"After spa, Chana joined the Order of Guadalupe nuns, changing her name to Domenica. This is all thoroughly documented for public examination," the doctor said in the frustrated tone of a dad describing all he had done for a rebellious teenager. "We encouraged her. We paid for her schooling at the Convent of the Order of Guadalupe. Everyone on staff wanted her to be happy in her new dedication to God. Now it seems our efforts to reach her were not as successful as I'd been led to believe."

"Can you describe the Antigua Method for me, Doctor?"

Domenica knew that man. She couldn't place him but she had seen his face before. Was he an old family friend, perhaps, a long-lost character from her childhood? Perhaps he was someone she had known, one of the tech crew from her brief, terrible stint with the *telenovelas*. Perhaps he was a teacher from one of the improvisational acting schools that she had attended, or a farming *compañero* of her father's in Oaxaca who—

Domenica gasped.

Those thoughts. Those memories. Whose were they?

She made a fist until her knuckles blanched, as if wringing those strange memories from her brain.

Acting school? Whose upbringing was that? That wasn't her. That wasn't her childhood of walking up the flower-lined path to her Catholic grade school in the suburbs of Mexico City. Her days after school were spent in the study of the pre-Columbian Anahuac Empire and its reemergence in the rising party, the Holy Renaissance. *Telenovelas?* Oaxaca? Farmers? She winced, trying to make sense of the craziness that had made its way into her head.

"The Antigua Method was state of the art for its time," said the psychologist, "and in my opinion has yet to be disproved. Raghib and Gunderson have thoroughly mapped the faith centers of the brain. It is within the pathology of cerebral development for the mind to encounter and examine its own self, then its own death. Around the age of seven years, the brain provides hardware, if you will, to embrace the paradox of both the ego's mortality and its undying place in the cosmos. This is faith. A beautiful evolutionary development, essential for a reasoning species. For the faithless, the Antigua Method merely corrects faulty wiring in these underdeveloped regions of the brain."

"But it did not work in the case of Chana Chenalho?" asked the interviewer.

"The Antigua Method replaces one pathology with another," said the psychologist. "Like crooked teeth, if the braces are removed, the old dental pattern will sometimes reassert itself. So with the brain." He turned and looked into the camera as it slowly zoomed toward his face. This was all scripted, Domenica realized with a rush of fear. They were trying to invade her mind. "Sister Domenica's conception of the Virgin is nothing more than a phantom image dancing across the synapses of her broken mind. A conglomerate, I have determined, of old matriarchal family members—her grandmother, specifically, might be whom she pictures when she 'sees' the woman in white. I want to help Domenica. *Mexicanistas,* if you know the whereabouts of Sister Domenica, please, report to your priest or to a Holy

Renaissance medical volunteer." His face hardened into concern and pity. "Please, help me find Chana Chenalho. If you see her, contact the *servicio sagrado* office in your neighborhood."

Offscreen, the interviewer breathed, *"¡Que puro!"*

Domenica struggled to her feet and looked at Pirate. "Get your stuff. Let's get the hell out of here."

"Something tells me," Pirate said, snapping the camera into its carrying case, "we're not going back to the convent."

"No," Domenica said, "we're going into the hot zone."

Pirate laughed. "Old Antonio told me I'd be back."

CHAPTER

14

"YOU'RE CLEAN. Congratulations." The *medica* at the International Airport smiled at Stark through her face shield after reading the last of his test results. "You're one of us."

Stark checked the clock on the wall—0700. He was exhausted, having spent the better part of his first night in Ascensión examining airport operations and, with Rosangelica's help, coordinating them with the Task Force, soon to be under Stark's command. Wearily, he picked up the white Racal-plus suit that he'd been issued. "It's been a while since I put one of these on," he said, slipping his feet through the suit's legs and into the boots. He shimmied the waistband up to his hips, then realized he'd gone about the process all wrong. The locks at the wrist cuffs dangled out of his reach as he gripped the waistband in place. "Um."

The *medica* held the shoulders of his suit while he shrugged inside, then locked his neck collar. She even held his gloves for him as if he were a toddler getting dressed for winter. "You'll get used to it," she said, snapping the air tanks onto Stark's back. She fitted the helmet over his head, sliding it against the suit's collar until it caught with a click and hiss. "Ready?"

He nodded. *"Empuédame."* Power me up.

She closed the collar, then hit the power.

Immediately, the suit puffed, making him look slightly rounder, the lines of his compact body indistinct. His ears filled and popped, and it was almost as if his hangover popped too. *Nice bonus for wearing this bag.*

Rosangelica, already suited, appeared at the entrance to the bathroom-cum–exam station. "All clean, Estarque?" Rosangelica said, though the Spanish word she used was *"blanco"* not *"limpia,"* as Stark would have expected. *Are you white, Estarque?*

A bit of leftover racism from the Spanish colonial era, Stark imagined, casting a nervous glance at the dark-skinned *medica*.

"There's an *aerobus* waiting," she said, her voice high and chirping through the suit's speaker. "*Ándale*. We leave at seven-thirty."

Stark followed Rosangelica out of the VIP Exam Room, then stopped. "What do you mean 'we'?" He had presumed that once they'd issued protocols on how global shipments of vaccine were to be handled that the *sabihonda* would see how boring his work was and choose to leave him alone. "I thought *we* were parting ways here."

"The senior members of your Task Force," Rosangelica said, still walking, "are planning to meet you on the way to the Majority Cloister in Torre Cuauhtémoc. Everyone is here. You and I were the last to arrive."

It was so loud in the airport concourse that Stark had to run after her and ask her to repeat her last sentence. The International Airport was solely for medical shipments and transport, per Stark's orders in transit, so trucks and ambulances had turned the airport's corridors into cacophonous roadways, as queues of ground transports moved medical supplies from the tarmac inside. "But I'm here now. Safe and sound. I don't need you anymore," Stark shouted over the roar of passing trucks.

"It's already arranged. We'll be in Torre Cuauhtémoc, the La Alta tower where President Orbegón has gathered the core of the Holy Renaissance— the Majority Cloister," Rosangelica said, leading Stark to a set of giant air locks covering the airport's foot-traffic exit. A line of people in ill-fitting Racal-plus suits or gloves and clamp masks were waiting to pass through the air locks. "The Ministry of Health is there. So is the National Institute, and of course your Outbreak Task Force. Orbegón wants to monitor your progress closely."

Plastered across the airport's windows were posters playing the Mexican national anthem and calls for Anahuacs to reunify Texas to *La Patria*. Many posters showed stylized pictures of the President for Life, high-contrast images of his rectangular moustache, chevron eyebrows, and signature spectacles. EMIL EL OLVIDADO DE DIOS, read the posters, their *pilone* prayer nodes blinking ineffectually. Emil the Damned. *Siempre rezamos por su alma.* We pray for his soul always.

"What a load of crap," Stark said in English.

Inside her helmet, Rosangelica's low voice was threatening. "You're not in Bastrop anymore, Doctor."

"Mexicans really believe that line about an Anahuac Empire?" The Holy Renaissance dubbed every pre-Columbian discovery in North America— whether an Ojibwe fire pit in Saskatchewan or an Olmec boulder head in Veracruz—proof of the once-sprawling Anahuac Empire. Proof of Mexico's ancient dominance over the continent. "Or does everyone know that just government garbage?"

"Cut it, Estarque."

He had to know how deep her loyalties ran. "Do *you* believe it?"

Rosangelica led Stark to the queue filing through the massive set of exit air locks, big particle arresters that panted and sighed like giant lungs. Stark's ears didn't fill as he passed through the air lock. The pressure in his suit was stable, he was glad to see. "I believe in *El Olvidado de Dios.* That's what I believe," said Rosangelica.

"The hell you talking about?"

"I believe in Orbegón. Emil." Rosangelica had shifted to Spanish, and said it like she knew the man. "Emil is *El Olvidado de Dios* because he takes all of Mexico's sins upon himself. The wars. The killing of criminals and other low elements." Ahead of them people stamped their feet on chemical pads and raised their arms for a blast of bleach across their suits. "He's the savior-scapegoat of a deeply Catholic country."

This gonna be my constant companion, huh? Stark thought, passing through the ALHEPA. *Ain't that wonderful.*

Outside the airport, beneath the full glare of the Mexican sun, Rosangelica looked up and down the unloading zone's roundabout, lined with *aerobuses* and swoops, searching for the one she wanted.

"This way. They're down here."

Stark saw eight people in Racal suits standing before a bloated *aerobus.* Six of the suits were like Stark's, white with cube helmets and broad, clear face shields. The other two were black and red with the shepherd-staff seal on the back. Holy Renaissance officials.

As the eight people noticed Rosangelica approaching, they turned to greet the pair. Stark shook hands at once with Jarum Ahwaz, who now sported a well-trained handlebar moustache and a powdering of gray hair since the last time Stark had seen him in Atlanta. Jarum was a Palestinian from the Pan-Islam Virological Institute and had been a frequent advisor to the Doctors Without Borders Commission, a group that the CDC's Central Command worked with closely. "Dr. Stark," Ahwaz said in English, "I regret no time for poker in this outbreak. It's a very bad one."

Stark assured Ahwaz that, if possible, they would find time to relieve the Palestinian of his cash.

The other face Stark knew was precious to him, one with which he identified the most gruesome moments of his life. Dr. Isabel Khushub from Pakistan.

"What did you say?" Rosangelica asked.

Stark had muttered his thought aloud. *What a relief.*

Stark had worked with Isabel in the old days when he was with Special Pathogens, and Isabel was a viral pathologist for Mexico's National Institute— back when she was known as Dr. Isabel Fuente Niebla. Circumstances—or astrological phenomena, according to her—constantly threw Stark and Isabel together, outbreak after outbreak; but he hadn't seen Isabel for over a year, not since the Imhotep Outbreak in Cairo. Quashing the smallpox epidemic had earned Isabel Khushub an impressive book deal in the virus's wake, and reading her book had made him feel close to her—though he was in Wisconsin and she, Punjab. But here she was, not the compassionate mind behind a well-written book, but Isabel herself, with all her glorious contradictions—her blown-glass elegance, filthy mouth, cutting mind, and maddening superstitions.

Isabel was speaking with one of the men in a Holy Renaissance suit. Stark strode toward her. "Dr. Khushub," he said loudly. "I finally read *The Mummy's Curse* last winter. We'll have to confer about your portrayal of me."

Isabel turned to face Stark. The bulky antiviral suit and aquarium helmet couldn't conceal the woman's polish. Briefly, she lifted her arms akimbo, as if to catch Stark, or embrace him, perhaps, then folded them across her chest again. She was looking at him, she recognized him, but Isabel's eyes guttered and went dead. "I thought I knew you well enough," she said, in an even voice, devoid of humor, "to paint an accurate picture, Dr. Stark."

The hell that supposed to mean? Stark thought, still smiling. Was this professional jealousy of some kind? Ridiculous. Bela's stellar expertise as a wetcoder put her in the same constellation as Joaquin. Stark ignored the comment and mugged, jutting out his chin, so that his two-day beard rubbed against his face shield. "Do I really have a lantern jaw?"

Isabel turned away as if he hadn't spoken and gestured to the stolid, cliff-faced man in the Holy Renaissance suit. "Do you know the Minister of Health, Dr. Xavier Sanjuan?"

Still puzzling over Isabel's coldness, Stark's mind collided against the phrase *Minister of Health Xavier Sanjuan.* "Excuse me?" He slowly turned to Sanjuan, eyes still on Isabel. "*Who* is this?" He finally looked at the fellow, who was a head taller than Stark. "Where is Diego?"

Sanjuan handed Stark a memboard, almost by way of greeting. Stark accepted it, and the man told him, "Dr. Alejandro accepted a promotion into President Orbegón's inner circle."

Stark felt like he was standing in a room whose doors and windows kept shifting position. First Isabel's prickliness, now this. He'd been spoiling for a knock-down-drag-out fight with Diego for the last two days, and having it snatched away made him angry. "A promotion?" He was about to inquire if that was wise, but figured Sanjuan wasn't the person to judge. "That's absolutely the most absurd thing I've ever heard."

Minister Sanjuan was an athletic man with a top-heavy build and a clipped, mechanical precision to his movements. He smiled confidently at Stark, clearly untroubled by the American's opinion. "I understand you had quite an adventure getting here."

"Cargo planes. Jailbreaks. Border crossings." Stark was speaking, but, really, he was worried about Diego. He slipped Sanjuan's memboard into the pouch at the small of his antiviral's suit back. "Very adventurous."

Minister Sanjuan gestured to the round man wearing the other red-and-black Racal suit, standing before the *aerobus.* Secular Mexico's eagle-and-snake crest was on his shoulder. "Dr. Stark, this is President Orbegón's Chief of Staff, *Jefe* Roberto Cazador. He's here to make certain that the Task Force transfers easily to your authority."

Stark nodded to Cazador, trying to hide his revulsion. If Americans like the puppet seller in Houston sometimes portrayed Orbegón as a clown, it was only to soothe their fears of Cazador. "*Jefe.*" Stark forced a grin. "My pleasure."

"Please. I'm Roberto," said Cazador, warmly clasping Stark's hand in both of his, a gesture that put Stark at ease against his will. "Welcome back to Mexico, Dr. Stark."

Though he had become something of a statesman in recent years, Chief of State Roberto Cazador had first built an international reputation as party assassin during Emil Orbegón's rise to power. Cazador's name was attached to the deaths of two thousand Purépecha nationalists in Chiapas, after they rallied to demand autonomy from Holy Renaissance Mexico. The man was a butcher. It was too easy to forget, so loose and comfortable was his manner.

Stark willed himself to look away from Cazador. La Alta's towers shot up from downtown Ascensión, he could see in the distance. "Things have changed since I was here last."

Cazador followed his gaze, and said, "Our shining city in the heavens. Eight million people, so close to God." He gave Stark a champion grin. "La Alta will be rather different from your grandfather's cooperative farm in Wisconsin, yes?"

Stark imagined he was supposed to feel threatened by Cazador's intimate knowledge of him. It worked. But it also served to rile Stark's patriotism. "Probably," said Stark in English. "Mexico ain't run democratically with an open membership and a guaranteed return of profits, right?"

Cazador shook his head pityingly. "An American romantic?" he replied in Spanish. "You cling to notions like votes and elections—as if those little levers were *ever* hooked up to anything."

Minister Sanjuan laughed on cue.

"We voted Land Reform in," Stark said, returning to Spanish.

"Thank you for that," *El Jefe* said. "You reformers chased your biggest corporations to Mexico—and your middle class, of course, followed the money to us."

Stark was about to say, *birds of a feather,* but he already regretted stepping into this lame tennis match. "According to my calculations," Stark said, "viruses aren't political. We're all in the same boat here, *Jefe.*"

Cazador and Sanjuan, in a tense pause, stared at Stark, their eyes pairs of headlights. "Well put. In any event, we're pleased that you arrived safely in *our* boat, Doctor," Cazador said, "and we appreciate the effort you made to get here. Did you place yourself amidst hooves?"

¿Métese entre las patas de los caballos? Stark puzzled over the translation. "Once more, please?"

Rosangelica broke off her conversation with Isabel with an abrupt turn of her body, and said to Stark, "The phrase means, were you in over your head? No, *Jefe,*" she said, nodding slightly to Cazador by way of a bow, "he was with me. It's an honor to finally meet you face-to-face." Her Mexican accent suddenly became so pronounced that Stark had to lean forward to catch every word.

"Likewise." Cazador's smile was so kind, so calm that Stark shuddered. "*Brava.* Your capacity for finding your way to the eye of a hurricane is shocking, Rosangelica."

Rosangelica said, "Perhaps I could have a word with you after the conference?"

Cazador's face registered apprehension, but his chuckle sounded like a bow bouncing across cello strings. "One might think you were making your way to the eye of *this* hurricane, too."

"No," said Rosangelica, "I'm here because I have volunteered to act as Dr. Stark's personal attaché, *Jefe.*"

A cagey choice of words. Rosangelica used the passive tense, as if to say that it was out of her hands. Chief of State Cazador, however, was the highest-ranking bureaucrat they'd yet encountered in Ascensión. *If Cazador didn't do it, then who OK'd her volunteering to be my attaché?* Stark wondered and by the frowning and flicking of his hazel eyes, *El Jefe* was wondering the same thing.

"Please, everyone, take a seat in the *aerobus,*" Minister Sanjuan interjected, indicating the vehicle's open door.

The *aerobus* was shaped like a giant ladybug, with a small cockpit for the driver and his armed guard and a large circular chamber behind. In this larger room, the floors were elevated and carpeted with rich brocade, and silver-tinted windows allowed a 360-degree view over the top of the forward cab. A single padded seat ran the circuit of the bus's wall and a circular table with imbedded screens and memboards was positioned in the center. Stark sat on the padded bench and scooted on his rump to make room for the other passengers.

Of the eight people waiting for him, Stark had met everyone except the driver, the guard, and one last fellow, who didn't have the self-important air of a medical doctor. The stranger appeared to be a Mayan Indian and walked just behind Cazador, making it difficult to tell if he was acting as bodyguard or simply another member of the Task Force currently taking orders from the Chief of State. This unnamed man was the last to enter the *aerobus,* and when all seven passengers were seated, Cazador told the driver to take them up.

CHAPTER

15

STARK HAD NEVER SEEN the spires of Ascensión before. By the strata of smog and smoke capping the mountain valley, the city's ion-scrubbers weren't working properly, but Stark could still see the seven gleaming, green spikes soaring above the pollution. The towers seemed too close together, rising from the floor of the Valley of Mexico like densely packed bristles and shooting two thousand meters into the sky. It was an illusion of distance, Stark knew. Each tower was at least a kilometer away from one of its mates. "Is La Alta's integrity still intact?" he asked.

"Still the safest place in Ascensión, yes," said Minister Sanjuan, waking the screen in front of him.

"And the *pilone* net?" Stark asked.

Rosangelica cut off the Mayan gentleman who was about to speak, saying, "Still inoperable."

There was much to discuss, but Stark was wondering when the transfer of power would occur. Experience told him to expect a careful bureaucratic speech about the limits of powers that were being granted to a visiting CDC epidemiologist. Despite the Holy Renaissance's infamy for pomp in war and crisis, Stark assumed the power transfer in this case would be done cleanly and secretly, so that the Task Force could get on with its mission. He kept quiet and felt the purr of the *aerobus* as it flew toward the sheaf of towers.

"Tell us your assessment of the situation so far," said Cazador, leaning toward Stark. "We expect that you've been monitoring our progress in transit, yes?"

The last thing he wanted was a medical consultation with politicians. "I'm still missing large pieces of the story, so an assessment would be hard right now, *Jefe*," said Stark. He turned to Isabel and Jarum Ahwaz. "Could one of you update me on Pathology? I'm confused by what I've read so far."

The two pathologists balked, each looking to Cazador, then waiting for the other to speak, until Jarum cleared his throat. "Please to go, Bela. My Spanish is poor."

Isabel gave Jarum a caustic glance. "*Pendejo* twit." She turned her face toward Stark and focused somewhere on the table before him. "It's—we're glad you're here, Henry David." She coughed and began again. "The epidemiological data that we need remains unorganized in any sort of database that we can use."

"I'll work on that," said Stark.

"However," continued Isabel, "the epidemiological team at the university cobbled together a decent if incomplete base of information for us, sourced from patients brought to the overflow hospitals."

"And what have you been able to determine?" asked Stark.

"According to the chicken reports, it originally took four days for the first dengue-5 patients to arrive at Zapata Hospital. But now," said Isabel, "we're not dealing with just two serotypes of the virus, dengue-5 and airborne dengue-6. Because dengue-5 has mutated into viable, subsequent generations, and because the new generations continue to emerge every ten to twelve hours, it's as if we're dealing with scores of dengue serotypes—any combination of which can create a dengue hemorrhagic syndrome—either airborne or non-airborne, and mutated from either dengue-5 *or* dengue-6. Big Bonebreaker can now kill in four hours instead of four days."

Stark nodded. He felt his hands growing slick inside their gloves. *We in trouble.* "How is Pathology discerning between the various generations? Or *are* you?"

Isabel's eyes met Stark's, as if in reluctant appreciation. There was something else in her gaze. Regret, perhaps, or apology. What was wrong with her? "Pathology always calls the newest generation—that is, the most recently discovered generation—Zed. Its parent's generation is Y, the one before that is X, and so on. As new generations are discovered, the Pathology database is automatically updated." Again her eyes flicked up to Stark's to make sure he was following her. "But my instinct tells me that the earliest generation of dengue-5, 'Generation One,' acted differently than the mutations we're seeing now. It's probably simpler, more like the natural dengue we know and love. Finding a sample of Generation One, or approximating it myself in a wetcode lab, may be our best shot at creating an effective nanophage. Because, right now, with multiple hot zones giving birth to multiple viral strains, all of which are breeding at different rates depending on where the virus finds agreeable hosts—" Isabel gestured as if releasing a dove from her hands. "We can never be one hundred percent certain which generation we are actually seeing at any given moment."

Jarum Ahwaz added in halting Spanish, "For example, this day, university reports that older generations—arrive—arrived—are arriving—*after* younger generations. That is how strange and without hope we are."

Stark picked up a memboard, tapped open a screen marked GENERA-TIONAL ANALYSIS and compared it to the information he'd read last night. The viruses were breeding too fast, faster than anything Stark had seen before. Ahwaz was right. Strange and without hope. "What do you recommend?"

"We're wetcoding a nanophage," Jarum said, "but it will hunt only for the most recent generations, beginning with Generation Zed. As newer generations discover—*are* discovered—new nanophages will have to be wetcoded."

Nanophages were Joaquin Delgado's greatest gift to public-health agents. Sprayed over hot zones with a swoop jet or a *barco,* released in water and food supplies, or injected into the population as part of a vaccination program, nanophages worked like an epidemic feeding on a specific virus. But they would be a stopgap measure with so many mutations to account for. Certainly, the terrorist counted on this.

Stark said, "Isabel, your work on wetcode for enhancing T cell antigen recognition. Update me."

"I was hoping it would help us here." She nodded. "But it's a failure. It turns the lymph system into jelly."

Stark wanted to console her, but he simply nodded in regret. "What happened?"

"We couldn't find a way to recode without killing the simulated human body," she said, dismissing what must have been years of work with a wave of a white-gloved hand. "A urinal bag of wasted fucking time."

Cazador rumbled in appreciative laughter, while Jarum Ahwaz pointedly turned his head away from Isabel in disgust. A Parisian-educated Palestinian of dignified lineage, Jarum rarely swore in his own language, let alone Spanish. Born in Mexico but living in Pakistan, Isabel, meanwhile, could draw from two cultures for her love of swearing. Stark smiled. *The Khushub and Ahwaz Comedy Show hittin the road again,* Stark thought.

Stark was girding his loins for the subject of Zapata Hospital's records, when the driver's voice buzzed from Cazador's suit. "We're passing over the hot zone, *Jefe.*"

"Please look, Dr. Stark." The Chief of State pointed and his voice was grim. "See what has happened to us."

Stark craned his neck to look out the *aerobus* windows, down into the grimy lattice of La Baja Ciudad. Beneath islands of smoke and smog, he could see neighborhoods stretching off to vanishing points in all directions—old Mexico City. He was surprised to find that, after civil uprising, street wars, and two viral outbreaks, he could still see the city as he knew it.

Stark turned back to the group and realized that all the Mexicans were staring at him. "I don't see the hot zone," he said.

"Take us down," Cazador said to the driver. "Show us Zapata Hospital."

The *aerobus* banked into a downtown descent lane, dropping through the thin layers of soot, down into the darkness between La Alta's magnificent spires and La Baja Ciudad's old Tower of the Americas, Pemex Building, and other modest skyscrapers that made the old skyline.

As soon as they dropped through Ascensión's veil of pollution and floated toward the *centro histórico,* Stark could see ground zero. It stretched some eight kilometers across in a wide arc of smoke-scorched, abandoned buildings, funeral pyres, and carcasses of torched vehicles, as if the viruses had been explosions of hellfire and sulfur. The *aerobus* passed over the *zócalo* and its bomb-blown banks, where the worst of the street clashes between *Los Hijos de Marcos* and Holy Renaissance troops had taken place. Corpse-removal teams nearly had the wide, paved plaza clean, but nothing could be done for the Austrian-style National Palace and its gray colonnade, or the cathedral with soot streaking across its standing walls and fallen façade. The Aztec pyramid, El Templo Mayor, reconstructed by the Museum

of Anthropology during Mexico's more secular days, sat alongside the National Palace. With a ring of plumed serpents at its summit like a pagan
crown, the pyramid surveyed the wreckage of the old Catholic church with
ironic majesty: El Templo Mayor was now the tallest structure on the
Square.

Floating over Avenida Venezuela, the *aerobus* took them toward Zapata
Hospital. The army and city militia had erected walls and hurricane fences
across every street in a twenty-block arc around the hospital. A hot zone
within the hot zone. The region within seemed a Dantean nightmare. Pro-
cessions of Mortuary teams filed below and some stopped to yell at the
aerobus.

They hovered over a little checkpoint clinic, placed inside a bank of hurricane fencing that ran around the eight-kilometer-wide hot zone. Stark
hadn't asked for a physical barrier around the hot zones, of course, and it
horrified him to think of the people trapped within. But the part of him that
had seen urban outbreaks before, that had kept death close as a companion,
looked down at those barbed-wire walls and admired the cruel, practical
mind that had ordered such a thing. "Whose idea was that? The fences, I
mean?"

The Chief of State stared back at him blankly but Sanjuan couldn't hide
his pride. He had given that order.

Well done, bastard.

The *aerobus* came about and sped toward Zapata, just a few blocks away.
An astonishing amount of debris ringed the ten-story building. Its long
bank of windows was shattered and the pieces lay like a green pebble beach
before the atrium.

"Why the street fighters—would to destroy the hospital?" asked Jarum.

Rosangelica gave a tart cluck of her tongue. *"Maricones estúpidos."*

With the same note of derision, Minister Sanjuan added, "Rioters
thought the Holy Renaissance created the virus and released it at Zapata."

Stark clamped his mouth over the question that popped to mind, but
then he thought he'd better ask it, after all. "Has it been proved that this outbreak *wasn't* a government operation?"

Sanjuan faced Stark, and his furious expression told Stark that this had
not been discussed, nor would it.

Cazador placed a hand on Sanjuan's huge shoulder and gave him a
friendly laugh. "Easy."

The *sabihonda*, however, wasn't on Cazador's leash. "In the middle of Mexico's greatest military action, you think," fumed Rosangelica, "a leader would release a bioweapon on his own people? Who sold you your degree, Estarque?"

Stark crossed his arms. "My doctorate? La Universidad de Oaxaca, actually."

He was rewarded with a smile from Isabel and a furtive wink from Jarum. Even the stony-faced, unnamed Mayan cracked a smile.

Cazador put his left hand flat on the table, right in front of Stark. "I assure you, Doctor, the Holy Renaissance did not create, store, or release these viruses."

But you still got Zapata records quarantined, thought Stark, looking at Roberto Cazador for a long, uncomfortable pause, wondering if this was the moment to confront him. *Why you do that?*

"Please," Cazador said to the driver, "take us farther down Avenida Venezuela. I want the Coordinator to see how *los bajadores* are dealing with this outbreak."

The *aerobus* floated down the street, toward a clinic in a crumbling blond-stone supermarket. It wasn't a Task Force perimeter operation. Indeed, there was no organization at all. It looked like a third-world infirmary from a CDC textbook, a twentieth-century Ebola hot zone dropped in the middle of a modern city. Bodies arrived in parades of litters. Through the plastic bags that encased them, Stark could see naked corpses with bloated abdomens and tin hearts pinned to their chests. Those carrying the dead ranged from *medicos* in gloves and useless surgical masks to family members who could not bring themselves to leave their loved ones—not even here, in hell. As he watched, Stark realized that no one was carrying newly infected patients into the supermarket clinic. In the street, a line of bonfires gassed the sky with oily smoke.

"Not much has gone right, but at least we've managed to impress on *los bajadores* that proper disposal is essential," Cazador said. "Maybe now that we have a beachhead with the perimeter clinics and dedicated outbreak hospitals, we can begin to help these field clinics."

"Maybe," Stark said. He gazed down into the bonfire before the supermarket/clinic. As fresh bodies in bags were placed on the hottest part of the fire, the plastic melted back to reveal arms and knees at tortured angles. "Take us down lower. I want to look inside that supermarket."

As the *aerobus* descended, the clinic workers nearest the fire looked up with hopeful eyes peering over bandana masks. Inside the dark market, light from holes in the ceiling angled down, and Stark could see that all the beds inside the clinic were empty.

Stark sat back in his seat, exhaling sharply. "I've seen enough," he said. "There's no need to show me the other clinics."

Rosangelica strained to see what Stark had seen in the market.

Minister Sanjuan pointed up the street. "But there are eight more clinics. They'll need to be incorporated into your plan eventually."

"This is lost ground," Stark said, shaking his head.

"Lost ground?" Sanjuan sneered. "You don't even know about the circuit doctors and other medical volunteers who're working the hot zones day and night."

Stark noted Cazador watching Sanjuan with furtive glances. *Maybe Sanjuan's performance ain't for me.* The Minister obviously had something to prove to Cazador, and Stark wondered what it was.

"Please, Doctor, be realistic," Stark said. "The only good thing about megaviruses is that they overeat their food supply, then die of starvation. That's what happened in that clinic," he said, pointing at the empty beds. "*That* is no longer a viable part of our response."

"But it's all *los destitutos* have, sir."

"Now, now let's keep our heads," said Rosangelica, trying to sound reasonable. "Stark, let's see what Sanjuan has to show us. It's the least we can do."

Stark would have to correct any presumptions the *sabihonda* had about becoming his medical assistant. "We are in the middle of a deadly emergency," said Stark, "but I still haven't heard about efforts to determine who patient zero was. That's my first order of business, not a tour through hopelessness."

"Dr. Stark," Cazador began, "this devastation requires that we sensitively—"

The *sabihonda* cut him off. She leaned forward and brought her elbows onto the table like a viper coiling into position. "Why are you taking this nihilistic attitude," said Rosangelica, "now that you're finally here? Why?"

"I am *not* being nihilistic. I'm being efficient," Stark assured her with a sideways glance at Cazador. Not wanting to get sucked into whatever political game was being played at this table, he said, "If you want to put on a dazzling medical performance for your people, don't worry, I'll give it to you, *Jefe*. But, please, follow my script and don't distract everyone with misguided sentiment for the dead."

In the quiet of the *aerobus*, six Racal-plus suits whirred and clicked like a watchmaker's studio.

Stark was surprised at his own callousness. He wanted to relieve the tension, explain his strong feelings about the horrendous task at hand, but the coldness he felt after looking at all the empty beds wouldn't crack. He opened his mouth to speak, but just then, Cazador called to the driver, "Up!"

And, like that, the seething pressure in the *aerobus* snapped.

Isabel edged herself up to the table, and Jarum leaned forward, gripping his left thumb in his right hand. His poker tell, Stark noted. He always held on to that thumb when he was bluffing with a crap hand. Meanwhile, the *Jefe* and Rosangelica both leaned back from the table, Cazador with a hand on his beer belly like a favored pet.

Sanjuan sighed, and said, "I think it's time you finally took a look at that memboard I gave you, Dr. Stark."

With the tension in the *aerobus* shifting, a new round in the mysterious game seemed under way, and Stark felt suddenly vulnerable. Sanjuan was testing him for some reason, so Stark looked down at the memboard and read. It was the same g-print that he had read on board the Dulce. He scanned the initial codons again.

> AGTTGTTAGT CTGTGTGGAC CGACAAGGAC
> AGTTCCAAAT CGGAAGCTTG CTTAACACAG . . . 60

"I read this on the flight into Ascensión," he said.

"And what do you think?" asked Sanjuan.

Stark put the report down and touched the memboard screen blank. "Well, I'm not a geneticist, but the tropism sequence is unusual, probably unnatural. This looks bad, but someone else will have to explain what it means."

Sanjuan's scowling gaze didn't waver and Cazador looked at Stark as if he knew to the penny how much money he had in his pocket.

"It looks bad, you say," said Sanjuan, his voice dry as gravel. "*Yo te conozco bacalao aunque vengas disfrazado.*"

Stark translated to himself: I know you, cod, though you come disguised.

He didn't wait for Rosangelica's explanation of the saying; it seemed plain enough. "If you have something to say, Minister, please be honest with me."

"Honest? *You* want *us* to be honest?" said Sanjuan.

"President Orbegón has taken a great political risk bringing you here," said Cazador. "We were hoping to get something more decisive from you than 'it looks bad.'"

"Not in this outbreak." Stark kept his eyes on Sanjuan as if the man might lunge at him. "These prints are state-of-the-art genetic snapshots but they're useless because they're genomes of mutated virus. Generation Zed, from what I can tell?" Stark dismissed the memboard with a flick of his hand. "If we were talking twelve hours into the outbreak, or if we had Zapata's records, we might have a prayer of analyzing this virus. Until we find the earliest, the first generation, fancy g-prints won't help us."

Isabel looked wounded, and Jarum's eyes bugged with anger and confusion. Stark assumed he had been too blunt, but did scientists of their caliber want handholding? The *aerobus* sailed out from beneath the shadow of a tower and the sun suddenly seemed hotter. Stark wondered what was happening at this table.

"I disagree with your assessment." Minister Sanjuan leaned forward and folded his hands on the table, the international gesture of a disenchanted bureaucrat. "Unlike you, Dr. Khushub here has discovered something quite decisive with the information at hand. Doctor?"

She may have dubbed him "the Patron Saint of Plagues" in her book, but Isabel was the real hero of the Cairo outbreak in Stark's opinion. Stark had spotted the common denominator in the first smallpox patients—all young boys hired to help in the robbery of a burial crypt where the virus was preserved in a mummified corpse. But Isabel wetcoded the nanophage that ended the outbreak in a matter of days. A good thing, too. Egypt had no smallpox vaccine stockpiled. "Let's hear it, Isabel."

Isabel's eyes flicked up and down from Sanjuan to the table before her, as if she were delivering a speech to the Minister, not conferring with Stark. "The tropism sequence is unnaturally brief, as you say, Dr. Stark," Isabel said. "Dengue-5 doesn't attack or breed the way it should. As a result, it has defied the typical approaches for determining pathology."

"But you were able to find alternate methods?" Stark asked, allowing hope to brighten in his voice.

"With help, yes," Isabel said. She lifted her hand to the unnamed Mayan-looking fellow who had been sitting through the meeting so far as a patient observer. "This is Ofelio Xultan," said Isabel. "He's the Chief Engineer of the *Pilone* Network."

Ofelio blinked a slow salutation at Stark, then placed his memboard in the conference table's dock and tapped the screen. Stark's memboard showed this:

```
AGTTGTTAGT CTGTGTGGAC CGACAAGGAC
AGTTCCAAAT CGGAAGCTTG CTTAACACAG
CTGTGTGGAC CGACAAGGAC AGTTCCAAAT
CTTAACACAG AGTTCCAAAT CGGAAGCTTG
CTGTGTGGAC CGACAAGGAC AGTTCCAAAT
```

"The virus's tropism sequence," said Stark.

Ofelio Xultan had such a sober, neutral delivery that Stark imagined the man could sound professional even if his clothes were on fire. "One might *assume* this is the tropism sequence," said Ofelio, but he shook his head. "This g-print isn't from either strain of dengue, however."

"Oh," said Stark, feeling stupid for speaking so quickly. He read the sequence again, more carefully this time. Like the stripped-down genome of dengue-5, this sequence had no extraneous DNA. "It's not natural, whatever virus this comes from."

Ofelio held Stark's gaze, but in his peripheral vision, Stark could see Isabel and Minister Sanjuan sharing a pointed look. Ofelio said, "Actually, this sequence was not taken from a virus at all."

The *aerobus* came about and circled a tower whose giant base was decorated with red and black Stations of the Cross, in plumed and boxy Aztec style.

"If you wanted to prove how little I know about wetcoding, you win." Stark wondered why he was receiving a viral pathology report from a computer scientist. "I can't tell what this sequence signifies."

"This sequence appears in only two places in nature: in a specific immune response unique to Native Mexicans, and in the protein sheath of dengue-4," Ofelio said. "With this snatch of code, the immune system can identify the dengue-4 virus and mount an attack on it."

A doctor wouldn't have put it that way but Stark understood. "So this is the code that native antibodies—probably immunoglobulin cell, IgG anti-dengue-4, perhaps?—use during specific antigen recognition?"

Isabel and Jarum Ahwaz nodded, solemn as hunted mice.

It didn't make sense. With tropism pared down like this, the response would be *too* specific, like radar that scanned only for missiles of a certain color. He frowned at his memboard for a moment, trying to discern what Ofelio was getting at. "Are you saying that the virus is tropic for Mexican Indians only?"

"Yes, but the range is not as limited as you might think," said Ofelio. "Unlike the United States, which ethnically cleansed its natives, the Spanish intermingled with the natives of Mexico. Thus, the word *'mestizo,'* which means mixed. Mexico is 71 percent mixed. Another 10 percent is Indian. That means that over 80 percent of Mexico could be susceptible to Big Bonebreaker."

Stark looked at Isabel. "That doesn't match up. Euros and Anglo-Americans contracted the disease, too."

Ofelio tensed. "The sequence you're looking at was taken from a cybernetically enhanced organ that underwent viral therapy."

Stark raised his hand to touch his brow, but the face shield was in his way, making it look like he was saluting Ofelio. "Ah." He sighed, as if this sequence of codons was a blade of light across his mind. "The *pilone*. This sequence is from the *pilone*?"

The *aerobus* stopped moving and hovered in place above the rain-forest preserve in Chapultepec Park.

"Yesterday, I ordered a three-pronged investigation of the *pilone* network's failure," said Ofelio. "The team working on the core couldn't give me anything. Nor could the bio-net team. But Dr. Girardo Castillo was the surgical pathologist whose team performed autopsies on seventeen victims of Big Bonebreaker. His findings were key. Here's the Castillo report." Ofelio tapped his screen, sending it to Stark's memboard. "To sum up, each victim's *pilone* wetware had dissolved into so much blood after contracting Big Bonebreaker."

Stark scanned the Castillo report. "The airborne virus was *designed* to attack the wetware—specifically."

"Actually, the immune system attacked the wetware," Isabel said. She shifted to English briefly for Stark's benefit. "The virus was designed to disable the wetware's 'self' status so that the immune system would identify the *pilone* as 'not self,' and expel it from the body."

Stark said to Isabel, "The terrorist was targeting the nationwide network. Is that what you think?"

"Exactly. *Mestizos* are not his aim," she said. "Foreigners without a shred of Native Mexican DNA in their bodies can still have the *pilone* surgery if they receive Delgado's viral therapy, as we saw from the North Carolina case. Indeed, viral therapy alters their histoimmunity, effectively 'indianizing' them, as Joaquin Delgado put it."

Isabel paused for a beat. She gave him a look that was imploring, almost lovingly poignant. It was so unexpected that Stark glanced away, then realized the group had fallen quiet and was glaring at him again. He looked back, and Isabel's loving expression had dissolved to something imploring and sad.

"He doesn't understand," Jarum said, straightening his suit, as if anxious to pull himself out of it. "He's innocent. For the love of God, someone just tell him and end this ridiculous game."

Rosangelica and Sanjuan hissed at Jarum to be silent.

Innocent? Stark watched Jarum's face for a clue. "Tell me what? What is this?"

"We pulled up Universidad Catolica in Monterrey archives," said Isabel. "This tropism code, down to the codon, was the very sequence that the young Joaquin Delgado used in his groundbreaking viral-therapy work that made the *pilone* possible."

Stark scoffed. "Joaquin?" He laughed. "Joaquin made the *pilone* possible?" He put his hands on the edge of the table, holding it as if for support. "Joaquin didn't go to school in Monterrey. He matriculated in Barcelona."

Stark looked at the faces of the others at the table. They were all scowling at him—even Isabel, now—as if he were an imbecile.

"No. That's a lie he told the world. Delgado was born and raised in Monterrey," Rosangelica said. "He got his degree just before the Holy Renaissance came to power and was an outspoken critic of Orbegón while he was mayor of Monterrey."

Stark's mouth opened into a square of astonishment. He squinted at

Rosangelica, unable to make sense of what she was saying. "Dr. Delgado is from Spain. Born and bred."

"His parents, perhaps. But Delgado is a Mexican by birth," Rosangelica said, grinning, enjoying Stark's shock.

Joaquin wasn't Mexican. He prided himself on his Spanish heritage. This could not be. It was absurd. He always bragged to Stark that he could trace his family back to a medieval lord in the Estremadura of Spain, that he adored his parents' Barcelona home and would never sell it, that the Spanish culture was so much older and nobler than Mexico with its horrid treatment of Indians and its brutish bent toward fascists like the Holy Renaissance, which he despised, and how they had stolen work of his when he—

Stark's mind walled off the thought. No. It simply could not be. No, no. "This is not what Joaquin would do. This is not how he would handle—"

"Listen to me, Henry David," Isabel said. She was reciting a prepared speech, he could tell. "Last night, three *sabihondas* in Dr. Xultan's service hacked into Joaquin Delgado's home drive. The evidence they gathered is damning. Delgado purchased dengue-4 cells and cloned them one year ago. The drive had built-in defenses that could not be overridden, but they learned that much and have the records of that purchase. Here's the report. The receipts. Testimony from the Sri Lankan dealers who sold him the cells. We both know, you and I, that Joaquin has a history of hatred for the Holy Renaissance—"

"So do you, Bela," Stark blurted, ignoring the report on his memboard.

"—a motive, and, most importantly, the unique skill and knowledge to make this disaster happen." Her face was an impassive oval behind her helmet's clear plastic shield. Finally, she cleared her throat. "And if Joaquin is a suspect, then you're automatically a suspect, too, Henry David."

He opened his mouth to retort, but outrage and betrayal had stopped the thought flow in his brain. Isabel might as well have stabbed him. In the past, colleagues might have questioned his statistics or his lab work, but never his honesty. It tormented him that the accusation should come from Isabel, the woman for whom he'd once considered leaving the United States. This accusation could only have been more devastating coming from his own grandfather.

Sparks seemed to spray before his eyes, as he managed to say, "Bela—that's—no."

Sanjuan said, "Dr. Stark, do you understand what Dr. Khushub just said? You appear to be collaborating with Joaquin Delgado. You appear to be a bioterrorist."

Out of instinct, Stark increased the flow of oxygen in his suit to keep from blacking out. The flush of cool air refreshed and cleared his mind and, immediately, he thought of Earl, the intern he'd discovered in his room two days ago. Grandfather was right. The Holy Renaissance had been checking him out in advance of inviting him. If that was true, then they had to suspect he was innocent, too, since there was no evidence for Earl to gather. "I assure you," Stark said, grasping on to that thought, his voice croaking, "I had nothing to do with this. The first I heard about it—"

"Joaquin Delgado told you to study in Oaxaca, so you went to Oaxaca," Cazador said. "He recommended you for the Centers for Disease Control, so you joined their Special Pathogens Branch. Joaquin helped create the CDC's Central Command, and you became its coordinator. Joaquin Delgado all but built you in his laboratory, Dr. Stark." El Jefe's tone was reasonable, though a strain in his voice betrayed his anger. "And the morning of the outbreak in Zapata, you spoke to Dr. Delgado by sat phone. We have a record of it."

"Yes, that's true and I—"

Cazador interrupted in a cutting bark. "Explain! Why were you talking to the terrorist the morning our people began dying like vermin!"

Stark flinched. "I always—Joaquin was telling me—" He couldn't say the words. He couldn't admit it. Couldn't speak. The Ghana outbreak was a lame stab in the dark, and Stark knew it, deep down, but he hadn't been able to conjure the doubt in Joaquin. There had been just enough of a thread to make the Ghana connection seem plausible, but now that theory, that hope, collapsed like a scaffold of support inside Stark.

While he searched for his voice, Stark glanced down at the report that Isabel had sent him, showing what the sabihondas had found. She was right. It was all there, including slides of cloned dengue-4 cells time-stamped with Joaquin's registry.

Cloning. The first step in wetcoding the virus. Joaquin's private business was to consult with hospitals. It was a desk job, no, a job that was conducted over steak dinners and rioja. Joaquin had no professional reason to buy and clone viruses.

Let alone that virus.

He planned it. The bastard. Jesus, he planned it for years. Joaquin knew I'd call, what I'd ask, how to spin me.

"Joaquin Delgado told you what?" Ofelio said, leaning forward, intrigued by Stark's lengthy silence. "Finish your thought, Dr. Stark."

Stark shook his head. His blind spot—his love for Joaquin—was humiliating in its grandeur and folly, and he loathed that it was on display for beloved colleagues and strangers alike. He still couldn't admit it. Joaquin had played on his blindness as coolly as if Stark were a stranger, an enemy. As if their friendship were nothing.

"Tell us, Henry David," Isabel said.

The kindness in her voice unlocked the words and Stark said, "He told me about an outbreak in Ghana and I took the bait." Stark clutched the seat. "He sucker punched me. It was a terrible mistake."

"Oh, it appears to be more than a mistake," Sanjuan said. "It appears to us that you deliberately misled—"

"Stop," Stark said.

"—your own investigation. Can you prove—?"

"I said *stop*. Stop right there," Stark said, mustering his nerve. "You proved Joaquin's involvement to me. Now you must prove mine. Wait, Minister, listen to me," Stark said, shouting over Sanjuan until the man fell quiet with Cazador's hand on his arm. Stark was falling back on the anger he'd felt for the past forty-eight hours, remembering it and letting it guide his words, though he was still hot and breathless with confusion. "Because *you* seem to be the ones obstructing this effort. You ignored Pedro Muñoz. And I think you knew there was a chance that he was right about this virus. You suspected from the beginning that mosquitoes didn't spread Big Bonebreaker. You had to, because your team was headed by Miguel Cristóbal, who's incapable of the incompetence required to misdiagnose a simple vector."

Rosangelica's empty metallic eyes had their typical, sedate gleam, but Stark was beginning to understand her strange expressions better. Rosangelica seemed torn between two visions of Stark, one as savior and the other as demon.

"I say you played on our confusion to further the goals of your old teacher," Sanjuan said. "A nanophage for typical dengue, when you knew it was atypical? I don't think *you're* capable of that incompetence."

"Yes, I was grasping. I admit it," Stark said. His cut lip ached from all the talking. "But you"—he stabbed his finger in the air at Sanjuan—"*you* bet your people's lives and lost thousands. You owe Mexico an explanation of what you're hiding about the outbreak."

"We aren't hiding anything," Minister Sanjuan said as if Stark were swinging wildly at him.

"Then put Zapata's records on our memboards. Now."

Silence.

Sanjuan and Rosangelica leaned forward, seemingly ready to leap upon Stark, and Cazador was about to defuse the tension once more, an affable smile seeping across his face yet again, when Stark interrupted them all.

"I killed a man in order to get here in time to help you," Stark shouted. He kept his gaze on Sanjuan. His throat clamped shut, and his cheeks burned red behind his blond beard.

Cazador spit, "What bluster."

Sanjuan narrowed his eyes and his nostrils flared in an expression that Stark read as either distaste or shock—or both. "Please, Dr. Stark. No histrionics."

Rosangelica unclenched her fist and laid her hands flat on the table. "No." The animalistic coil in her muscles unwound. "It's true. I saw him do it."

Cazador and Sanjuan stared at Rosangelica, then shifted their gazes to Stark.

Isabel whispered, "How? What happened?"

Rosangelica spoke with ease in her low, throaty voice. "He shot a man who meant to keep him from reaching San Antonio," she said. "Then he released me from jail."

Cazador looked as if the American had just removed a mask, revealing himself to be someone utterly different than the *Jefe* had expected. "Why then did you say in your report that *you* saved Dr. Stark from jail?" asked Cazador. "Why didn't you mention a killing?"

"Porque la carne de burro no es transparente," Rosangelica said.

A mule's hide isn't transparent. After puzzling over that one, Stark decided, *She didn't trust me either—till just now.*

"I didn't want to make a hero of him before determining his association with Delgado," said Rosangelica. "I wanted to see if he would tilt his hand. But it's clear to me that he is truly destroyed by all this." She glanced sidelong at Isabel, and said, "Dr. Khushub's accusation has wrecked him, I'm relieved to see."

"Maybe Stark killed simply in order to infiltrate us," Sanjuan said, unable to see Stark as anything but a terrorist, "to continue a campaign of subterfuge."

"No, believe me," Rosangelica said, "he's not a cool killer. And when it matters most, when he's under duress like this, Stark can't lie. No, the farm boy is just a farm boy, exactly as he seems to be."

Watching Cazador digest that last piece of information, Stark realized he suddenly had a very expensive feather in his cap with *El Jefe*. Rosangelica's word. Stark turned up the volume on his speaker since he didn't have much breath for speaking. "I have a plan for ending this epidemic. A sketchy and optimistic plan, but I have one." Stark let that sink in, watching Cazador lean his bulk back toward the table. "But you have to trust me. So. For the record," said Stark, taking a deep breath and letting his voice wheeze into the room. "I haven't seen Joaquin for two years and the first I heard about this outbreak was two days ago. If you don't trust me, I'll find my own way back to the US."

Sanjuan and Cazador were still chewing on Stark's admission of murder and only seemed to half hear his declaration of innocence. Ofelio Xultan looked satisfied and Isabel now seemed disgusted by herself, this meeting, and the people in it. She stared at the middle of the table, then looked at Sanjuan, giving him a short nod. "For the record, the Minister asked me to observe your response to this accusation. I feel like a bloody, fucking Judas dragging you through this, but Minister Sanjuan wanted to be sure of your integrity before proceeding."

Cazador turned to Sanjuan, and said, "Are you satisfied?"

At that moment, the *aerobus* driver drafted an empty ascent lane for the Majority Cloister's dock a half kilometer up.

"No, I don't trust him," Sanjuan said, "but I trust Rosangelica. So I'll take the *sabihonda*'s voucher."

Out of the corner of his eye, Stark saw Rosangelica sag back in her seat, sated.

Pulses of traffic sent streams of glittering swoop jets and *barcos* into the docking bays of the high towers. The *aerobus* sailed up the shimmering silver-green cliff face of Torre Cuauhtémoc, and a shock of sun electrified a bank of gilded balconies. Then, plunged into shadow, Stark found himself in a La Alta docking chamber with wooden barrel-vaulted ceilings overhead like a medieval church. No more political games of intrigue. No more guessing if he would be accepted. Henry David Stark was finally in.

CHAPTER

16

ATOP THE FIFTEEN-FOOT-HIGH wall that enclosed the little courtyard, a watchman wrapped his trench coat's skirts around his cold legs, while behind him the Gaijin Butoh Troupe prepared in the chapel for Epidemic Theater.

Through the branches of an arching oak, a cloud-board could be seen in the dusk, floating against the side of a skyscraper overhead, eclipsing its minaret crown. The cloud bulged around the tower like an amoeba and re-formed on the other side, reigniting its eerie, orange light.

YOU ARE IN A QUARANTINED NEIGHBORHOOD, read the cloud. PLEASE REPORT TO THE NEAREST PERIMETER CLINIC AT ONCE.

Every evening, the watchman sat on this wall in the shade of the oak, nearly invisible, watching the day's last march of the dead pass Sor Juana's chapel. Stretchers, wheelchairs, biers of old loading pallets, and upon them, the dead and dying, with loved ones carting them off the street before sun-fall. In the hot zone, no one was safe on the streets at night, when looters made their rounds and rape gangs emerged to test their immunity. Worse were the government's *ejércitos de la luna,* moon troops, who came out at night to shoot the infected. Last night, from this very wall, the watchman saw seven soldiers wearing black Racal-plus antiviral suits, carrying heavy *Sangre de Cristo* class rifles. They stalked across Isabela la Catolica Avenue, emerging from one shadow, then vanishing into another, ghosts hunting down the hot zone's last bit of life.

Witnessing the day's last march from this wall was the watchman's way of allowing himself to leave it, after fourteen or fifteen hours of hauling bodies.

From where he sat, the watchman could also see the stage through the nineteenth-century chapel's bombed-out wall. A spotlight cut a bright circle on the black floorboards, and he could hear dancers shuffling and talking in the dark. Seconds later, a naked female figure stepped into the spotlight, plaster white makeup covering her from shaved head to bare feet. She stood with her chin resting on her chest.

Epidemic Theater would begin when she was in her skin.

"Your dance is everything now," Hiro, the troupe's leader, said from the shadows, and his Japanese accent added to the watchman's sensation that he was no longer in Mexico. A second later, Hiro appeared near the spotlight, his red-shirted torso floating legless along the stage. "So dance," Hiro said to Yvonne, "your body remembering."

The skin of Yvonne's freshly shaven head gleamed in the spotlight, as her shoulders hunched forward like a feeble old woman's. Her left arm began trembling as if a current rattled through it.

Even though he hadn't been a lover of theater in his previous life, before it erased itself and began again in chaos, the watchman found this strange dance form hypnotic. Back then, before Ascensión fell, his tastes ran more toward soccer and historical novels, not obscure, Japanese theater. He liked to tell his coworkers that they never had to worry about his filing red sheets on them—he didn't like trouble, dissonance. But there was something about *butoh*—something profoundly troubling and dissonant—that he found comforting now.

Walking just outside Yvonne's harsh spotlight, Hiro's feet waded in darkness. "The body's sole ambition is to claim you for its own," he told her, watching Yvonne's arm, which continued to shake as if with seizure.

No matter how he tried, the watchman couldn't count how many nights he'd been here, in the hot zone. It was at least three, but less than twenty. Astonishing how, after Zapata Hospital was compromised, civilization collapsed so thoroughly that even the walls between day and night had eroded. Now he dwelt in a half-lit unlife of hauling dead bodies, igniting bonfires, tending to the infected, then returning here, to "the cell of sanity," as Hiro called it.

Trying to count the days back, he started with Saturday evening, when everything changed. The night that patients started appearing at Zapata, while searching for the lost notes he'd taken on the effect of this retrovirus upon the first patient's histocompatability, he had chanced across a curious report in a dead doc folder.

Reality started crumbling in that dead doc file.

The report was written by a *sagrado servicio* officer named Xavier Sanjuan, composed on-site at Zapata and sealed with his Epidemic Intelligence Services code. Unfortunately for Sanjuan, he didn't realize documents written on the hospital system were automatically triplicated.

Our initial tests prove that we have a crucial opportunity here, not a crisis, Sanjuan had written. *My people believe the virus targets an immune response in Native Mexicans. It occurs to me that this condition, if allowed to propagate, may alleviate long-standing economic concerns in the lower city of Ascensión, and in Mexico.*

It felt a great act of cowardice, copying that document in his personal files, disguising the title. He should have sent it to the media. He should have sent it to, well, *someone.* In the hours that followed, the watchman felt craven and small, hinting about the atrocity like a sniveling gossip to his colleagues. But he couldn't just say what he knew. Couldn't blurt it out in the press conference as every instinct in his body told him to do. If he did that, he knew the consequences would be swift and total. If he was lucky, the Holy Renaissance would disappear him, rearrange his brain, and drop him in the Peruvian province, where he'd wake up as a church gardener or a mad street-corner evangelist. After filing a dissenting report to the Ministry of Health's assessment of Big Bonebreaker's vector, he felt lucky that he got away with a mere demotion.

And besides, it was simply too horrible to contemplate, that these words should be typed and sent from a hospital while human beings were bleeding and shaking like that.

All his coy hinting and surreptitiousness had amounted to nothing. The night that the airborne virus compromised Zapata's integrity as a hospital, he was assessing a new round of patients. These people, oddly, did not have mouth pustules, a notable change in symptoms that he'd wanted to tell Dr. Stark about. Alejandro's pathetic dengue conference was nothing but political grandstanding and he was blackballed anyway, so he had slipped away to confer with the dengue ward's attending physician. When the Code

Blue Klaxon sounded and the hospital's rarely used loudspeaker announced that people were rapidly dying of massive bleeding, he knew that his own prophecy of a coming dengue hemorrhagic fever outbreak had come true.

He only stayed in the hospital long enough to receive bloodwork affirming that he was clean, all the while wondering if this could have been prevented had he spoken up like a man. But after he was deemed clean, he fled the hospital with scores of others—*medicos* and patients alike—pressing through the military cordon outside and into the mass panic that clogged the streets beyond. Weapons fire lit the underbellies of faltering cloudboards, and a blaze or a war was raging in the National Square.

Running by the corner of Isabela La Catolica and Izazago Avenues, he'd seen a group of hipsters dragging trunks and backpacks toward a bombed-out chapel on that intersection. Without thinking, he ran with them. A Japanese man in dreadlocks and muscle shirt slammed the gate shut behind him, clapping him on the shoulder as they ran to the cloister together.

That night, as attack boats screamed over the nearby National Square, Gaijin Butoh Troupe's leader, Hiro, inaugurated the first performance of Epidemic Theater.

It was the first time the watchman had ever seen *butoh*. The gestures and movements of the dance seemed bizarre, like the delirium tremens of a drunkard. Later Hiro explained that it had originated in post–World War II Japan, in a society nearly as rigid as the Holy Renaissance's. During Hiro's first performance, an attack *barco* had roared low over the Sor Juana chapel. His dreadlocks shook, and his mouth tightened into a purse of bitterness. His eyes scanned the ceiling in absolute terror. The *barco* passed. Still, Hiro had stared at the ceiling, like a child unable to forget the nightmare, and that fear transformed into a hunching, quivering dance, a palsy of subtle gestures. Hiro was a specter signaling across the void between worlds. Arms clutched close to his stomach, face twisting into expressions of agony, then mad delight, Hiro seemed both disciplined and yet totally out of control, his body a fantastic, nonsensical thing. It hypnotized the watchman, a man who knew too well the limits of the human body. He had decided then, watching Hiro dance, that he would stay with the Gaijin Butoh Troupe until the quarantine was lifted.

Yvonne's left arm trembled until it seemed to rise on its own accord, parallel with her shoulder.

"Your body is giving you this moment," Hiro said, coaching Yvonne.

She let her arm twitch, elbow cranked at an unnatural angle, then she wiggled her fingers.

Hiro winced. "Freeze."

Yvonne stood with her left arm in the air, as though embracing an invisible partner around the shoulders.

"You aren't here," Hiro said. "You just left."

"I know."

"You are intending."

She nodded.

"What were you intending?"

Yvonne answered quickly, as if she had been expecting this. "I'm just too aware of—" She looked through the ruined wall to the cloud-board with its quarantine warning floating above the chapel. "I wanted to do something beautiful."

"*Butoh* doesn't 'do' anything," said Hiro. "Besides, you are already beautiful." Hiro stepped into the glare and rubbed her bald scalp playfully. "And very ugly." The watchman imagined the sound of her stubble scraping under Hiro's callused hands. "Your immune system suffers Big Bonebreaker into itself every day," said Hiro, "and every day your body dances by killing that virus. Dance the dead plague. Your immune body remembers it. Forever. You just let it remember, remember, remember."

An interesting strategy. The watchman's was the opposite: forgetful oblivion. He couldn't even count the days, his strategy was so effective. Last night, he and Hiro were sitting together on the chapel's stage, drinking shot glasses of *pulque,* looted from a bodega.

"Are we immune?" Hiro had asked him.

The watchman didn't know why he, Hiro, and the other dancers had survived viruses with an 80 percent mortality rate. But, in an attempt to answer his new friend, the watchman described how the body identifies a virus, then rallies a response to kill it. He described how that virus is then entered into the immune system's memory, so that the body would have a better chance of spotting and killing that same virus in the future.

"My body is killing this virus?" said Hiro. "It will remember how to kill it in the future?"

"That's right. At least, I think so. With these viruses—"

Hiro shushed him loudly and lunged for his notebook. The watchman looked over Hiro's shoulder as he drunkenly scrawled:

"Our immune bodies will dance the plague forever.
"Our bodies will always remember."

The watchman didn't want to remember. He didn't want to think about mouth pustules, tetravalent vaccine, or Sanjuan's *crucial opportunity* and his own pitiful response to it. He didn't want to remember anything except *butoh*. But, like most Mexicans, he *was* Catholic, so beneath his forgetfulness, he trusted that there was a working system in the cosmos. In Mexico's case, he had faith that there was a massive, cultural response under way against the virus. Maybe it was nothing more than bodies surviving and working hard to help other bodies, but he decided that if he was immune, for whatever reason, it was his mission to haul corpses from houses to street corners, to comfort the infected with their swollen lymphs, which clustered in the armpits like nests of toads. He would say prayers with the dying, hold their hands when the seizures came. And he'd build funeral pyres from the wood of abandoned tenement shacks. He'd go as far as the Plaza de Toros, the bull rings, in search of healthy people, and he'd watch in horror as the bulls, monsters of the Xajay bloodline, fought in the streets, goring and then eating one another. He would even burn the body of a fellow field-clinic worker whose symptoms first flared as they washed sheets together. Day after day and on into the many nights, until exhaustion made a blurry smear of his mind, then he would return to Sor Juana's chapel for stolen *pulque, butoh,* and sleep.

But the oily-sweet smell of those horrifying bonfires clung to his sinuses, and he couldn't misplace himself so easily. The bodies followed him back to the chapel-turned-theater and merged with the bodies of the dancers, so that the diseased corpses became the muscular arms and bulging calves that turned and flexed on the spotlit stage. The wiry beards and delicate clavicles. Creased brows smooth at last. Skinny froglike legs. Jiggling bellies. Hairy hands. After Epidemic Theater finished for the night, the relentless dead followed him to his bed of wool blankets, and he slept, dreaming of loose change scattered from upended pockets. Moles on anklebones. Blue, parted lips. Fingers fattening around wedding bands. Caesarian section scars. Tattoos. Watches keeping time on still wrists.

Sitting on the wall, the watchman could hear people on the avenue dragging something. Emerging in a pool of moonlight, two women in old-fashioned surgical masks were hauling a litter up the sidewalk toward him.

From his quiet perch he could see both the litter-bearers struggling and Yvonne, alone now, a steady white flame burning in the dark.

The person borne by the litter bearers was in late-stage onset symptoms; the watchman could tell by the uneasy thrashing and twisting of limbs. Though he might have leapt down to help them, he decided to stay on the wall, in the shadow of the arching oak. Once the seizures started, there wasn't much time left, so he held his breath as the dying person passed beneath him.

Onstage, Yvonne, painted white, looked new and pure, her slim back and teacup breasts turning in the spotlight. He watched as she shivered and pivoted to look over her shoulder with an expression of pained surprise.

The dying person below caught his eye. A teenage girl with dark liquid dripping from her nose—blood rendered black in the color-sapping moon— and around her mouth a crescent of pustules.

The watchman stood, hand on the heavy limb of the oak, bewildered.

Mouth pustules?

In his endless days of hauling bodies, he hadn't seen a single chapped lip, canker sore, or mouth pustule. Not since the day he fled Zapata.

"Stop, please," he shouted.

The two litter-bearers spun in fright, almost dropping the sick girl, trying to pinpoint the direction of the man's voice. "Who is it? Who's there?"

"I'm a doctor," he said. "I won't hurt you. I just want to know how that person caught Big Bonebreaker."

"Are you joking?" one woman said. "Come on, let's hurry and get her home."

"Please," he said, "she's obviously been in the hot zone for days. How did she finally get it?"

"She caught it from a group of flagellants who came to her house begging for help," the woman shouted back. "They broke in and infected her. Now come down and help us or leave us alone."

"Better hurry, then. It's getting dark." The watchman sat down again, letting the oak's shadow swallow him up.

Looking back at the dancer, he wondered if he had the nerve to present his credentials at a perimeter clinic and tell them what he'd just found.

Somehow, the virus is still being spread from a primary source.

Yvonne was at last dancing *butoh,* the watchman could see. Ash white makeup, shaved head, Hiro, this insane cell of sanity, the dead's march, and her own remembering body all had conspired to erase the person named Yvonne. With tottering steps and uncontrolled tremors in her plaster white hands, she was a leap beyond human now—a phantom, an angel, or some very other thing. As the watchman slipped down the wall and away into the dark, her body claimed her, and she intended nothing, nothing but the whim of her alabaster form.

CHAPTER

17

DR. JOAQUIN DELGADO had stood at the podium, resting his long hands there without looking up at the audience. He introduced himself quietly into the microphone, said he was from the CDC, then fell quiet.

He was quite tall, young HD noticed, and his slightly stooped posture made him look like a man with tiring pride, a brilliance burdened with a thousand enemies and a man who believed himself worthy of the enmity. A modest farm kid, HD couldn't decide if he admired this about the guy or not.

Osterholm Hall in the University of Wells-Fargo seated three hundred, but only half of it was filled. Local doctors and college administrators filled the front three rows, and graduate students made up the rest. Most presumed that Delgado's revolutionary advances in virology would direct their own work: employing viral therapy to repair the damage of heart disease, drug and alcohol abuse, postsurgical trauma. Muscle tone enhancement without exercise. Total memory restoration. The possibilities of harnessing the virus seemed endless. HD, considering grad school, was enticed by virologists who were creating urban immune complexes. These city-sized laboratories, located in the viral hotbed of southern China, would monitor the seasonal diaspora of influenza and create nanophages, Delgado's breakthrough contribution to modern medicine, for each new mutation of flu as it appeared, killing it before it could emigrate.

Joaquin Delgado turned to the blackboard behind him and picked up a blue piece of chalk. He drew a big circle and slashed a vertical line through it. In the left hemisphere, he wrote THEM in square capitals, and in the right, US. Then he turned back to the audience. "Who is 'us'?"

Looking at that diagram, HD found himself groping toward a life-changing thought.

Later, Joaquin would say that the young man looked as if he were crawling out of his skin to be recognized. Delgado nodded. "Who is 'us'? You, with the crew cut."

HD started to speak, but his voice cracked. He made a vague, inclusive gesture that could mean everyone in the room or everyone in the world. Then he cleared his throat, and said, "The immune system."

The professors in the first three rows turned to look at HD, whose grades were barely average and who rarely spoke in class.

"Thank you. Yes. We are the immune system"—he made the same vague gesture that Stark had made, drawing a laugh from the audience—"we men and women in this room. The health organizations around the world. Immunologists and epidemiologists. We fight for both the survival of individual bodies and the body of the species. This struggle," he said, with a slight nod to the chalk diagram, "is in the body, eternally, waging itself, even in this very room."

Delgado leaned on the podium and looked up under heavy lids. "Most of you, students and doctors alike, came to hear me speak because you are fascinated with"— Joaquin turned and touched the chalk word THEM— "viruses. You will probably devote your life to virology because you Americans are rugged individualists, undaunted by spending long hours alone in laboratories over freezes of replicating viruses. *Bueno*. Even Milton found Satan more fascinating than God."

Delgado paused as if expecting a laugh. When none came, HD thought he saw the man wince, perhaps at his own clumsiness.

"This is the greater work. Public health," he said, pointing to the word US. "Defending and maintaining the greatest good for the greatest number." He straightened, but even with his head held high, he looked like a man whose pride exhausted him. "Epidemiology is a medium in decline, falling away as new technologies emerge. Analyzing statistical data, calculating a chicken report by hand, organizing immunization programs. These are not breakthrough tasks, are they? Nor is entering a hot zone to clean human filth, but it is the noblest work."

Sitting in that plastic seat in the lecture hall, HD felt a charge of energy rattling in his hands, as if his body were actually shaking something off.

HD had grown up with a deep allegiance to his grandfather's cooperative farm and the people there. It had created a hyperawareness in him, surrounded as he was by the strange array of people who were perpetually drawn to Nissevalle Farm. With US agriculture slowly starving for lack of oil even before gold mold destroyed it, many Midwestern cities had drained into rural communities in search of food and jobs during HD's childhood. Nissevalle became a beacon not only for farmers who wanted to farm, but spoiled old-timers accustomed to a steady supply of food, avant-garde artists turned rural hayseeds, neo-Jeffersonians, intellectuals fleeing the sinking isle of America's collegiate class, urban Land Reformers, Australian war refugees who'd fled one frying pan only to land in another, disabled people whose government aid had evaporated, misfits, orphans, former dot-commies, and the unemployed mass that had been marching into the countryside for years. As a kid in this environment, HD had grown into a role that the *quop* desperately needed, the one member who could look into all the different lives of people in his *quop* without judging. The Wisconsin Rosetta Stone Grandfather called him.

But watching Delgado deliver his lecture, the child's awareness expanded outward from the circle of his childhood—from farm to globe, and the selfishness of a career in virology to the selflessness of epidemiology. From person to species:

Us.

Isabel Khushub cleared her throat noisily, and said, "¡*Caray!* Don't make me repeat myself, Henry David."

Stark looked at her reflection in the elevator door before them—her biohazard suit a warble of white in the glass—and smiled thinly. She looked older than thirty-eight right now, older than she had in Cairo a year ago.

So did he, Stark noticed. Not just tired. Old.

She said, "You're thinking about him again."

"Bela, stop it. I'm not."

Screaming swoops and parachuting penny-drops fell past their boost and down through the vast, central shaft of the tower. Isabel, Rosangelica, and Stark were being lifted through the Federal Cloister of Torre Cuauhté-moc.

"Rosangelica is right about you," Isabel said.

The *sabihonda* stopped eating and looked at Isabel, tamale poised before her chin. "What am I right about?"

"What is she right about?" Stark asked, annoyed.

Isabel slipped her memboard into the pocket at the small of her back and pressed the heels of her hands into her eyes. "You're a shitty liar."

Standing next to her in the boost, Stark could feel the humming jolt of Isabel, wound tight as she was on coffee, adrenaline, megadoses of vitamin C, huge volumes of pathology data, fear, and guilt. She'd apologized to him repeatedly over the last three days, but it did little to soothe her—or him. Probably because Stark was still trapped in an echo chamber of his own regret and guilt. "Sorry, Bela. Tell me what you just said."

"The viruses are mutating too fast for us to respond with effective nanophages." She propped her reading glasses on the tip of her nose and slipped her memboard back in hand. "I'd say our 'phages are seventy to eighty percent effective, which is a pile of laughable shit."

"Fantastic."

"Even if we had ninety-nine percent effective 'phages,' that one percent would allow the viruses to break free," Isabel said. "I'm beginning to think that 'phages' are the wrong approach."

Stark was about to ask why Isabel hadn't said this in the meeting they'd just attended, the Ministry of Emergency Management, but he knew why. Ministerials weren't the place for communicating bad news backed by hard evidence. Such meetings were cheerleading sessions, where politicians kidded themselves that the outbreak was being tamped down, and too much time was devoted to bishops blessing the proceedings. The truth emerged in transit from one meeting to another, or, like this, at the wrung-out end of another bitter day of bad news. "What's your assessment of Vaccination? Are they helping?"

All three of them snatched at handrails in the boost, as the elevator slowed for horizontal traffic. An enormous statue the color of polished lead dominated the hollow space in this section of Torre Cuauhtémoc, its blank eyes gazing down watchfully over the villas, terraces, and balconies of La Alta. Outside their boost, Stark could see a saber hilt the size of a barn.

"No. To put it bluntly, it's not. We're fucked," Isabel said.

Rosangelica held the tamale away from her body as the boost shot upward again. "But daily mortality has dropped. *Something* must be working."

Isabel's sneer was queenly. "Fifty-eight hundred dead in Ascensión alone. You call that *foquin* 'working'? I call that horse shit raining from heaven."

Rosangelica opened her mouth as if to retort, then bit the tamale instead.

The only thing that lifted Stark's spirits these days was watching people get rocked on their heels by Isabel's prosaic cursing. "Omnivalent vaccine is finally hitting the perimeter clinics," he said. "I have two hundred thousand doses of tetravalents coming in this evening from Bombay. Vaccination teams are ready to take those doses into the street tonight. That will slow the viruses down some."

"But Pathology has shown," Isabel said, releasing the handrail as the boost regained its previous speed, "that vaccines are just staving off the inevitable. The viruses are mutating so fast that they dodge around vaccinated sections of Ascensión, then double back to start claiming lives again."

Stark had read this morning that Mortuary teams were finding corpses with vaccination marks on their arms. "What's the answer, Isabel?"

She shook her head. In all their years of working together, Isabel had never said *I don't know.* The boost was plunged into darkness as they rocketed into the residential floors.

"It gets worse," Isabel said as gold utility lights blinked on.

Stark folded his arms. "Of course it does."

"Unless we come up with an effective 'phage or vaccine," Isabel said, "the viruses will break free in four to six days. They'll mutate so that tetravalents are ineffective—even omnivalents won't be able to identify the new viruses correctly. We could get mortality down to one death per day and it *still* wouldn't be good enough. That's how virulent these viruses are."

So. There it is, he thought. *Four days.*

After a day of reorganizing and streamlining the public health response in Ascensión and bringing Outbreak Hospital Administration, Perimeter Clinics, Inoculation Program, Wetcoding and Pathology, Microbiology, Vaccination and Clonufacturing, and Mortuary Assistance Teams under his command; after another day of leashing the Ministry of Emergency Management, the Joint Information and Joint Operations, Joint Epidemiological Committee, Disaster Coordination, and Emergency Operations Centers; and after a third day, today, of being brought up to speed on the *Pilone* Network Task Force's work to bring the net online, Stark was right back to the paralyzing thought he had as he disembarked from the *aerobus* in La Alta three days ago.

Joaquin Delgado had already won.

He looked me right in the eye and lied to me and I ate it up, Stark thought, staring at himself in the elevator door again. *Might as well have shot me in the face.*

As of noon today, fifty-eight hundred dead, that number was climbing, and the worst was yet to come.

Four days away.

Light flooded the boost as it slowed toward their floor in the Triforium section of the Cloister, where the elite of La Alta lived; all the foreign VIP members of the Task Force were housed here. The boost stopped and its doors parted. As Rosangelica stepped out, a large family waiting to get on stepped back in unison, the father bug-eyed at the sight of the *sabihonda*'s disfigured face.

Stark and Isabel followed in her wake, stepping out into a cobblestone street lined with live oaks and walls painted flat orange, rose, and terracotta, with wrought-iron gates leading in to neighborhood villas. Isabel touched his arm kindly. "I'm sorry, Henry David."

He gave a little shrug at her touch, not wanting kindness from her now. "Rosangelica," Stark said, "are you carbed and Connected?" The meetings with Ofelio Xultan had left the *sabihonda* as drained as she was in Bastrop.

Rosangelica daintily dabbed the corner of her mouth. "*Compuesto.* Opposite. *Foto. Topes.* I am now."

"I'm giving an order to Isabel that I also want you to give to the World Health Organization, the Central Asia Immunological Society, and any other society remotely associated with the International Congress of Immuno—"

Isabel turned her body as if she meant to tackle him. "What? No, Henry David."

"—Congress of Immunology, anyone who was involved in Dr. Khushub's—"

"You can't be serious. No."

Stark made a slashing gesture at her. "Bela!"

Isabel looked saddened at first, then, as blood suffused her cheeks, angry enough to hit.

Rosangelica looked back and forth between the two, relishing the tension. "What's going on here, Doctors?"

Stark knew that shouting at Isabel had changed everything between them, with the colossus of her guilt still hanging in the air. He tried to lighten the mood. "Don't interrupt me when I'm talking to my cyborg, Bela."

"Talking to your cyborg about what?" Rosangelica said.

"I want all parties involved with Dr. Khushub's immunological recoding project to resume work—right now."

Rosangelica didn't say anything, but her eyes, with their metallic glint, shifted to take in Isabel's reaction.

Isabel was as tall as Stark, so she could look him in the eye, even look down on him if she summoned herself—as she was doing now. "It never worked. Never, Henry David. Not once. *Never.*"

"But, Bela, look at where we are and—"

"Its chances won't improve under *these* conditions."

"I'm entertaining all ideas," Stark shouted at her.

Again, Isabel looked astonished, whipped. "How dare you—"

"Wait, wait," Rosangelica said. "Everyone calm down. What are you proposing, Estarque?"

"Complete recoding of the immune system so it can identify particular pathogens from a supplied matrix of information," Isabel said, then sighing through her nose to show her disgust. "That's what Henry David is proposing. It's a *valemadre* red herring on which I piss with all my might, but he's willing to risk it for—for—I don't *know* why he'd risk it."

"Bela, you just got done saying we were out of options. We have four days. Listen to—"

"But I never thought in a thousand shit-covered years that you'd consider *that.*"

Rosangelica's rapacious eyes followed the conversation as if she were looking for an opportunity to pounce. When she found her opening, she said, "And what is immunological recoding?" It was a Biology 101 question, so when neither doctor even looked at her: "You won't explain it to me? *Pues, bien,*" and lapsed at once into a spate of Rodriguez's aphasia. "Uncle. *Nunca.* Noontime. *Nadie.* Proposed last year. Anoint. *Encomienda.*"

"You never really tried it, Isabel," Stark said over the aphasic mantra. "You don't *know* that it wouldn't work."

"All my sims came up negative, every single *foquin* one, for months upon months!"

"Scratch. *Hache. Riesgo*. Whisk. Wetcoding the immune system to improve its disease-fighting capability, right? Creating a matrix of viruses and nanorecoders that would genetically alter all the various immunological systems in the body simultaneously for the purpose of identifying newly emerged pathogens." Her eyes focused on Isabel. "My God, you and Joaquin Delgado explored that together."

Isabel said, "Exactly."

"And you both determined it didn't work," said the *sabihonda*.

"*Thank* you," said Isabel, eyes blazing with triumph at Stark. "That's right, *sabihonda*. It didn't. You read who papered my research? Postlethwaite in Kenya and Wong in Detroit. Wetcoding the immune system doesn't work. I shit on my own dead theory. Twice."

"You wrote that your tests killed simulated patients," Stark said, still yelling. "You said that's why you never tried it on human subjects, Bela."

Isabel gave an astonished laugh. She looked at Rosangelica for support. "Killing the test subjects means it's time to move on, wouldn't you say, *sabihonda*?"

"Durable. *Durango. Ojalá.*"

"I read the notes on your sims last night," Stark said. "What you and all your peers ignored was—"

"Why were you reading those?" Isabel shouted. "That son of a thousand syphilitic whores Delgado wrote them, not me!"

"I know. That's *why* I read them," Stark shouted back.

Rosangelica stopped babbling in her satellite language and lowered her silver eyes to Stark. "Dr. Khushub is right. I couldn't find a single paper suggesting anything worth pursuing in the human immune-system-recoding sims."

"But look at what Joaquin says here." Stark hefted his memboard and brought up Isabel's own files, then shot them to her memboard. Rosangelica went aphasic again in order to follow along. Stark read, "'The human-recoding sim subjects died of gross hemorrhaging as the old lymph system was destroyed by the new. Augmented T cells were present in sim blood assays, and the desired nanorecoders may indeed have been created which could have recorded the process of differentiation and used to augment other immune systems, but the process destroyed the simulated autoimmune system and its sim human subject.'"

"All the sim subjects died," Rosangelica said, face aimed at the nearest windows, reading. "The matrix was a failure because it couldn't possibly account for every nuance in the vast array of systems and cells employed in the immune system, according to Khushub and Delgado." Then, as if trying to get through to a crazy person, she said to Stark, "Why are you being such a stubborn ass?"

"Because it worked! 'Augmented T-cells were present in sim blood assays, and the desired nanorecoders may indeed have been created'!" Stark shouted, a little spit on his lips. "You calculated a slim chance that the matrix would be successful, Bela, but stopped your research when the hammer came down from your peer reviews."

"Henry David, your brain turned to cow shit on that goddamn farm. We couldn't *foquin* do it outside of sim," Isabel said, calm tone belying her scatology. "Immune-system recoding isn't worth the piss of useless dogs."

"You never tried it on a live person."

Light through the ceiling of rain-washed windows made the street seem submerged, silent as the bottom of the ocean, even as a herd of schoolkids scampered past.

Rosangelica raised her eyebrows at him. It was a new expression— neither bemused nor curious. Stark realized he had finally shocked the *sabihonda*.

Isabel's angel face looked hot with anger. She was watching Stark, but he had the distinct impression that she was not seeing him. As if he were wearing a mask, Stark could see how it was to be a stranger in her eyes.

"So," the *sabihonda* said, "you would need a human volunteer in order to create this matrix?"

Stark nodded his head sadly. "I know."

"And who would do such a thing? No one," Isabel said, a knife-edge slitting through her words. "Besides, we'd still need patient zero for the wet-coded T cells to differentiate effectively."

Stark knew she was right about patient zero and differentiation but he pressed, nonetheless. "Who would do it?" Stark asked. "A hundred would do it in this country, right, Rosangelica? For *La Patria*. For Emil the Damned."

Rosangelica looked down the long street, seemingly torn between pride and dismay. She sighed. "Good papist Catholics. Passionate humanists. Maybe even radical insurgents," she muttered. "Yes, you could find a hundred volunteers, Estarque."

Isabel's face turned a pale green as she seemed to sense that her brief alliance with Rosangelica was ebbing away. "You can't be serious."

Stark wanted to list all the people he'd spoken with, all the doctors worldwide he'd consulted, all the roadblocks that had been thrown in his path while looking for anything to smother this prairie fire of an outbreak.

The biggest? he thought, looking sidelong at Rosangelica and recalling his meeting with her and Cazador. *Mexico itself.*

"Don't keep pressing me about the Zapata records," Roberto Cazador had said yesterday, warning Stark with malice.

They'd met in the Chief of State's suite. Rosangelica stood spinning a sixteenth-century globe under her finger, while Cazador sat behind his enormous kidney-shaped desk.

El Jefe sipped coffee, and a cigar was smoldering in a conch-shaped ashtray. "Give us a little more time to secure the hospital," he said, trying on a warmer voice.

Stark demanded, "Why? Why won't you give the Task Force all the information we need?"

Cazador leaned back in his chair, smoothly revealing the holstered gun beneath his armpit. Roberto was old-style, twentieth-century fascism. He was a fat-cat Chicago ward heeler, a *decamisado,* a union buster, a Dixiecrat, a neocon, a brown shirt. Cazador, himself, was a one-man outbreak, disappearing *indígenas* by the thousands. He stared at Stark with a delighted twinkle in his warm, brown eyes. "I absolutely understand how important this is," he said, still friendly. "The insurgents, *Los Hijos de Marcos,* own the hot zone around Zapata. They are well armed, they've looted the hospital for antiviral protection, and they are emboldened by that radical nun, who has openly joined them. Would you care to organize a mission into the hot zone, Doctor? Hundreds of troops? Equipment? Transporting the wounded and infected?" *El Jefe* didn't allow Stark to say yes. "I've called up five units from our Ecuadorian army. Dr. Isabel Khushub says that the Ecuadorians cannot contract the disease. Different Indian genetic stock and unConnected to the net. They should arrive within the next three days, and they will secure the *centro histórico* hot zone and Zapata Hospital for you, Dr. Stark."

Stark stepped backward toward the llama-hide chair and lowered his head as he sat, wondering how he could get the Chief of State to see that they didn't have three days at the rate the viruses were spreading.

But as he sat, he watched Cazador from beneath his brows, and the Chief of State offered his eyes to the *sabihonda,* in a questioning, almost beseeching look.

Jefe Cazador nodded his head once, slightly. *See?* he seemed to say. *It's taken care of.*

"Henry David," Isabel was saying, "go ahead. Do it. Maybe you're right and it's the only path to pursue. But don't ask *me* to do this. Please."

The whole situation was surreal to Stark, madly, infuriatingly bizarre. Cazador was deliberately creating a maze that looped Stark back to the same dead ends—no Zapata, no patient zero, no early mutations to work with, no end in sight to the outbreak.

If I had nothing, that something, but I don't even got that.

Stark wondered where Joaquin was right now—a villa in Spain, or maybe he really was in Austria, monitoring his former student's lack of progress and laughing. Did he pity Stark's pathetic flailing in the face of the master's greatest work? "I don't have time to coddle you, Bela, we need this to start—"

"Coddle me?" Isabel sneered in revulsion. "You *want* me to kill? Do *you* want to sacrifice a human being?"

All Stark's disgust for Joaquin, his hatred for being affiliated with the man, came spilling out and spewing over Isabel's quaint moralism in a gush of sarcasm. "Oh no, I wouldn't ask you to sacrifice *anything,* Doctor. I expect you to hang around like a '*foquin*' lab coat while ten thousand people die. Good? You and Ahwaz can simper and preen over how to name the mutations and whether or not patient zero would help," Stark said, "and that's all I'll ever ask of you again, Bela."

Though it was still May, the summer rains had begun, and the high glass windows overhead cast rippling shadows of water over the empty, faux cobblestone street and its line of gates.

Isabel said in English, "You're a fucking monster." She took several long strides, heading toward her rooms down the street, then, over her shoulder she shouted, "Bend yourself over and fuck yourself to death for all I care."

They watched her disappear into a gate down the way, as swoop jets and *pesero* buses sailed past the street's balcony.

"Well," Rosangelica said cheerfully, "I, for one, am impressed, Estarque."

Stark ignored her and walked to his apartment, just two gates down from the elevator.

"Though I think alienating the scientist you need to actually *perform* the recoding—"

"Shut up, know-it-all," Stark said, and subvocalized his password to the gate, sliding inside his apartments, to leave the *sabihonda* in the dark and silent street outside.

The apartment that the Ministry of Health provided him was lavish to the extreme. Brandy-colored, seemingly hand-hewn beams of oak. White-marble walls veined with raspberry red. Custom sunlight from any time of day you liked. Stark couldn't help but gawk when he'd first arrived ("Is that marble? Is that oak?" he'd said in wonder, looking at the ceiling. "It's *plasceron, naco*," Rosangelica had retorted, using the Spanish word for "hick.") Stark had never been in such a room, let alone while working an outbreak. He was more accustomed to Trexler tents with air pumps breathing jungle heat, or if he was lucky, getting a clean hospital room to sleep in. This apartment had four rooms, a bathroom with a vast Jacuzzi, and a kitchen the size of Nissevalle manor's—all for one person.

Stark set his memboard on the kitchen counter. *Bela*, he thought, already regretting how cold he'd been with her. At least she had sworn at him as she stormed off. It was when Isabel stopped swearing that you knew she'd written you off. Stark poured himself a fat scotch from the fully stocked liquor cabinet. Three days and he was already on his second bottle.

Just when he'd dropped into the overstuffed chair by the windows looking out at the Valley of Mexico, the gate said to him through the house speaker, "Visitor."

"Tell Rosangelica I'm not interested," Stark told the gate, voice echoing in his glass.

"The visitor says it is an emergency," the gate said.

The monitor, which had been showing images of that nun, Sister Domenica—apparently the only thing that Mexican television showed—flashed a picture of his caller.

"The hell?" Stark said, sitting forward.

CHAPTER

18

"Who are you?"

The hooded figure bent close to the gate. "Dr. Stark, please. I'm an old friend. Let me in."

His visitor's face was unidentifiable under the flagellant's leather mask he or she wore, and the person's mouth was so close to the gate that the voice squelched in the speaker. If this really was an old friend, Stark couldn't recognize who it was.

"Open," Stark told the outside gate.

He stood and opened his front door with its noisy particle arrester in place. A moment later, the flagellant appeared—a man he guessed, watching him on his memboard. "Come in."

The man walked inside, pausing in the particle arrester. "Thank you, Doctor," he said, his elbows lifting, letting the vacuum get a good pull on his whole body. "I've been looking forward to this moment."

Stark stood several feet from the flagellant, but, good God, the smell of him. Soot, gas, and the horrific sweetness of burning flesh. The smell drilled through Stark's sinuses, right into his memory.

Sudan.

The skid-37 outbreak, the smell put him right there again, when he'd built his one and only funeral pyre. Fourteen bodies had needed disposal, but the ground was rock-hard from drought. The sun, relentless. So while flop-eared goats watched from a pen, Stark and three volunteers piled the corpses and doused them with gas.

"What do you want?"

The man reached up and pinched the zipper at his chin and drew it up over his nose and between his eyes.

Laughter kicked up in Stark, a galloping hysterical roil. "Oh my God."

The man tossed the hood-mask onto Stark's kitchen table. "Is that scotch?"

Still laughing, Stark handed Pedro Muñoz the glass in his hand.

Muñoz, dour as winter, looked down at the drink. "Pour me a fresh one, Doctor."

Stark couldn't stop laughing as he pulled the bottle out of the liquor cabinet again, and clinked ice into a clean glass. "Oh, my God."

He put the glass down in front of Muñoz as the younger man sat at the kitchen table. The delight and wonder that Stark felt wasn't mirrored in Muñoz's haunted expression, though. Something terrible had happened to Muñoz, too terrible for a happy reunion over drinks. The young doctor, urbane yet earnest in their conversations four days ago, now seemed slightly feral, his eyes skittered anxiously and he had the air of prey. Muñoz held the glass of scotch with grave seriousness, pressing his lips together, wary gratitude on his grimy face.

Nonetheless, Stark felt like a long-lost brother had finally come home, and for a moment, the scaling mortality rate of Big Bonebreaker, Isabel's betrayal, Joaquin's phone call fell away. He tried to staunch his laughter, but couldn't, as he dropped into a chair across from Muñoz. "How," Stark said, "in the world . . . ?"

Muñoz ignored him and drank deep. He let out a whoof of air, savoring the burn. "Boy."

Stark had a hundred questions, and wanted to loose them all, but if he'd needed a drink after *his* day, he imagined Muñoz must feel like a man in a desert. He could let the man enjoy his scotch without yapping at him like a hysterical puppy.

After a few more sips, Muñoz let out a shaky sigh. "Well, that's a little better."

"You were listed as dead, Pedro."

Muñoz seemed struck by that thought, amazed. "Good. That's good," he said. "You know, the last four days were scary, but nothing like trying to sneak into La Alta just now." He tilted the glass back until he was kissing ice and closed his eyes in rapture as the cubes touched his mouth.

"You've been in the hot zone all this time?"

Muñoz nodded solemnly, pushing his empty glass at him.

Stark refilled. "How did you get up here?"

"Let's just say you have some security holes in your perimeter clinic."

"Goddamn hallelujah," Stark said in English. Then in Spanish, "Thank God."

Muñoz cracked a smile finally. "To their credit, Clinic Number Three on your perimeter identified me as immune and asked if I'd be part of a study."

"As ordered."

"They bought me a ticket upstairs, dosed me with a tet and an omni, then I swooped up," he said, scotch loosening him a bit, "joined a line of flagellants long enough to get that hood, then risked a boost up into the Cloister."

"How did you know where to find me?"

"I asked who was heading up the Task Force and a nurse told me. I already knew where VIPs stayed in Cuauhtémoc."

"A nurse?" Stark said. "It was supposed to be highly sensitive info that I was here. Black letter. Top secret."

Muñoz laughed at Stark. "Please. The Holy Renaissance? They couldn't keep Diego Alejandro's death a secret. I mean, I heard that one down in La Baja."

Stark's joy sputtered and went out, staring at Muñoz and realizing that the young doctor wasn't kidding. Stark had been sending angry notes to Diego's address for three days, demanding a meeting, or at the very least an explanation of his behavior at the beginning of the outbreak. "What?" he said. "Diego?"

"Yeah," Muñoz said. "I heard he was 'promoted.' Everyone in Mexico knows what that means."

Stark felt dim and gullible. Maybe he was, but none of the Mexicans working side by side with Stark had bothered to explain it. Too many other deaths to worry about, perhaps. Stark didn't think he could take any more terrible news this day. He stood and walked into the living room, where the view of La Baja at night showed that grids in distant sections of the city were finally lighting up whole neighborhoods.

"Oh," Muñoz said to Stark's back, "you didn't know."

Stark couldn't deny it. His first thought had been to call Joaquin to tell him about their friend. He put a finger to his injured lip. "No."

"I figured—" Muñoz stood and brought Stark his drink after topping it off. "Sorry, Dr. Stark."

"Forget it." Stark made a hand gesture like he was waving traffic past him, then took the scotch. "Call me Henry David."

Muñoz raised his glass. "Here's to survival."

Just twenty minutes ago, he would have sneered if anyone proposed a toast like that. But it sounded like a possibility, now, looking at Muñoz in his filthy trench coat and soot-smeared face. "Absolutely. *Salud.*"

"*Salud,*" Muñoz said. He took in the room for a moment, casting his eyes about, maybe looking for something, or maybe hoping that something he feared wasn't there. "Look, I'm risking a lot being here. But I came because I have something to tell you," Muñoz said. "There's something that I saw in the hot zone."

Stark took a long pull on his scotch. He knew he would have to face what was happening in La Baja eventually. The pyres. The street fighting. The complete lack of public health inside the barricaded hot zones. "What did you see?"

"I've been hauling bodies and treating infected people down there for four days. I'm no pathologist or geneticist, but there's a symptom I haven't seen since Saturday night," Muñoz said, "when the first patients started arriving at Zapata. It changed on Sunday, the symptom did. It stopped appearing in new arrivals."

Stark's heart hammered, suddenly aware that he had the doctor who'd been on the dengue case long before Diego Alejandro slapped a quarantine on the hospital's records. "Tell me. What was it?"

"I saw mouth pustules on a body just last night."

Stark's lips parted slowly. "I heard about pustules on my flight. Cristóbal wrote about them."

"Right." Muñoz seemed relieved that Stark understood the significance, and he became less wild-eyed. "Your people in the clinics may not note the symptom if they haven't been told to look for it. All I'm going on is

Cristóbal's speculation that mouth pustules might be a symptom helpful in identifying patient zero."

The hell? Stark thought and crossed the room to retrieve his memboard. *Why we seeing such early generations now, four days into this thing?*

"Mouth pustules," he said to his memboard, and like that, he had fifteen pages of notes. "Jesus, I can't believe it. I had the info right here. I just didn't know what to ask to find it." He looked at Muñoz. "I've been warring with Cazador for days to let me into Zapata's records."

Muñoz stepped back suddenly, a spooked animal caught in the open. "Cazador?"

Stark acted casual, hoping to calm Muñoz. "He hired me, Pedro."

"How much contact do you have with Cazador?"

"Pedro," Stark said, "I'm not going to turn you in. I'm not going to tell him I saw you. Jesus, *El Jefe* has far bigger things to worry about than what a staff epidemiologist thinks is going on here."

This seemed to satisfy Muñoz for a moment, but then his eyes flicked back to Stark, clearly trying to discern if he could trust the American to tell the truth. "Look at Zedillo."

"What?"

"A clinic in the northern part of the city," Muñoz said, left hand grabbing the right and wringing it. "You don't need Zapata's records. Patients were pouring in all over the city. Do you have Zedillo's records?"

Stark was glad he finally had a Mexican epidemiologist to speak with, let alone the unique man himself. Stark simply didn't have the knowledge of Ascensión to dissect the flood of epidemiological data this outbreak was generating. Stark tapped in Muñoz's suggestion, and there it was. "Jesus, I got info from before noon on Sunday and I didn't even know it. Look at this. From Clinica del Norte. Patient Father Gasapardo. Age fifty-seven," Stark read, excited. "Felt sudden sharp pains in his stomach while watching SD. Visibly bloated abdomen. Prob gastritis." Stark looked at Muñoz. "No, probably massive internal bleeding from DHF onset symptoms. Clinicians." Then he read the last line. "Mouth pustules."

Muñoz spread his hands, *There it is.*

"Three patients were admitted to Clinica del Norte in rapid succession, right after Patient Gasapardo was treated. Where is that clinic?"

"It's on Calz de los Misterios," Muñoz said, eyes gazing upward for a second, as though locating the street in his mind, "five blocks south of the Basilica."

"The Basilica. Cristóbal's notes and now these both mention the Basilica."

Muñoz stopped wringing his hands. He sat down in the overstuffed burgundy sofa. "Interesting."

"Those four appear to be the earliest in the 'mouth pustule' category," Stark read, scanning through his search results. "And yes, two patients expressing mouth pustules had been at the Basilica that morning."

"And the other two were at Sister Domenica's sermon," Muñoz said.

Stark stared at Muñoz like he was a magician. "How do you know that?"

"SD in Gasapardo's file that you just read."

"That schizophrenic nun everyone's talking about? Sor Demonica?" Stark didn't understand what Muñoz was getting at. "What's the connection?"

"I don't know," Muñoz said, walking to Stark's netmonitor and turning it on. Not surprisingly, there she was—stock footage of her sermon on the slopes of the volcano Popocatépetl. "But that's Sister Domenica. And she's connected to everything in this country, it seems. She predicted the volcano's eruption last year. The flooding in Panama province. Even Big Bonebreaker."

Stark recalled watching one of her prophecies on the Dulce jet. She'd given a rather disturbingly accurate description of dengue hemorrhagic fever, though Stark had chalked it up to the coincidence of biblical imagery and *any* calamity. "I saw some of that, yes."

"The first patient I saw was a prostitute named Barrientos or Barracon," Muñoz said, trying to remember. "She was kind of obsessed with Sister Domenica. I presume she must have caught it while attending one of her sermons."

Stark watched the nun on-screen—a woman who could have been twenty or fifty. She spoke with charisma, or at least, she obviously had a chemistry with the crowd on that mountainside. Too much Catholic hell and damnation for Stark's taste.

Muñoz's eyes drifted to the netmonitor again. "Did you hear she prophesied that the creator of the virus was a Spaniard?"

Stark smirked. "You're pulling my leg."

"Hair." Muñoz laughed at him. "In Mexico we say 'you're pulling my hair.' Anyway, Domenica used the word 'augmented' before any medical personnel."

"Unbelievable," Stark said. "That's Joaquin she's describing."

"Joaquin?"

"Joaquin Delgado. One of the best wetcoders alive. We know he's the one who created the viruses," Stark said.

Stark looked back at the image of the nun and didn't look away for some time. Outside his window, the sun set, a bloodred coin falling behind mountains. Stars ignited in the Mexican sky, and Stark's calla lily lamps lit themselves. Elsewhere in Torre Cuauhtémoc, Stark could hear a band playing the Holy Renaissance anthem, *Land of Milk and Honey,* complete with congas and meowing trumpets. Screens shuffled forward on the netmonitor showing more stock footage, this time of Domenica walking upstairs to the Capilla del Cerrito.

"Holy shit," Stark said, as the rival pope's new Basilica came into view behind and below Domenica in the shot.

"She was there," Muñoz said, spreading his feet, leaning forward. "She was at the Basilica, too."

Stark's vision went black for just a moment. Then he felt as if someone were lifting him by the shoulders. When his sight came back, he was standing in the middle of the living room with a gloved hand upon his brow.

Muñoz was staring at him from the couch with a worried, confused look on his face.

"That woman is everywhere. She's always on the monitors. Always." Stark flipped up the volume and tapped the monitor's screen. Windows shuffled and showed a tight close-up of the wide-smiling nun, sitting in a cramped room, whispering into the camera, cruddy lighting. "Joaquin would have been intrigued by her prophecies." Then, like the sensation he had when Sanjuan told him that the virus targeted an immune response in Native Mexicans, suddenly Stark felt as though a shaft of light were shining on him, as if he were staring into his old teacher's study and catching glimpses of his secret, profane work in there. *I see. Oh, I see it now.*

There was a second, very strategic reason for Joaquin to wetcode a virus that targeted *mestizos.* Yes, it would unlock the *pilone's* Self status in the body, keyed as it was on the *mestizo* immune response, and spur the immune system to attack the *pilone* wetware. But also, as a non*mestizo*, Joaquin could carry the virus without fear of contracting it. As a Spaniard, he could walk through the streets of Ascensión, infecting people at will, and no one would look twice at him or presume he was a foreigner.

And dengue. *Sí. Perfecto, maestro,* Stark thought. Endemic to this region, the virus would appear to be a native, too. Accomplished liars and masters of disguise, Joaquin and his viruses, both.

The image on the netmonitor showed the nun in full habit with the blue mantle of the Order of Guadalupe. *"A Spaniard created this virus,"* she was saying on-screen. *"A second Cortés has come to Mexico."*

Stark couldn't believe what he was hearing. Somehow she knew. She couldn't possibly know, but she knew. *She would have been too much for him to ignore.*

Standing at the netmonitor, Stark hefted his memboard and thumbed up the Cristóbal report again, searching for the section he had read on his way into Ascensión.

"Nurses at Zedillo Clinic told me that they admitted a steady number of patients with gastritis, stomach ailments, and mouth pustules yesterday, May 14. All of them had been to see Sister Domenica last night and left feeling nauseous."

"I've been thinking about this outbreak all wrong," Stark said. "Big Bone-breaker's pathology might show that the viruses target *pilone* wetware, but outbreak patterns show who *Joaquin* was targeting." Until now, Stark hadn't allowed himself to project his image of Joaquin into this abomination and couldn't picture him doing these terrible things. But now Stark could see his reasoning, his cunning, and even his old friend's blind spots emerging in the epidemiological data.

"Joaquin is hunting Sister Domenica," Stark said.

"You mean he *was* hunting her."

"I mean he *is* hunting her," Stark said. "That's why you saw mouth pustules, Pedro. You were seeing more patient zeros, not just early generations. Joaquin is down there somewhere. Probably looking for Domenica."

Muñoz stood next to Stark, looking back and forth between the netmonitor and Stark's memboard. "He *is* still here."

Stark tapped in a new searcher to his memboard, this one looking for mouth pustules in Mortuary team reports. When several lit up, he highlighted the most recent one. "Tuesday May 17," Stark read to Muñoz. "Cleanup crews reported to a compromised field clinic and found eighteen corpses, three, notably, with mouth pustules. They discovered that all the patients and staff within had died the day before." Stark muttered, "That was Monday, then."

"The *medicos*? Dead in their own clinic?" Muñoz said. Then he spread his hands when he got the answer. "Ah. The *medicos* were the ones with mouth pustules. Right?"

"Right." *It fits,* Stark thought. *It all fits Joaquin just so.* There were two aspects to the man: the scientist and the Catholic. The attack on this field clinic fit Joaquin's scientific approach: Disable any medical personnel that get in the way and the hospital where the Dengue Conference takes place; design the virus to look like dengue under the 'scope and take advantage of the misdiagnosis. All were reflections of Joaquin's nimble and maneuvering mind. But the other half of the outbreak fit Joaquin the good Catholic: infecting loyal followers of the Holy Renaissance at the rival pope's Basilica and at the sermons of the disturbingly prophetic nun. She would have perplexed Joaquin deeply, and maybe confounded both the measured and passionate halves of him, set them one against the other.

Muñoz said, "He was here as recently as yesterday, in the hot zone near the National Square."

"A perfect place to hide," Stark said, looking down at the spray of lights below, "down there, immune among his viruses."

"If he's still here, Stark, you can still capture unmutated virus," he said. "You can get Generation One."

Pedro, you right, Stark thought, looking at him, feeling grateful for the first time in days. "But we can't just wait around for the right patient to show up." He could see, clear as an open highway, what the next course of action had to be. He didn't know what Muñoz had planned for himself now that he'd left the hot zone, but it would be better if he didn't know what Stark planned to do next.

"Joaquin might be after Domenica. But I'm more worried about the street fighting," Stark said, trying to throw Muñoz off the previous train of thought.

Muñoz smirked. "What's that got to do with—?"

"It's interfering with a decent survey of the viruses' morbidity rates," Stark said, letting his voice go cold and brittle. "We'll have an easier time finding another patient zero if we can quell the uprising in the hot zones."

"You didn't mention that as a concern before," Muñoz said.

"This plague is a test for Mexico," Sister Domenica was saying on-screen, arms spread in a gesture of pleading. "And only a precious few will pass."

Out of the corner of his eye, Stark could tell that Muñoz was watching him. The skin on Stark's face felt like a cold, stiff mask as he avoided looking directly at Muñoz. If he met his eyes right now, Stark would feel too guilty for lying to him—and there was no time for that. *I gonna tell you everything later, buddy. Right now, I got to keep some things to myself.*

CHAPTER

19

STARK ASKED ROSANGELICA to meet him at a *sin piel* café on the Cuauhté-moc rotunda, overlooking the tower's main shopping district and sports center.

Sin piels were "no skin" establishments, certified by the Ministry of Health, assuring customers that meals and beverages sold here had been prepared by workers wearing level-four antiviral suits. On the rotunda, there were at least ten such cafés and restaurants. Their balcony-side decks were dotted with expatriated Americans and Persian men in turbans. These days, Mexico had a slightly more foreign look, Stark noted, as he walked from the elevator.

The *sabihonda* was seated near the railing of the rotunda's balcony. Below, a soccer match was under way on a shockingly green field, all the players wearing gloves, faces covered with skintight clamp masks. White sunlight slanted down from frosted-glass ceilings overhead, a pleasant breeze trimmed the air, and the boyishly slim Rosangelica, in her narrow duster and boots, sat in a pool of cool light, sipping espresso, watching the game.

"Let me get a drink, then I'll join you," Stark said, glancing at the field as a cry came up from the thin crowd below. He placed a lugall under her table.

Stark went to the bar, situated in the middle of the café's deck. He asked the counter worker for a cappuccino, selected his bottle of water for the coffee and a packet of grounds, then signed the café memboard stating he accepted responsibility for the risk of drinking this coffee. When the cappuccino was prepared, he carried it over to Rosangelica's table. "Like trying to get data out of Zapata Hospital, ordering a drink in this town."

"Very funny." Rosangelica sipped her espresso. Her clamp mask hung around her neck like an ugly scarf. "What's with the luggage?"

"I'm going to tour the perimeter clinics after I'm done here," he lied.

"Oh? Do you need me with you?"

"No," Stark said. "I don't. But I need to ask you something before I go."

Rosangelica sat forward and brushed her hair back from her forehead, revealing the ripples of subcutaneous wiring rooted beneath her hairline and worming toward her eyes.

Stark unstuck his clamp mask from his face, let it dangle while he sipped his coffee. "I need you to get the classified patient records out of Zapata Hospital."

"Me?" She frowned in bewilderment. "You know I can't get those records until the hot zone is secure."

"I heard *El Jefe* say that, yes. But I'm testing a theory," Stark said.

Rosangelica seemed ready to sit back in her chair, then rocked forward again, as if she couldn't decide whether to take Stark seriously or not. Her eyebrows made a shallow V over the bridge of her long nose. "Those records aren't accessible by satellite. I couldn't get them even if I wanted to break the law."

"OK." Stark wiped coffee from his upper lip. "That proves part of my theory."

Rosangelica looked at him from under her eyebrows. "What the hell is your theory?"

Stark took another coy sip of coffee and decided he could now push the *sabihonda* a little harder. "I didn't think you could get me the info or you already would have done it."

"Oh really? Your theory has a hole in it." Rosangelica picked up her coffee and set it back down again. "It presumes I would defy a Holy Renaissance imperative."

"No. My theory is that you *make* Holy Renaissance imperatives. Or at least you make your own, which would explain what you were doing in that Bastrop jail cell," said Stark. Before she could contradict him, he unsnapped his lugall and slipped a memboard out, then hastily shut the valise again. "Here's the thing, Rosangelica. I've done everything I can do to stop this outbreak without a dossier on patient zero. I need someone to go down to Zapata and get it for me."

Rosangelica's head snapped back in surprise. "And you think I'll volunteer? No way. The riskiest thing I plan to do today is sip this coffee at a *sin piel* and double my bet on *Los Capitalinos* down there," she said, jerking her thumb toward the soccer match below. Then she took a pensive breath, and said, "I won't go until the black letter on Zapata is lifted, anyway. It's against the law."

"Mexican law is irrelevant to me, Rosangelica. And it doesn't seem to apply to you at all."

"Let me put it another way," said Rosangelica. "Entering Zapata is against the wishes of those in power."

"Now we're getting somewhere," said Stark, setting down his cup, ready to press his case. "Who is in control of this situation, Rosangelica? And what do they want? Their wishes do not include stopping the outbreak, apparently."

"Yes, they do, actually."

Stark picked up his cup and sipped. "So tell me what's happening, Rosangelica. Is Orbegón insane? I can't think of another reason for keeping those records sealed."

Rosangelica's long hair, worn loose today, almost made her look normal as it fell over the distortions on her brow and temples. Her voice, however, was all *sabihonda*, full of intimidation and venom. "He has kept them sealed in the interests of national security. Cazador explained that to you. I'm not at all pleased that the Task Force coordinator has taken an interest in Mexico's national security."

She wasn't going to bite on going to Zapata, but Stark kept baiting her for his backup plan. "And you won't violate national security? Even if I ask you to? Right?"

"Of course not," she said with a wary frown.

"Of course not. Your job is protecting national security, right? And I'm willing to wager that you have a great deal of license in carrying out that job."

Rosangelica leaned forward again, ignoring her coffee, eyes drilling into Stark's. "You know I have an aunt who plays guitar, Doctor?"

"Pardon me?" said Stark.

"An idiom. It means, what the fuck does this have to do with anything?"

Rosangelica spread her hands. "Where are you going with this moronic theory of yours?"

"Let me tell you my moronic theory. My theory about how the virus is spreading, that is."

She put her fingertips on her mug. "I thought Ahwaz and Khushub already determined how the virus spreads."

"They determined tropism, yes, what the virus hunts. I'm doing the epidemiological work. How the epidemic physically communicates from person to person. Look at this." He laid the memboard on the table and called up the spreadsheet showing admission times for all the infected patients with mouth pustules. "My theory says that Generation One patients form pustules around the mouth. As you can see, all the earliest patients developed this symptom. No others did."

Rosangelica read for a moment. Nodded. Then shook her head. "Generation One? What's that?"

"Generation One means Joaquin Delgado. It's like his fingerprint on a dead body. Generation One means that the person caught the disease straight from whatever means Joaquin Delgado used to deliver his viruses."

Rosangelica's face blanched as she read the spreadsheet a second time. "You have a trail to follow?"

"Yes, I do," Stark said, then tapped open a searcher saying, "Basilica. Domenica."

The spreadsheet filtered out some of the later patients, but the majority remained.

Rosangelica looked as if Stark had just showed her tea leaves. "I don't get it. What's this mean?"

"All the patients listed here," Stark said, pointing at the list of earliest Big Bonebreaker patients from Clinica del Norte, "were either at Sister Domenica's mass on the fourteenth or at her Basilica sermon on the fifteenth. I think it means that not only was Joaquin here, in Mexico, but he was targeting the nun."

Rosangelica couldn't keep her jaw from slackening. "He was *here*?"

"That's my theory."

"You and your damn theories," she said. She looked down at the memboard as if reading, but Stark could see he had played to her outrage perfectly. She had a lingering distrust of Stark, obviously, but the mere mention of Joaquin Delgado was working on her resistance beautifully. Just when he was about to prod her a bit further, Rosangelica said, "OK, Estarque, you have my attention. How do we prove he was following the nun?"

Stark wasn't quite convinced he had dazzled her with enough medical statistics to make his pitch, but it was now or never, he figured. "The high, nonvirus mortality rate is messing me up."

"What do you mean?"

"The fighting between the Holy Renaissance troops and the insurgents."

"I see." He could tell she was struggling to keep up with him.

"I can't tell for certain who is dying of what, Rosangelica. We need to clear away the fighting if we're going to determine where and how Joaquin was spreading the disease."

"You need the uprising in the hot zone to stop."

He had her by the gills now. "I need the conflict in the hot zone to end, yes. I need *you* to stop the fighting."

Rosangelica's eyes went cold with disbelief. "What? Me? I have no control over that," she said. Then she sneered. "*Las indígenas* have been fighting the Mexican government for decades, centuries. And now they're backed by cash and clout from abroad. I may have powerful connections, Stark, but I can't just—"

"I want to find this Sister Domenica and have her transmit a message of truce to the city," Stark said, pointing at the terrace floor. "From here. From La Alta where she can show the city her commitment to unity. Once she does that, I want to hit this town with everything we have—empty the supplies of any vaccine that has a prayer of working and flood the streets with every medical worker we have. We have to clear away the dust so that we can find Joaquin's trail, or this virus is going to keep spreading." It was such a good plan, Stark almost believed what he was saying for a moment.

Rosangelica scrutinized Stark, seemingly impressed with him. "Whose side are you on, Estarque? Tell me true. *Los Hijos de Marcos* seem more like your match politically than the Holy Renaissance." She paused and narrowed her eyes at him. "Some say your being here is a security risk. People think you're here to garner some legitimacy for *Los Hijos*."

With firm anger in his voice, Stark said, "I don't help anyone wage war. Run a check on my farm sometime. You'll know what I am by seeing where I come from."

"I know. The little co-op towns in the Midwest are little hotbeds of liberalism," Rosangelica said. "Land Reform and democratic control of capital. Sounds like *Los Hijos*'s agenda to me."

Stark longed for a time when the key cooperative principle of *one person, one vote* wasn't considered radical. Democracy was messy and complex, but it was exactly what this paranoid country needed. "You have to overcome that thinking if my plan is going to work, Rosangelica," he said. "We have to find Domenica, and both she and the Holy Renaissance must come together to create peace in the capital, because peace equals public health for Mexico. It's that simple."

Rosangelica closed her eyes for a moment and thought out loud. "It *wouldn't* embarrass the Holy Renaissance to woo Domenica back into the fold, as it were. Maybe you're onto something there. It might even help Emil internationally." Rosangelica went aphasic for a moment, whispering *"gatos"* over and over. Then her eyes cleared and she looked at Stark with new appreciation. "So you think I have the power necessary to convince the President for Life to extend an olive branch to the nun. That's your theory, eh?" She smiled. "It's a pretty good theory."

Oh my God, Stark thought. *I right about her.* This woman controlled Mexican war drones on the Guadalupe River, policy regarding political enemies in Ascensión, maybe the Holy Renaissance itself, for all he knew. Was she really going to make this happen? The red herring he was offering her was turning into a real course of action—and maybe a good one. He kept pressing. "But for any of this to work, you have to find Domenica so that I can convince her to come to La Alta."

"You? You'll convince her?" Rosangelica laughed.

"Yes," Stark said. "It has to be me. She won't trust anyone from the Holy Renaissance."

"I'm not a public face. She might trust me."

Stark swallowed his fear that the *sabihonda* would simply kill the dissident nun given the chance. "Do you want to try?"

"No, I think you're right. I think you and I should try to find the nun together and you should do the talking. The *servicio sagrado* has a pretty good idea of which neighborhood she's in, but she keeps moving. Maybe I should find out what they know and pinpoint her."

"But if the *servicio sagrado* finds out—"

Rosangelica blinked a slow, reassuring blink. "Don't worry. They'll never find out what I'm up to."

"Then you'll do it?"

"It's better than any plan currently before Emil. With the *pilone* down, the Blues are massing faster than we are on the *Tejas* border. The Minister of Defense will support this," said Rosangelica. "But tell me, did you ask Cazador to offer clemency to Domenica and he turned you down?"

"No, I didn't want to waste any more time, so I came straight to the true power source."

Rosangelica seemed ready to contradict him, frowning and shaking her head almost shyly. But then she turned the corners of her mouth down and her eyes sparked. "OK, Estarque. OK." She stood up. "Where can I find you in, say, two hours?"

Two hours. Perfect. "I'll be on my way back from the perimeter clinic," he lied again.

"I'll call you on your phone."

Stark watched her out of the corner of his eye as she stood, finished her coffee, and got into an elevator.

Fleetingly, he wondered if Rosangelica really could get Sister Domenica into Torre Cuauhtémoc. That would certainly be some sweet icing on the elaborate cake he was baking. But for now, all he needed was this brief time without Rosangelica breathing down his neck.

And perhaps best of all, she didn't seem to know about the resurrection of Pedro Muñoz—let alone his new position working the sentry lab in Torre Cuauhtémoc.

When the elevator doors closed and Rosangelica had disappeared, Stark grabbed his lugall and dashed to the nearest bathroom, located between the decks of two *sin piel* cafés. He removed his Racal suit from the lugall, fitted the neck ring and hastily shimmied into the legs, and clamped the helmet over his head. Then he grabbed his lugall, filled with memboards and a couple push packs of omnivalent vaccine, and ran as fast as he could in his cumbersome suit to the nearest docking bay.

He had two hours without fear of Rosangelica's interference.

"My ID chip," Stark said, handing it to the nearest dockworker. "I need a *barco*."

The dockworker scanned Stark's chip into his memboard. "American? Max clearance. *Caramba*," he sneered, leading Stark to a queue of red-and-black skyboats. "You don't know how to drive one of these, do you?"

"Um." Stark glanced down the line of bulbous vehicles, intimidated by the memory of one hitting the Texas highway at high velocity. "Really, I'd rather have a skycycle," he said. At least his one adventure on a 'cycle hadn't ended in a twisted heap. "I just need to get to Torre Juárez."

The man pointed to the far end of the docking bay. "There's one down there beyond the line of *barcos*. Keep the speed up on that one. It likes to stall in updrafts."

Stark got on the 'cycle that the dockworker indicated, then revved it up. He waited for his bay's green light, then, when no one else departed, he rolled the 'cycle forward with care, down the ramp, and off into the great gulf of air outside Torre Cuauhtémoc.

CHAPTER

20

STARK SKIMMED OVER the rooftops of La Baja Ciudad on his skycycle, noting that no stoplights were lit below, no business signs blinked with old-fashioned neon charm, and no music (so prevalent in La Alta above) throbbed from street-corner sound pods. The only sound was his bike roaring over the empty desolation of a noncity.

Even without the riot's destruction, the streets surrounding the National Square, the destroyed cathedral, and Zapata Hospital were in rapid urban decay. Façades of warehouses crumbled, and famous streets—Paseo de la Reforma, San Juan de Letran, and Balderas—coursed through neighborhoods that looked more like third-world slums than the streets of the richest city on the planet.

But the richest city on the planet, Stark reminded himself, towered overhead. Down here, old Mexico remained.

Stark eased the 'cycle over Venezuela Avenue in dips and stalls, flying it like a badly made paper airplane. This skycycle, unlike the People's Army of East Texas's, had Mexico's locust-eye override, which kept the rider from making the kinds of fatal navigation errors that Stark was making. Based on the eye-brain connection in locusts, which kept the insects from smacking into each other in a swarm, the skycycle's "eye" saw and responded to dangers thousands of times more quickly than Stark's unwieldy brain ever could. So even though Stark should have somersaulted down the avenue in a fiery, disfiguring crash, instead, the 'cycle corrected his landing angle, applied a jet of airbrakes, and a heartbeat later, he was rolling down the empty street toward Zapata Hospital.

He found an abandoned convenience store near the hospital campus to hide his 'cycle, even though he had seen no one on the streets other than a staggering line of flagellants near the National Square. He killed the engine and collapsed the wings so that they folded neatly against the side of the bike. Then he rolled it into the completely looted store and, after removing his lugall, positioned the cycle behind an overturned shelf.

Zapata Hospital, a six-story white-concrete cube, was just down the street, glowing in the midday sun like a block of ice refusing to melt. Stark walked toward it beneath the tattered awnings of deserted buildings, not for the shade but for the cover. The silence was ominous, he felt naked and obvious, walking down this empty street in his antiviral helmet and suit, and he didn't like the idea of anyone watching him enter the hospital. As he inched closer to Zapata, he could see that its atrium, a large, open reception area whose glass walls had all been shattered in the rioting, was exposed. Fire had gutted the entrance, and carcasses of furniture and toppled palm trees hunkered in the center. Stark looked up and down Venezuela Avenue, then crossed the street. Peering into the shadowy hospital, he clambered into the atrium, the boots of his Racal suit crunching glass and the bones of burned ceiling tiles.

He went to the reception desk, which had a counter and an enclosed office behind it, assuming that the records and other data he needed would be accessible from here. But just as he feared, the computer had been immolated. Stark leaned into the little office adjacent to the desk and found another computer, but its monitor was smashed and the main drive had been cracked open. Bullet holes perforated the wall behind it.

Stark put his lugall on the reception desk and opened it. He took out his map of Zapata's floor plan, tapping the edge. "Backup computers," he said. The sound of his own voice, loud in his fishbowl helmet, made him jump. Immediately, a route traced across the surface of the memboard, from the atrium, through the hallways in a red line that bent this way and that in right angles, then ended in a star on the second floor: COMPUTER LABORATORIES, read the memboard. Stark oriented himself. The hallway he needed was on the other side of the burned-furniture mountain. He took one last look at the sunny street and the gutted convenience store where he had hidden his skycycle. Then he turned away and walked into the hospital's dark hallway.

Ten steps into Zapata's darkness, Stark was nearly blind. No windows or open doors offered any light in this hallway, nothing but the dim wash of light in the reception area behind him. He'd been foolish not to find a flashlight before fleeing La Alta to come here, and he was reminded of what his grandfather had said to him, leaning out of the milk truck window. *Don't jump into the middle of anything and bullshit your way out, like you usually do.*

Stark kept one hand on the left wall as he walked and stumbled over what seemed like either kites or signs—he figured they were fallen ceiling tiles, but he couldn't see them. *Ain't never gonna learn to look before you leap,* he scolded himself.

When he reached the end of the hall, Stark stopped. Remembering the map, Stark figured he had reached the intersection of the main hall and the elevator bay. There would be elevators to his immediate left and across the hall, too, directly in front of him. The stairwell he needed was just to the left of the far elevators, somewhere in the blind darkness before him, so he followed the elevator bay, dragging his left hand along the wall. He took a few steps and then his heart dropped away as his hand passed across an empty space. Stark stopped; he couldn't move. He heard something to his left where the wall should have been. Water dripping far below. A hollow rush of air. *Open elevator shaft,* he thought, refusing to move forward, as if he might be sucked into this empty shadow.

What happened to the doors?

Stark willed himself to move, keeping his left foot shuffling forward and his hand tracing the black emptiness. Another open elevator. Then a third. It felt like someone had ripped the sliding doors out of the elevators' frames. Why would someone need elevator doors? That thought bred a scarier one. Was someone here, in the hospital, now? His suit's exhaust pump made a sound like a breathy sigh—a deafening noise in the silent elevator bay. Stark imagined that if anyone else were in Zapata, they would hear him coming long before he heard them. Stark walked past the elevators until he found a doorway with a real live door. He pushed it open and felt the floor beyond with his toe, relieved to find solid ground. He stepped through. The noise of the exhaust pump echoed in a space stretching far above and far below.

Stark decided he was in the stairwell and found the handrail and steps. His heart lightened and he sighed deeply, walking with more confidence now. The stairwell switchbacked upward and Stark soon found himself at the doorway leading into the second floor.

He was grateful to find the hallway's fluorescent ceiling lights still flickering. That bode well for the computer lab: This floor probably had its own generator. Six gaping elevator shafts yawned at him here, too, and Stark realized he was looking at the elevators from which Miguel Cristóbal and his team had emerged while Stark consulted with Pedro Muñoz. *That ain't even a week ago now,* Stark thought. He found the conference room where dengue-6 must have been released, an ALHEPA filter fitted over the door. Stark read the panel, MAX QUARANTINE—DENGUE 6 ACTIVE, and, with a violent shudder, imagined the ugly scene on the other side of that door, and backed away.

Stark took out the hospital map, but in the half-light all he could see was the crazy red line, angling like the letter of an alien alphabet. He held the map so the strobe could illuminate it. The lab he needed was at the other end of this long hall.

Stark had never been comfortable in hospitals. As an intern, he had spent a lot of time in them, but rarely as a professional epidemiologist. He was a Wisconsin *quop* boy, accustomed to a very different architecture: cramped quarters, noisy hallways, hot kitchens boisterous with political debate. While Stark appreciated the cleanliness of a hospital, the fact that they housed hundreds of people—doctors, nurses, orderlies, secretaries, patients, babies—while still maintaining a creepy illusion of emptiness felt deeply wrong in the core of his bones. The countless unoccupied rooms and their vacant beds. The unblemished floors that looked as if no human had ever trod upon them. The long corridors that seemed to stretch off into vanishing points. These images came into Stark's dreams, usually in nightmares, where Stark was a boy, again looking for his grandfather somewhere in the tidy maze of a hospital.

But Zapata was far worse than any of his recurring nightmares.

Stark folded the map, put it in the pocket at the small of his back and was about to head down the hallway when he heard something from the stairwell behind him. Or maybe it was from one of the elevator shafts.

A shushing sound. A whisper, maybe, or a foot sliding on the ground.

Stark stood stone-still for a long time, straining to hear, but there was nothing more. He could have come armed, but after what happened in Bastrop, Stark never wanted to hold a gun again in his life. He started down the hallway, taking big cartoon steps to keep his hard-soled boots from tapping too loudly on the tiles.

Then he heard footsteps.

Stark stopped walking.

A lonely whistle sounded from the stairwell behind him. Two notes, one high, the next lower, like someone whistling for a dog. Stark looked over his shoulder but he couldn't see anyone emerging from the stairwell. He stood still as a deer, but he couldn't hear very well over the sounds his suit made: the pump's hiss, the pressure gauge's quick waltz of clicks, the constant creak of the plastic coverall. But there it was, another footstep. Then more whispering. He couldn't discern words but the tone was definitely conversational.

Question?

Response.

Agreement.

Someone was following him. The voices fell quiet and all Stark could hear was his suit. Spooked out of his skin, he ran down the hall and when he reached the computer lab, he ducked inside and listened at the door.

I should not have done this! he told himself. *I should not have come here!* He was an idiot to come without a flashlight or a gun, without a guard, without a team of twenty or thirty bodyguards to protect him. He decided Roberto Cazador was the smartest man in the world to call up foreign armies before coming into the hot zone. Stark picked up the nearest object that he might use as a weapon, a computer keyboard, then flattened himself against the wall by the door. His brain kept repeating those two sentences until they danced into a crazy little rumba rhythm in his brain. *I-should-not-have* done THIS! *I-should-not-have* come HERE! He waited, listening, computer keyboard held like a plank, ready to brain anything that entered the room.

When no plague-infected monsters leapt into the computer lab, Stark swallowed his fear and slid away from the wall. The hallway outside was still empty. *Hospitalophobia gettin the better of me,* he decided. He watched for a few more minutes, then cautiously turned his attention to the task of starting up a computer. The lab was full of terminals, and grounded strips blinked red. Looters had taken chairs, desks, even doors, but they had left the computers on the floor. Stark supposed that in *pilone*centric Mexico, computers weren't much more than filing cabinets that broke down more easily.

Stark put down his keyboard-club and went to the nearest terminal, flicking it on without a problem. The system ran a virus check, which made

Stark laugh humorlessly, then its screen read, *El sistema se funciona bien.* The system is operational. Backup generators had protected these computers from any surges during the riot's blackouts. Stark found the dengue files from icons on the desktop, and when he found the storage of files dated May 14 and May 15 (the last files available), Stark removed the memboard from his thigh pocket, whispered his name to it very quietly, and winced at the series of loud wake-up tones. He looked over his shoulder: Still, no one in the hallway. Then he plugged the memboard into the terminal.

YOU ARE REQUESTING BLACK LETTER FILES.
PLEASE ENTER YOUR HOLY RENAISSANCE ID CHIP TO CONTINUE.

Stark entered his Task Force ID code, hoping it would work or this ghastly excursion would be for nothing. A moment later the Ministry of Health logo appeared on screen. On a template so bright that Stark jumped, the computer read:

WARNING. CONDITIONAL ACCESS GRANTED.
THE MINISTRY OF HEALTH IS NOW BEING ALERTED TO YOUR REQUEST.
PLEASE WAIT.

Stark knew there were no fiber-optic connections to Zapata's records. Would they have secret connections for the sole purpose of ratting on intruders like Stark? He glanced back at the doorway, still nothing, then looked back at the computer monitor, shifting his weight from one foot to the next. He had to get to a bathroom soon. The suspense was excruciating.

ACCESS GRANTED. MINISTRY OF HEALTH ALERTED.

Stark started in fright, but immediately began downloading files like a thief shoving silverware into a swag bag. He took all the dengue cases from the first two days of the outbreak, then pulled up a searcher and downloaded any case file or document that contained the word *"dengue."* After that, he took patient records and interviews, nursing staff reports, pathology reports, phlebotomy reports, and Pedro Muñoz's letter of dissent to Zapata Hospital's administration. He even took a document labeled "Grandmother Muñoz's Tripe Soup" from the Staff Epidemiologist's personal file. It would

take a while to download it all, but Stark didn't want to risk needing anything once he fled the hospital.

Just then, from the hallway outside the computer lab, a man called in
singsong Spanish, "Where are you, you little fucker?"

Stark stood up straight. His head twisted about frantically looking for
another exit, then realized there was no other way out of the lab. He picked
up the memboard. It was still downloading. THREE MINUTES UNTIL TRANS-
FER IS COMPLETE, read the screen. His instinct was to leave the memboard,
or better, rip it out of the main dock and run. He looked back at the door-
less entrance. Stark was standing in full view if anyone passed. Terrified beyond the ability to react, his brain retreated into its little rumba rhythm
again.

Footsteps shuffled toward the gaping doorway. "Are you in the computer
lab?" said the singsong voice.

Then that lonely, two note whistle again.

Stark felt a quick, warm trickle down his left thigh before he could control himself.

Two young men appeared at the doorway. They were desperate-looking
fellows, wearing wet bandanas over their faces and oven mitts on their
hands. Both wore smoke-stained Sanborn's restaurant uniforms. One carried a makeshift spear made from a broken lamp stand. The other carried a
wide set of pretty gauze drapes serving as a net.

The thing that Stark focused on, more than their crazed dress, was the
fact that both had native dark skin. *They're* indígenas, thought Stark. *Indígenas alive in the hot zone.*

When they saw Stark, standing there like the statue of an astronaut, the
men threw themselves back against the far wall of the hallway. *"¡Chinga!"*
swore the drapery man. *"¡Ejércitos de la luna!"*

Stark realized they were hunting, and whatever the net man meant by
armies from the moon, they apparently weren't expecting to find a suited in-
truder in the computer lab. The absurd irony of it rinsed away Stark's fear.
Two Native Mexican men in the hot zone, wearing nothing more than bandanas and oven mitts, faced with an immune *norteamericano* wearing a
state-of-the-art antiviral suit. *"Soy un médico,"* said Stark.

"¿Un médico? Ridículo." The lampstand spear-carrier ducked his head as
he pushed himself away from the wall. *"¿Qué haces en este hospital?"*

The *tu* form of address that the man used could have implied anything from friendship to insulting familiarity, but Stark was glad he'd used it. It broke the tension. "I'm looking for information that I need to help stop Big Bonebreaker."

"*¿Si?*" said the spear-carrier. "*Haltará el plago nadie pero Dios.*"

Stark smiled. "Then I hope I can help God stop it."

The spear-carrier liked that answer but the drapery-net-man didn't trust Stark. He looked ready to scream and finally tugged at his friend's arm. "*Vámanos, flaco, vámanos.*" Then he could not stand it anymore and ran off down the hallway.

Before turning and following his friend, the spear-carrier said, "*Onare a Santa Domenica, la patrona de los plagos. Ahora ella está la sola quien escucha Jesuchristo.*" Then he crossed himself and vanished from the doorway.

Stark remained at the doorway until he couldn't hear their footsteps anymore. Then he returned to the memboard and waited for it to finish downloading. Outside the hospital, he could hear the two men shouting to each other as they ran down the street.

Pray to Saint Domenica, the Patron Saint of Plagues, the man had said. *She's the only one Jesus listens to now.*

A strange noise filtered down the hallway as Stark disengaged his memboard from the computer. He stuffed it into his lugall, then walked to the lab entrance and listened. It came from the elevator shaft.

A clarinet.

It was a whimsical little tune, like a Jewish wedding song. Stark took his memboard and walked slowly toward the music. When he reached the elevator bay on this floor, he stopped and cocked his ear toward the dark, yawning shaft. The clarinet warbled. The hallway lights flickered.

Then the music stopped.

In the caesura came a bellowing scream, man or woman, Stark couldn't tell, but it was wrenching. When the scream ceased, the clarinet started playing again. Stark leaned into the elevator shaft and shouted, "Hello? Do you need help?"

The clarinet music stopped again.

After a long pause, a measured voice called down, "Yes, I need some help. Please, come up here."

Stark didn't like the sound of the voice. It sounded healthy, calm, and rational—not the screamer's voice. "Where are you?" Stark called.

The sound of footsteps echoed in the shaft. The man's voice was closer, calling directly into the shaft. His voice went from neutral to plaintive. "We're on the seventh floor. We need help. Hurry!"

Oh my God, thought Stark, remembering the floor plan of the hospital. *Surgery is on the seventh floor.* He didn't understand what was happening up there, but he wanted no part of it. Stark edged toward the stairwell.

The man's voice came again. "Where are *you?*"

Stark entered the stairwell and tromped downstairs without pausing to listen.

A moment later, a door slammed open somewhere above him. Then footsteps resounded as someone flew down the steps after him.

Stark ran blind down the long, dark hall, bashing into the ceiling tiles or kites or whatever they were, almost falling. When he'd burst through the reception area and into the fully lit street, Stark ran to the store, located his 'cycle and jumped aboard. While he feebly yanked at the key, spinning it in the ignition, he looked back at Zapata and saw a figure skidding to a halt in the shadowy atrium. Stark saw the person from a safe distance, in the blaze of the midday Mexican sun, but that did nothing to still his hammering heart.

The figure was holding a clarinet in one hand and something long and sharp in the other.

A moment later, Stark was roaring down Venezuela, throttle opened. A moment after that, he was coming about over Zapata Hospital and sailing back to the sanity of La Alta.

CHAPTER

21

HIS NAKED WAIST wrapped in a scratchy, white towel, Stark was sitting on a plastic-covered couch when Isabel arrived with a fresh pair of boxers and pants for him. She stood in the blood screening room's air lock, appraising him with droll eyes.

"Don't say anything, Bela," Stark said.

"I'm glad you called me. This is quite an opportunity," she said dryly, "seeing you like this."

"Don't."

"Don't what? Make fun of a celebrity doctor for wetting himself?" she said. "I wouldn't dream."

The bloodwork technicians glanced at Isabel as she entered the lab; but their faces were blocked by their helmets, so he couldn't tell if they were laughing at him. Stark pretended to be absorbed with the memboard that held all the Zapata information he'd stolen. He *was* absorbed with the memboard. "I had a temporary lapse. OK?"

Plopping his clothes in a stack on the sofa beside him, Isabel said, "Not quite ready for big-boy pants, eh?"

They hadn't spoken since yesterday, so Stark was relieved to hear Isabel's invectives. He didn't know if that meant she was considering the recoding project, but the lighter mood was welcome—especially after what he had just seen in Zapata.

"Come on. These might be symptoms you're suffering from," Isabel said, her professional voice taking over and shifting to Spanish. *"¿Qué pasó?"*

"It's not a symptom," sighed Stark, humiliated at discussing his "accident" in Zapata. "I took a skycycle over to Perimeter Clinic Seven. I—uh—wasn't used to driving it." He glanced at her with sheepish eyes. He hated lying, even white-lying, to Isabel; it made him feel like all the death around him was creeping closer, especially after their heated words yesterday. He couldn't wait to be alone with Isabel, to show her what he had found in Zapata's computer banks. He needed her, especially her, to see what he had seen. "How much longer until we get my blood results?" Stark asked the assay technician.

"You're the one who insisted on a complete assay, Doctor. Just a few minutes more." The technician, for whatever reason, had taken an immediate dislike to Stark.

Isabel looked Stark over, curious. "Everything all right at clinic seven?"

"Fine. As far as I can tell. I'm just pregnant, that's all."

Isabel laughed. "What?"

Stark meant to say *tengo verguenza* (I'm embarrassed) but lapsed and chose the easy cognate, *estoy embarasado,* a novice Spanish speaker's mistake. He *was* rattled.

Isabel lowered her eyebrows, smiling. "Are you all right?"

He wasn't all right. No. He had gone to Zapata to find patient zero and instead had found something so outrageous that he could barely fit it in his brain. In English, Stark stammered, "I'm embarrassed. Embarrassed. *¿Comprendes, novia?* I just—I have a lot on my—oh, *here*." Stark shoved his memboard at her. He couldn't hold it back any longer. Sitting on the Zapata data was like being dealt something ominous, aces and eights, the dead man's hand, but he didn't have the fortitude to maintain a poker face.

At that moment, an orderly arrived with a new Racal-plus suit. Stark had asked for his other one to be thoroughly cleaned with antivirals.

Isabel smiled broadly at his discomfort. *"Pobrecito."*

While they waited for his assay, Isabel read the report that Stark had pulled up for her. It was marked BLACK LETTER across the top. She glanced at him, eyes rounding, then continued.

Dolores Barracon. Prostitute. Treated and released for fever and flu May 14 Zedillo Satellite Clinic. Readmitted 5:00 A.M. Zapata May 15. GP speculates dengue, so Epidemiology was contacted. Blood draw. Assay nonconfirming. Refer to Cruz. Primary: Pedro Muñoz.

Stark had loaded the report with links to the blood draw results and genome prints of this woman's virus, everything Isabel would need, he hoped, to create an effective T cell in the recoding matrix.

Isabel typed something into his memboard and handed it back to Stark. *How did you get this? It's classified.*

"I'll explain later," said Stark. He hit the genome print's link and a cascade of A's, G's, C's, and T's spilled across the little screen. Then he hit MUTATION which compared Patient Barracon's virus to the virus that Pathology had dubbed Generation T, their earliest known generation of dengue-5 to date. It was a simple computer function to determine that the two viruses were 34 percent similar.

Isabel sucked in her breath quietly, as if recognizing a rare bird in flight. "You think this might be Generation S?"

Stark glanced at the technicians in the room. After Muñoz's revelation that a nurse had told him about Stark's role on the Task Force, Stark felt surrounded by ears and eyes. He typed, *Better than that. It's either Generation One or Generation Two.* He handed the memboard back to Isabel and watched her expression as she realized their research and prospects had just taken a great leap forward. If this really was patient zero, as Muñoz had asserted last night, the question was, did Barracon's blood contain unmutated virus, straight from the trough, or were they still a step behind Joaquin Delgado? Isabel looked down and the silver light of the memboard reflected across her face shield as she read the genomic report. "Henry David," she said after a moment. "This isn't what we hope it is."

Stark had imagined that this would take several hours to analyze. "What? Why? How do you know?"

"Mutation markers." She showed him the screen but he watched her face. "Wetcoded viruses can't mutate without leaving markers. It's like a flaw in a printing press. All subsequent copies will have mutation markers." She winced. "And this genome has them."

He typed angrily, *But I'm sure that's patient zero.* He wasn't ready to tell her about Muñoz, yet.

She may be, Isabel typed back. *But she lived long enough for the virus to mutate.*

Stark deflated. The risky trip into the hot zone felt like a snipe hunt. "This still has to be worth something, right? Tell me that much."

Isabel sighed deeply and her breath rushed inside her helmet. *Oh yes. It's at least Generation Two. With Gen 2, I can predict what JD originally scripted in Gen 1. Not 100 percent. But close.*

Stark read her words. "How close, Bela?" asked Stark. "What percentage effectiveness?"

Isabel thought for a moment, called up the genomic print, and thought some more. "Maybe a nanophage with 95 percent effectiveness, if I get lucky."

It wasn't good enough. With only three days left before the next wave of infections hit, scattershot nanophages weren't the right strategy, as Isabel herself had said yesterday.

The option of the immune-recoding project floated before him—only this time, an even greater urgency raced in Stark's heart. Isabel had to see what Stark had found in Zapata.

"I want to show you something," he said. Then he brought up the file called "Grandmother Muñoz's Tripe Soup." He hesitated a moment, wondering if he should keep that to himself, confirm with Muñoz that it was what he thought it was, but realized he couldn't, realized he needed Isabel to help him bear the reality of it. "Here." Beneath the recipe's heading was a second heading, which read COLONEL XAVIER SANJUAN'S EPIDEMIC INTELLI-GENCE SERVICES REPORT TO THE HOLY RENAISSANCE.

"Dr. Stark," the snotty technician said, "you're white. Leave whenever you're ready. Please."

Isabel looked like she was shrinking inside her suit and helmet as she read, unable to mask her loathing. "What *is* this?"

"Read." Stark picked up his Racal-plus suit, his shirt, and clean clothes. "I think you'll agree we're obligated to move quickly. Let me change, then let's find Ahwaz."

The changing room was nothing more than an old broom closet. It smelled like bleach and sour antivirals. Stark kept smacking his wrists against the walls as he wrestled into his new Racal-plus suit and wondered what should be done with that memboard filled with Zapata information. They would have to download the pertinent files that Isabel needed—namely, the genomic analysis of Patient Barracon's virus.

But how to handle Sanjuan's EIS report? Delete it? Stark could appeal to no authority in Mexico. Yet as a policy statement advocating genocide, the report seemed too volatile for one person to erase or ignore. An old, quiet voice in Stark, the part of him that had grown up on his grandfather's farm in Land Reform America, wanted to protect the people targeted by this report, wanted justice. Revenge. *They let it go,* this old voice fumed. *Bastards let the virus spread just like in the Tuskegee syphilis study. Bastards should pay.*

But the archly practical Special Pathogens agent dismissed that voice. Stark couldn't afford to be a jailed whistle blower when Mexico needed him to be the best virus hunter he could be. Nor could Isabel resist any longer. The best way to make the Holy Renaissance pay was to stop the outbreak and expose this information afterward.

When Stark stepped out of the changing room, Rosangelica was standing by the ALHEPA air lock, her thin body leaning against the wall like a rifle.

Stark froze, hand on the closet doorknob. The Zapata computer terminal's warning flashed across his mind's eye as if Stark himself had a *pilone* connection to the hospital. *"The Ministry of Health is now being alerted to your request. Please wait."*

To hide his shock at seeing the *sabihonda,* Stark immediately bent over and fussed with his ankle locks. Out of the corner of his eye, he could see the memboard in Isabel's hand, perched there, brimming with damning evidence that could either get him killed or bring down a government or both. When he stood upright, Stark let his face go passive, slack, his eyes drowsy. "Rosangelica, hello." His stomach felt like a teakettle ready to whistle.

The medical staff had all found jobs on the opposite side of the screening room away from the *sabihonda.* She turned toward Stark, and he could see by her expression that she was excited about something. "I tracked you down," she said with a curt nod, seemingly pleased with herself.

He waited for her to speak again, explain herself, and give him a clue as to whether or not she knew he had been to Zapata. He came to stand by Isabel, next to the couch, and casually put a hand on her shoulder.

Beneath his hand, Isabel started. He glanced down at the memboard to see what she was reading. It was still that bastard Sanjuan's Epidemic Intelligence Report. Black Letter. He caught the words *solution to the indigenous problem.*

"Can we talk, Stark?" Rosangelica said.

She sounded eager, not her usual deadpan neutral voice. Stark was frightened of what made her eager. (*Access granted. Ministry of Health alerted.*) He inclined his head toward Isabel. "I was hoping to talk to Dr. Khushub about a recent breakthrough. Can it wait, Rosangelica?"

"A breakthrough?" She sounded surprised, honestly surprised—which was good. "I haven't heard anything new from the health boards. What breakthrough?"

Isabel was a pathetic liar but smart enough to know not to try. She looked up from the horrors contained in the EIS report, eyes blank as empty saucers.

"We're not sure what we have," Stark said. "That's why we haven't posted any reports yet." He was trying to sound frustrated, then decided to lay the groundwork for future lies. "I hope that it's Generation Two."

"Two? A number designation instead of a letter?" Rosangelica nodded. "That does sound promising."

"I hope."

"What would that mean?" Rosangelica asked.

Stark was so paranoid that he couldn't bring himself to look Rosangelica in the eye. He wished he could rub his face and hide behind his hands for a moment. Instead, he shut his eyes, playing the role of exhausted researcher. "If we're lucky, it could mean a very effective nanophage."

"And T cell," Isabel said. She showed Stark her eyes and her furious resolve. "The recoding project suddenly seems a more viable option to me."

Stark caught his breath. *Generation Two increases our odds of a successful recoding matrix, too.* Stark wanted to shout with joy when he realized what had put the fire back in those glorious eyes. Isabel Khushub, the woman who came riding into Cairo like the cavalry when it looked like smallpox was going to explode unchecked across the planet, was finally here and on his side in Mexico. *Goddamn hallelujah, baby.*

"Adorable. You two kissed and made nice. In that case, you will *definitely* want to hear what I have to say, Estarque," Rosangelica said, raising her thumb. *Out.*

Damn her. She could sound eager one minute and harsh the next. She gonna accuse me of something?

Stark said to Isabel, "Can we talk later, Doctor?"

As though released from a trap, Isabel quickly stood. "Of course. I should get back to the Institute anyway." She took a step away from the couch, leaving the memboard where she had dropped it.

"Please," Stark said, offhanded, smothering his own jolting fright, "why don't you go ahead and take that memboard? We'll discuss all the ramifications after you've had a chance to read it more thoroughly."

Isabel had no subterfuge in her. She looked like he'd asked her to pick up a scorpion. "Yes," Isabel said without moving to take it. "I can take the memboard."

"Consult with Dr. Ahwaz about this too, please," Stark said as he scooped it into her hand.

Rosangelica turned, leading them out of the screening room. Light from a high clerestory of stained-glass windows threw blue-and-yellow light down on the trio, and bells clanged as a gaggle of clamp-masked nuns on bicycles passed in the hallway's road.

Stark put a hand on Isabel's arm and gently pushed her, cueing her to get moving. "I'll call you when I'm free, Bela. We'll have plenty of time to talk later."

"Fine. That's just fine." As if unmoored from Rosangelica, Isabel started walking slowly down the hall, then, once she was a few yards away, broke into a run for the nearest elevator. The last bike-riding nun had to swerve to avoid hitting her.

Rosangelica pointed down the hallway, the opposite direction. "Let's go. We have work to do."

The *sabihonda*'s apartment was located just off Torre Cuauhtémoc's Triforium with its halls of pointed arches. Not merely the home of Mexico's Majority, its corporate elite and political power center, the Triforium was the Holy Renaissance's home turf. Cardinal de Veras and his rival church were here, and, the rumors went, the Orbegón family residence, too. Stark and Rosangelica entered a terra-cotta-tiled courtyard with palms and birds-of-paradise bobbing under ceiling fans and a slanted glass roof of red and orange.

Inside, Rosangelica's apartment was posh, just like Stark's. Her windows faced east, so the light was diffuse at this time of day, making the dark, wooden molding of her rooms ominous. As she turned on lamps, Stark couldn't read her expression. He braced himself for an onslaught of accusations. Get him alone, away from his ally Isabel, probe him. Pathology of the *sabihonda*.

After flinging back the drapes that had covered the east windows, Rosangelica went to her closet and removed a rifle case.

Stark coughed. "What do you need a gun for?"

"I spoke with my superiors," she said, "and they agreed." She removed another lugall that looked too small for clothes and books—probably ammunition by the metallic clank within.

"Agreed to what?"

Rosangelica frowned at him as if he were ill. "What do you mean 'to what'? To your proposal. To grant Sor Domenica free sanctuary in La Alta."

Stark sat down hard. He'd forgotten all about his "proposal," which had primarily been a means to get Rosangelica away from him for a few hours. He hadn't hoped in his wildest fantasies that the Holy Renaissance would actually agree to that. He listened to the clank of the ammunition packs for a moment, gathering himself. "Free sanctuary, eh? Then why do you have a Matador class rifle?"

She laughed at him. "What kind of idiot would go into the hot zone without a loaded gun?"

Stark watched her load it, slipping three different sizes of magazines into six separate chambers. The gun's power cell had the *pilone* symbol on the side, the jagged lightning bolt, and Stark wondered what sort of gun the Matador was. "The Holy Renaissance agreed to allow Domenica to make a broadcast appeal to the insurgents?" Stark asked.

"That's right. If we can find her this afternoon, we can broadcast tonight."

Stark tried to keep his thoughts from spilling out of control. "So we have to find her. OK." His inclination was to delay, go back to his room, plot. But there was no time. This was working too well. "OK then. OK. How *do* we find Domenica?"

With the rifle loaded, Rosangelica spread her hands as though revealing her winning hand. "No worries, Estarque. I know exactly where she is."

"You do? How?"

"Her long-range trinity boosts," she said, tapping her forehead. "I've been searching for her all afternoon while talking to—to my superiors. Domenica has someone very good protecting her. Very difficult to triangulate on the ground and pinpoint her signal. But I did it from orbit once I got clearance. *Sagrado servicio* really wants to know where she is, but she's as good as dead if I tell them." She zipped up her Matador.

"And this is on the level? Cazador won't disappear her once we get her back to Ascensión?" Stark said. "What assurances do I have?"

She smirked her most condescending smirk. "None."

Stark gripped the arms of his chair.

"But," Rosangelica said, laughing at his discomfort, "if we can convince Domenica to convince the insurgents to put down their arms, then the Holy Renaissance will give her sanctuary. It's in everyone's best interests, right?"

Stark edged forward on his seat with an eager lurch of his body, about to make his next flood of requests: a full-media broadcast for Domenica, Orbegón at her side, the whole dog-and-pony show so that Joaquin could see where Domenica was. But suddenly Stark saw the hole in this half-assed plan of his, a hole so wide it filled him with dread. "And if Sister Domenica doesn't agree?"

Rosangelica stared at Stark for such a long time that he wondered if she'd heard him. "You can't have it both ways, Stark," she said finally. Slow blink. Dead eyes.

Stark's chest went cold and his hands sweat. *Don't jump into the middle of anything and bullshit your way out, like you usually do,* the grandfather in his brain was saying.

"That nun is fomenting civil unrest by siding with the insurgents." Rosangelica swung the lugall full of ammo back into her closet. "You said yourself it was impeding your investigation."

Imagining that he was on a field trip to help a wetwared secret agent kill a psychotic nun, Stark wondered if the outbreak had slipped beyond his grasp. "I'll just have to convince her of the right thing to do, I guess."

"I guess you will." Rosangelica hefted her gun case.

CHAPTER

22

LONG AGO, Filomeno Mata Avenue was probably a bustling, volcanic brick-paved alley between façades of crumbling Old Money. The street might have housed modest businesses in the last century or important families in the century before that. While its buildings were still beautiful with Austrian scrollwork on the lintels, Mexico's New Money had obviously digested and forgotten this little avenue with the rise of La Alta's wealthy Gallery neighborhood, the gilded Triforium, and their *plasceron*-patios in the heavens.

Just a few blocks from the hot zone's ground zero of Zapata, this cobble-stoned Mata Avenue seemed more than forgotten. It was beautifully dead.

"Mata 11. That's her safe house, I think," Rosangelica said, standing on the sidewalk beneath a chipped and weathered stone balcony. Because of her too-straight posture, her Racal suit looked like a marionette, turning this way and that, rifle slung over one shoulder. She was scanning the street's addresses, embossed on brass plates on every blond-stone building. "It should be right here."

They had lowered their *barco* onto Tacuba Avenue and walked, looking for Filomeno Mata, where Rosangelica's satellites had told her she would find the vanguard of *Los Hijos de Marcos* and the trinity boosts that Domenica used for broadcasts. They passed the old National Art Museum and walked through its plaza, past a neat stack of twenty or so bodies near the statue of the ancient and hated Carlos IV, last Spanish king over Mexico. A man walked around the pile of corpses with a can of gasoline, dousing it. Carlos looked on.

Stark craned his neck as he passed, watching the gasoline splash. "Mata 11 is that way, I think."

"Yeah, I know, it's probably at the corner," Rosangelica said. "I have a map right in front of me."

Stark turned away as the man lit a match. He heard the whoosh of gasoline igniting. Stark told himself not to look back, but he did anyway. The stacked bodies burned, and skin ran like wax. Fatty soot unfurled from the bonfire and blew over Carlos, rendering him a silhouette in smoke.

"Did you hear me? I said, I have a map right in—"

"Yes," Stark said, nausea making his voice croak froglike for a moment. "Can we stay on task, please?"

Rosangelica lifted her face and the filter of her gas mask pointed at the sky. The greasy smoldering from a hundred bonfires lay like a lake of smoke in the sky, and the fans of the nearest La Alta tower, Tower Juárez, were drawing it in. "Look at that."

Stark didn't look. "Let's go."

Rosangelica kept her head craned back as she watched the smoke rise from the bonfire. "You know the instances of influenza and other common diseases in Ascensión have lessened since putting the tower filters on maximum output?"

"Mira," Stark spit. "I read all that. My epidemiological team wrote all that. ¡Vámanos!"

Her mask remained aimed at La Alta. "Touchy."

"Look, I just want to get off this street and find the nun." The black plume from Carlos IV's bonfire sailed over Filomeno Mata so that Stark couldn't avoid seeing it in his peripheral vision.

"Oh," said Rosangelica, following him toward the street sign that read Mata. "I get it. It's the pyre that bothers you. It's all finally getting past your filter."

Stark glared at the sabihonda, but she was right. He shouldn't have looked at that bonfire. The afterimage (red as coal skin liquefying) was still on his eye, and he could feel it stiffening him like clay in a kiln.

Rosangelica led the way down Filomeno Mata, looking for addresses set above narrow doorways of these seventeenth-century buildings. "You'd think these places would be more clearly marked. Bajador inefficiency. Que triste."

Stark fanned the air in front of him though the smoke was high overhead. "Shocking. The safe house doesn't have a street address."

"*Tss*," Rosangelica hushed him. "Take. *Sencillo. Plátano.* Pulled up another map." She sounded exasperated. "*Bueno.* I see it now. Eleven is right there." Rosangelica pointed to a building that might have once housed a telegraph office or an old Internet café, Stark imagined.

He followed the *sabihonda* to the unmarked door and stepped into a small lobby. A stack of unopened liquor crates leaned against one wall, and black tables and chairs were piled in the little foyer, as if this were a restaurant's private storage and not a storefront. They could hear chains and gears cranking to life behind the foyer's shut elevator doors.

"Someone's coming to greet us?" suggested Stark.

Rosangelica unshouldered her Matador. "They must have been watching us from above."

The doors opened and revealed an empty elevator car—empty except for a ratty Christmas poster of Orbegón with graffiti glasses and horns, and a balloon coming from his mouth saying "*¡Feliz Navidad, puta!*"

Just as Stark was trying to make sense of this message, a gun fired. The lobby's plate-glass window shattered behind them, and suddenly, Stark's face was pressed against the clear shield of his helmet after throwing himself on the ground.

"Down! Lie down!" shouted a man from the staircase.

Rosangelica scrambled to the ground next to Stark.

Several people entered the lobby, boots crunching over the shattered glass of the window. A tall man with curly red hair appeared in the doorway, and wearing an old black-rubber gas mask that shoved his hair back into a clownish halo around his head. He came to stand next to Rosangelica and kicked her hard in the ribs. "Stop accessing your sats right now!"

Stark glanced at the *sabihonda*. He didn't understand how the man knew she had satellite access, but he feared she would jeopardize their chances of meeting Domenica if she didn't do as the men asked. "Rosangelica, don't—"

"Hey!" The red-haired man looked at Stark. "So it *is* Rosangelica!" He jammed the gun barrel into the back of the *sabihonda*'s neck, crinkling the fabric hood. "I'll blow you right into the ground, right down to hell where you belong, whore of Babylon!" Then he swore a litany so creative and biblical that Stark couldn't follow him.

Rosangelica screamed. She sounded like a cat getting doused with water. "Stop it! Stop it! I'm not accessing!"

"What's happening?" shouted Stark. "What are you doing to her?"

Rosangelica groveled, clutching at the man's boots. "Stop it, please!"

"Satan's little whore," he said, flipping her over with the toe of his boot so that he could aim the gun in her face. "Came for the bounty you put on my head, is that it? Think you can bag me like a rat?"

Rosangelica's screaming continued until a second man appeared next to the redhead, looking down at the woman and glancing at the gunman under his eyelids. "Pirate, stop."

The gunman grabbed Rosangelica by the Racal suit bunching at her shoulders and hauled her to her feet. "I should kill her. I should kill her. It's the right thing to do. I should kill her. She'd have killed me. I should."

"Pirate," whispered the gunman.

"If I don't, Orbegón himself will show up to arrest the saint." Pirate's eyes were white Ping-Pong balls, bugging at Rosangelica through the goggles of his mask. Stark could see that, like worms beneath the surface, the skin around his eyes rolled and puckered.

He a sabihondo!

"If I kill her, I bet the whole war in *Tejas* grinds to a halt," Pirate shouted.

"Domenica won't like it if you kill anymore—"

"This *sabihonda* probably just alerted the whole city's militia to where we are, José!"

"I didn't access! No one knows we're here!" said Rosangelica, going limp in Pirate's grip. "You got inside my sats too fast!" She caught her breath, and said, "I swear. Check my path. I swear it."

Stark raised his helmet off the ground and looked at the two cyborgs. *Who this guy? He some sort of radical Rosangelica?*

Pirate's gun went off. Plaster rained down on Stark's head. He covered his helmet with his hands.

In the echoing quiet after the gunshot, Pirate said, "OK. Aborted path. But I got a node-dog on you, whore. It bites. You felt that. You know this gun, too, don't you?"

Rosangelica shut her eyes as if the gun were a blinding light. "I know that gun."

"Shut up. You don't know this gun," Pirate said. "I installed *i.a.* in its injection magazine. Me and the gun are brothers and we're twice as fast as you and your little Matador. Oh. But you found that out already. Access in my presence or mess with the tracer I put on your node, and the gun will target *you* and fire before I can even think," he said. Then a light from the gun's targeting eye blinked twice in her face, as if winking, identifying her. "Got the rules straight? OK. Who's with you, Rosangelica?" She relaxed in his grip and opened her mouth to speak, but he shook her again, as if to remind her how frightened she should be. "Who did you bring me?"

Stark had never heard Rosangelica sound so feeble, so terrified, as if she might burst into tears. "That's Dr. Stark—of—of the Centers for Disease Control."

"What? Henry David Stark?" Pirate handed Rosangelica to a third man. "Turn over, Dr. Stark."

Stark rolled onto his back. He was shaking as he looked up into Pirate's goggled and masked face.

"A Dr. Stark just checked out of docking bay nine in Torre Cuauhtémoc twenty minutes ago. Destination: hot zone." Pirate sighed and the barking pit bull in his voice softened. "All right. Why are you here, Dr. Stark?"

Stark wasn't sure what the right thing to say was. So he decided to try the truth. "I asked Rosangelica to help me find Sister Domenica. I need Domenica to help me end the outbreak."

In a low voice, Pirate said, "How do you expect Santa Domenica to help you?"

Stark shook his head. "I'll say what I have to say to Domenica herself."

"I'll hear you out. If it's worthwhile, I'll contact her."

Stark figured Pirate would never let them see the nun if Stark told him the whole, dangerous plan, so he reverted to the lie that he had told Rosangelica. "I need to stop two outbreaks. One is viral. The other is violent. I need Domenica to join ranks with the Holy Renaissance and ask for an end to the civil unrest in Ascensión. The Holy Renaissance has already agreed to offer her clemency."

The five other men and women in their makeshift suits scoffed loudly. One woman laughed like a mule and another man whistled his derision with a single piercing note.

But Pirate was listening. By his worried eyes, he saw the situation more clearly than his confederates did. He stepped closer to Stark and spoke low, "How many have died in the fighting?"

"I have absolutely no way of knowing who is dying of the virus," said Stark quickly, seizing on Pirate's question, "or who is dying in the street war." Which was true. "Until I can discern between the two outbreaks, I can't stop Big Bonebreaker." Which was only partially true.

Everyone in the room fidgeted, annoyed. The insurgents seemed to be losing patience with Stark, and Rosangelica clearly wanted to do the talking but her metallic eyes kept drifting to the gun targeting her.

Pirate shook his head in displeasure. "You came here with the most politically dangerous person in Mexico. I'd be doing *Los Hijos* a huge favor by killing her and I could include you in that execution for good measure, *guero*." His eyes blinked rapidly with uncontrolled anger. "Why should I believe a thing you're telling me, Dr. Stark?"

Because I'm on your side! Stark wanted to say. *I want these bloodsuckers to pay for their policy of genocide and I want to see Orbegón dead from massive DHF hemorrhaging!* But Stark needed to get through this with Rosangelica alive and trusting him, so he composed himself, saying, "Mexico is currently dying at a rate of nearly one thousand people per day, so you have no choice but to listen to me." Stark wasn't as defiant as he would have liked to sound. He was too scared that Pirate would ignore him. "The Holy Renaissance understands this. They know that they have to close ranks with Sister Domenica to stop this outbreak."

"You're a fool," said the woman who had laughed like a donkey. "The Holy Renaissance sees you as the means to imprison the Plague Saint forever. Or worse."

"No," Stark said. "With the virus running rampant through Ascensión, the Holy Renaissance sees that neither you nor they can win." Stark swallowed, and said, "Which means they apparently understand the situation better than you do."

Pirate was all bluster. The *sabihondo* considered Stark's words, large eyes scanning the ground, blinking rapidly. Pirate didn't want to be an insurgent. Stark could see he had taken on the role against his will. That was obvious in his little-boy posture and sad expression. After a pause, he gave Stark his hardest, most *macho* look, but the truth had already been revealed. "You know what happens when the epidemic ends, don't you, *yanqui*?" He pointed to Rosangelica with his gun. "You know what Orbegón has planned for the United States?"

"I was in *Tejas* before I came here," said Stark.

"And still you work on the tyrant's behalf?"

"I'm saddened by what Mexico has allowed itself to become, but, Pirate," said Stark, feeling hot in his cool Racal suit, "Big Bonebreaker will eat until it dies of natural causes if I don't stop it, and I can't do that without Domenica's help."

Pirate adjusted the gas mask. Then his goggles. He glanced at his compatriots, who were poised, practically on the balls of their toes, waiting for him to decide. Finally, Pirate's sigh whistled through his filter. "José, take my gun and keep it trained on the *puta primera,*" Pirate said, handing the rifle to his second.

Stark wondered if Pirate was making a mistake, leaving Rosangelica out of his sight. But by the way Rosangelica stared at Pirate's gun in the other man's hands, she wasn't wondering the same thing.

"Get in, Stark," Pirate said, pointing to the elevator's open doors. "I'm taking you to see the saint."

The elevator creaked with rust and disuse and came to an abrupt halt that almost knocked Stark off his feet. When the doors opened, he found himself face-to-face with a Lockheed-Pemex pyramid logo. A door-sized air lock prevented him from leaving the elevator. "Where did you get the ALHEPA?" he asked, impressed.

Pirate opened the air lock for his guest. "Got it from an abandoned field clinic by Chapultepec Park." Beyond the air lock was a little room whose other exit was yet another cutting-edge air lock. "Be so kind as to remove your suit."

This was Stark's second suit of the day. "Will I get it back?"

Pirate removed his gas mask. He was a good-looking young man with a Roman nose and a week's worth of beard. The subcutaneous wires around his eyes veined and shifted as he grinned like a wolf. "I don't steal, I forage."

Stark unlocked his cuff and collar locks, letting hisses of air into the room. "Some might call taking ALHEPAs stealing."

"That's the chief benefit of working for a saint," said Pirate. "Instant absolution."

"You keep calling her a saint, but . . ."

"A title of affection," Pirate said, waiting as Stark shed his suit. "Neither Cardinal de Veras nor the Vatican has officially recognized her, but the people know what she is to them. *La Patrona de los Plagos,*" he said. "Domenica has just one rule for visitors and comrades. Don't ask her about the prophecies."

"Why not?" Stark asked, draping his suit over a bench. He found a spritz
bottle marked bleach and disinfected his suit and helmet.

"They are precious to her and not up for debate. That's part of why she
has not been canonized. She refuses to verify or renounce her visions," said
Pirate. "Believe them or don't, it's all the same to her. Now. One last question."

"Yes."

"Whose side are you really on, Doctor?"

In the clean, neutral protection of the air lock, all viruses, wetwared
spies, and fascist officers of the Renaissance at bay, Stark finally felt safe
enough to tell the truth. "I always appreciate," he said, "a spirited struggle
against superior force."

Pirate smiled his wolfish smile. "Then let's go."

The air lock opened into what was either a dance club converted into a
church or a church that had crossbred with a nightclub. An old bar ran the
length of one wall on the left-hand side of the room, and an ancient disco
ball lay broken like a cracked egg on the right. The windows were sealed up
with thick gobs of plaster over the glass and frames and black wooden floors
and black walls made it look late-nineties American *noir*. The far wall was
devoted to the *Virgen de Guadalupe* as she had once been worshipped in
Mexico, before the Holy Renaissance: A kind image of the dark-skinned
Madonna, as she had appeared to the Nahuatl Indian Don Diego, seemed to
beatify this dark disco. In an arc over her head were painted roses, and
spikes of gold suggesting a halo crowned her. Candles lit the altar before the
Madonna's painting, and before the altar sat twenty-five young men and
women. Most were praying, though many sat with plates of food and bottles
of water. A shocking number of US M-32 machine guns sat piled against
one empty black wall.

Los Hijos de Marcos, Stark thought.

Pirate turned to Stark. "This used to be a gay bar. The oldest in Ascensión. Can you believe that?"

"Gays in Mexico come well armed."

"Part of life in the hot zone," Pirate said. "We shelter the *contralunas* here,
the street fighters who take on the Holy Renaissance moon troops. Have you
heard about *los ejércitos de la luna*?"

"Someone mentioned them to me earlier today."

"They're conducting a pogrom in La Baja, murdering the poor and *los in-dígenas* who survive Big Bonebreaker." He raised his finger. "Don't let any-one tell you otherwise: The Mexican government has been fighting its own Indian populations since the arrival of the conquistadors." He nodded to the guns as he stepped away from Stark. "There's *our* spirited struggle."

Stark watched as one man, a slender *indígena* with a deeply lined face, counted the weapons and boxes of ammunition. He looked rather old, but tough and resilient like a bullwhip. He had an unlit cigarette between the fingers of one hand while he wrote down numbers on paper with the other. Stark noted a black ski mask in the man's back pocket, a symbol of Mexican rebellion as old as Stark's own grandfather.

The man caught Stark looking at him and gave a slight wave with the hand holding the unlit cigarette.

Pirate whistled sharply through his teeth. "Everyone, we're packing up! We're not in immediate danger, but I'll be breaking down the particle ar-resters and air locks in forty-five minutes."

The crowd of people before the painting of the Virgin stood and swarmed toward Pirate. "*¿Qué pasó, q'pasó?*" What happened? They empha-sized the O so that it sounded like a chorus of "oh-oh" to Stark. They gawked at Pirate and Stark, waiting for explanation.

The old *indígena* turned to Pirate, held the hand-rolled cigarette as if he were about to smoke it, and considered the *sabihondo* through squinting eyes.

"You all know where the next safe house is." Pirate clapped his hands, but no one moved.

The *indígena* lifted his cigarette and called out, "*¡Vámanos!* You heard the know-it-all."

At once, the room boiled into action, but before they dispersed, Stark could see heads turning as someone pushed through the crowd. When the force that cut that wake appeared, Stark immediately recognized her, but he wasn't prepared for her presence. Standing before her was like standing in the presence of a queen, though she was shorter and older than Stark ex-pected, with streaks of gray in her long, braided hair.

"Antonio, what is this?" she said to the weapons man. She had reading glasses that hung on a chain around her neck. "You give the order without telling *me*?"

Antonio gestured to Pirate with his cold cigarette. "The know-it-all has been out hunting."

Domenica spread her hands and shrugged, looking back at Pirate. Her eyes flicked like wet matches on his face, but when she met Stark's eyes: fire. "Dr. Stark?"

How does she know me? He nodded to the nun, unable to form a greeting or an introduction.

"Dr. Henry David Stark came here with someone who was helping him track you down," Pirate said.

"A *sabihondo*?" asked Antonio, stepping closer to Pirate on well-oiled work boots. "Or should I say, a *sabihonda*?"

Pirate nodded. "That's right."

Domenica crossed herself.

Old Antonio looked like he really wanted a drag off his cigarette. "I'll get the weapons packed," he said, loping away on his long stride.

As Domenica looked at Stark again, her eyes went from black and blazing to two wet drops of ink. "Why?" She implored him with a voice filled with sadness. "Why would you bring Rosangelica straight to us, Dr. Stark?"

Stark wanted to ask how she knew his name, or Rosangelica's for that matter; but clearly Domenica and Pirate had already accelerated beyond the need for such questions, and he felt compelled to keep up with them. The church of insurgents hustling around him and breaking down their safe house added to the feeling that he was standing still in their presence. "I—I didn't bring Rosangelica to harm anyone."

Domenica suddenly looked at Stark as if he were a phantom bearing a message. "What *are* you doing here?"

The back of Stark's neck felt icy cold. He had the distinct feeling that Domenica already knew what he was going to ask her. "I came to ask you a question. A favor."

Pirate waved for Stark to be quiet. "Wait." He motioned for Domenica and Stark to follow him. "Come."

He led them past the bar and past another air lock. Beyond was an old kitchen, though now it served as a mini–hot lab. Through the kitchen door's windows, Stark could see two people in suits analyzing slides beneath DA scopes set up next to an industrial dishwasher. Pirate hit an intercom switch, and said, "We're breaking down! Finish up and start packing."

Domenica and Pirate led Stark to what must have been an old office. It had been soundproofed with multiple layers of cardboard and Styrofoam. A small sat camera and several other pieces of equipment that Stark didn't recognize sat with blinking green lights on a beat-up desk. A console near the camera had a memboard attached. Stark saw that it read, TRINITY BOOST = NO LINK.

Pirate took a hand-printed sign that read QUIET! and put it on the outside handle of the studio door, then shut it behind him as he left.

"All right, Dr. Stark, you've got my attention," Domenica said. She sat down on the upholstered sage green couch positioned before the camera.

Stark looked at the camera. "We aren't really uplinked, are we?"

She grinned the famous, too-wide smile. "No, Doctor. We're alone, I promise." She indicated a rolling chair with a wide seat and deeply curved back. "Now let's talk about this favor you want to ask me."

Stark sat. He folded his hands. He looked up into the nun's face and saw that she was looking at him as if she were waiting for him to pronounce a death sentence. "You knew I was coming, didn't you."

"I was told something. But this is the wrong time, I thought." She concentrated hard for a moment, then shook her head and clasped her hands between her knees like an awkward adolescent.

The cyborgs were bad enough; now he was dealing with someone who heard a whole different frequency of voices in her head. "I need you to help me end this outbreak," Stark said. "You're the only one who can do it."

Domenica touched her chin. "Me? Why?"

Though there were moments of breakthrough and success, most of epidemiology was a statistical game, supported by the tedious examination of hard evidence. Stark had never strayed further from the game than he had in this outbreak, this moment. "Domenica, I haven't told anyone what I'm about to tell you, but I swear to you that it's the whole truth as I know it," Stark said, "even though you may hear me say otherwise later. Do you understand?"

"You're dealing with people like Rosangelica and *El Jefe*," Domenica said. "Lying is a misdemeanor sin."

"OK. Here it is. The virus was designed and wetcoded by a terrorist—a colleague and a former friend of mine. His name is Joaquin Delgado and he's a Spaniard just as you—'foresaw,' I guess. His viruses attack a Native Mexican immune response and the *pilone* wetware, making your country about eighty percent susceptible to the virus. I am certain that Joaquin is still here, still walking through the streets of Ascensión, probably through this very hot zone, looking people in the eye and infecting them. For all I know he could be one of your people, in this very building."

She sneered in disgust, her mouth agape. "Among my people? Why would you suggest such a thing?"

"Because Joaquin Delgado is after you, Domenica." Stark went on to explain how early Big Bonebreaker patients had attended Domenica's mass at the Church of Our Lady of Perpetual Sorrows. The Basilica workers. Father Gasapardo and the others. He explained how he had gone to Zapata Hospital himself based on all this information and found patient zero, despite the Holy Renaissance's best efforts to thwart him. He explained how he and Isabel had discovered Generation Two with the information he stole from Zapata. "Now, that's the truth as only I know it, Sister, and it's as close as we've gotten to Joaquin without having the man himself. But it's not enough. We need virus fresh from Joaquin's body to end this outbreak. We need Joaquin." Stark wanted to touch his injured lip. Healing nicely, it hurt when he spoke too much, and speaking Joaquin's name aloud made him want to be quiet now.

Domenica's hand rested on her chest, just below her throat for a long moment. Together, they listened to the faint, faraway sounds of mobilization beyond the badly soundproofed room, the crank of the freight elevators, and the shuffling of boots as men lifted heavy loads together. Stark watched Domenica closely. Her jaw clenched as she thought about everything Stark had told her. "You think he's still after me?"

"If the statistics don't lie, then they show—"

She shook her head frantically. "No. Tell me what you *believe*. You know him personally. Is he still after me?"

Stark sat still and realized that his upper body was nodding, not with affirmation, but with his pulse. "I don't think he'll stop searching for you until he finally lays a hand on you." Stark smirked at himself. "How's that for prophecy?"

Domenica examined Stark with her ink-drop eyes, so dark and wet that it seemed they would bleed down her cheeks in trails of black. Suddenly, her face hardened into a semblance of the queenly woman who had greeted him moments ago. "You want me to act as bait, don't you, Dr. Stark?"

"Yes, I do. I want you to come with me back to Torre Cuauhtémoc."

Stark turned as if he might see the towers from this secret room. "I want you to appear on a netcast so that Joaquin can see where you are."

She looked cornered. "Antonio and *Los Hijos de Marcos* won't like that."

"Antonio—who is he?" asked Stark.

"The old fellow who was counting the guns. He's a Purépecha elder and leader of *Los Hijos*," said Domenica. "Is there no other way? Can't you make a cure? A vaccine?"

"Modern medicine is miraculous," said Stark. "But Joaquin knows all our tricks. We need the virus to make a vaccine. We need Joaquin to get the virus." He sighed deep, saying, "And we need you to get Joaquin."

Domenica considered Stark for a long, uncomfortable moment, during which he felt certain she could see through him to the foam at the back of his antiviral helmet. Finally, she said, "You're a farmer."

Stark's head shot back as if she'd jabbed him in the face. "Yes. That's right. Well, I grew up on a farm."

"You're a farmer," Domenica said. "I've worked with farmers from New Mexico to Nicaragua. It's in the way you speak, your hands, the way you stand."

Stark imagined Grandfather saying that American agriculture was doomed if Henry David was a farmer. "I grew up on a cooperative farm"— he smiled—"in Wisconsin."

"I worked on a *quop* in New Mexico," Domenica said. "All certified heirloom seed."

"That was my grandfather's initiative in the push for Land Reform," Stark said, seizing the chance to brag.

"Oil and food are at a premium these days. Orbegón doesn't hide his lust for the United States' arable land," Domenica said, "and if Mexico breaks through *Tejas*, they won't waste time with your gold-mold-infested farms. They'll come for the functioning cooperatives and Land Reform farms." Those eyes. Those penetrating, damning eyes. "Why help them take your land, Dr. Stark?"

Stark lifted one shoulder, a shrug of defiance and dismissal. "I'm a dumb American. They don't frighten me."

"They frighten us, Doctor." Domenica scooted forward and took his hand in hers. "What *does* frighten you?"

Stark felt sardonic, angry that she was playing nun with him, trying to "reach" him. "What if Joaquin has already left Mexico and we're too late to do anything about it?" He raised his eyebrows at her. "How's that for scary?"

Domenica looked so comically frightened with her dark eyes and large mouth that Stark laughed.

He took his hand back and pointed at her. "What scares me is you not coming back to La Alta with me, Domenica, because if you and I don't stop Joaquin," Stark said, "then he wins, and this is the end of Mexico." He stood up and suddenly felt the pressing urge to flee this place and get back to the National Institute. He glanced at the soundproofed door, heard running outside, then gave Domenica his best urgent look. "Please, Sister. We don't have time to talk about politics and farming anymore."

She stood and looked wobbly, light-headed. Stark offered his hand but she refused it. "I can see that." She went to the door and opened it. Outside, Pirate and old Antonio were talking and Pirate locked eyes with Domenica.

Domenica said, "I'm going with Dr. Stark."

Pirate lowered his head and closed his eyes.

"What? Where are you going?" Antonio asked, his voice hard and resonant.

Domenica put her hands on Antonio's and Pirate's shoulders, and they walked down the black hallway together, with Stark walking slowly behind. "I have to explain something to you two."

CHAPTER

23

NO ONE LIVED in the Villa anymore. That was the family's old name for the house of walls painted bright yellow, of hydrangea gardens and potted rubber trees. An open roof and three floors of balconies looked down on a patio of rust-red tiles—a sunny, peaceful retreat in what was once the banking district of downtown Mexico City.

Joaquin Delgado came to the Villa after stumbling down highways jammed with cars fleeing the city and lined with dazed penitents holding, as he did, heavy whips in one hand. The priest with the black-wool robes and deep eye sockets called to those in the cars, begging them to join the procession. The sound of lashing and gasps of pain became the whole world. The magic number was thirty-nine. Thirty-nine *Aves*. Thirty-nine lashes.

But each member of that mad procession died, either from blood loss, or with buboes bulging like clumps of poisonous mushrooms in their armpits and necks. Soon, even the insane priest who had guided them, screaming his bizarre chant of Spanish and Latin, lay down to die on the side of the highway. The fanning skirts of his cape were spread like black wings, his final *Ave* a wet, coughing prayer.

Walking. Walking. Walking. Walking in a life-circle.

Back to the Villa.

Congested downtown life had vanished, and now traffic rivered in every direction from the city. Whole neighborhoods, like this one, were lonely with the sound of wind blowing newspapers in somersaults up empty streets. The lock on the Villa's door was easily forced. Someone had recently abandoned the house, leaving with it pictures of a family of four children, three *indígena* housekeepers, a mother. Not Joaquin's family, but a comforting nucleus nonetheless. The furniture in the living room was lustrous *mundo-baroque* of dark, hard rain-forest wood. The rubber trees nodded in desultory breezes—bigger, broader in leaf, but somehow true to memory. They leaned toward Joaquin as he walked onto the patio. The red-ceramic floor tiles were the same. He lay down and pressed his hot body against their cool surfaces.

Then the dreams came again. *Walking. A colonnade of doors and an angry snap of leather and wire. Thirty-nine times. Then a prayer to San Felipe, Patron of Ascensión.*

Joaquin scalded the smooth tiles with his body. When he shifted to find a cool spot, the shell of scabs on his back cracked open.

"*Virus y veneno y virus y veneno,*" *the mad, dead priest intoned, taking Joaquin's good hand, dragging him to his feet, and guiding him down the colonnade of doors. Cape swirling, he stopped and opened one to reveal a small sailboat tossing on a river of lava, coursing down a mountain slope.* "*You are different from all the others,*" *the vampire priest said.* "*You understand that immunity is a matriarchy. That you are poison.*"

"*Virus sum,*" *Joaquin agreed and wrote it on the wall of his childhood bedroom.*

"Wrote" *it? No, he would* write *it. That hadn't happened yet.*

Joaquin pushed his body away from the tiled patio floor. The sun had extinguished itself, and his body shivered in the cold, mountain night. He had never seen stars from his childhood home before, but with this part of Ascensión powerless, he could see a spray of silver overhead. More cracks opened in the scabs upon his back, and he felt breeze on fresh blood as he went into the Villa. He walked upstairs, found that his old room had a child's bed in it, and fell asleep on its cold sheets.

Another door, down the colonnade. Turquoise sky vaulted over a hill of lion-colored grass, and the smell of sagebrush scorched the wind. Like the center of a flaming jet, the sun became a crown of spikes jutting from the heavens. Joaquin stood looking at the sky through the magic door.

A woman stood on the hill's dry hay, looking up at the shining corona. Over her head she wore a light blue shawl with a yellow hem, embroidered with stars. Her smile was bright against her dark skin, a swath of cream in coffee. She lifted her hand, beckoning him. "*Do you know who I am?*" *she asked in her musical voice.*

There was a metaphysical force in the world, Joaquin knew. He had jokingly called it the "Matriarch," in his days as a graduate student in Monterrey, but, in lecture, he alternately called it the Virgin of Guadalupe, Mother Mary, or even Tonanzin, an Aztec mother goddess. The name was arbitrary to the young Joaquin; the Matriarch's power was not: Immunity. "Yes," Joaquin whispered, "I know you."

Joaquin smelled roses as she lifted her shawl and draped it over her shoulders. She pulled him into her arms and they looked at the magnificent sun together. The Matriarch was selfless, existing only to protect and defend. But she was utterly self-indulgent, too, an enclosed soul. She was fearful of foreigners and fiercely tribal—reactionary, slumbering in repose when there was no enemy, but crushing in her response when a foe intruded on her sacred earth. "You can always call on me," she whispered, stroking Joaquin's arm, "whether you have a wish or a problem. Call, and I shall come."

Joaquin twisted in her arms and looked into her oval face. She was the greatest advocate of humanity. In Joaquin's work as a viral therapist, however, the Matriarch was ever his adversary. "You would help even me, señorita?"

The beautiful woman looked up at the heavenly display. But when she looked back, she had a white visage with hollow eyes, lascivious tongue, and snapping fangs. "Oh, oh, yes, especially you, my dearest." *Scowling into his face, a word was written backwards on her forehead.*

Joaquin recoiled, but she had him in her arms now. "No!" *cried Joaquin, trying to pull away. This woman was a petty advocate for humanity, at best. She stood at the body's gate, the high priestess of a destructrix cult, standing against the virus, never understanding the irony of her existence, never learning from the exchange between her precious self and the viral enemy, except to catalog its DNA in the sacred scrolls of her memory.*

The Matriarch held Joaquin in her iron embrace, yelling, an operatic scream rising in vaulted thirds, and her breath was fetid with the smell of viruses and death devoured. She squeezed him until Joaquin's breath escaped in a heave. "You're killing me," *he gasped.*

She laughed a husky, aroused laugh. "I must know you." *Suddenly he recognized the backward word on her forehead: It was his own name.* "Never fear. Am I not here, I that am your Mother?"

Fever dreams, Joaquin thought, surfacing from sleep's lava. *The Matriarch comes for me when I'm weak. Joaquin would never dethrone her with his work, for her power was a legacy. She was all mothers, from across time. She was a list of the viruses killed, bacteria eradicated. The sum tally of a mother's active immunity was logged in the memory of her lymphocytes. When those cells crossed the placenta into the fetal bloodstream, a pregnant mother conferred this bestiary of viruses and bacteria to her child—along with the bestiary from her mother before, and her mother's mother in an ancient litany. Without this matriarchy, Joaquin knew, there would be no immunity in the world. Mother to daughter, mother to daughter—here is what our bodies know. Here is what we have fought and killed, for generations before you were born. Take my blood. There. Now you are protected.*

She was strong and he was too weak. He could never overthrow her and she would never abdicate.

But she could be fooled.

"Help me," wheezed Joaquin into her ear. "Ave Madre."

The Matriarch faltered. Her grip slackened. The rotten breath exhausted and that kind voice of shimmering arpeggios and incense returned. "Oh, my poor child."

Far away, a rhythm of codons infected an old Spaniard in London, like a tune played in another room. The old scientist sat bent before the gel screens in his workroom, scrolling through genomes, J. S. Bach tolling his uniform measures from the computer.

"My poor, poor baby," cooed the Matriarch, coddling Joaquin. *"Come to me."*

Searching for a viral vehicle in which to mount tools to aid patients in postsurgical recovery, the old scientist examined the genome for the fourth serotype of dengue, found nothing of use, then moved on to the Potosi virus, then the Machupo. Green Bay flu. Adenovirus. But as he searched, an unexpressed code rattled in the old man's mind, railing against the orderliness of the other viruses and the perfection of Bach's concertos. What was it? Was it from a natural genome, dengue perhaps, or a code of his own design? Where had he heard it before? He pulled up that genome again, dengue-4, and watched it cascade down his liquid screen, but couldn't find the sequence that haunted him. Codons beat like drums in a song whose name escaped, but whose rhythm snagged the memory, the body.

He finally remembered what the sequence was, and Joaquin shoved himself away from his computer. "God bless me." He folded his arms, eyes shut, picturing the sequence on his mind's screen. It wasn't a genome, as he had thought, but a *break* with genome. It was a rhythm that had been drilled into his head as a graduate student at La Universidad Catolica in Monterrey, Mexico. Young Joaquin's task had been to develop a method of convincing the body not to reject newly developed wetware. He couldn't find a universal passkey past the "matriarchy," as he thought of the immune system, but the resourceful, callow researcher found the next best thing. Since nearly 80 percent of *mestizos* drew their native blood from six Mexican *indígena* nations (Otomí, Mazahua, Mazatec, Nahuatl, Mixtec, and Zapoteco), he discovered a serviceable sequence in the MHC I complex, a body's self-identifying protein. With neutered viruses targeting the native sequence, he was able to develop a therapy that would trick the average Mexican's immune system into thinking a foreign entity (in this case, a newly developed brain implant) was actually part of the body's own system—thus "indianizing" any body.

Self and Not Self. Blur the line. Fool the Matriarch.

Joaquin erased the Machupo genome from his silver gel screens. He silenced Bach and stood listening to the broken rhythm that had been playing in his head, beholding its fractured perfection.

The Native Mexican sequence was *in* the dengue virus's DNA. Unexpressed and rearranged, yes, virtually useless, true, but like an Inquisition-era cathedral in modern Mexico, or broken Mayan pottery in the heart of Spain, the sequences were present in virus and human protein both. Twin DNA in diametrically opposed cells. Perfect.

"You are killing me," Joaquin whispered to the Matriarch.

"Pobrecito." *She sighed and relaxed, accepting his embrace, melting into his arms. "How could I have been so careless as to harm you, my baby?"*

Absent from his own body's movements, the old man picked up his suit coat, his keys, locked his offices, and walked down to a seaside café. An ocean storm was skimming the Catalonia coast. Lightning broke in its dark blue heart. The scientist sat at his favorite table near the window. By the time he had received his espresso, the war plan was manifest, leaping from his mind like Minerva from the cloven skull.

Joaquin removed the Matriarch's blue mantle, let it fall from his hand. "You wanted to make me your enemy." He ripped away her dress and shoved her to the ground. He drank in the sight of her ripe breasts and trembling limbs. "You wanted to kill me."

She did not flee from him, but she wept. "I know."

He threw himself on top of her, and said, "Now you will help me."

When the Spanish conquered Mexico, they took something more precious than gold. They took for their children the immunity of the vanquished Indians. Cortés was the first to steal this immunity when he took his *indígena* bride, a woman named Malintzin Tenepal. *La Malinche*, history would call her. A female Judas. Cortés and Malintzin's child was the first *mestizo*, the first modern Mexican; and the children of the first conquistadors, with Spanish fathers and Native mothers, were graced with the immunological mysteries of survival in Mexico.

Otomí, Mazahua, Mazatec, Nahuatl, Mixtec, Zapotec.

Which was the original DNA sequence, the viral code or the human one? Joaquin wondered, watching bright sardine boats cut their white sails against the blackening sky, fleeing before the Mediterranean storm. No matter. This was the answer, and it swarmed over a split in Joaquin, stitching shut his soul over the wound of Mexico. It had been decades since he felt anything like hope. As the *wunderkind* student, Joaquin believed his work on the *pilone* would be a weapon against that rising fascism of the new party, the Holy Renaissance. Mexico was vibrant with a populist political rebirth, artists, and millions of skeptical students, none of whom would stand for Orbegón or de Veras's perversion of the Catholic Church. The *pilone* would be a tool for intellectuals, researchers, and academicians—a fluid library coursing through the minds of millions. Joaquin joined the opposition to counter *Be fruitful and multiply*, the Holy Renaissance's battle cry. But members of Orbegón's party came to power in Monterrey and seized the *pilone* research from La Universidad Catolica, crushing Joaquin's dreams of a truer renaissance in Mexico.

"The viral therapy is just a shortcut," he'd warned Orbegón, then the brash mayor of Monterrey, pleading with him not to start work on a *pilone* net. "It isn't finished."

"*Ya basta,*" joked Orbegón, stealing an old *indígena* battle cry. It would be enough, and he was right. The *pilone* network would help the dictator-to-be leash Mexico, and Orbegón's future was lashed to something more dynamic than patriotism. Hope collapsed in Joaquin as he watched young Catholics ignore the admonitions of Pope Santiago I, crossing into de Veras's Catholicism and signing up for the implant surgery, paid for by the Holy Renaissance.

Joaquin's hips drove forward between the Matriarch's spread thighs. She pleaded with him to stop, but he would not stop until he had taken her, until he had given her everything.

Orbegón had personally offered Joaquin an office in the Holy Renaissance. Colleagues at La Universidad wanted to use the methods Joaquin pioneered to implant even stronger hookups, with denser central servers, DNA-based computers, satellite relays. They also wanted to use his viral therapy to "indianize" non-Mexicans, so that anyone could use the *pilone*. It never crossed Joaquin's mind to accept the offer. He left Mexico the day after Orbegón officially changed the name of Mexico City to Ascensión, less a religious name than an arrogant acknowledgment of the dictator's rise to power.

Time healed nothing. Though half his life had passed since then, Joaquin still despised Orbegón for perverting his science, his church, his adopted country. He hated the Mexican people for their weakness and greed. He hated their willingness to have their minds and bodies infiltrated by the dictator. He hated de Veras's church, which implored Mexico's women for more children, to make their country the Western Hemisphere's sole superpower with an even bigger population. He hated it that he was responsible for finding the genomic sequence that made the mark of the Beast, the *pilone,* a reality.

The dark sky and water made a mirror of the seaside café's window. Joaquin had grown accustomed to looking away from his reflection in these later years, unwilling to see the deep circles under his eyes, the slight sag of flesh on his throat. The *wunderkind* was gone. His smooth, young face and long ringlets of raven hair appeared only in old photographs now. Joaquin had fled Mexico, the United States, and field epidemiology, one after the other—all in various forms of protest, supposedly. But all that running had merely transformed the angry young man into a timid old scientist with a comfortable business and a roomful of industry awards. It made him as melancholy as Quixote at the end of his opera, crying his final aria over an ironic blast of brass, unwilling to face either his own reflection in the Knight of Mirrors' armor or the fantastical world that the Don himself had shaped.

The vampire priest appeared. "Look what you have done." He guided Joaquin away from the sun-scorched, grassy hill where he had raped the Matriarch. "Evil boy!" He slammed the door shut on that hill and handed Joaquin a whip. "Now. Again. Thirty-nine more."

The dream lash fell and his own hideous scream woke Joaquin. He remembered that he was back in his childhood home, back in the Villa, as his father had called it. Joaquin looked at his fist and opened his hand. He was carrying a little crucifix, which he set on the table next to his bed.

Joaquin went to the bathroom and found a box of things marked BAÑO in capital letters, as if prepared for a move, then left in haste. He cleaned his back as best he could with linens, then lowered himself into a tub of water mixed with a bottle of hydrogen peroxide. He could barely stand the sting, the lap of water on his cut back excruciating. After letting the bloody water drain from the tub, Joaquin dried himself. Like a somnambulist, he walked downstairs in search of food and found three ripe avocados and a netmonitor. He hooked up the monitor in his bedroom and lay on his stomach while he cut open the avocados.

A netcast of the preposterously tall President Orbegón was on. Ascensión had been quarantined, and the international community had quarantined Mexico. Good. In the capital, sixty-seven hundred had died since the outbreak began—nearly ninety-eight hundred nationwide. Orbegón declared that he had allowed agents from the Pan-Islamic Virological Institute to visit the devastation in Ascensión. But he declared that America and the EU had started a war by releasing Big Bonebreaker into Mexico, and he demanded to see the work records of all their wetcoders for the last two years.

Joaquin cut the pit out of an avocado.

"Our critics have claimed," Orbegón was saying, "that we are oblivious to the plight of the poor, that we deliberately underestimated the virulence of Big Bonebreaker when it first appeared. Nothing could be further from the truth. We are struggling with technology beyond our knowledge, friends, dispatched upon us by an outlaw nation desperate to recapture its past glory. I extend my hand to those Mexicans who have been hurt most by this plague, in both apology for our ineffectiveness and in hopes that you will join with me in rebuilding our great capital. Mexico is always growing, ever expanding. There is always a place for you at Mexico's table."

"Ever expanding?" scoffed Joaquin. "Like a cancer."

"A vocal critic of the Holy Renaissance has set aside her arguments and joined with us today," Orbegón said. "Sister Domenica is the most popular religious figure in a very religious land. Her compassion for *los destitutos* is worthy of Santa Teresa of Calcutta. She has joined us in the Federal Cloister to deliver a message to all of Mexico, and she has our blessing to speak her heart."

The camera pulled back, and there she was.

The nun.

Joaquin stopped moving, a halved avocado in one hand, the slippery pit in the other.

"Thank you, Mr. President," she said in her high, violin voice.

"The Holy Renaissance is grateful for your cooperation, Sister," Orbegón said. Their voices were like an absurd duet in Joaquin's ears, Orbegón's comic bass to the Malinche's searing soprano.

"Mexicanistas," said Sister Domenica. She wore Cardinal de Veras's symbol, a tin heart of Jesus the Conquistador, on her deep blue blouse. The traitor. The traitorous bitch. "I am here with President Orbegón today to beseech *Los Hijos de Marcos* and the *Indígena* Insurgent Army to suspend their aggressions toward the Mexican military, particularly in the hot zones of the capital. You have nothing to gain in this conflict, *compadres.* The president's Outbreak Task Force cannot mount an effective response to the virus while you fight."

Joaquin edged closer to the monitor, wincing with the movement.

The nun's face went smooth with a peacefulness that seemed to sigh from behind her eyes. *"Mexicanistas,* this virus was created to target a genetic code inherent in Native Mexicans, which means it will attack *mestizos* and *indígenas* alike. Mexico, you must stop fighting yourselves and admit this one great truth: The virus does not discern between *blancos* and *indígenas.* What divides the *indígena* from the *mestizo* cuts Mexico in half."

She made it sound as if the viruses were created to kill Indians, as if Joaquin were a racist. *I wanted the* pilone, *not Indians.* Joaquin set down the pitted avocado. *I wanted to destroy the government that you're protecting, Malinchiste!*

"That which infects the *indígena* infects us all," she said, raising her voice until she was almost singing.

A disturbance of voices shouting dissent and approval rose somewhere behind the cameras. Domenica was playing a dangerous game, Joaquin figured, pretending to "join" the Holy Renaissance, only to use this press conference as a means to push her pro-*indígena* agenda.

The emblem of Torre Cuauhtémoc behind her, Domenica shouted over the shouting in the studio with: "What kills the *indígena* kills all of Mexico!"

Orbegón, behind the nun, looked anxious for his safety as a commotion broke out behind the cameras.

It was the pilone *I was after,* thought Joaquin. *I am not a racist.*

A heartbeat later, the tumult behind the cameras passed. Domenica said, "Though it does not have a cure—yet—the Task Force is responding swiftly and with all its might. They are exhausting all supplies and all their energy now, mounting a single, massive response. Because the world has quarantined us, we must stop quarreling and save Mexico ourselves."

This was CDC talk, CDC language. Immune system as *leitmotif*. Health institutes mounting responses with swiftness and unity of purpose. Joaquin cracked his knuckles. *Mexico is secretly doing business with a US agency. I wonder if they pursuaded Henry David to come here, after all.*

"Hold your rosaries up tonight. Say thirteen *Ave Marias* at sunset for the Blessed Virgin of Guadalupe. Obey the curfew. Obey the military rule in the hot zone, *Mexicanistas,* and follow the orders of Emil Orbegón and his Task Force."

Joaquin tried to stand up but couldn't. He looked hard at the screen. Was that really the same girl he had seen at the Capilla? The one who had called for resistance to the Holy Renaissance? "How dare you, *Malinche*? How dare you in the midst of this atrocity betray your people and side with that devil?" Joaquin screwed his eyes shut and rubbed his face. "The world is backwards and upside down if God has sided with her and the dictatorship."

"A cure is coming, *Mexicanistas.* I swear to you. This is God's promise spoken to me through the woman in white." Domenica took a step back and stood side by side with Emil Orbegón. She put her arm around him in a half hug.

Orbegón shouted, "We will have the *pilone* network functioning within days, my friends. *¡Viva El Renacimiento!*"

Joaquin flinched in disgust. The woman whom the Virgin had chosen was hugging that despot, that fiend. God shunned Joaquin, but He would send the Virgin to that nun, and send that treacherous, profane, *Malinchiste* to the tyrant.

The pilone *net will be back up in days.*

Joaquin turned away from the screen. He stood up and went to the window that overlooked downtown Ascensión. With ion-scrubbers disabled, the city was smoky and dank, as filthy as he remembered it when he was six. Nonetheless, the shining spikes of green, the towers of La Alta, remained like nails driven into the bones of Mexico. Sixty-eight hundred deaths in a week and it still wasn't enough to alter Orbegón's skyline.

"God spoke to her. To *her*?" Joaquin clapped his hands and stalked away from the window, then back, gripping the sill in fury. "Why would You choose a traitor?" He pushed himself away from the sill again and picked up the monitor with great effort. He staggered with it for a moment, then threw it out the window, watching it burst and smoke in the street. His crucifix pin followed a moment later. A moment after that, his fail-safe syringe full of palitoxin sailed out the window. "*I* am fighting the true epidemic in this country, and I'll fight God to eradicate it, if I have to."

The netmonitor was gone, but in his mind's eye, Joaquin could see the tower's emblem, a portrait of the last free Nahuatl chief raising a red-and-orange fist behind them. Joaquin said that tower's name aloud.

"Cuauhtémoc. Cuauhtémoc. Cuauhtémoc."

Joaquin felt a wet trickle on the back of his calves. He pivoted carefully at the waist and saw red dots flecking the backs of his legs. His vision misted. His mind shifted. Later he remembered taking a step toward the bed.

Doors led through doors, and those doors opened onto confusing, fevered passages. Joaquin walked slowly through the maze and finally opened the last portal. He saw himself lying in his childhood bed, his back so badly flayed and scarred that he seemed burned.

Disease. Overpopulation. Starvation. War upon war upon war. Nature had been attempting to expel humanity from this poor valley forever. Now she could finally expel the human infection with the arrival of Joaquin's progeny. "Am I not a part of nature? Are not these viruses mine?" Joaquin said, walking to his own sleeping body, touching his back, dipping a finger in the blood where his children played. "Am I not here," he said, looking at the bead of red on his fingertip, "I that am your Mother?"

On the wall above his bed, he wrote two Latin words in blood.

Virus sum.

"I am poison."

The first game was over. He'd won. But the *pilone* net was now under repair and his children were still breeding in his veins. A new hunt was under way, a new mission. Infect Domenica, defy God, and once his children were stampeding through the dictator's city in the heavens, he would count himself the victor in that game too.

PART
IV

CHAPTER

24

IN DEATH, the infected lung cell destroyed the virus that had poisoned it.

"Look what has happened to me," the lung cell said.

Defeating this virus was a victory. But it was too late to help the rest of the body; the virus had already bred. Other lung cells did what they could, however, to alert the body by gathering bits of the destroyed cell and presenting them like a dying murder victim clutching the attacker's kerchief. It presented these viral bits to the bloodstream, demanding justice. "Look!"

Two days earlier, the immune system never would have recognized even the shattered pieces of the virus. Two days earlier, the powerful antigen would have mutated and spread unimpeded, killing the body within hours.

But vaccinia from an omnivalent serum floated here. So, cued that something had gone wrong, a newly formed T lymphocyte stopped to examine the attacked cell and its offered evidence. It scurried over the surface like a spider looking for an anchor point for its thread and found the offered viral protein bits. It recognized the virus, having been taught by the omnivalent vaccine what to look for. The immature T cell then sprouted, differentiated, using the information it gathered from the destroyed virus in order to mature into a white blood cell with the ability to kill viruses just like this disassembled one. One T cell couldn't do much against a rapidly spreading virus, however, so this cell cloned itself. Geometrically. Thousands of identical T cells spread through the body, hunting down their one prey, wherever the virus had found purchase in the body—lung cells, muscle cells, or even floating harmlessly in the blood.

Guillermo slept extra soundly as the armies in his bloodstream engaged. He'd contracted the virus from a unique body that birthed eight octillian viral cells every day. An Episcopalian priest and a corpse-removal-team volunteer, Guillermo had come upon this extraordinary body by accident, in a pleasant little courtyard with terra-cotta tiles and rubber tree plants. Guillermo accepted a bottle of water from this body in thanks for helping the man put ointment on his flagellated back.

A microscopic battle began when Guillermo took the water. For unbeknownst to him, the extraordinary body had spit in the bottle and resealed it. The viruses in the water were Generation One, right from the epidemic's source. But the vaccine in Guillermo's blood had a key, a code. It bore a sequence of codons that gave the body a fifty-fifty chance of grabbing this virus by its shell and cracking it into harmless pieces.

That's how the T cells could identify and kill these viruses. They attached themselves to the invaders, lysing them with cytotoxins and eradicating them from the tight, closed system of the body.

Guillermo slept a deep, black sleep as his body rallied its energies to seroconvert, turning this deadly, viral infection into nothing more than a swarm of T cells. His mother did not know what was happening to her son when she stuck her head into his room at the end of the day.

But the chickens noticed.

As well as a minister, Guillermo was a public-health volunteer. Accordingly, he was fitted with the universal, antibody-monitoring chips that *medicos* jokingly called *"gallinas"* (chickens), or universal antibody reports. Along with tens of thousands of other *capitalinos,* the chips relayed information regarding mass seroconversion to a ring of *i.a.*'s in the National Institute of Public Health. The *i.a.*'s translated the information into a landscape of the city's pathogens and the population's responses to them.

Along with a small handful of others who'd fought off the most potent generation of virus, Guillermo's immune response appeared on the antibody report, like this:

<1%: Unknown IgG: viral: retro: max virulence.

They destroyed the virus with their own bodies and the aid of the naked DNA vaccine. This destruction was too late to help the rest of Ascensión, of course, but the universal antibody report did its part, displaying the information that the dying cell had displayed to the T lymphocyte, like a dead victim still clutching the murderer's kerchief.

The Joint Operations Coordinator, a Dr. del Negro, did his part, too, reading the universal antibody report with care and deducing what the American Task Force Coordinator was up to.

CHAPTER

25

"SISTER, IF WE could begin? I must leave within the hour in order to deliver a speech at the University of the Americas."

"Santa Domenica is busy," Sister Evangelista said. A stiff, little wire of a woman, she was Domenica's self-appointed bodyguard since Friday night, when the young nun arrived in La Alta. "Give her a moment, she is watching—"

"Shh," the nun hissed. "Just wait! Wait a minute both of you!"

The netmonitor showed a stage. The spotlight was so bright and harsh that it seemed to crackle when it hit the corpulent baritone's white, ruffled shirt and blue squire's hat. He stepped forward to deliver the most famous aria in contemporary opera, his pouting lips parted, his chest thrown out, and he unleashed the shearing note that Domenica wanted to hear. He unleashed the word *creo* and with it, Sancho's and the audience's passion for the Don. It was Sancho's moment. He had betrayed Quixote by helping him, by turning him over to the priest who wanted to cure him. But the question remained, did Sancho believe in the Don's imaginary world of the Glorious Quest, of righting the wrongs committed by giants and sorcerers? *Creo.* The word swelled out of him in that magnificent note, high in the baritone's register, painful, crying out in equal parts regret and conviction.

But it disappointed Domenica. She desperately wanted to share Sancho's catharsis and declaration of faith, but only felt her distance more keenly, the passions of the opera remote, the monitor a wall between them. The Order of Guadalupe's dining hall suddenly echoed with quiet mediocrity now that the hyperbole of *El Quijote* was over. "Compared to the *pilone,* the netmonitor is a very sad medium for opera. I can't feel it," she said, struggling for words. She placed her hands on her heart, then her stomach. "Here. Where the music should be."

Dr. Benito was just as insistently curious as Sancho, but not nearly as delightful. "I'm sorry to rush you, but may we please get on with my inquisition?"

Inquisition. Has he no shame?

The three were in the candlelit refectory where the Sisters of Guadalupe took their meals, sequestered from the crowds in Our Lady of the New World Church. Beef stew and red wine still sat on the communal dining table where Evangelista had set them. Domenica poured two small glasses and asked the older woman to leave. "I'll be fine, *señora,* I promise."

Mother Superior Evangelista was a small, brittle *abuelita* with the air of an attack-dog trainer. But in just two days, the severe Evangelista had fallen in love with Domenica, calling herself the nun's *jefa.* Mom. "I'll wait over here and watch the television," *la jefa* said. She was old enough that she still called netcast "the television."

Dr. Benito said, "Please wait outside, Mother Superior."

Evangelista departed with a sniff and a slammed door. She would wait just outside, Domenica knew, and ladled the psychologist a bowl of soup. "What do you want to ask me?"

Benito fussed with his robes of black and red as he sat at the knifenicked wooden table. He had a strapping build that the robes couldn't hide, but his movements were surprisingly small and rodentlike. "Do you remember me, Sister?"

Domenica knew who this man was. While she and Pirate were hiding out in the hot zone, trying to find a way to connect with Old Antonio and his street fighters, she'd seen this man on netcast, telling Mexico that Domenica wasn't Domenica, that the nun was really an actress. "I know who you are."

"Yes," the psychologist said, "but do you *remember* me?"

It was hard to say. Domenica wasn't sure of what she remembered anymore, which of her two childhoods was hers, or which identity, Chana or Domenica, she should identify with now. She looked at him hard. His face was familiar—she thought so the first time she saw him. "I might."

Benito began stammering, then he stopped and started over, though he still sounded nervous. "I'm the doctor who coordinated your case—the Antigua Method—we performed it on you thirteen years ago. The faith-realignment procedure." Benito watched her carefully. When Domenica said nothing, he continued. "I would like to understand what happened to you after the surgery, Sister."

"My visions." Domenica nodded. "You want to know about my visions."

"Yes."

"So do I," Domenica said, sniffing the steam from her bowl. "It doesn't make sense, does it? If I was the actress Chana Chenalho—"

"You *were* Chana Chenalho."

"Then did you give me my visions?"

The man pursed his lips for a moment. "I don't know, Cha—Domenica. I don't know. That's what I want to find out."

Domenica had long avoided talking about her visions, even with Pirate—she didn't want them questioned or lessened in any way. But this man had clues about her two identities that she would need if she was going to build normalcy into her life—now that she'd left *Los Hijos,* now that the visions were over.

After a spoonful of stew, she said, "It was after vespers, about twelve years ago."

Dr. Benito tapped something on his memboard, then tilted back his head to look through his old-fashioned bifocals. A light on the side of the memboard blinked, indicating it was recording. He nodded to Domenica. "Had anything like it ever happened to you before?"

Domenica stopped eating and thought about that. Of her two distinct sets of memories—one of a wealthy, white Mexico City upbringing, a child-hood under strict adherence to the Roman Catholic Church; the other set, rural, *indígena,* with parents who loved her and encouraged her to pursue acting in the capital city. The first set of memories belonged to Domenica. The second was apparently Chana Chenalho's. "I think that was the first time ever."

Benito's tone became fatherly. "Tell me about the first time, then."

"One Friday morning, after vespers," Domenica said blithely, though she had seldom told this story, "I was dressing, when it seemed the sunlight was brightening on the floor of my cell. It got warmer, too, as if a more powerful sun were shining outside."

That mountain nunnery had been the most peaceful place that either Chana or Domenica had ever experienced. The air, clean. The sunlight, milky and pure. She had loved sitting in her window and watching the shadows of clouds sweep over the amber valleys and desert plains below. That morning, Domenica had gone to her east window feeling flushed and heady, wondering why the sun seemed so bright. She looked out over the shoulder of the distant peak and saw a crown of light surrounding the sun like the directions of a compass drawn on an ancient map.

"I saw this strange light in the sky and thought I could smell roses, so I turned away to see where the smell was coming from," Domenica told Benito. "That's when I saw a middle-aged Indian woman sitting on my bed."

"Una indígena?" Benito frowned. "Who was she?"

Domenica said, "The Virgin of Guadalupe."

Benito repeated himself, clearly incredulous. "An Indian woman? The woman in white is Indian?"

"Yes. Her dress was like something my—something Domenica's great-aunt would wear—cotton gauze. Her sandals were cut from old tire treads. I asked who she was, if she was lost."

Domenica recalled how sweetly the woman in white had smiled at her. "Sweet girl. No. I—am not lost. You lost—me—but in Mexico," the woman said with a halting Nahuatl accent, "things don't stay—buried forever."

Domenica had turned away for a moment to look at the sun and was trying to figure out how the woman had entered the room unnoticed. "Excuse me? What did you say?"

The woman laughed at her and pointed out the window. "See that?"

Popocatépetl, the volcano, was in clear view, its white faces shining beneath the crowned sun. "Popo? Yes, I see it."

"It will—tip—and pour," she said, cupping her hands around her mouth and pronouncing each word with care, as if she were in a loud, crowded room and wanted to be sure that Domenica understood her perfectly. "Warn the people—who have ears."

"Warn them about what?"

The woman in white lifted her hand. "You—you are interfering with me—don't interfere with me. I have—I have three—important things to tell you. Three of them."

Domenica gave an obedient nod, willing to hear what this poor *indígena* had to say.

"First, I tell you—that death is on that volcano. That—death is there. Tell those with—ears."

"Is it going to erupt?"

"Stop that! Stop interfering, I said! Three hundred and twenty. That's how many—the volcano wants. Three hundred and twenty."

Domenica shook her head, irritated that the woman in white didn't say what she meant. "Three hundred and twenty deaths? Is that what you mean?"

The sun dimmed. Her cell darkened. Domenica looked out her window but saw no clouds, no morning, mountain haze. The corona folded itself into the sun, and the smell of roses drove itself into Domenica's head. She held her forehead in her hand, and when she looked up with watery eyes and running nose, the woman in white was gone.

Her first Marian migraine, as Pirate later called them.

To Benito, Domenica said, "I was convinced. Immediately."

"Of what?"

"Of her identity."

"But she was an *indígena*," Benito said. "Why would you think she was Santa Maria?"

"The Virgin of Guadalupe *was* considered to be *indígena*. Father Hidalgo rallied the people for Mexican independence under the banner of the Virgin because she looked like them: native; dark." She allowed a bit of scolding to enter her voice. "It's you in the Holy Renaissance who turned her into a European."

"I'm not—is that what you intend?" Benito asked. "To rally the people under a banner?"

He sounded neutral, not hostile, but Domenica supposed this was the real reason for this meeting. The Holy Renaissance was analyzing her, an outsider, an insurgent, who had entered the pure Federal Cloister. Even if they weren't going to disappear her, they at least had to determine Domenica's political motives. Her ties to Old Antonio and *Los Hijos* were too valuable and had been widely reported, no doubt by that *Malinche* Rosangelica. "I wouldn't be in La Alta if I wanted to rally the people, Doctor. Wealth kills revolutionary ferment."

"I don't know about that," Benito said with a wry smile. "'What kills the *indígena* kills Mexico.' Your words are uttered all over La Alta, now, all across Orbegón's empire. I saw that painted across a poster of Emil the Damned up in the orbit launches at the top of Cuauhtémoc."

"Dalliances of the rich and bored, I'm sure." Domenica pulled her braid from beside her neck and let it fall straight down her back. "If the wealthy of this country truly wanted to do something about the well of poverty in which *las indígenas* have been thrown, it would have been done decades ago. *Los altadores* don't have ears, as the woman in white would say."

Benito seemed grateful when Domenica brought up the woman in white again. "What did you do after that first visitation?"

"I tried to tell my sister nuns about Popo erupting," Domenica said. "I told them I had a dream. But they paid no attention. So I went to the village that supplied our cloister with flour and shoes. I found a bicycle repair shop, and spoke with a young *indígena* boy who might believe my story. I told him that the Virgin of Guadalupe had come, warning me about Popo. About a week later, I got news on the *pilone* saying minor shock waves indicated an eruption of Popocatépetl. That night, Popo's top exploded, and a *campesino* village was caught unaware. Two hundred and ninety one people were killed."

"So," Benito said, a mix of relief and disbelief in his voice, "her prediction of the death toll was wrong."

"Well, later, when the woman in white came back to deliver the Guatemala prophecy," Domenica said, "I asked about that. 'The volcano only took 291,' I told her. 'You said it wanted 320.'"

Dr. Benito leaned forward, a hunger in his eyes, and Domenica realized that this is what he was looking for. Details. Evidence. Proof. "And what did she say?"

"The Virgin said, 'Twenty-nine people had ears.'"

Benito's face went placid for a moment, then he tilted back his head as if savoring that detail upon his tongue. Finally, he looked back at Domenica, and said, "And what do you believe, Sister? Why does the woman in white come to you?"

"It doesn't matter what I believe."

He reached for her hand as if she were slipping away from him. "I think it does."

She gave him a probing look, and he took back his hand. This wasn't about what she believed, Domenica realized. This was about him, the psychologist, and what he wanted to believe. "Why does it matter to you?"

Benito gestured quickly, like an accountant trying to explain an error in his books. "Is the woman in white just a woman from your family, as my colleagues have posited? Or did *I* create you? I mean, your visions?" He calmed his hands, folded them, and his voice grew heavy. "There are people in Ascensión who put up their guns or go to war at your command."

"Do you feel guilty about my visions? Is that it? You want to know if you created Mexico's civil war?" Domenica said.

"No, not per se, but—" He fell quiet. Then he said, "But look at you. You're a walking conundrum. You could be either *mestizo* or *indígena*, Sister." Benito's jaw was slack and his head shook slowly, side to side. "What *are* your visions, in light of the fact that you might not be yourself?"

Domenica wondered what it would mean if she answered that question with any sort of honesty. She had no doubt that this "inquisition" would determine her level of freedom for the rest of her life, so her words mattered now more than ever. *Am I really Chana?* She wanted to ask him. *I have Chana's desires for audience and theater, for justice and equal treatment for Native Mexicans. I have her memories, a mother who wanted something more for Chana than campesino life. I remember a house with tin cans rolled flat to cover bullet holes in corrugated metal. Was that me? Am I* indígena? *If I think that I am, is that enough?*

Domenica stirred her soup. If she was Chana, then she was merely playing the role of white, visionary nun—a lifelong act of street theater. If so, then what was to be made of her Catholic school memories? The nuns who encouraged her to sing in front of her classes, who saw in her a bride of Jesus Christ, who spared *mestizo* Domenica the punishment that her *indígena* classmates so often received? Was that life a lie instilled in her by Mexico's "restorative psychologists" and later whispered to her by her own mind?

The Antigua Method, Benito had said in his netcast interview, *merely corrected faulty wiring in these underdeveloped regions of the brain—these faith centers.*

"Tell me, Domenica," Benito said. "Tell me what everyone wants to know."

After spa, Benito had said, *Chana joined the Order of Guadalupe nuns, changing her name to Domenica. This is all thoroughly documented for public examination.*

She felt her ears burning so hot that she wanted to cover them. "If you don't know, then I don't know either, Doctor."

Another barrage of questions seemed to well in the psychologist's eyes.

His face, she imagined, was a mirror of her own, a visage of wonderment and quandary. Finally, he said, "I came here because I have to make a decision about whether or not to give you something."

Domenica barely heard him. Her thoughts were swirling on themselves. So the woman in white was nothing more than the phantom of a broken mind. True? Or was this agent of the Holy Renaissance deliberately trying to misdirect her, encouraging seeds of doubt planted long ago by his Antigua Method? Her hands were trembling in confusion and she felt a quiver in her stomach and throat that said she would either start laughing or crying in a moment. "I can't help you. I'm not clear. And I—I should go."

"No." Benito stood. He looked at the door where Evangelista had departed. "Wait." He reached into a pocket beneath his robes, saying, "I'll go. I came looking for answers about something to which there can be none." Then he set a small red tube on the wooden table beside his half-eaten bowl of soup and grabbed his memboard. "I've upset you and you should rest."

She nodded with little tremors of her head, but said nothing, couldn't look him in the eye. When she heard the door of the refectory shut, Domenica took the red tube, about the length of her finger, and opened it.

Inside was a hand-rolled cigarette.

She laughed, astonished, and looked at the door, wanting one last word.

Old Antonio's roll, she could tell—no one could roll a cigarette so perfectly—a mate to the one he carried, unlit, always.

She held the cigarette between her fingers as he did.

I won't light this, he'd told the Purépecha elders in council when he first rolled it over a year ago, when the Native Council had decided to seek funds abroad for arming *Los Hijos* against Orbegón and his Holy Renaissance. *But smoking it will be the first thing I do, when the Holy Renaissance falls.*

Unraveling the snarl of implications and possibilities in this situation fueled her to laugh even harder. A turncoat in the ranks of the Holy Renaissance? "I can't know anything for sure, anymore," she said through seizing fits. "I just can't know. Nothing. Anything."

Sister Evangelista was suddenly at her side, looking at Domenica, who was laughing hysterically while holding the unlit cigarette.

Something wet hit Domenica's hand. She looked down and saw a drop of water. The laughter wasn't laughter. She was crying fat tears and she hadn't even realized it.

Evangelista said, "Come. Let's get you back to your room, dearest."

Domenica could now hear the crowds that overflowed outside the church, hoping to see her. Some were singing Domenica's favorite hymn, "Go Ye Moneychangers Go." Some were chanting *Aves* in unison. Domenica could even hear the snick of flagellants' whips.

Domenica watched herself sob in her detached mind's eye as *la jefa* led her through rear hallways, away from the crowds hoping to catch a sight of her.

I am not insane. I know what I know, Domenica told herself, seizing the one thought she could grasp. *Hitler. Augmented plague. What the woman in white predicted came true, and I know what I know,* she thought, laughing and weeping her way to her dormitory cell.

Don't I?

CHAPTER

26

"How long were you stuck in the hot zone, Doctor?" The young woman gave him a concerned frown as she led him toward the labs. With lanky limbs and girly bangs, she had the air of a puppy perpetually glad to be reunited with its owner. "You were really out there, weren't you? Way out there. I can tell."

"Yes, I was out there all right," the doctor said, following close behind her. They passed doors that looked into old classrooms with desks and chairs cleared out. Chalkboards still bore syllabus adjustments or phrases in Arabic and Chinese. Eight days ago, this was Las Aztecas Community College. Now it was Perimeter Clinic Four.

"Do you know how long you were 'out there,' if you don't mind me asking?"

The doctor's fingertips tingled from the pinpricks given to him in the bloodwork station. "Six or seven days, I think."

The orderly flipped her wrist out to the side when she spoke, a little girl's gesture. "Why were you there?"

"When the military barriers went up around the hot zone, I was trapped inside," he said. "I couldn't get out, so I thought I'd better help the people who were less fortunate than I."

"Your tests showed that you're immune. Did you know that? You couldn't have known that. I think you're a very brave man," the orderly said. She was of indeterminate age—anywhere from eighteen to thirty—though young enough to let awe and attraction mingle without shame. "I could never have done that. Even if I knew I was immune."

The doctor noted how the equipment was placed as she led him deeper into the perimeter clinic, analyzing its operation, trying to guess what tasks the administration would ask him to perform. This hallway seemed to be storage for a dormitory. Extra beds were loaded in every classroom. Sheets and pillows. Cleaning supplies. "You would have done it, *señorita*," he said. "Your conscience wouldn't have let you do otherwise."

"By the way," the young woman said, "that ape Santiago back in the bloodwork station didn't introduce us. My name is Marta Serra." As they walked, she held out her slim, once-manicured hand. Now the formerly shiny nails were rough and her skin chapped from constant washing.

The doctor looked down at the bare hand in wonder. "Call me Reynaldo." He took a deep breath and managed to talk himself out of an irrational urge to slap Marta for not wearing gloves—but there were standards to uphold. "Maybe I've been in the hot zone too long, but do orderlies always go without gentex around here?"

"I know. I'm cheating. But it's nice to pretend things are back to normal, isn't it?" said Marta, withdrawing her hand, a sheepish look on her face. "That probably seems horrible after everything you've gone through. But we've had no new patients this morning. Can you believe it? The Head Epi says we'll probably stay clean until the next wave hits us in a couple days. We're lucky. We don't get it nearly as bad as Perimeter Clinic Eight. What a hellhole that one is. Hey! Listen!"

Marta stopped walking and turned her face dreamily toward the ceiling. An airy, *conjunto* tune of accordion and guitars waltzed down the hall from the laboratory.

"That's progress," she said. "*¡Radio Bajo!*" Marta tapped her temple where Joaquin had noticed the absence of a zigzag scar. "Those of us off the *pilone* appreciate radio. Someone down on Insurgentes restored the signal. The city is waking up!"

The *conjunto* music faded, replaced by a breathy woman's voice telling Ascensión citizens to avoid the downtown and to attend the inoculation seminars in their neighborhoods. *The city is waking up,* he thought. *But as long as the* pilone *network stays down, it can't wake up very quickly.* Joaquin folded his gloved hands and followed Marta. His back was healing, sore, but he tried not to let it show as he walked.

"Here we go. Infirmary Alpha," she said, opening the door into a gymnasium with four long rows of white beds. "This is where you'll be working for the next few days. Though, depending on what kind of doctor you are, they might have bigger plans for you." She smiled at him eagerly. "Have they said?"

Joaquin paused after entering the infirmary and squinted. Overhead lights lit the room so brightly that he felt as if the crisp, white beds and waxed floors were abrading his eyes. Air conditioners had been removed, and all overhead vents, the seams of the window frames, and various cracks around the room were splattered with a thick, white sealant. It astounded him that this dormitory could exist, just a few blocks from the hot zone where the epidemic reigned in filth and squalor. He pinched his eyes, and they watered under his fingertips.

Marta let the door swing shut behind them and the radio voice now sounded far away. "What is it?" She put a hand on his shoulder when she noticed his tears.

Joaquin flinched before he could stop himself.

"Are you having a reaction to your shots, Doctor?"

He hated this room but he loved standing here. After smelling nothing but pyre smoke, household bleach, and the stink of his own, self-inflicted wounds for almost a week, this beautiful room rendered the very purity he'd wanted from his whip. He'd spent his entire adult life in such order and cleanliness, and he found himself longing for it. "Such a fragile place."

"Sit down, Dr. Cruz," Marta said. "Take it easy for a minute." She led him to the desk and pulled a chair out for him. "All the beds are made and the lab doesn't have our materials ready anyway. Please take your mask off. We're safe in here. Relax."

Joaquin sat and peeled off his clamp mask, letting it dangle. He rubbed his brow and brushed back the curly, black locks from his forehead. He hadn't seen a mirror in days, but he imagined he was grayer than when he arrived in Mexico. *Was that plane flight from London just two weeks ago?* Joaquin pretended to be emotional, out of sorts. It wasn't hard. After whipping himself as he had, he was lucky to be alive. He was lucky to have had someone chance across him, the minister who helped him. Joaquin's back still hurt but he hid the pain and his sore left hand. Joaquin took a measured breath. The desk smelled of coffee in a self-warming cup—stale, slightly burned, and delicious.

"Are you still hungry, Dr. Cruz? I don't think the commissary will close for another few minutes, so if you need more to eat, I could—"

"No, I'm full, thank you, *señorita*. The fresh bread you gave me was—it was—" Joaquin couldn't speak as he remembered the warmth of the crust dissolving in his mouth. "Is there coffee?"

She opened the filing cabinet and pulled out a capped mug for him. The mug was slightly warm and he cupped his hands around it. He pried off the lid with his good hand and sipped. His first coffee in many days. A bitter, plunging taste. He shut his eyes.

"Hard to believe what this place might look like if a new wave of infections hits," Marta said, glancing around the dormitory. "Hope the lab certifies us soon."

Joaquin opened his eyes. The infirmary did have the air of calm before battle. Ten-gallon water dispensers sat by each bed. A phalanx of stainless-steel carts was loaded down with swabs, alcohol, antiviral wipes, red-lined plastic garbage cans for bio-waste, blue spray guns of tetravalent vaccines and painkillers. And every bed sat neatly made with folded corners and black restraining straps dangling on the floor. Joaquin said, "What is the laboratory bringing us that we don't already have?"

"These are going to be early, stage-one patients," said Marta, nodding toward the beds. "No bloody patients at first, just those with fever and seizures. They'll move our team out and bring in a hazardous-waste team once the unit advances to stage-two—hemorrhaging." Marta shuddered. "Then Mortuary comes in after that. We rotate with three other infirmaries in this Clinic. Hard to believe this was a mortuary two days ago, huh?" She let the clean silence speak for itself. "Our job is to tend to patients and look for the ones with mouth pustules."

Joaquin stiffened. "Why?"

"I guess that's a sign of Generation One dengue-5. We'll use those blood spinners to isolate the virus if we find mouth pustules." She pointed to a bank of pheresis machines, not unlike standard viral assays, though Joaquin did not recognize the model. "The lab is bringing us a new kind of genosorbent that can help us—I mean, you—take instant DNA readings."

Though he was mostly angry and frightened hearing all this, Joaquin had to admit he was impressed, too. This was not the response he was expecting to see once he'd weaseled into a perimeter clinic. This was much more innovative, much riskier—tailoring new tools for the outbreak. Genetic analyzers right in the clinics? A cunning breakthrough. This wasn't the steady, stalwart approach Cristóbal might have taken, nor would the Mexican National Institute approve using untested gadgetry. No, this was way too radical for Mexico, which expected immediate and incontrovertible results for its solid *peso.*

If Henry David weren't literally attached to the Central Command in Wisconsin, Joaquin might have thought it was Stark. But that wasn't likely. *Mexico ain't inviting me,* Stark had said. *Won't neither.*

"I'm not familiar with those," Joaquin said, indicating the new pheresis machines with a nod.

She glanced at the cleft in his chin as she spoke. "You wouldn't be. They're new."

"Really? How new?"

"They just came in two days ago." Marta beamed, as if she had thrown them together herself. "Dr. Ahwaz and Dr. Khushub refitted them. It makes their work of creating virus hunters a lot easier. They can wetcode one in a single day, thanks to those dogs. Can you believe that?"

They're wetcoding nanophages in a single day? A single day? *A single* day? Joaquin's eyes burned with fury and envy as he stared at the assays beneath the raised basketball backboard, each with a pair of circular spin chambers, making them look like a line of giant mechanical owls staring back at him. He forced himself to stop thinking about smashing the machines and destroying this clinic. "Isn't that just amazing?" Joaquin whispered. When he was an undergraduate, it sometimes took months, years to isolate viruses effectively. *Now dingbat Marta can do it in minutes.* "Will they use that on my blood test, too?"

"No, they didn't find measurable antibodies, remember?" She laughed. "You're white as the rest of us."

"Oh right, of course," Joaquin said. Despite this advance, public health officials would always be reliant on old-fashioned immune-system assays to detect the actual, initial presence of a virus. And since he was immune to his own disease, they'd found only traces of antidengue white cells—circumstantial evidence of the army hidden in his blood.

"But I heard things aren't going well," Marta said. "We're at sixty-nine hundred dead, but the Task Force is expecting an even bigger spike tomorrow or the day after."

Joaquin studied Marta closely. "How do you know that?"

Marta said, "Dr. Khushub said so when she showed us how the spinners work. She's trying to create a 'phage that will stop the next wave of infections."

Isabel? Joaquin couldn't picture her here, not in the field clinics he saw down in La Baja. No. She wouldn't be in La Baja, that was for certain. *She must feel very safe wherever she is, or that obnoxious diva would have fled town days ago.* Isabel was most certainly high above, in the paradise of La Alta, in Torre Cuauhtémoc and the Federal Cloister. Along with the Ministry of Health. Along with that *Malinche* Domenica.

At the thought of the nun, Joaquin glanced around the infirmary looking for a netmonitor, as if Domenica might be here, looking over his shoulder. The nun. The insidious nun. "So why are we taking instant genomic reads, Marta, if mouth pustules tell us all we need to know?"

She shrugged. "They want genetic prints of the oldest viruses they can find." Marta put her feet up, resting them on the corner of a white bed. "The *first* ones. That's what they want. The generation closest to the terrorist's blood. They say there's a reward for the person who isolates the generation of virus that he needs." She winked at Joaquin. "Want to bet that I'm the one who puts it into a blood spinner first?"

Joaquin smiled at her cuttingly. *They know the virus's primary source is here,* he thought. *I can't let my children loose haphazardly anymore.* He tugged at his gloves, grateful for the first time for their protection. *They may even know it's me.*

Just then, the infirmary doors swung open, and Marta immediately turned her back so that she could scoop on gloves from the desk's dispenser. A tiny woman strode into the infirmary, wearing an abbreviated Racal suit—particle-arresting clamp mask, small tanks on her back, and a plastic shirt with belt lock. Behind her were two men and two women carrying ALHEPAs for the gymnasium doors. Joaquin stood as if he'd been caught picking a lock.

"*Ai,* Marta," the woman wearing the *Racalito* suit said. "You're on report. If I see you without gloves again, I'm knocking you down to Mortuary. Now get down to the blood station for a full round."

Marta spun and showed the woman her gloved hands. "I've got them on, Dr. Garcia!"

"Go. And get back up here as soon as they pass you," Garcia said. She gave Joaquin such a stiff look, he almost stepped backwards. "What are you doing in here?"

"I'm—" He had to catch himself. This woman with heavy eyebrows and a faint moustache had the presence of a nun, and Joaquin's first reaction was to tell her his full Catholic name. "I'm Dr. Reynaldo Cruz, ma'am."

For such a stern woman, her smile was rewarding and bright. "Oh, Dr. Hot Zone, yes. I'm the head physician, Dr. Filomena Garcia de la Costa," Garcia said. "We don't shake hands in Perimeter Clinic Four, but allow me to say, I'm proud to have you on my team, sir."

Joaquin's breath came back to him. "Thank you. That's kind of you."

She barely paused for him to speak before continuing. "When I found out that you had survived in there a week, I told Central Staffing, 'I want Dr. Cruz.'" She turned to the four men and women lounging in the doorway. "Get the locks in place, niños. Let's start pumping all this polluted air out of here." She waved Joaquin to follow her out of the infirmary, back into the hallway where *Radio Bajo* was playing more old time *conjunto*. They stood in the hallway and spoke while the team of *"niños"* secured the first particle arrester. "There's some dissent on the Task Force. First they wanted us to withdraw and bring our team up to La Alta. Then they changed their minds because the other Clinics are starting to fill up again. I want to be ready just in case they ask us to close up shop. What's your background, Dr. Cruz? They tell me you worked in Zapata but that an army officer saved you."

"I didn't have to ask him or anything. He just—"

At that moment, the door leading back to the bloodwork station opened and another woman stepped through, wearing a full Racal suit in Holy Renaissance black. "Garcia," the woman said through the suit's speaker, "we have patients. Is the infirmary ready?"

"Mouth pustules?" asked Garcia.

"No, no mouth pustules yet."

"Momentito," Garcia said. "Dr. Cruz, this is Dr. Florencia Ramos, the head of Perimeter Clinic Eight."

Joaquin opened his eyes and smiled at Dr. Ramos.

The suited doctor saluted him by way of greeting. "My pleasure. What do you practice, Doctor?"

"I was in genetics at Zapata," Joaquin said. It was now time to make his play for the head physician's trust. "But I also tailored Zapata's computer system for its unique epidemiological needs."

Garcia examined him skeptically. "Computers?" The word sounded like an anachronism, the way she said it. "You're a geneticist *and* a computer man?"

He flashed his best smile at her. "What can I say? I'm good with code."

Garcia was distracted, momentarily, but not by Joaquin's beauty. "Our new Joint Ops coordinator, a man named del Negro," she said, "seems to think our mission is collecting data."

"Sounds like an epidemiologist. I've worked with them before as a data cruncher."

Garcia nodded, thinking. She was smart, Joaquin could see. She was curious about him, maybe even a bit dubious. But Joaquin's résumé was irresistible, and under the circumstances, she obviously couldn't take time for lengthy job interviews.

"Dr. Ramos, take Cruz to Systems," Garcia said finally. "Del Negro wants chicken reports collated with our findings. Maybe Cruz, here, can handle that so the rest of us can concentrate on—" Garcia paused, standing in a stilted pose, mannequin-like.

Dr. Ramos took a shaky step forward, as if she meant to embrace Joaquin.

Joaquin stepped backward. "Doctors?"

Garcia seemed ready to topple, and Ramos stumbled back to lean her forearm against the wall. Garcia swooned so badly that Joaquin held out his hand to her. Suddenly her head jerked to the side in a violent spasm. So did Ramos's. Then both women leaned their full weights back against the wall.

"What's wrong?" Joaquin shouted. "Tell me what's happening!"

Down the hall, someone dropped a metal pipe. A woman swore. All four workers erecting the air lock were swaying on their feet.

From the lab, Joaquin could hear the female announcer of *Radio Bajo* saying, "What is it? What's happening?"

Joaquin stepped away from Garcia, but then she raised her head, and her eyes were glassy for a moment. They cleared and she looked up at Joaquin with a feeble smile. "What's wrong?" she said.

"Hey," one of the young men by the air lock said, "hey, it's up. It's *up*!" He gazed off as if he could see far beyond the walls of the old community college.

Joaquin's stomach clenched in terror.

"I noded in!" another orderly said.

"Me, too!"

"Attention, *bajadores,*" the sultry *Radio Bajo* announcer said. "We have *pilone*. If you're cut, you're in, as we used to say in Monterrey."

Both doctors paused as they obviously checked their wetware, eyes scanning in the empty air before them as though reading. They looked at each other for confirmation, then at Joaquin.

"I'm sorry—I," Joaquin stammered, "I'm not—I don't have the hookup."

The two doctors looked away as if he simply did not exist, enraptured by whatever wonders the *pilone* was showing them, Joaquin imagined. "What a blessing," Dr. Ramos said. "This is all going to be so much easier now." She turned away. "We can explore *pilone* land later, everyone," she called down the hall. "Right now we have infected patients." She turned to Joaquin. "Help them get that up, will you, Dr. Cruz?"

As he turned to walk down the hall, he heard Ramos say to Garcia, "We'll need to be in constant contact with the infirmary. Get a *pilonista* to attend Reynaldo Cruz."

Joaquin felt the clinic compressing around him, as if tendrils of wetware were closing in and snaking out toward him. He couldn't remember if he had seen a *pilone* scar on Reynaldo Cruz's body. If so, could someone here discover the man's node? Could people tell Cruz was dead, just by trying to contact him? Joaquin's posture stiffened and the scars on his back hummed with pain. He forced himself to relax but feared he only managed to look nauseous as he approached the four orderlies. "*Bueno,* let's—" His voice constricted as if a cold hand were gripping his throat.

"Are you all right, Doctor?" an orderly asked.

"Let's get to work," Joaquin rasped, nodding. "I have so much work to do today."

CHAPTER

27

"REMEMBER HOTEL CHOLERA?" Isabel said to him, sprawled in her bed, arm thrown over her eyes.

Stark could smell sour laundry and roses as he came into her dark bedroom. Isabel's gate had let him in. "Ah, such a nice trip down memory lane."

Hotel Cholera was what Isabel and Stark had called their tent, their cots, and their meager clean water supply. The Holy Republic of Mexico was wrestling Colombia from what remained of the Federal-Cartel Alliance armies, and cholera had broken out in Tres Esquinas, the longtime flash point for Colombia's near century of drug wars. Stark's barrack-sized tent was pitched outside the reconstructed city among deep green coffee plants. The Pan-Islamic Virological Institute had sent her to code nanophages in the safety of a lab—but she came out to the field and never balked at working with Stark in the clutter and filth of the outbreak. A godsend. Her nanophages hunted down *Vibrio cholerae* in the small intestines of officers in their barracks, coffee pickers with wicker baskets around their necks, working faster than a vaccination program ever could for cholera. He had also appreciated working with a doctor who said precisely what she thought, describing harsh emotions and harsh situations with equally harsh swearing. As the tasks of cleaning up the hot zone were ticked off his list, Stark had felt his heart turning to Isabel Khushub.

"You could have had me, then," Isabel said now, red mouth moving beneath her arm in the dark bedroom.

"I could have you now," Stark chided, hand still on her leg.

"Go ahead." She was still groggy from a sleep-shot last night. "Wake me when it's over." Isabel dropped her arm and smiled at him. "Are we still in Mexico? Is it still Big Bonebreaker? Haven't we moved on to something nice and simple like a rhinovirus?"

Stark smiled at her and noted how haggard and skinny she looked. The recoding project's sims were eating her alive. "Sorry, Bela. Still here. Jarum is waiting for us. We need to get to the National Institute as soon as possible."

"With my Venus in Taurus and your Mars in Scorpio, we should have had babies together, Henry David," she whispered. "You should have spirited me away to your communist collective and given me baby after baby."

"I know." He didn't think so, really, but he wasn't about to contradict her now. "But it's a cooperative, not a commune." He kept tracing his nails over her exposed leg, knowing this relaxed her. "There are six principles of cooperation, did you know? Principle One: democratic control of capital. Principle Two—"

"How long have we known each other, *novio*?" She smiled, arm still over her eyes, seemingly grateful to interrupt him on cue.

"We met seven years, umpteen viruses, and a squad of bacterial infections ago."

"I shit on the empty heads of girls who marry too young." She sat up and touched his bright, yellow beard. "We could have had thousands of babies by now."

"You have kids, Bela. You love your boys."

"I know. I wish you and I had children, though. A farm full of our babies in Wees-kohn-seen."

It always sounded so exotic when Isabel said the name of his home, or talked about the fantasy of them together there. But the thought always made him laugh. *Isabel? In the* quop? *Like a peacock in an ice-fishing shack.* It was always just a lovely diversion in the middle of horror.

The fantasy was an oasis now, because the sims were nightmarish. Even Stark had to admit it. The first morning and afternoon of inputting data had been fine. That was Saturday. Sunday and Monday morning were grueling as Isabel reconstructed her version of Generation One. But last night, the first sim showed in excruciating detail what would happen to a living person. The three networked *inteligentsias artificiales* named the sim patient Debora1, and described her in unnerving detail. A teacher with brown eyes, blond hair, two children, a sweet job selling tea, and the description of her death was awful. Her body shed and emitted its natural lymph system, making way for the new, with a set of symptoms shockingly similar to hemorrhagic fever. Stark asked Ofelio Xultan to tone down the *i.a.*'s verisimilitude, but that would have taken hours that they simply did not have.

Worse, when they tested Debora1's simulated body for wetcoded white blood cells and the potential for a successful recoding matrix, they found that the new immune system didn't survive long enough to bud wetcoded T cells, let alone create a matrix for recoding immune systems. Isabel modified her version of Generation One, reconstructed from the prints that Stark had stolen from Zapata, but it didn't help Debora2. She died as quickly as Debora1, and Isabel Kushub had left the lab last night looking threadbare, drunk.

While Stark watched Isabel's mood and resolve break over the last two and a half days, he had the growing awareness that he had to hold himself together now—their traditional alliance of love and intimate support was completely drained. He was alone. There were no personal mentors or colleagues left to call and beseech help. Anyone with expertise was already here, already working hard, already overwhelmed. Four days ago, standing on Filomeno Mata Avenue, Stark had stared up at the greasy smoke that had once been a small group of people—a little coterie of human beings, crowding together not on a street corner or in a concert, but gathering midair—and had been given a taste of his own mind cracking.

The hardest thing he'd ever had to do in order to stop an outbreak was on an endangered primate reserve in Tanzania, where researchers suspected an emergent virus had leapt from Lusk's mangabeys to humans. At first, Stark had quarantined the mangabeys to keep them from infecting the other endangered primates on the reserve. But Joaquin Delgado's pathology report, written from London, showed that the emergent virus was mutating rapidly, and that the mangabeys, with their long, almost human bodies and Mark Twain facial hair, were uniquely qualified to ensure that the virus would leap to humans. They had been cloned to perfection, after all, from the last wild mangabeys—hampered immune systems intact.

So Stark gave the order to euthanize the last of a species.

But that was simply a letter he had to write and sign. He didn't have to watch it happen. Here he had to interview the sacrifices, make sure they were the physical specimens they needed. "Three nuns from this tower have agreed to meet with us," he said.

Isabel picked up a glass of water from her bedside and stared at it. "Nuns."

Zipping his coveralls, Stark said, "Hermenia is one. Geraldina is another. I can't remember the third. Roberto Cazador gave me their names."

"And they know what we did to Deboras 1 and 2?"

"I told Cazador, yes, and he told the volunteers."

"Oh, Henry David, how can you call them volunteers? As if there could be no coercion in this situation. As if nuns of all people could clearly consent to—"

"Stop it, *novia*," Stark said, picking up his Racal-plus and holding it by the waist and slipping in his feet. "We've been down this street."

She drank. Her dark eyes were bloodshot over the rim of her glass as she stared at him with accusation.

Stark imagined being put on trial—either a court of law or a medical ethics board—to answer for this brutal endgame. The mathematics of trading one human life for many. Part of him wished someone would haul him off before the project went any further—before he had to make that choice. "Don't think it doesn't bother me."

"I know it does," she said. "But you never act like it. You and Joaquin. You have poker. And him with Pluto at midheaven, he has chess. Either way I've been partnered with scientists who see human genetic recoding as a test of skill instead of what it is."

Stark wriggled his hands into his gloves. "And what is it, Bela?"

She raised her hand and let out a sardonic laugh. She set her empty glass down with a loud thunk. "It's death. It's all death. *Valemadre, valemadre,* death, death, and—"

"Bela, stop." He didn't like growing impatient with her, but he needed a dram of her strength and nerve now, not her wilting despair. She was every bit the wetcoder that Joaquin was, but whether it was Pluto at midheaven or just *cojones* the size of God's, Joaquin had something Bela didn't: a complete lack of guilt. "It's the only way out of this horrid, putrid situation, which will only get more horrific and more putrid if we don't do this."

Isabel sat slouched on the bed. "I know."

She wasn't fighting back, the way she had when they first argued about the recoding project. The realization depressed him. He pushed. "I say damn the consequences. I say damn us to Mexico's idea of hell for killing a volunteer. I accept that. Now get your coveralls, Doctor," Stark said. "It's time to go."

Naked on the bed with her shoulders slumped over her crossed legs, Isabel looked like a skinned animal. Her eyes rose to him, pleading. "Don't be that way with me now."

He snapped his wrist and ankle cuffs in place. He reached for his helmet and slipped it on over his head. "I don't mean to hurt you." He snapped the locks closed at his collar. "But you said yourself we could see a tidal wave of infections starting today or tomorrow. If that happens, I think I'll fall apart if I allow myself to feel it the way you feel." He clicked the speaker on so that his voice was loud and clear in the bedroom. "And we can't both crack and disappear. Not now." Stark picked up her underwear from the floor and handed it to her.

Ignoring him, she stood from the bed and picked up her coveralls from their place on the oak dressing table. "Your mother has a dick. I don't need underwear *or* your condescension."

"Who's condescending?"

She tugged on the coveralls, wrestling needlessly. "I'm not vanishing, either. I am all too here," she said, and there was force in her voice again. "As long as I'm here, I'll *foquin* do it." Wisps of hair spidered around her long braid, which she'd slept in, and she scowled at her leggings as she jammed her toes into them as if angry with her own feet. "If for no other reason to prove that my wetcode is *always* better than Joaquin Delgado's."

CHAPTER

28

"*Mexicanistas,*" President for Life Emil Orbegón was saying from the monitor.

Stark and Muñoz were waiting in the National Institute's atrium for a consultation with Jarum and Isabel. "Shh," Stark told Muñoz, who was talking to a member of the Mortuary team via cell phone. The *pilone* net had been up for two days, but most of Mortuary, whom Muñoz was ordering to load bodies in grocery warehouse freezer lockers before the heat of June hit, didn't have the Connection. "Here it is. Here it is."

Muñoz said into the phone, "I'll call back." He looked briefly at the keypad, trying to make sense of the Farsi notations, then hung up.

On the netmonitor, Orbegón sat with a bank of fluffy peonies behind him. He wore neither a suit nor clamp mask and lush sunlight fell over his tanned face.

"Sun?" Muñoz looked at the wet windows of the immune complex's atrium. "A man can't trust his own eyes."

"*El Sol Real.* Gives you any kind of sunlight you prefer, anywhere in La Alta. It's all the rage," Stark said, grateful to have Pedro Muñoz as his companion. They could be perpetually amazed at La Alta together.

"I come before you today bringing you very good news concerning the state of Big Bonebreaker in the capital," Orbegón said. "But first, I want to take this opportunity to honor a patriot. Colonel Xavier Sanjuan, the Holy Renaissance's former Minister of Health."

"'Former'?" Stark said. "Did he say 'former'?"

"Shh!" Muñoz hissed. He picked up his coffee cup and memboard, and joined Stark on the couch, slapping his legs to make him move.

"—with Mexico's gratitude," Orbegón was saying, "to reward Minister Sanjuan with a more important post."

Stark and Muñoz glanced at one another. Neither acknowledged it, but the truth behind Orbegón's announcement hung in the air. The writer of the "crucial opportunity" that had stalled Mexico's initial response to Big Bonebreaker was dead.

"At least we don't have to worry about Sanjuan recognizing you anymore, Dr. del Negro," Stark said, using Muñoz's *nom de guerre.* In his five days as Joint Operations Coordinator (overseeing La Alta sentinel clinics with the seven perimeter clinics in La Baja), Muñoz had never bumped into Minister Sanjuan—Stark had made sure of that. For most hours of the day, "Dr. del Negro" was in a clinic near the docking bays of Torre Cuauhtémoc. It was when he ventured into the National Institute, higher up in the tower, that he pressed his clamp mask tight against his skin and kept his helmet low over his brow.

"Minister Sanjuan saw Mexico safely through the first week of this horrible crisis," Orbegón continued, with deep seriousness in his voice. "But with the outbreak now reaching a critical stage, we see fit to promote Minister Sanjuan to a position within our inner circle, to advise the president on medical matters within the military, to safeguard our soldiers against possible viral attacks on the *Tejas* border." Orbegón raised the back of his hand to the camera and bobbed it once, the Mexican gesture for honored thanks. "Xavier, you have the Holy Renaissance's deepest gratitude. Good luck in your new position."

The atrium door opened with a hiss as the ALHEPA vacuums started up, and Isabel walked in. Behind her was Jarum Ahwaz. Both were looking uncharacteristically upbeat.

Isabel stood in the ALHEPA calling over the rush of the particle arrester. "Did you hear about Sanjuan?"

Jarum stood waiting for her to enter the room. "Whenever you're ready, Doctor."

Isabel looked over her shoulder and made a face at him. "This isn't a *foquin* nightclub. You'll get in."

"Yes? Well, it's a HEPA filter, not a car wash," Jarum said, trying his hand at a little sarcasm in Spanish. "You don't have to stand there and—"

"Would you two quit it?" Stark shouted.

As Isabel and Jarum took seats near the netmonitor, Emil the Damned listed the Task Force's accomplishments over the last nine days: *pilone* net functional; 520,000 vaccinated in the states surrounding the *distrito federal* (thanks in no small part to the *pilone* going up two days ago); rabid outbreaks isolated in Cuernavaca, Cholula, and Managua where *pilone* users were fewer; and Ascensión's mortality rate was down from nearly 2,000 deaths per day at the height of the outbreak to less than 150 per day over the last seventy-two hours. Orbegón gave all the credit to former Minister Sanjuan.

"But I must be completely honest with you, *Mexicanistas*. We have reached a critical juncture," Orbegón said. "An even greater danger than we've already experienced is directly in front of us. If a cure for Big Bonebreaker is not found immediately, we may see even more loss of precious life. That's why the Holy Renaissance has called in one of the greatest scientific minds of our time, Dr. Henry David Stark."

The four doctors in the room leaned back in their chairs and looked at one another as if their roller coaster car had just lurched forward.

"Dr. Stark's track record as a Special Pathogens agent is superb, having worked the famous Borna epidemic in Guangzhou, China, and most notably, the smallpox outbreak in Egypt." Orbegón gave an absurd nod of his cinder-block head. "His efforts to stop the virus are already under way, and if anyone can stop Big Bonebreaker, it's Dr. Stark."

Stark stood and turned off the monitor with an angry punch.

"If I may?" Jarum said with real concern in his voice. "I believe they're setting you up, Henry David."

Muñoz laughed at Jarum with a mix of reproof and mockery.

Scrunching up his eyes, Stark did the math and decided that they were already operating on borrowed time. Five days ago, Isabel had predicted that a new wave of infections would hit in four to six days. Current rates of vaccination and efficacy levels of Isabel and Jarum's new nanophages had obviously bought Mexico more time—but those efforts were merely staving off the inevitable. In twenty-four to thirty hours, the viruses would breed three more generations and completely mutate, rendering the weekend's new nanophages useless. Joaquin's twin demons were unforgiving, so Stark walked himself through the worst case scenario: By tomorrow mid-day at the latest, a tiny percentage of dengue-5 and dengue-6 would worm free and breed. The collective immunity of Ascensión would give way, the perimeter clinics would clog with bodies by tomorrow night, and, with omnivalent vaccine caches about to be used up, Big Bonebreaker would spread unchecked across Mexico the day after tomorrow.

When Stark opened his eyes, he could see that his three colleagues were looking at him with pity. They saw what he saw, and the daily rain beat against the windows.

"Update, Recoding Project?" Stark said to Isabel and Jarum. Through a *plasceron* window, Jarum's bank of three *i.a.*'s gleamed black against the white of the laboratory. Black-and-white photographs of Jarum's three daughters, pencil-colored by his oldest, hung on the frame of one computer. "What happened to Debora3 this morning?"

Jarum and Isabel seemed to negotiate who would report to the Task Force Coordinator with a series of glances and, finally, Jarum, ever the gentleman, deferred.

"Not good, but not a total loss," Isabel said. Her voice was clear, hard, and it worked on Stark like a tonic. "My original conclusions are bearing out. There's no way to save the volunteer *and* keep the target lymphocyte cell viable," Isabel said, almost as if this were good news. "They are at cross-purposes in the procedure."

Stark made a little noise of affirmation and straightened. "Did you try infecting Debora3 with your new working model of Generation One?"

"Yes," Jarum said. He did not seem quite as energized by their findings as Isabel did. "But only the real Generation One virus would render more effective results."

For a moment, Stark's mind flitted to Sister Domenica. *She safe?* He glanced at his cell phone, briefly confused, as always, by the Farsi keypad (tens of thousands had been donated by Iran when the *pilone* network went down). No calls. It was an obsession, now, checking for calls from the Convent of Guadalupe.

Stark looked up from his phone and caught Muñoz staring at him, the same scrutinizing stare that he'd been giving Stark lately, the same stare that Muñoz had given him when the two were deducing Joaquin's pattern of targeting Sister Domenica together. *Pedro, you seeing through me?* Stark wondered, returning Munoz's stare. Predicting the second outbreak, seeing mouth pustules as symptomatic of early viral mutations—the man obviously had an antenna on him to rival the nun's. Had Muñoz determined Stark's plan to capture a sample of Generation One? Perhaps. No, *probably*. Stark wished he could be open with Muñoz—he admired him, truly liked him. But after Isabel of all people had accused Stark of helping Joaquin Delgado, Stark felt he could trust no one. That no one could trust him, either. A plan to lure Joaquin into the open, no matter how logical it might be to do so, would probably simply appear as conspiracy in Ascensión's culture of paranoia. *Sorry, Pedro,* Stark thought, and looked away.

"The old system still won't accept the new long enough to allow T cell differentiation or the matrix to learn from that differentiation," Jarum was saying. "I calculated a success rate of 15 percent for this matrix."

"Well, 15 percent," Isabel said, surprised, impressed, "is better than I ever got, Jarum. Well done."

Stark was surprised by Isabel's note of optimism. *So, 15 percent sounds good to her?* He bit his lower lip. *Hoo, we so screwed.*

"But," Jarum said, "I have something new to go on for the matrix."

Isabel sat back, crossing her legs, annoyed. Typical consultation with Jarum and Isabel, Stark thought. The left hand ever outdoing the right.

Jarum touched his memboard's screen, pulling up his morning's work. "I went back to Dr. Delgado's original notes on Isabel's project, archived at Barcelona Technical." He folded his arms and spoke to Isabel, probably thinking that Stark and Muñoz wouldn't really understand him anyway. "Delgado's supposition that virus and immune response are evolutionarily linked provided me with a few insights to Protein Three's codon arrangement. I took the liberty of stealing several more arrangements right from dengue-5's genome and inserting them into the matrix. It wasn't enough to save Debora3." He smiled. "But then, I considered what you discovered about dengue-5, Isabel."

Isabel nodded. "Which was?"

Jarum's voice thrummed with excitement. "Histocompatibility. The moment that virus and immune system meet and exchange identifications is where—"

"Piss on that. We've gone through that," Isabel said. "It's not about rejection, it's about compatible systems—"

"We didn't make it *thoroughly* compatible. The tropism sequence!" Jarum said with a little strangled noise of excitement. "Remember?"

Stark looked at Muñoz for a translation, but he shrugged. Jarum and Isabel were speaking their own shorthand now.

"The scrap of Native Mexican DNA in the virus's tropism sequence, telling it what to attack?" Jarum said. "I believe it's a passkey that works both ways—not only for the virus to target the immune system but for the immune system to identify the virus. I believe it's a base code even for the very surface proteins of the virus, which Joaquin stripped down so far as to be unrecognizable by a Native Mexican immune response. But he couldn't do away with that one last code. *That's* what we need for the recoding project to be a success."

"Jarum, that would require entering that sequence into every shitty little cell in the *foquin* body involved in T cell production," Isabel said.

"Can we afford to pin our hopes on 15 percent?"

Isabel shrugged in exhaustion.

"I already provided the structural foundation for this new code with the work I did on Protein Three," Jarum said to Stark, making his pitch when Isabel relented. "Personally, I think this is the right direction."

Stark was distracted by a shadow passing across the atrium window, and, a moment later, the *sabihonda,* in long coat and boots, barely paused in the particle arrester as she entered the room, the skirts of her black cloak rustling. Rosangelica glanced at the faces of the four doctors as if she were scanning the pieces on a board, midgame. "What's happening here, Doctors? Three volunteers are awaiting instruction in the recoding project labs."

Stark leaned back, hands behind his head. "We were about to discuss the Task Force's next plan of attack."

"A *new* plan of attack? Really?" Rosangelica said, her voice singsong with sarcasm. She pulled up a chair and sat backwards, legs spread, leaning her elbows on its back. "What a surprise. Maybe skulking around Zapata Hospital put the fear of God in our Task Force Coordinator?"

Oh damn. Stark had wondered when this moment would come. *They know.* Out of the corner of his eye, Stark could see Muñoz lowering his head to let the crown of his helmet block his face. "Afraid? Of what?" Stark said, trying to keep cool. "I broke quarantine and I got the information we needed regarding patient zero."

"The ends justify the means, eh? You'll get no argument from Emil

Orbegón on that score." The *sabihonda* was clearly relishing the tension in the room. "But how can I trust you when you lie to me like that?"

"Yes, how to trust someone who breaks a ridiculous law in order to save lives?" Stark laughed but he knew it sounded forced and furious. "It's a mystery."

She closed her eyes. "We'll settle up over lawbreaking later, Estarque. And with you, Dr. del Negro." Those silver pupils shone at Muñoz and Stark felt his breath leave him. "Or are you going by Muñoz again?"

Muñoz bowed his head, unable to look Rosangelica in the eye, Stark could tell. He was about to insist that Muñoz's name was del Negro, but he told himself that Rosangelica wouldn't be chatting like this if she knew about Grandmother Muñoz's Tripe Soup recipe or that Stark and Isabel had read Sanjuan's genocidal recommendation. If the *sabihonda* knew, they would have already been drawn and quartered, and realizing that, he felt a bit braver. "Rosangelica, the grown-ups are busy," he said. "We can't play spy with you right now."

Rosangelica gave a twisted smile. "What's the new direction, Estarque?"

Stark explained what Jarum had proposed, that the base code from Joaquin's Monterrey work had provided hope for creating a more effective T cell, but that the time it would take was almost prohibitive. "However," Stark said, "we have over twenty WHO-affiliated wetcode labs worldwide willing to help us. Coordinating with them—"

"I'll be brutally honest with the Task Force," Rosangelica said, cutting him off and pausing. "We don't have the time, as Dr. Khushub admirably put it, to enter that sequence into every shitty little cell in the *foquin* body."

"Sons of whores." Isabel let out a shocked gasp as she heard her own words coming from the *sabihonda*'s mouth.

Stark's mind reeled in fright for a moment. *Rosangelica got a bug on us.* His eyes flitted over the memboards, their suits, the speakers in the atrium that allowed them to speak to *medicos* in the hot labs, the computers, the netmonitors. Who knew how many ways the *sabihonda* could have tapped their conversation? Stark felt even more grateful that he had never uttered aloud his plan to use Domenica as bait for Joaquin to anyone but Domenica down in La Baja.

Rosangelica suddenly seemed like a bird of prey in that chair, perched but ready for flight. "The United States has managed a twenty percent troop buildup since the start of the Big Bonebreaker outbreak. We're on the verge of being outmanned at the border. Emil wants a quicker end to this outbreak," she said. "One hundred fifty deaths a day and another delay from the Task Force are not satisfactory."

Stark had relied on rudeness as a tool his whole career. The petty needs of governmental figures nearly always required that an epidemiologist browbeat and humiliate them into understanding the limits of their power during an outbreak. Though Rosangelica scared him to his bones, he let Stark, the Special Pathogens agent, take over. "Rosangelica, did you read the morning medical boards?"

Rosangelica blinked slowly, pondering him. "Yes."

"Then you know it has been established that political pressure has no effect on dengue-5. I believe it was Dr. Huffenpuff who proved that."

Raising her chin, lips pressed together, Rosangelica clearly had more to say, but instead she smirked at him. "You don't think Emil would pull you off this Task Force?"

"Domenica and *Los Hijos* stopped the civil unrest that Orbegón couldn't," Stark said, throwing punches for the hell of it now. "Troop movements? Please. Let's move on."

"You are in no position to talk shit with me, Stark."

"And you're no doctor. Shut up or leave. Those are your options."

Rosangelica grinned at Stark like he was a piece of fruit she intended to devour. "You're a good flirt, *papi*." Glancing at Jarum and Isabel, she said, "You're the two I trust now. I want to talk to you about this proposal later. I can't sign off on it, Doctors. It's dangerous."

Rubbing his hands together like he was wringing wet towels, Jarum's eyes were wide, his mouth, firmly pursed. He was too aghast at the whole situation to respond.

Isabel gathered herself, and cursed, *"Me cago en la tapa del organo y me revuelco encima de la mierda."*

She a cuss-poet, Stark thought. That one was so bizarre, he couldn't even translate it.

"Are you insane?" Isabel shouted. "We can't rush into this with only a 15 percent chance of success."

"I disagree, Dr. Khushub," Rosangelica calmly replied. "You have as many shots on goal as you like. Three volunteers and a 15 percent chance per shot is better than delaying further."

Like the high barbed-wire fencing he'd seen around the hot zones when

he first arrived, Rosangelica's "roll the dice" attitude grimly appealed to the
cold tactician in Stark. But killing human beings as they had just killed
Deboras 1 through 3 would crack Isabel—and perhaps others. "No, Rosangelica. That's absurd. I'll talk to Cazador. He'll understand that a higher percentage of success is preferable to—"

"Cazador now reports to me, Stark. Which means ultimately, you report
to me, too."

Isabel scoffed. "Henry David doesn't report to mules fucking on a beach,
sabihonda, and we won't kill indiscriminately. Do you have wetcoders in the
wings ready to take our places?" She put a hand on Jarum's shoulder. "Do
you have anyone who can recode the entire immune system?"

Rosangelica's pause was long enough for Stark to say, "Leave. You're in
the way, Rosangelica."

"We don't have an answer of how to proceed," Rosangelica said, "and I
don't leave policy discussions."

"This is a medical consultation and you aren't helping."

To everyone's surprise, Rosangelica relented with a sigh. "A few volunteers," she said, standing up, walking to the door, "or several more hundred
dead." Before leaving, she looked at Stark, and said, "I don't trust you.
There's something behind your delay, and I intend to find out what it is."

Only one window in the atrium looked out onto the inner, hollow shaft
of Torre Cuauhtémoc where *peseros* and swoop jets climbed and dove, their
beacons blinking red and blue. Through that window, Stark could see the
massive epaulets and bearded chin of the Federal Cloister's gigantic military
figure. Stark suddenly realized that Orbegón's naming Stark publicly and
Rosangelica's hostility were interlinked. The Holy Renaissance was preparing to disappear him.

"I laugh while I shit on these *foquin* pederasts," Isabel murmured to no
one in particular.

"I'll contact the WHO-affiliated laboratories," Stark said to the other
three. "Get me all your recent findings, Jarum, and your recommendations
for how to proceed." He stood. "I have to meet with the volunteers and
make sure they're ready."

Isabel, for her part, seemed relieved that they had a path that didn't lead
straight to killing human guinea pigs, so she finalized plans with Jarum to
coordinate with WHO.

Stark left the atrium and headed for the nearest boost, the boots of his moon suit clopping on the cobblestone street. As he waited for the boost to arrive, Muñoz appeared next to him.

"That was awful," Muñoz said.

"Are you worried?" Stark asked.

"Of course."

"I guess that shows you're smarter than I am."

That look was back, Muñoz's cutting stare as if his eyes were trying to peel back the very skin of Stark's face. "I have something I want—that I need. Something I want to ask of you," Muñoz said.

The boost arrived and they stepped in after a group of men in gloves, clamp masks, and tuxedos exited. "What is it?"

The doors closed behind them and they plunged downward. Outside the elevator, they could see the giant statue's hands, resting on giant biceps as though hugging its giant self.

"Are you what you appear to be?" Muñoz said.

The boost kept falling and a swoop jet shrieked by. "What kind of question is that?" The layers of distrust around him were confounding to Stark. "After what Rosangelica just said to me? You ask me a question like that?"

"I have a feeling," Muñoz said, "that I know what you're up to."

Could Rosangelica hear this conversation? And if she did, would it matter, if she and Orbegón had already made up their minds about Stark? He stopped the boost. Outside, the wounds in the giant hands looked all too real.

Stark didn't think that Muñoz could have really deduced that he was trying to trap Joaquin. But the man had proven himself to have more than just a deductive mind, so Stark took out his phone. "What's your number?"

Muñoz checked his phone, realized it was all in Farsi, then gave his number from memory, frowning in confusion.

Stark tapped in Muñoz's number so that it would ring differently if Muñoz called him. He looked up to see if Muñoz had seen what he had done, and the younger doctor nodded. "Call me if you bump into anything of interest, Doctor."

Muñoz looked back and forth between the phone and Stark. "That doesn't really answer my question."

"I can't really answer your question." Stark resumed the boost's descent, and a moment later, they were spilled out on the street where Stark was to meet the volunteers in the National Institute's clinic. "Are you coming with me?"

"Actually," Muñoz said, "I was hoping you would come with me." He took a few steps, looked back at Stark, then walked into an adjacent clinic where his own Joint Operations offices and "fever rooms" were located.

Stark glanced at the doors to the Institute, anxious that the volunteers were waiting for him, then followed Muñoz into the Joint Operations offices, a bustling hub that coordinated the perimeter clinics with La Alta's medical line of defense.

It seemed more newsroom than medical staff, Stark thought, as doctors, clinicians, and communications specialists hustled around him.

Through the crisscross, Stark could see why Muñoz had brought him here.

Beyond the triple-coated, *plasceron* "glass" of the Joint Operations' assay labs, or "fever rooms," sitting on an exam table in a red-and-black antiviral suit, was Sister Domenica.

CHAPTER

29

EVER SINCE DOMENICA'S ARRIVAL in La Alta, she'd sequestered herself in the Convent of Guadalupe. Stark felt a pulsing dread as he wondered what she was doing here, in Muñoz's fever room. "Is she all right?" Stark said.

"She's fine. I promise. We just needed a safe place to talk with you." The panic that had turned Muñoz icy and silent when the *sabihonda* said his name was starting to dissolve, and he spoke kindly now.

Stark said. "'We'?"

"She has a request, Henry David. Well. *We* do."

Muñoz led Stark into the clinic and Domenica looked up as she heard the assay lab lock open. Her ominously dark eyes gleamed at Stark from within the helmet. "It's good to see you again, Dr. Stark," she said, standing. "Thank you for agreeing to see me."

It had been refitted for bloodwork and immune-system assays, but the clinic had originally been a veterinary hospital. Posters of puppies and kitties yapping and meowing were on the walls, and, as Stark approached Domenica, Muñoz walked around the room, touching each to render them silent.

The last time Stark had seen Domenica, she was giving final orders to Old Antonio and a group of street fighters four days ago. It was surreal, seeing her painted in red and black. "Please, sit."

Domenica wasn't accustomed to the biohazard suit and it kept bagging at her legs as she tried to adjust her position. Muñoz came to stand next to her, offering his hand. "This thing," she said, frowning down at the suit. Then she looked up at Stark, and the deep, foreboding gaze returned. "I asked Dr. Muñoz to bring you here because he and I have grown close in recent days." She turned her face to Muñoz as if she were going to speak with him, but said, "We want to ask a favor of you."

"Name it, Sister," Stark said with a shrug. "I owe you more than I can ever repay."

"I was hoping you'd see it that way," Domenica said. She seemed swallowed, digested. Muñoz had hinted yesterday that something psychological and physiological were clashing inside the woman—probably due to a botched "faith lift." Whatever Sister Domenica was confronting, something in those haunting eyes told Stark that she was staring so deeply inward that she might never look away. "I hear the Outbreak Task Force is divided," Domenica said, "over the immune-system-recoding procedure."

"Yes, you could say that," Stark said, feeling that he was about to receive another lecture on the morality of the recoding project. "Dr. Khushub doesn't think it will work, but she's on board out of duty, or maybe out of friendship to me." Stark added hastily, "But even Isabel agrees that this is the best chance for a 'cure.'"

"In that case," Domenica said. "I want to make an appeal."

Stark mentally arranged his arguments, ready to defend the procedure. "Go ahead."

"I want you to allow me to be your first volunteer."

Horrified, Stark stepped backwards into a countertop, his hands colliding with neatly arranged infrared thermometers and one-touch blood scanners. The cold resolve and disaffection he'd been relying on so heavily these days began to wither, shrinking beneath the glare of her intent. "That's just—you understand what the procedure would do?"

Domenica said nothing, and her dark eyes gave nothing away. Muñoz, however, slowly nodded.

"You want to do this, Domenica?" Stark said.

"Of course I don't *want* to do this," Domenica said, scolding. "But *I* should be the one to perform this service, not women who have no idea what's happening here."

"And what *is* really happening here, Sister?"

"I've been putting my life on the line already," Domenica said, a pinch of bitterness in her words.

"Sister," Stark hissed at her, mortified to hear that very secret piece of information spoken aloud.

"It's OK," Muñoz said to Stark. "This is a level-six hot lab."

Stark relaxed and apologized. Even if their biohazard suits *were* bugged, they were safe in here—basic turn-of-the-century antiterrorism protocol made certain that nothing—microbes *or* information—could get out.

Domenica turned her attention back to Stark. "All I'm saying is that you should select a volunteer who knows what's at stake."

"A compelling argument," Stark said. He thought for a long moment, seriously weighing Domenica's appeal. The pros and cons balanced for a brief moment, but then he said, "No."

"No? No what?"

"No, I won't accept you as a volunteer," Stark said.

Muñoz sounded surprised. "What?"

"We intend to create a viable immunocyte," Stark said, looking at Muñoz sidelong, "not a martyr."

"Well, what you 'intend' is irrelevant," Domenica said. "You *will* create a martyr. What you have to decide is if the first volunteer will be Holy Renaissance, or . . . someone else."

Mexico and her symbols, Stark thought. The Virgin of Guadalupe. Hidalgo's torch. The boy martyrs who killed themselves rather than be taken alive when the US sacked Mexico City in the 1800s. Domenica was right. If Isabel and Jarum successfully created a recoding matrix, whoever died in this procedure would be immortalized in Mexican myth. Stark admired Domenica, and Muñoz, too—perhaps more than any other people on earth. They didn't have to be neutral—and they refused to be. "You're assuming too much about my politics. I sympathize. Believe me. I do."

"I know you better than that," Domenica said. "You more than sympathize. I saw your eyes when you walked through our safe house, when you met Old Antonio. I know you appreciate a spirited struggle against superior force."

Stark laughed. That's exactly what he had told Pirate upon entering the safe house. But he fell quiet.

Domenica said, "Do you know why old Antonio carries that unlit cigarette wherever he goes, Doctor?"

"No matches?"

"He rolled it at the beginning of the dengue outbreak," Domenica said loudly, speaking over Stark's glibness, "and promised his Purépecha elders that he would smoke that cigarette when Orbegón fled Mexico and a new world began." Domenica lowered her voice in a dramatic, conspiratorial whisper. "If I told you *Los Hijos de Marcos* and Old Antonio's *contralunas* are poised to take the capital, I think that would fill you with pride, Henry David Stark."

"Maybe," he said. She'd pegged him pretty well. Nothing would give Stark greater pleasure than to watch Mexico rise up and destroy Orbegón, Cazador, and Rosangelica—their Kafka-like suspiciousness; their cruel effi-ciency; their faith lifts, spas, and work ranches; their beloved war in Texas. "Look, I'm no Mexican. I'm just a doctor. This is your fight, not mine," Stark said. "I'm here to stop Joaquin Delgado, and after that, I plan on going home to harvest spinach before the summer heat."

Domenica stood, stepping with confidence this time, and stood before Stark, placing a hand on his arm. Her eyes were so expressive, so penetrat-ing, that he wanted to step away, but the counter was already at his back. "Pedro says you know," she said with reprimand and supplication in her voice. "Pedro told me you know about the Tripe Soup recipe."

The EIS Report. Sanjuan's gift to Orbegón, for which he probably paid with his life. Stark felt Muñoz's surgical stare on his skin again, and he thought he understood it a bit better now. If Stark were in Muñoz's shoes, he might be parsing the foreigner's loyalties, too.

"You know what this government is capable of doing to *las indígenas,* the people who are close to the land," Domenica said. "*You* can't not side with us, Henry David."

Stark's mouth parted and he slowly shook his head, but in dismay, not in refusal. He felt checkmated, the board a locked grid of powerless pieces. He imagined his grandfather scolding him in disgust, as he said, "I can't." He clasped his hands. He shut his eyes. "If I interfere, and Cazador or Rosangelica get wind of this, they will interfere with me, and Mexico can't afford any more interference from the Holy Renaissance." He raised his hands as if warding off more argument, though Domenica and Muñoz were both silent, fixed as fence posts. "Domenica, I want you to leave. I need to talk to Pedro in private."

"I'm sorry, Domenica," Muñoz said to her back, from across the lab. He gave Stark a biting, disappointed look and Stark could tell he had been thoroughly diminished in Muñoz's esteem. "I'll contact you at the convent later."

Domenica watched Stark for a long moment with those deep-seeing eyes. "You can change your mind," she said to Stark, "and I expect you will."

Once Domenica had left the lab, Stark turned on Muñoz with anger. "Why did you do that to me? Why did you put me on the spot like that?"

Muñoz hesitated, but raised his eyes and answered, "I wanted to see for myself where you really stand."

"We don't have time for political games, Pedro." Stark shook his head in disbelief. "Rosangelica's *or* yours."

"Dr. Kushub was right about you." Muñoz nodded, appraising Stark.

Stark was so furious he lapsed into English. "The hell that mean?" He caught himself, and in Spanish, he said, "What do you mean by that, sir?"

"You are a completely amoral person." Muñoz folded his arms, defiant, like he was preventing Stark from entering a gate at his back. "She's right. You're so amoral that you're completely opaque to me."

Stark's mind went blank with confusion. *Me? Amoral? Bela said that?* He tried to rally an angry retort, but, just then, Muñoz stiffened as if yanked to his feet by his collar. He stood still, in a pose of listening. *That damn* pilone *makes puppets of all of em. Even Pedro.* Annoyed, he said, "What is it now?"

The red light over the hot-lab door lit up and another alarm light went on over the receiving desk table in the office outside and, simultaneously, a computer beside Muñoz stopped scrolling chicken reports and read ALERT. Outside, in the offices, the medical staff was looking in at Muñoz and Stark, waiting for an explanation.

"It's a compromise! Where?" Stark demanded, ignoring the alarm, the curious faces, and that last stab of a comment from Muñoz. "Where is it?"

"Damn." Muñoz's eyes refocused and blinked at Stark. "There's been an accident in La Baja. Perimeter Clinic Four. It's been shut down. A doctor was infected."

Stark's stomach clenched, threatened to squeeze its contents up and out of his throat. *An accident? Hope he right about that.* But that thought died an early death. Stark was about to remove his cell phone from his back pouch, then thought better of it. Muñoz, Connected, could tell him everything more quickly. "A *doctor* was infected?" he shouted over the alarms. "Who? A coordinator? Who?"

Muñoz's eyes scanned the empty air. "Head doctor—Dr. Filomena Garcia de la Costa—she has it—Big Bonebreaker. Confirmed." As soon as Stark wondered if there were indications that it was Generation One, Muñoz said, "Mouth pustules. Garcia has mouth pustules, Henry David."

"Have they quarantined the clinic?"

"Damn!" Muñoz growled, snapping his head to the side in anger. "No. Dr. Ramos has initiated Retreat Procedure."

What the hell? Stark shouted, "*What* Retreat Procedure? Why? To *where* are they retreating?" He dragged Muñoz by the shoulder to the hot lab's exit.

"Federal docking bay. Perimeter Four staff have been ordered to the Joint labs there."

"Why?" As they ran out of the Joint Ops offices, Stark instinctively grabbed a push pack loaded with omnivalent vaccine, bleach, and infrared thermometer, then seized Muñoz by the arm again. "Tell me who ordered a protocol change."

Muñoz shouted, "Would you shut up? Let go of me! I'm trying to find out!"

"Well, tell me what's going on! You have to be my *sabihondo,* Pedro," Stark said as they ran down the crowded street to the boost. "Contact Francisca de Verano. She's the phlebotomist for the Federal Cloister's docking bay. She's one hundred percent. No infections have gotten by her. Tell her to meet me there but *not* to take a blood draw from Garcia until I arrive."

"She's on her way," Muñoz said, stopping suddenly and rising on tiptoes to avoid a toddler who'd broken free from his mother.

"Why did they retreat?" Stark said, more to himself than Muñoz. "I gave specific orders to quarantine in this situation! Isn't anyone paying attention to my script?" Stark was so angry he could see his facial hair on his cheek flexing with his pulse. "Call her, Pedro," Stark said. "Call—I mean—'node' Ramos or whatever it is you do with that oyster in your brain. Tell her to stop the retreat, get back to the Perimeter, and quarantine her staff!" He pushed past four young men with baby carriages strolling with maddening slowness from the elevator and impatiently guided Muñoz in. He immediately hit the CERRADO button, and the boost doors slid shut over the angry faces of teenagers waiting to board outside. He and Muñoz found themselves between a group of ladies with cello cases and clamp masks. "Tell Ramos that no one can leave Perimeter Clinic Four until I say so! The virus has to be contained there! Anyone with anything like any symptoms we ever heard of!"

The women with cellos edged as far away from Stark and Muñoz as they could manage in the cramped boost.

"It's too late. They closed the gap and re-formed the perimeter line immediately." He shot Stark a look of apology. "The *pilone*. We're too efficient for our own good. Most of the Perimeter Four staff has already been processed out of their Joint labs and moved up."

"Moved *up*? Where, here? Tell them to stop what they're doing!" Stark said in frustration, desperation. He felt like his guts, his very innards, were spilling out of his body, through his fingers. Who could have done this? Who could have given such orders?

The certainty of the answer almost strangled his raging anger.

Joaquin could have changed the protocol if he had access to a perimeter-clinic computer. Maestro *knows code.*

Was this it? Was this the moment Stark had been waiting for? If it were really Joaquin, he wondered if it was time to shift into the "Joaquin script" now, the script of responses that Stark had kept mentally, preparing for the day when "Patient Minus One" finally emerged from the chaos and murk of the hot zones.

"Pedro, when we get to the docking bay, double-check that basic handling protocols were followed in this retreat. You're going to be the one to determine how this happened. Read the logs before they were uploaded on the *pilone* net. Find out if any new doctors were added to the roster recently."

Muñoz's eyes burned as he realized what Stark was suggesting.

And I gonna make sure we get blood samples, he thought. *Big ones.*

The boost dove into a palm-lined esplanade, and when the doors slid open, Muñoz and Stark dashed out, shouting through their suits' speakers for a passing tram to wait. They leapt aboard and the tram picked up speed in the open ground of the esplanade, scattering a flock of doves. The phlebotomist would do this the old-fashioned way, Stark decided, watching the flock's shadows soar up the giant sandals and hem of the enormous Jesuchristo statue's robe. He would see to it that the patient gave up a barbaric, full pint of blood to make certain they had ten times as many samples as needed, in case Joaquin *was* responsible for this infection, in case he had emerged at last, and the infected doctor had Generation One.

This my Holy Grail, at long fucking last? Stark wondered, watching the flock vanish against the enormity of the scabbard high overhead. *Or we just seeing the beginning of the end for La Alta?*

Stark resisted barking more questions and orders at Muñoz, since they couldn't do anything else until Muñoz had determined what really happened. As the tram rounded a bank of palm trees and entered the docking-bay tunnel, Stark could see thirty or forty septic troops barring the way and a swarm of antiviral suits beyond. His breath felt like lead in his lungs.

Stark and Muñoz jumped from the tram and presented their credentials to a soldier with a *Sangre de Cristo* rifle on his shoulder. "We're with the Outbreak Task Force," Stark shouted. "We need to get into the dock!"

"Talk to Captain Berenguer," the soldier said, waving Stark toward the heart of the commotion. "The docking bay is under his jurisdiction since they just brought an infected doctor up here."

Stark flashed his credentials. "Does anyone else have the virus?"

"Go ask a doctor, *guero*. You're clear. You're clear. Move it."

Stark and Pedro ran past him into the turmoil of the docking bay, where big-gun tanks were nestling into their air cushions and soldiers marched double time, lining up at the various tunnels leading out into the esplanade of the Federal Cloister. Stark looked at the laboratories and sole clinic where the commotion centered, a hive within the hive. "Oh man," he said, looking at the swarm of bodies between him and the labs.

"I'm off to find the reprocessed patients," Muñoz said. He took out the phone and shook it before Stark. "I'll call you if I find anything."

Stark wished him luck, then forced his way into the throng, making for the blood-draw rooms. As he did, he peered into the face shields of helmets around him, examining eyes, looking for the face of Joaquin Delgado.

CHAPTER

30

"I'M DR. HENRY DAVID STARK. Where's Dr. de Verano?"

The phlebotomy station was a mill of white Racal suits, rifles, and pivoting helmets, but through it emerged a woman who seemed grateful to hear Stark's voice. "I'm here, Doctor!" A woman in clamp mask and gloves shoved herself through the mass of soldiers. "I can't get in to see Dr. Garcia! They won't let me see her!"

"Good. I asked them not to." Troops continued to pour into the outer chamber of the phlebotomy station and though they wore military septic uniforms, their presence was a danger to the quarantine's integrity. "We don't need all these soldiers here," Stark said to a wall of backs. "Can someone please get them out of—?"

But his words were just noise in his own helmet. The soldiers were listening to *pilone* orders, oblivious to the sound of one doctor talking. The room continued to fill with soldiers.

Stark cranked up the volume on his suit until it squelched like a bullhorn. "All military personnel, out!"

Helmets and face shields turned in his direction.

A tall man strode toward Stark as if he meant to knock him down. "Who the hell are you?"

He was the only military suit in the room not carrying a gun. *Officer,* Stark figured. "I'm the Task Force Coordinator, and I am here to—"

"Identification?" The officer held out his hand.

Stark's first reaction was to slap the man's hand away, he was so impatient to get into Garcia's cell. The patient was safely quarantined, the phlebotomist was ready, and Isabel or Jarum had speculated that Generation
One became Generation Two in a matter of hours. "Look," Stark said, "we
don't have time to play army. I'm—"

"Identification," the officer repeated threateningly.

Slow down, Stark told himself. The virus was mutating, but it would be
hours before it reproduced. The response may have been wrong, but, thanks
to the *pilone* network, it had also been swift. Stark had time. *Throw this dog a*
bone and he gonna get out of your way. Stark reached into his back pouch and
pulled out his credentials again.

Inside the officer's helmet, Stark could see a wide nose, and the man's
thick black moustache contrasted with the white of his coverall's hood.
Glancing at the ID chip, the officer said, "You're the American?"

"Only because Mexico's best were killed nine days ago in Zapata Hospital," Stark said, defensive.

"I know," the officer said. When Stark held out his hand to retrieve his
card, the officer made no move to return it. The officer tilted his head back
and looked down his wide nose at Stark. "I was at Zapata that night. I'm
Captain Ulises Berenguer. I handle Ascensión's military response to these
outbreaks."

Stark was about to make his plea for the captain's help when another
throng, a Holy Renaissance entourage, pushed its way into the clogged
room. At the center was a figure of great prominence, Stark could tell, by the
way the red-and-black uniforms cut a wake through the soldiers.

Cazador.

Stark thought, *Like a kids' soccer game here, players all running to the ball.*
"Stay close to me, Doctor," Stark told de Verano. "I don't want to lose you in
this crowd."

Francisca de Verano stood behind him and put her hand on his shoulder. Stark appreciated the contact.

"*Jefe* Cazador," Stark shouted. "Is that you in there?"

A speaker-voice answered, "Dr. Stark?"

Stark bobbed his head back and forth trying to get a look at Cazador.

"Doctor? Where are you?" The red-and-black septic suits parted and
Cazador emerged from his retinue, belly first. "What the hell is going on,
Stark? How did this happen?"

"A lapse in protocol. That's all I know."

Cazador raised his hands as if they were little wings ready to carry his big body away from this crowd. "Why did you call for military up here?"

"I didn't," Stark said. He wanted to hide the fact that someone, maybe Joaquin, had changed the script, but he wasn't sure how long that could possibly remain hidden in a city full of wetwared people. The great machine of Mexico's *pilone* culture had come to life and moved with such terrifying unity of purpose that it might prove, ironically, his greatest obstacle. Stark shut his eyes, quickly recalled the true script, and said, "I called for military in the docking bay but not here, not in the labs."

"Do you *want* all these soldiers here?" Cazador asked, cutting through the explanation.

"Hell, no."

Cazador's face paled as he accessed his *pilone* node.

At once Berenguer spun and shouted for his unit to exit and regroup outside the phlebotomy station.

Cazador thinned his own retinue down to two people, asking the rest to wait outside with Berenguer. Then, Cazador turned to the room's quarantine cell and looked through the window at Dr. Garcia. "Is she the only one who was infected?"

"Dr. Mu— *Someone* is determining that," Stark said.

"I heard she has mouth pustules?" Cazador peered into Garcia's room. "That means Generation One, I hear?"

Stark said, "That's de Verano's job to find out." Stark lowered his voice to a deep, serious whisper. "My hope is that Garcia can be our volunteer for the genomic recoding procedure. If she has Generation One and if she consents, we'll have an excellent chance of creating the lymphocyte we need." He nodded to Dr. de Verano. "Once she has samples, and if all goes well, we could clone a very effective nanophage within twenty-four hours. A vaccine, too."

"I want this to happen," Cazador said. "You have my total support, Dr. Stark. What do you need from me?"

Smelling the politically promising whiff of *cure*, Cazador seemed ready to ignore the breach in protocol regarding the outbreak script. "Stand out of the way and allow de Verano to do her work, *Jefe*."

As Dr. de Verano prepared to enter the quarantine cell, the outer chamber's ALHEPA hissed again, but when Stark turned, ready to shout at anyone he saw, Rosangelica was standing in the particle arrester. She stood looking at Cazador with a strange expression—furious, maybe fearful, but darkly intense. She ignored Stark so pointedly that he felt certain she was staring at him.

Stark couldn't tell what passed between the *Jefe* and the *sabihonda* but, like a pressure drop, something in the room changed. Cazador's posture became rigid. He adjusted the oxygen on his suit and stepped backwards as Rosangelica walked into the room. Then, a heartbeat later, the *Jefe*'s two-person retinue walked out of the phlebotomy chamber without so much as a look from Cazador.

"Dr. de Verano?" Rosangelica said to the phlebotomist.

"I'm Francisca de Verano, *señorita*." Francisca met the *sabihonda*'s gaze then lowered her eyes, not out of respect, but shock.

"Please excuse us a moment," Rosangelica said with stiff politeness. "Wait outside, till I call for you."

"No," said Stark, holding de Verano's arm. "She's not going anywhere. I need her now in order to take—"

Rosangelica walked over and broke the contact between Stark and de Verano, then led the phlebotomist to the air lock. "Go."

Stark, his voice edging into its upper register, said, "What the hell do you think you're doing?"

"I'm cleaning up after myself," Rosangelica said. After the doctor left, she turned and began shouting. "Why is an infected patient up here? In La Alta?" Rosangelica pointed to Garcia's cell, still yelling. "Who gave the order to bring an infected patient here, Dr. Stark?"

The *sabihonda* was angrier than he'd ever seen her—scary, out of control angry. He'd wondered briefly if Rosangelica could have changed the protocol at Perimeter Clinic Four. Rosangelica's loyalties were difficult to parse at times, but ultimately, she was a patriot. She'd do nothing to compromise Orbegón. *No, it ain't Rosangelica who changed the script,* Stark thought. His eyes drifted to Garcia, thrashing in the quarantine room. *She got Generation One straight from the source.*

It was Joaquin.

But he couldn't let that detail out just now. Not with a furious cyborg and a partisan assassin breathing down his neck. Stark swallowed his pride, and said, "It's the standing Retreat Procedure."

Rosangelica seemed surprised, as if she had expected Stark to shirk responsibility. If it weren't for her metallic eyes, she might have looked heartbroken. "You asked for this?"

"Stop it, Rosangelica. Let's move on to the immune-system-recoding procedure," he said, staring hard at her, forcing her to look at Dr. Garcia, convulsing in the quarantined room.

Cazador stepped toward Stark, inserting his belly into the conversation. "Explain yourself and let's get on with this," he said. "Why bring Garcia to the last clean refuge of Ascensión? You must have a reason."

Stark couldn't explain the change in the outbreak script, not without also explaining that he had never given the order, not without explaining that he had tricked them into befriending Domenica, that he'd been luring a Typhoid Mary toward La Alta without telling them. "We operate by rules. We have to adhere to a plan," he said. "Now, if you'll call Dr. de Verano back, we can—"

"You *changed* the script, Dr. Stark," Rosangelica said.

He felt as though he could hear the virus seroconverting while they argued. "She has mouth pustules," Stark pleaded, knowing that his credibility had eroded, that anything he said now was only static and noise. He had lied too many times, and although he had lowered the epidemic's daily mortality rate from thousands to hundreds, all Rosangelica and Cazador would see were the lies. "If she contracted Generation One," Stark said, nodding to Garcia, "if she consents, we can use *her* to recode the necessary immune response."

"A maneuver that you sought to delay just this morning," Rosangelica said. "What changed? Why did you change the outbreak script?"

Cazador seemed about to defend Stark, then stepped backwards, retreating from Rosangelica's line of sight. Some unspoken *pilone* debate was still passing between the two, and by Cazador's flustered air, Rosangelica was winning.

Stark trembled so that he couldn't speak without a slight quiver in his voice. "Look." This was it. Poor Dr. Garcia, body wracked with seizures in the other room, was the endgame. Stark couldn't lie or plead or scream his way out of this confrontation with Rosangelica. "I admit changing the outbreak script was risky, but it worked. We have the patient we need. Here. Now," Stark said, wondering when his lies within lies would stop. "We have an opportunity to wipe out these viruses. If we don't come up with a cure, we'll be overwhelmed all over again and the virus will mutate completely out of our control."

"I think your concern for Mexico is *bullshit*," Rosangelica said, using the English word. "Your code is on the protocol change. You brought her here deliberately," Rosangelica said. "You risked infecting the heart and nerve center of Mexico by bringing her into the Federal Cloister. Where the Holy Renaissance is headquartered. Where Emil Orbegón lives."

Cazador's big body turned toward Stark and he peered blankly at him from under heavy lids, seeping hatred and violence.

As if a tide were rushing from him, carrying Cazador, Garcia, and Joaquin away, Stark stepped toward Rosangelica with hands raised. "Wait. Wait."

"He can't be trusted," said the *sabihonda,* passing her hand in front of Stark's face, wiping him away. "There's no way to know for sure if anything he says is true. It's that simple."

"Rosangelica, don't be a fool," Stark said. "If I wanted to destroy Mexico, I'd have done it days ago."

"You *have* been doing it! You're doing it now," she said, her voice nearing a shrill cry. "This was no accident. *You* did this. You are working with Joaquin Delgado, who is *here,* in Ascensión, somewhere."

It felt like Stark's stomach was cracking open. *She knows. Oh, no, she knows.*

"And you *continue* to lie for him. You didn't change that protocol script. That code was changed from Perimeter Clinic Four while you were in the Joint offices with that Judas Pedro Muñoz."

Stark lifted his hands, wanting to bury his face in them, but his face shield was in the way. *Lying to a* sabihonda? He couldn't lie without a deck of cards in his hand—*never no good at it*—and now, confronted with his dim, flat-footed lies, he couldn't begin to fathom his own folly.

"Is this true, Dr. Stark?" Cazador asked.

"Of course it's true. Dr. Delgado changed the outbreak script. Stark let him, and now he's covering for him."

The walls of the lab seemed to constrict around Stark. "No," he said. *I didn't let him. I ain't covering.* But he felt a stab of guilt, because the *sabihonda* was right. That's exactly what he'd done.

Confronted with his own lies as if he were a microbe on a slide to be analyzed, Stark was exposed even to himself. For there, in the smallest recesses of his hopes, Stark had actually been secretly wishing that Joaquin would get past him and infect this rotten government from the feet of that ridiculous Jesus statue to the crown, Emil the Damned.

The *sabihonda* walked over to the outer chamber's bank of windows and polarized them with a touch, blocking out the view of the *barcos,* 'cycles, and swarming *militarios* in the bay. Warm noon sunlight rose in the chamber automatically. She held out her hand. "Give me your gun, *Jefe.*"

Another exchange passed silently between them on slow subcortical *pilone* waves, and Cazador, posture straightening like a man before a firing squad, raised his hand to a pocket in his suit and produced the gun that he had threatened Stark with last week.

"No. You can't. You can't," Stark said.

Rosangelica took the gun from Cazador and walked to the antechamber outside Dr. Garcia's cell. Cazador and Stark had their hands raised as if the *sabihonda* were robbing them.

When Stark made a move to stop Rosangelica from opening the door, she aimed the gun in his face until he stepped back. "Rosangelica," said Stark, wincing with the gun barrel in his eyes. "Yes, I admit it, I lured Joaquin here, but I did it so we could get his blood, so that we could clone a vaccine, so that—"

"Everything you say is a lie," Rosangelica said, gun still trained on him as she made sure her suit's various locks were fastened. "I was wrong to bring you to Ascensión, so I'm correcting my mistake. As of now, you are finished, Estarque. I just erased your security codes."

Cazador gasped. "*You* haven't the authority. I'm the only—"

"Quiet. I also just dissolved the Task Force," the *sabihonda* said. "I've determined that its decision-making process has been influenced by Joaquin Delgado himself. The new Minister of Health will have his hands full tonight."

"Wait, Rosangelica, wait!" pleaded Stark.

Ignoring him, Rosangelica passed through the two air locks and into the quarantined room where Dr. Garcia lay. Stark watched in horror as the *sabihonda* raised Cazador's gun, aimed it at Garcia's face, and pulled the trigger. The contorting woman was forced down into the bed in a bouncing jolt, and then she sagged and went limp, her arms still jerking akimbo.

Stark's mouth drooped open as his gaze lowered to the floor, unable to look through the cell window at that vicious tableau, the precious blood sprayed uselessly against the cell wall. Stark felt grateful for his whirring, clicking air-controlled suit. The silence might have crushed him as he waited for this retreating tide to carry all of Ascensión and Mexico away from him.

Codes erased.

Title stripped.

Nada.

Stark felt upended and emptied, like his knees might unlock beneath him. As he watched the *sabihonda* standing over Dr. Garcia in that little cell, a veil inside him unfastened itself and fluttered away, exposing someone far different than the man who had flown to Mexico a week ago.

From this moment forward, all deaths my fault, Stark thought.

Henry David, HD, the boy who'd grown up on the *quop* farm, couldn't comprehend the gigantic folly of Dr. Stark. Stark, the Special Pathogens agent, the CDC man, always had the finest intentions available, but they rendered him cold and calculating at best—a liar, cheat, and murderer at worst. He'd killed Howell for nothing. Garcia's death was pointless, too. And now he couldn't be trusted to help when needed most.

All that HD could think in this moment was, *it didn't have to happen like this.*

Cazador watched the *sabihonda* as if she were a vampire that had just fed on Garcia's corpse. "Will Rosangelica have the disease?" he muttered to Stark.

He hoped so, but Rosangelica didn't actually touch Garcia. *Besides,* Stark thought, *nothin alive could live in that thing.*

Rosangelica hit the speaker in the quarantine, and said, "*Jefe,* get me a new Racal-plus. I'll have de Verano examine me in the particle arrester." She turned back to the corpse, saying, "Get a Mortuary detail to destroy Garcia's body—do it *in* this cell. Don't remove anything but ash." She looked at them through the window and pointed at Stark. "Don't let the American leave. I'm taking him to the airport. He'll be on a jet within the hour."

"You're sending him back?" Cazador said.

"No," Rosangelica said, "I'm promoting him."

CHAPTER

THE QUARANTINE DIRECTOR, a *Oaxaqueño* with a bad lisp, signed Pedro Muñoz into the La Alta holding facility newly filled with Perimeter Four Clinic workers, saying, "Everyone's been tested, so you're safe in there, Doctor."

Three floors above the docking bay where Garcia had been housed, the quarantine facility was a complex of sealed apartments accessible only by elevator. Stark had asked for these rooms to act as quarantines, in case La Alta was overwhelmed by the virus. But in this scenario, with the clinic staff all uninfected but for Garcia, these apartments made a nice little retreat. Spanish dagger plants and cactuses thrived beneath the cheery wash of false La Alta sunlight, and down one corridor, Muñoz could hear the solemn back and forth of a joyless Ping-Pong game.

"Dr. Muñoz?" An earnest young *medico* greeted Muñoz on the other side of the bolted air lock. "Protocol requires me to request your identification."

Muñoz showed him his genbadge, signed in, and then the customary blood draw and pheresis ritual followed. After Muñoz had resuited himself, he told the *medico,* "I'm here to determine how Dr. Garcia de la Costa contracted the virus. I especially want to see logs that never made it onto *pilone* storage this morning."

"We retrieved our data cache before fleeing La Baja. I'll show you," the *medico* said, aiming the crown of his white helmet toward another air-locked room. "We're speculating that she contracted it from one of the new patients who arrived right before the clinic was compromised."

Muñoz followed him, memboard in hand, gazing at its screen. Accessing the security cameras from his memboard, he could see that the old Azteca College turned Clinic Number Four looked ironically serene. In fact, after tapping up the particle report from the clinic's ALHEPAs, he discovered only one area that had to remain quarantined in the building: Dr. Garcia's private office.

Entering the computer room with the clinic's data cache, Muñoz fell to the task of making certain that procedure had been followed, so that meant reading reports that hadn't yet made it to "wet text" on the *pilone* net. This had to be done manually at a computer terminal, and Muñoz was poor at typing on keyboards, let alone doing it with gloves on. He brought up the computer's screen interface and tapped the scroll on the right side of the screen, bringing him to the top of Garcia's log.

Muñoz found grim pleasure in reading the head physician's log from yesterday. Dr. Garcia was thorough, and reading her elegant attention to detail was oddly inspiring.

May 23. My personal items stowed: Skirt, O'Hara-brand shoes, rayon blouse. Blood draw normal. New gloves before and after. Checked clinic's four external door filters and low-pressure units starting at 1005. 1031 ALHEPA filters: clean (though a bit wheezy—called Support). Oversaw maintenance of new particle arresters in the main infirmary with Dr. F and Dr. T, and all three of us certified the level-six hot lab together. Began my rounds at 1114.

Muñoz smiled in admiration. Her notes were exact down to the brand name of her shoes. Garcia then went into her patient logs, but Muñoz ignored them. The *medico* said a patient must have somehow infected Garcia, but Garcia wasn't sloppy enough for that.

One way to find out more, he figured.

Muñoz's *pilone* Connection wasn't fast. Though he could receive almost anything with his Connection (and did—the Holy Renaissance propaganda engine made sure of that), he could only send short data packets. Glancing at the head physician's profile on the computer screen, Muñoz contacted Garcia de la Costa's node and sent her as concise a message as he could manage. It was hard to restrain himself from raining questions on her.

The *pilone* wetware tapped his language centers and his words or "phonemes" appeared on his VisionField. This wasn't necessary for *pilone* communication (Rosangelica, he imagined, could "think" to her satellites as if by telepathy) but it allowed Muñoz a modicum of privacy and self-editing.

>Garcia<, he addressed, >Well enough to answer ??'s?<

He was relieved to receive a response almost immediately. Garcia clearly had a better Connection, but with *pilone* net controls still shaky, her data packet hit Muñoz's wetware, sapping from his thalamus a cocktail of dopamine and other neurotransmitters—and a mild euphoria.

>Muñoz< Yes. I'm waiting for a blood draw. Who's the American?<

Henry David is there. Good, Muñoz thought. >Theorize please, dr: time/place of infection.<

>I feel like someone took a crowbar to my arms.<

Knowing that he sounded more abrupt than he would have liked, Muñoz repeated his request.

Her response came bounding back, filling Muñoz's wetware like a surge of enthusiasm.

>I lost my husband four days ago. I lost him.< >There's an officer. He's talking to the American. Can you tell them to hurry?<

The double-packet transmissions were dunking his brain in a dopamine bath. He knew he ought to stop transmitting and catch his breath, but he needed this information. >Not much time. Theorize please, dr: time/place of infection!!<

>What are they arguing about out there? Why don't they hurry and take this sample from me?<

Her fever was high and affecting her mind, Muñoz realized. It didn't make any sense to keep harassing her. >Must go, dr—poor connection—node out.<

How in the name of God could this have happened? Muñoz immediately pulled up the Outbreak Protocol, a simple piece of canned software that, when particle arresters registered pathogens in the perimeter clinics, would initiate the Task Force Coordinator's script, sound alarms, deliver orders via cell and sat phones. It was easy enough to see that it had been rewritten—

Stark would never call for infected patients to be lifted to La Alta—so Muñoz checked to see when the canned software was last accessed.

24 May. TFCHDS001ASDF/1205 hours.

Muñoz couldn't make sense of this. He presumed the pass code would have been Perimeter Four's own code, stolen by Joaquin Delgado. He read it again, and a third time.

It was the Task Force Coordinator's own code. It was Henry David's time stamp.

Henry David Stark? Henry David gave this order?

Muñoz read it a fourth time. Noon today, the timestamp read. That was while Stark, Ahwaz, Isabel, and Muñoz were consulting. Of course, Stark did have his memboard with him. Easy enough to give such an order mid-conversation, without anyone in the room knowing.

A falling, swirling sense of dread caught Muñoz, and he thought about the night that he'd snuck into La Alta, when he and Stark determined to-gether that Joaquin was still in Ascensión, still infecting people. They'd reached a curious moment, that night. One minute, Stark had been talking about mouth pustules and Generation One, the next, he was insisting they had to stop the street fighting. At the time, Muñoz had been so disoriented after five days in the hot zone, that he chalked it up to his own burning paranoia.

Then, yesterday, he read the chicken report that confirmed Joaquin was definitely still alive, still infecting people in the hot zone. *<1%: Unknown IgG: viral: retro: max virulence.* Citizens were encountering Generation One. Now, looking at Stark's timestamp on the retreat order, he looked at Stark's non sequitur that first night in La Alta in a completely different light.

The Holy Renaissance's initial distrust of Stark was correct. Stark is helping his old friend. He deliberately left an opening for Dr. Delgado to weasel in.

Didn't he?

Muñoz pushed himself away from the keyboard, squeezed his eyes shut so he couldn't read the gel screen anymore. It was ridiculous. Stark wasn't a pathological killer. Why would he do this? Genocide? To what end?

Henry David is the most amoral man I've ever known, Isabel had told Muñoz. Stark's longtime friend and colleague had said that.

Virgin Mother, what's happening here?

The particle arrester for the office surged to life as someone opened the air lock and stepped into the doorway. Muñoz didn't turn. This would be the nurse, he figured, come to give him the staff's immunological assay results.

"Dr. del Negro? I'm Marta Berra. Can I bother you a moment?"

Muñoz saw Marta's name while scanning Garcia's reports. A "careless girl" who had to be threatened with Mortuary detail to follow basic protocol.

"Are you busy, *señor*?"

He glared at her over his shoulder. Was she kidding?

"Dr. Reynaldo Cruz is here to see you."

Dizzying excitement flooded through Muñoz as he heard that name. He slowly turned in his chair. "What? What did you just say?" Cruz was dead, wasn't he? Isn't that what Muñoz had read when he checked the mortuary manifest upon arriving in La Alta? Reynaldo had been a good friend, one of the few doctors to sign Muñoz's letter of protest to the Holy Renaissance. Muñoz was about to leap from his chair, eager and full of hope for the first time in days.

But as his hands lifted and rested on the arms of his chair, an instinct stilled Muñoz, stopped him in place. It was as if he could hear a bone-thrumming bass note on the other side of the door.

Something's wrong.

"May Dr. Cruz come in, *señor*? He's in the hallway here," Marta said, turning and looking at someone standing to her left.

Muñoz feared that he could guess who was there in the hall, just beyond the particle arrester. He had come for the Joint Operations Coordinator. An intelligent maneuver.

"Are you all right, Dr. Muñoz?" Marta asked, stepping into the computer lab.

Muñoz turned away to hide his face by feigning engrossment in his gel screens. He decided that he had to be cool and collected, that he had to lie as well as Henry David Stark right now. He decided to *be* Henry David Stark, conjuring the American's demeanor, his cold, abrupt aloofness. "Of course, Marta," Muñoz said, back turned to her. "Send him in."

He heard someone enter the room, and then Muñoz spun back to the door in his chair. He looked up into the eyes of a creature from another world.

It was the man with the backpack, the orderly who had been at Zapata

Hospital the night Muñoz had appeared before the media with Minister Alejandro and Elena Batista. Muñoz recalled thinking that he'd never seen that orderly before. *But how fine, an orderly of his age.* The man now stood holding a stack of white bedsheets, wearing Reynaldo Cruz's genbadge on the outside of his Racal-plus suit. He said to Muñoz, "I just finished making the quarantine beds and wanted to let you know that the Perimeter Four staff can stay here tonight, if needed." He held his stack of sheets to his chest as if they were family linens. "You're Dr. del Negro, yes?"

Ahí está, Muñoz thought. *The man who brought a city to its belly is right in front of me.*

Dr. Joaquin Delgado was disarmingly handsome, with a perfect cleft in his broad chin, but he had black, thirsty wells for eyes and it took all of Pedro's willpower to hold the demon's gaze without flinching.

"I'm Dr. del Negro."

Marta turned her helmet back and forth between them. "Dr. Cruz was stranded in the hot zone for many days."

"Incredible," Muñoz said. "Were you working in a—hospital at the time of the outbreak, Doctor?"

"I was at Zapata," Joaquin said. He set the bedsheets on a counter, patted them, rested his hand there, and nodded his upper body, which he carried with rigid grace. Then he faced Muñoz, waiting for reprisal perhaps or a contradiction of some kind.

Muñoz lowered his hands from the armrest and folded them in his lap. Waiting. Waiting. Did the demon know that Reynaldo and Muñoz had had lunch every Thursday afternoon at a *taquería,* three doors down from the ambulance bay?

Joaquin closed his eyes. "I was there the night of the outbreak. An officer took me away to work at a clinic. He broke quarantine but he saved my life." Joaquin fussed at the hems on the sheets. "How are we faring? Did we contain the clinic's outbreak?"

Every word was a taken pawn, as if Joaquin were gobbling up a chessboard with his mouth. Muñoz felt he couldn't speak without feeding the demon pieces that he might later need. "I think so. Yes. I hope so. I do." That didn't sound much like Henry David Stark so he cleared his throat, and said, "I'm busy. What can I do for you, Cruz?"

Joaquin nodded his head in a little bow of deference, and said, "Marta, please excuse us."

"Oh, I'm sorry." She laughed at herself. "I was just waiting to hear more stories about the hot zone. You know, I heard someone say that Dr. del Negro here was in—"

"Marta," said Muñoz, in Stark's exhausted, impatient voice.

Joaquin said, "Go watch the Ping-Pong game. I'll come find you in a moment."

She laughed her nervous laugh, apologized two more times. Then she slipped through the ALHEPA and shut the door behind her.

As soon as the room had fallen into its cadence of clicking suits and chugging particle arresters, Joaquin said, "Can I be honest with you, *señor*?"

I'd be surprised, Muñoz thought.

"I wish I were a brave, young *macho,* but I am nearly fifty." Joaquin leaned his hip against the counter and folded his arms, hands on his biceps as if hugging himself. "I don't want this anymore. I don't want to see infected people anymore. I would rather make beds."

These words were said with such sadness that Muñoz heard himself say, "I understand, sir."

"I can tell from the reports that another wave of infections is likely to hit the lower city." Joaquin let his hands drop down to the edge of the counter. "I—I can't do it, *señor.* I can't go back to La Baja and watch it happen all over again."

Even this might be true. There was probably only one person in all of Ascensión who had seen more death than Muñoz himself, who'd beheld it in its fantastic whole, and that was Joaquin Delgado. "None of us wants that."

"*Señor,* would you assign me here. To La Alta. Please? Don't send me back to La Baja. I have all my documents. I've been tested twice since I've been up here. I'm clean."

Muñoz was incredulous. "You received actual blood draws?"

"Yes, twice. Clean both times." Joaquin placed his genbadge on the table next to the computer.

Muñoz looked at the picture of Reynaldo Cruz for a moment, then placed the dead man's badge in his memboard and sure enough, Joaquin Delgado was clean. For a heartbeat, he considered dashing to the phlebotomist's station and retrieving "Reynaldo Cruz's" precious sample. Even if this report was legitimate, however, Joaquin would have only given a drop, a pinprick, just enough to test his immune system and not the full pint or more that the immune-system-recoding procedure required.

Could Muñoz get away with requesting a third blood draw? Would Joaquin allow it? If only Muñoz knew whether or not Stark had already retrieved a sample from Dr. Garcia. Perhaps he should call Stark now. But then he thought of the time stamp.

24 May. TFCHDS001ASDF/1205 hours.

Stark and Delgado, Muñoz thought. *Does one know what the other is doing? Right now?*

His pulse felt like it was going to pound out of his veins. Muñoz glanced at his cell phone, which had Stark's emergency line tapped into it. Casually, he picked it up and turned it off.

I have to relax. I have to calm myself. I have to think this all the way through.

"Shall I come back later, Dr. del Negro?" Joaquin asked after a long, excruciating pause.

"Permit me to Connect?" Muñoz kept his eyes in middle distance, staring at his VisionField so that he would not have to look at those thirsty dark eyes. "I'll only be a moment."

Pretending to Connect bought him time to think, calm himself. Muñoz's heartbeat was still racing from Dr. Garcia's messages, and with Joaquin Delgado staring at him, he felt as though his heart might vibrate into a million pieces. He couldn't risk putting Stark in charge of Joaquin, his blood draw, or anything to do with Generation One. Muñoz would have to do it himself, but he'd still need help, still need a way to get a sample straight from Joaquin. *O heavenly St. Michael,* Muñoz prayed, *Lord of the heavenly host, you better get your limp dick to Mexico* ahorita, *because I got your man right here.* Ave Maria, ayudame por favor, Virgen de Guadalupe, mujer en blanco, tu—

Muñoz stopped praying.

Woman in white. Yes. Woman in white.

Maybe there was someone who could help him, after all.

Gracias, Virgen. Mil gracias.

Muñoz cleared his throat, and said, "I think I know what I can do for you." He stood and pushed in his chair. "Let's get out of this place, Dr. Cruz."

Joaquin was distrustful, Muñoz could tell. His eyes became thirstier, darker, for just a moment. Then he went back to playing the sad, old man. "I can just leave the quarantine facility? Just like that?"

"You're white, aren't you?"

"Of course I am."

"I just gave the order to release everyone with white blood draws back to Clinic Four," Muñoz lied. "Right now, I have something more important to do, and you can help me do it, if you want the chance to work in La Alta." Muñoz gestured to the door.

"Thank you, Dr. del Negro. I'm forever in your debt. Where are we going?" Joaquin smiled, rising to the bait.

CHAPTER

32

THE NORTH CORNFIELD was a blank span of snow except for a row of hopping footprints that stretched off into the shining white. As he stood by Experiment on the edge of the field, young HD could feel Wisconsin through his fur-lined jacket. They were tracking together, boy and dog, and Experiment was HD's best friend in the whole world.

That wasn't true, Stark reminded himself. Experiment was too cool for young Henry David. A disturbingly smart dog, Experiment was the most popular person in Nissevalle *quop*, everybody's best bud. The dog practically had a conversational command of English, so you could say to him, without a note of inflection, "Want to hang out?" and Experiment would appraise you with a sober eye, assessing your offer, and turn away with an air of contempt, continuing on his rounds (third-floor family rooms, common hall, water guys, Jan the Kitchen Duchess, garbage bins, and back again), unless you were doing something very cool.

Like tracking.

HD and Experiment usually followed the corn fence up into the bluffs, where the hills were like giant eggs, half-buried on end, bristling with pine. You could find all kinds of tracks up there. Mink, stoat, raccoon. Fox, coyote, and wolves. This day, the two trackers came to the road by the cornfield gate, and Experiment aimed his nose at the ground, following a scent across the frozen mud. He sniffed to the gate where the snow lay thick beyond, and looked back at HD, like, "Hey, dork. Over here."

It was a small rabbit, HD could tell, its small footprints frozen into the snow, heading straight across the cornfield. They followed it, HD high-stepping through the crunching snow and Experiment bounding with a happy dog grin on his black-and-white face.

Shooting out of the Torre Cuauhtémoc docking bay, Stark looked down into the burgeoning hive of La Baja Ciudad as he sailed above its network of crumbling neighborhoods. He wasn't over the hot zone, so vendors hemmed the streets below, and sidewalk restauranteurs made steam and smoke with their grills.

Feeling snatched and seized in this *barco* turned paddy wagon, Stark could finally imagine a return to Wisconsin, after all but erasing it from his mind. The discovery of vCaMV on his grandfather's farm seemed a distant nightmare compared to the relentless horror he'd beheld in this outbreak. It would be June, soon. Summer in Wisconsin. Tomatoes would be bulging green in the house gardens and the north cornfield would be shuddering with shin-high stalks.

"If we send him back," said Rosangelica, "we have to arrange getting him across the border." She was sitting on the other side of the *plasceron* window in a comfortable nest of velvet cushions, talking to a handsome man seated across from her. The man was rugged with his once-broken nose. His black uniform that made the whole *barco* smell like leather. An officer, Stark could tell, but not Mexican army. "Doing the right thing doesn't seem worth the trouble."

The officer hadn't said a word since jumping into the *barco* just before it soared out of the docking bay. He'd flashed an identification card that made the driver recoil and nod quickly as if threatened. "The 'right thing' is irrelevant," the officer said. "You might have to do it out of necessity, Rosita."

"Have to?" she said with a slight shimmy in her seat. It chilled Stark to realize she was flirting with a *servicio sagrado* officer. "Tell me what I *have* to do, *macho*."

The man stretched his legs between Rosangelica's. "The Americans know he's here."

Rosangelica put her hands behind her head and sighed at the ceiling of the *barco*. "I know." She unsealed her clamp mask and sipped from her glass. Stark thought the drink looked like tequila. "But this man is a state criminal. We could *vox populi* him. If I leaked the truth to *Ojos de Las Nuevas* and *Para Ustedes,* we could have a trial by *pilone* tonight. I bet his aggregate numbers would demand immediate action, and the Holy Renaissance would benefit from hanging a high-profile villain."

"True, but then," said the officer, "you'll have a reinvigorated enemy on the border."

"Probably. Probably," Rosangelica said as she sipped her tequila. "You got all the angles, don't you, Carriego?"

"What does the president say?"

"He hasn't. He's leaving it up to me."

Carriego laughed. "And you say I have all the angles."

"He's secretly hoping I make the wrong choice. Emil is playing me off of Cazador." Rosangelica glanced at Stark and dismissed him with a blink. "He's waiting to see if *El Jefe* has one last trick up his sleeve before putting his full trust in me."

"And the wrong choice," said Carriego, "is the one that restricts Emil."

"Always."

Stark didn't care who Rosangelica was secretly fencing with while Mexico burned in a viral fire. He didn't care who this Carriego was and how he fit into the behind-the-arras politics. None of it mattered, and Stark couldn't allow himself to think about what kind of trouble La Alta was in now. It was over, he realized, looking down at the useless push pack of omnivalent vaccine, alcohol, and bleach still in his hand. His help wasn't needed. Not his problem. No doubt the sims had been called to a halt, and Jarum and Isabel were put on planes home. Pedro would have to handle Big Bonebreaker now, if Cazador and Rosangelica didn't dispose of him first.

Stark shook his head and sat back in his seat, soothing himself with thoughts of snow and dogs, recalling how Experiment looked like a shaggy dolphin leaping in and out of that deep snow.

Twelve-year-old HD liked tracking, especially in winter, when he had fewer labor points to work for the cooperative. He liked looking at the footprints of an animal and imagining how its body moved, making those tracks. Rabbits' front paws always printed just behind the long, back feet, and HD could imagine this one as it darted across the cornfield in stretching leaps, front paws down between its legs, back feet raised but ready to land and launch the rabbit forward again.

HD looked ahead as he ran. The tracks were making for the border of the farm, the steep hills and slopes of green juniper beyond. Experiment let out a delighted, growling bark as he bounded.

"I called you, Carriego, because I was so furious, I thought we could just pop him and dump in the Gulf," Rosangelica said, loud for Stark's benefit. Her clamp mask dangled around her neck as she drank.

"Fish food?" said Carriego, leering at the *sabihonda*. "Just like Colonel Sanjuan?"

"I wish I could let you do it," said Rosangelica. "The fucking *valemadre* liar."

"Of course I lied," Stark said quietly, still looking down into the haze of old Mexico City.

Carriego flitted his eyes in Stark's direction, and Rosangelica peered at him down her long nose.

"You made it impossible for me to work openly," said Stark, his voice gaining volume now that he was coming clean. "To help Mexico, I had to lie."

Rosangelica jerked her thumb in Stark's direction, like, *Get a load of this guy*. "To help us, you had to conspire with a bioterrorist, eh?"

"I wasn't conspiring with Joaquin, I was tracking him," said Stark.

"Tracking him," said Rosangelica. "Uh-huh."

"I knew he would emerge eventually," Stark said. "I figured that Joaquin would eventually infiltrate one of the clinics and pose as a technician—clinician, computer analyst, phlebotomist—get hired on. I figured he would make his way into La Alta slowly over time, and that we would first hear about him from—"

"You don't lie very well," Carriego cut him off. "Why would you anticipate Joaquin coming to La Alta?"

Rosangelica raised her glass to Stark. "Because he had advance knowledge, of course."

"Because La Alta is—" Stark was about to lie and say because La Alta was where Orbegón lived. But he decided he might as well confess it all if he wanted a plane ride home. "Joaquin Delgado would come to La Alta because I was luring him there."

Rosangelica put down her drink.

Carriego took a slow breath through his nostrils that seemed to fill his body with anger.

"How," said Rosangelica, "could you have lured him?"

Stark met Rosangelica's eyes. "By conning you into bringing Sister Domenica to La Alta to act as bait."

Rosangelica obviously didn't like hearing this in front of the officer in black leather. She gripped her glass so hard that Stark wondered if it would shatter. "How did you know Joaquin would come for her?"

"I figured it out from the outbreak patterns," Stark answered. "Domenica's prophecies were a little too accurate for Joaquin's comfort, I figured. Spaniard. Wetcode. Describing the symptoms of hemorrhagic fever before the first patients hit Zapata."

Rosangelica and Carriego listened to Stark, rapt as children at a ghost story told by firelight.

"How could Joaquin let her keep talking in public, saying things like that, while he was in the middle of releasing his viruses?" said Stark. "So he improvised. He tried to infect Domenica at a church downtown, then at the Basilica, revealing himself to me in the process."

"Is he lying?" said Carriego. "Again?"

Rosangelica shook her head. "I can't tell what's real anymore."

"I tricked you into getting Domenica on camera in Torre Cuauhtémoc," said Stark, "but it didn't go the way I predicted. I messed up."

"How did you mess up?" asked Carriego.

"Joaquin changed my outbreak script, changed the rules of the game. I didn't anticipate that." Stark repositioned his helmet on his head, a nervous habit that showed up when he was angry. "I figured he would slip into the cathedral one night and steal his way to her cell, maybe infect her while she slept, like a kissing bandit. All we would know of his presence near Domenica would be the evidence he left in her blood."

Though he'd never been to a church, Stark felt relieved to confess his ghastly plan in this very Catholic way, accusing himself of sins, safely separated from his confessor by a partition. Stark had considered the plan clever. Clever to lie to the *sabihonda* and risk huge infection rates in La Alta. Clever to manipulate the great Joaquin Delgado. Clever to put an innocent woman in harm's way.

Cold, smart man, the young HD said to old Dr. Stark, *willing to add Domenica to the trail of bodies behind you.* The stack of corpses on the square before the National Museum with that putrid smoke rising up into the bronze face of Carlos IV. The thirteen boys in Cairo who died of smallpox. The brain-eating Borna victims, some slain by the virus and some shot with bullets in their madness, and the West Nile virus and cholera, Legionnaire's, Crimean-Congo, meningitis, yellow fever, Lassa fever, pertussis, EV-71, Japanese encephalitis, flu. HD had stepped off the co-op farm twenty years ago, embraced this life of death, and never stopped grappling with it, not once in the last two decades. With this confession, Stark considered himself finished with corpses and blood. He wanted true life now—whatever that was, wherever it hid.

"As a result, you let Delgado into La Alta," said Carriego.

"We *should* kill him," said Rosangelica, looking at Stark with new contempt, "for playing games with the lives of our citizens like this. Had you simply told me, Estarque, we would—"

"You would have put me in a work ranch the minute I mentioned it," said Stark. Sarcastically pretending to consult with Rosangelica, he said, "Say, I got it, Rosita! Let's bring a radical nun to La Alta and allow my former teacher to walk right in and start spreading the virus. Good plan, eh?"

Rosangelica fell quiet, either lost in thought or the *pilone* slipstream.

"You may have just bought yourself a ticket to that work ranch, *gringo,*" the officer said, watching Rosangelica.

For a flash, he pictured himself on the roof of Stark Manor at sunset, looking over the river mist in the Kickapoo River Valley. But after what he had just seen Rosangelica do to Dr. Garcia, he couldn't allow himself to hope for such a thing.

"*Gacetilla. Garganta.* Awry. Arguing. *Aero,*" Rosangelica chanted.

Then she turned her beaklike face to Stark, silver eyes wide.

Stark's heart clenched like a trembling fist. He pressed forward until his nose almost touched the window between them, locking eyes with the *sabi-honda.*

"What is it?" Carriego asked her. "You got news?"

"She's got news all right," Stark said. "She's receiving word from Pedro Muñoz."

Rosangelica reacted as if Stark were a conjurer making bouquets appear in his open palms. "How did you know that?"

"Pedro's in the cloister," Stark said. "He's with Domenica. Right?" The brief moment of imagining home, roof, and river valley fled, as Stark eased back in his seat, realizing he wasn't finished after all. He was about to be thrown back to the virus. "And I bet he knows where Joaquin Delgado is, too."

Rosangelica slapped the back of the driver's seat as if he were disobeying orders. "Forget about the airport, *cabron*! Turn around! Now! Back to Docking Bay *Aztlán*!"

"What is it?" shouted Carriego. "What's going on?"

Rosangelica kept shouting: "I'll clear the bay. Don't wait in queue for landing orders! If you airbrake for a second, I'll rip your throat out!"

They came about, and the giant wall of the sea-green tower seemed to swoop across the windshield. Rosangelica screamed for speed, and Stark sank back in his seat, thinking about what he found at the end of that trail of tracks across the cornfield, so long ago.

Over a yard of snow stretched between each footfall as the rabbit dug into a fierce race toward the pines at the edge of the field, and HD felt like he was on its heels in hot pursuit.

But then the tracks came to a sudden end, right in the middle of the field. HD stopped where they stopped, staring down at the snow, eyes wide.

Experiment spun around to look back at HD, betrayed, wondering why the dumb boy wasn't running anymore.

HD caught his breath as if he'd seen blood. Two feathered strokes in the snow terminated the line of tracks like abrupt punctuation. Huge wingprints like crescent moons were laid end to end in the rabbit's path. HD looked forward, across the untrammeled field to the distant stand of lonely pines where there would have been cover, safety.

But here in the cold, empty whiteness, there was just this angelic clap of wings, then nothing.

CHAPTER

33

DR. DEL NEGRO closed the ALHEPA door shut and turned the spin lock so that it ticked like a metronome, closing it. A gasp of pressure sighed audibly through the particle arrester beyond, and Joaquin was in.

It wasn't locked, merely shut, he noted, calming himself. Just shut, that's all. He stood with his head bowed, knowing that the nun was in here. Sitting on her bed. Sitting in the center of the room.

Allí está, he thought, without looking at her.

There she is.

"Sister, I've assigned a doctor to be your new personal physician," del Negro said, loping into the room. They were casual friends, Joaquin presumed. Beneath his helmet, del Negro had an unruly cowlick that dropped an S shaped curl of black hair in his eyes. "Dr. Reynaldo Cruz."

Joaquin lifted his head and looked at the woman sitting on the bed at the center of her cell. She was older than he expected, or perhaps the last week or so had aged her since he saw her at the Capilla. He was relieved that she wasn't scrutinizing as nuns often were, sizing up men as if for a war of wills. The so-called Saint of Plagues paid him no attention. Sitting cross-legged, she was watching *El Quijote,* the final act, when Sancho's aria steps out of the recitative with the Knight of Mirrors, as the squire agrees to betray the Don. The baritone was Carlos Diamante. The performance, April of 2055. Sounded like Al-Shiraz conducting. Not Joaquin's favorite.

"My pleasure, Dr. Cruz," she said.

The room was light and spare. No accoutrements, no furniture beyond the bed and the chair. No windows. The room's adjustable sunlight threw the equivalent of late-afternoon sun across the nun's bed, casting red light and her long shadow across the flower-tiled floor. A proclivity for the dramatic, Joaquin noted. "You enjoy opera?"

"I'm Mexican. I love *El Quijote*," Domenica said. She still had not met his eye. "I keep watching it, hoping that I will feel what I felt when I first heard Sancho sing."

Joaquin set down his lugall with the medical equipment del Negro had given him. *Characters do not sing,* he wanted to inform her. *Humans do.* Dilettante.

"I'll stay and keep you both company," del Negro said, sitting in a wing chair near the monitor. He did not turn his chair so that he could watch the opera. He faced Joaquin and nodded to him. "But don't mind me, Doctor."

"Hard to re-create that first encounter with a glorious aria, isn't it?" Joaquin said. He unpacked his stethoscope and blood pressure cuff. "The Don is a magical character, but not that magical, alas."

Domenica finally looked at Joaquin and smiled. Then she stood and turned off the monitor before Sancho could deliver the aria, the one expressing his anguish over betraying the Don and declaring his belief that Quixote had willingly fought the physician posing as the Knight of Mirrors, a battle that, in the end, would prove fatal to the Don's imaginary universe. Dilettante though she was, it spoke highly of Domenica that she loved that aria. The layers of meaning were complex, ironic. "'I believe he conquers my reason, even now,'" Domenica said, quoting it with a sad smile as she sat on the edge of the bed, facing Joaquin.

"Ah, very good." Joaquin showed her the blood pressure cuff, and Domenica began rolling up her sleeve. Joaquin stepped forward and made to sit on the bed with her, thought better of it, straightened awkwardly, then finally knelt at her feet on the floor. Their shadows stretched together across the room. He held her arm, so thin he could have snapped it like kindling, and took her pressure. "You are a romantic? You believe in fantasies?"

"Recently, I've been forced to accept unreality as reality," she said, her dark eyes glittering. "I suppose I am a romantic."

Joaquin's hands hurt he was so nervous, and he stole glances at Domenica

while he read her pressure. Domenica kept looking up from his mouth
whenever he looked her in the eye, as if she were contemplating a kiss, and
her blood pressure was in the high range of normal.

"Are you anxious about something, Dr. Cruz?" she asked.

He pulled the cuff from her arm and turned back to his lugall so that she
could not see his face. He was being foolhardy, vain. He shouldn't cat and
mouse, he scolded himself as he rummaged through his equipment. He
should infect a needle with the tainted cotton swab he'd spat upon, jab her
with it, and be done. "You're the most famous person I've ever met," Joaquin
said, trying on a nervous laugh as he knelt at her feet again. "Well, that's not
true. I once danced with Conchita Consuelo, before she became a star. Here
in Mexico City. Your pressure was fine by the way." By her left foot, he
placed a little safe-box for used needles and set a clean syringe on top of it.
"This first draw is to see if you carry the virus," he said, cleaning the crook
of her arm with alcohol.

Domenica said, "Ascensión."

"Hmm?"

"It's Ascensión now," Domenica said patiently.

Joaquin cursed himself, then forced a muttering laugh. "I guess I never
got used to that."

Domenica didn't seem to think his gaffe very strange. "If I contracted Big
Bonebreaker, Dr. Cruz, how fast would the symptoms set in?"

Joaquin gave del Negro a weary look, as if he did not like discussing
such dark topics with patients. Then he held the needle up where she and
del Negro could see it, like a sleight-of-hand artist showing his audience an
ordinary coin, and sterilized it twice with alcohol. "The fever would begin as
soon as your immune system started fighting the virus with macrophages."
He paused, shrugged, and answered her finally. "Within hours." Joaquin
sucked her blood into the syringe wondering if her hemoglobin would look
different, somehow, beneath a microscope. Could one see holiness in the
blood of the Patron Saint of Plagues?

When he had secured the sample and disposed of the needle, Domenica
asked him, "When did you stop whipping yourself, Reynaldo?"

That watery, fountainous noise that he had first heard during the riots in
the *zócalo* bubbled through the room, drowning out the valve works of the
ALHEPA. How could she know? Joaquin froze, as if he could feel the *espir-
itu sanctu* filling up the corners of this room. Was she prophesying? Could

she see Joaquin staggering alongside the insane priest, the heavy leather strap in Joaquin's unbroken hand? Could she see, after that, his rising fury and hatred for a pitiless God? He glanced briefly into the nun's penetrating eyes but couldn't look there very long. Over the roar of the boiling noise in the room, he whispered, "What makes you think I whipped myself?"

Her tone was not accusatory, but tolerant. "I've met lots of flagellants. It's the way you move your upper body," she said, "like you have a sunburn."

Joaquin held the next needle in his right hand. He curled his broken left hand against his stomach. "I joined a procession. Yes. In a moment of weakness."

"No, *señor.* I've never seen weakness in a St. John's Procession. Thirty-nine lashes, just like the Savior's. You were taking on Mexico's sins?" Domenica asked. "Or maybe you felt guilty about something?"

How vast was her prescience? Could she see him in that room in the villa, lying with his back flayed open? Could she see the words on the walls, the words that he'd painted in his own blood?

Virus sum.

I am virus.

The words were almost on his lips as if Joaquin were being compelled to admit his identity.

Then he recalled lying in bed and watching this very woman on netcast, standing with her arms around the despot, the man who'd stolen Joaquin's research on the *pilone.* He kept his eyes on the nun's arm.

Traitor. Judas. *Malinche.*

"Let me ask you a question instead, Sister," Joaquin said, hoping that deflecting her question wouldn't make del Negro suspicious. He had to restrain himself from taking her slender arm too violently. "Do you believe your own miracles? Or are they fantasies?"

A look of distaste crossed her face. She leaned away from him, her arm still firmly in his hand. "I don't discuss my visions, Dr. Cruz."

Joaquin couldn't be sure, but she sounded as if she wanted to add, *Especially with you.*

He removed the tainted cotton ball. "Please, Sister," Joaquin said. "I badly want to know."

Her posture was straight and perfect as she looked down at him holding her arm, haughty as a queen having her royal person attended. She nodded, finally, seeing something in Joaquin that perhaps instilled her with confidence. Or was that merely resignation? "I believe, Dr. Cruz, yes," she said, her voice sounding clear as a note from a violin. "Of course I believe what happened to me."

He wished he could draw that belief out of her body with the needle. He wished he could have just a drop of her confidence in God's benevolence, to study it, to analyze, to swallow, and absorb.

Joaquin could still feel del Negro's eyes on him. He swabbed another needle, not daring to swab it with the infected cotton ball yet. Joaquin slipped the clean needle neatly into Domenica's vein. "I mean, do you really believe that those messages came from God?"

She watched the syringe fill with blood, then looked away. "Yes. That's what I believe."

Blood swirled into the syringe's chamber. "You believe the plague was a test of some kind?"

"Maybe Domenica doesn't want to answer any more questions, Dr. Cruz," del Negro said, resting his pointy elbows on his knees.

"I don't mind, Pedro." She looked down at Joaquin, down her nose, like a teacher at a student, and said, "Yes. Of course. The plague is obviously a test."

He watched her face as he withdrew the needle. "Why do you think the Virgin comes to you?"

Clearly, she did not expect such a question. Her wide mouth and wide-set eyes, which had looked froglike to Joaquin only days ago, now seemed a countenance of graceful contemplation. He liked looking at her, understood why so many loved her, but forced himself to look down at the needle and secure the sample. "In the Book of Job," said Domenica, speaking so softly she sounded like she was whispering secrets in his ear, "God says 'Hast thou perceived the breadth of the earth? Declare if thou knowest it all.' I don't, Dr. Cruz. I only know what has happened to me. Not why."

Don't belittle me, Joaquin thought, securing the sample. He didn't want to hear platitudes and vagaries and Bible verses, especially from her. "Why," Joaquin said, "doesn't He come to anyone else? To Dr. del Negro—or me for example?"

"Later, in the Book of Job, God also says—"

"I'm not inferior to you," Joaquin said. He paused, rallied his composure with a terse laugh at himself. To cover the rash choice of words, he sweetened his voice to sound jesting, chiding. "I know Job, Sister. Very well as a matter of fact," he said, worrying that his anger had shown and that the nun might now fear him. He looked up into her face and he smiled at her until she smiled back. "At the end of that Book, you'll remember, God repeats what Job has already declared, that God is great and man is dust. Those words did nothing to answer the question posed. No?"

"And what was the question posed in Job?" the nun asked, rolling down her sleeve.

Joaquin got to his feet with a pinching pain in his back. He looked down at her, trying to give her the same pedantic stare she had just given him. "Why does God slay wicked and good alike? Why the hypocrisy? Why did God send the Virgin to you, yet still allow this plague to happen?"

Her voice was musical, but her eyes were hard. "You sound exactly like Job."

"This plague has made me sympathetic, yes," Joaquin said. "I think if Job were here, he would want to know why God used His divine power merely to speak through you, rather than to help the afflicted or, say, to confront the person who started this epidemic."

Domenica shook her head with sadness on her lips. "Job never got answers to his questions."

"That's my point," Joaquin said.

"That's *the* point."

"I simply want my day in God's court, Sister, *before* I die." Joaquin laughed, knowing that he had spoken those words a bit too loudly, with too much force. He smiled down at Domenica again to ease the moment, but she would not smile back this time. "I mean, all of Mexico wants fair representation. Because whether we confess or not, the same end comes to us. You see, Sister? Whether I admit my sin, or correct my wrongs, still I—*we* are kept at arm's length from God. We watch thousands die every day. We suffer. We doubt." Joaquin shook his head, marveling. "But you don't suffer, Sister. You have no cause to doubt."

Domenica clenched her jaw, angry at him, obviously, but unwilling to unleash her words. She composed herself, closing her eyes. "I suffer. I doubt."

"You just told me that you *believed*. It's easy when you bask in the glow of divinity, isn't it?" Joaquin pressed. "You get so much more than the rest of us, Domenica. You're a favorite daughter and the rest of us are stepchildren of the Almighty. Is that fair?"

She kept shaking her head. "I don't pretend to understand."

"No, you're just afraid to admit what you know is true. God is the ultimate consumer. He eats and eats and eats and He is never satisfied."

The nun was pretending to listen, but he could feel that she wanted to stand and run. He could see the air lock in her posture, its low pressure pulling her away from him.

"He is all the things I fought—*fight* as a doctor," Joaquin said. "God is rot. God is bacteria. He is pestilence and plague and the turning worm. No matter what we doctors do to undo God's appetite, no matter how we succeed and advance, God will eventually devour us all."

Del Negro was staring at him, and Joaquin faltered. But it didn't matter what that dupe thought. God was certainly listening now, here, with His precious mouthpiece sitting before Joaquin. Could God be goaded to respond to these poisonous words spilling over his beloved daughter?

"God will side with fascists," Joaquin said, lazily lifting his hand and pointing to Domenica. "He will anoint killers. When scientists perform beneficial deeds for mankind, populations skyrocket and God eats them like candy. When scientists perform accidents or even—even evil—when thousands die as a result, God doesn't stop it. No, he comes running to the trough to feed." His voice was loud, deep, satisfying in his throat like a flowing music after years of silence. "God is a disgusting glutton, devouring whatever plate is set before him—good, evil, blessed, profane—"

Domenica whispered, "Joaquin."

"How am I to make sense of it?" he asked. "The line between God and nature, creation and creator, evil and good, is so thin, so easily crossed, that it's hard to see which side—"

"Doctor, I want to give you something," the nun said. "I want to do something for you."

Joaquin caught himself, and he clenched his right hand. He'd said too much again. "You do?" He took a deep breath. He glanced at del Negro, who was sitting in his chair, pale-faced from accessing his *pilone,* Joaquin imagined. He glanced at the tainted cotton ball just out of his reach. "What do you want to give me?"

The nun stood, put her hands on Joaquin's plastic-covered shoulders, and urged him to his knees. He knelt and she raised a hand in benediction.

Joaquin's mouth parted and he blinked rapidly in total confusion.

"*Nuestra Señora de Guadalupe,* Holy Virgin, Blessed be the Fruit of thy Womb, Jesus Christ the Savior." The woman said the prayer so quickly that the words ran together. She begged the Madonna to protect and bless him for all the days of his life.

For Joaquin, the blessing was so unexpected, he could not deny or refuse it. The words acted on him like a spell, turning his muscles to wood, bones to marble. He bowed his head, and let her speak.

When the prayer was finished, Domenica raised his head with her hand under his jaw. The nun's face was flushed and pretty. He looked into her eyes and crossed himself.

Then she tenderly unsealed his clamp mask, let it drop against his collarbone, and held his face in her hands. She bent, and touched her lips to his.

Skin to skin.

Joaquin tried to speak but his voice wouldn't come. He could not make sense of the kiss. "You shouldn't have done that."

"You deserve a blessing. Whether you intended it or not," Domenica said, "you've made everything right."

Del Negro leaned forward in his chair as if watching a matador raise his curved blade. The nun placed her hands on either side of the kneeling Joaquin's face. Everything white in the cell was rouged with the light of a false setting sun.

Footsteps sounded outside the nun's dorm room. Many voices, shouting. One rose above the others. "Muñoz! Goddamnit, which room are you in?"

Joaquin recognized the voice. An old friend. A student. A cascade of realization fell over Joaquin, and he shoved himself away from the nun, throwing her to the bed and quickly wedging himself between del Negro and the air lock.

Del Negro pushed back his chair and immediately dropped into a crouch. "In here!" Del Negro shouted at the door. "He's in Domenica's room!"

"Where?" that voice answered. "Which door? We can't find you!"

Joaquin kept his body turned toward del Negro, but he reached back and twirled the ALHEPA's spin lock all the way tight. Then he removed the pipe from the handle and hefted it in his good hand. Just then he heard footsteps right outside the air lock.

So did del Negro. "Joaquin locked the door!" he shouted. "Pull the air lock apart!"

Joaquin looked at the nun, lying on the bed where he had shoved her. *She tricked me! She* wanted *the virus.* He lunged at her and found del Negro in front of him, ready.

"Pedro, don't fight him, we have—"

Joaquin lashed out at del Negro. A low, sickening thud sounded from pipe meeting skull.

Domenica cried out, "Pedro, no!"

Del Negro crumpled around Joaquin's knees, as if del Negro could drag Joaquin down into unconsciousness with him.

The pipe fell again and again on the treacherous doctor's zigzag scar. "You led me here!" Joaquin shouted. Even after del Negro's hands dropped, unable to protect himself, the pipe continued to fall. "You led me right to her!"

Like the figures of a code, blood swirled across Joaquin's coveralls. He stood straight and looked at the nun. She screamed and tried to run past him to the door, but he sidestepped in front of her and she backpedaled away from him.

"You lied!" Joaquin said. "You're God's own precious one and you lied!"

Behind him, he could hear the ALHEPA filter being swiftly pried apart.

"Joaquin!" that well-known voice shouted from beyond the air lock. "Leave them alone!"

Domenica ran to her table and seized a slender candlestick. She turned to face him with her weapon.

In a leap, Joaquin was in front of her. "How could *you* lie?"

She brought the candlestick straight up, catching him under the chin, but all it did was gouge him.

That voice came from inside the room now. "Joaquin!"

He brought the pipe sailing down on the crown of the nun's head, and, as if her feet had been swept out from under her, Domenica collapsed.

Joaquin stood over her, straightening her head with his foot. He was ready to bash the life out of her so that the Holy Renaissance couldn't isolate his beloved children from her blood, when suddenly, a hot coal burned into the back of his knee.

He fell backwards, pain ripping up his leg. The agony of landing flat on his flagellated back was nearly as awful as the searing pain in his leg.

What happened? he thought. Or maybe he said that.

His ears hurt, too. The sound of a gun blast echoed through his mind.

That was when Joaquin realized he had been shot. The red sunlight hurt his eyes as he wondered why he wasn't passing out.

A moment later, a face loomed into his field of vision. White. Pasty. A scrub of blond hair.

"I wondered if you might be here," said Joaquin.

CHAPTER

34

SOMETHING IN THE WAY he fell reminded Stark of Joaquin, but the man Rosangelica shot now seemed like a beached ocean thing, a broken crab-creature that did not belong in this world of oxygen and light. The way it lay on its back, wincing and sucking in air through gritted teeth. Its left hand broken, deformed. Streaks of white shot through the matted, black hair.

Stark couldn't look at the wounded thing anymore, so he turned away in disgust and saw the officer, Carriego, about to enter Domenica's cell. "Stay in the hall," he shouted.

Carriego backed out, the shield of his helmet reflecting dramatic red sunlight back into Domenica's room.

Stark went to Muñoz, looking at the injury to his head. There was no point in taking his wrist, feeling for a pulse. The amount of blood was confounding.

Sister Domenica, however, was trying to drag herself up by pulling on the bedspread.

"Domenica is hurt!" Stark shouted to Rosangelica, as he knelt to examine the nun. Domenica's face was a wash of blood from the split skin of her forehead. "Head injury. Rosangelica! Get a level-four team up here! And tell them to bring two extra suits." He looked back at Domenica. "Oh shit," he said in English, "I shouldn't have—wait. Just lie down. Relax."

"I'm OK," Domenica whispered, sounding like a sleepwalker. She allowed Stark to prop her in a sitting position. "It looks bad, but I have something in me now."

Stark only half heard what the nun was saying. He'd glanced at Rosangelica, who was standing over Joaquin, looking down at him. *"Fecha. Cuchillo.* Faker. Get up here. *Fayuca."* Her handgun was held loosely and she seemed to be waving it toward his face, as if toying with aiming and firing. "Done. They're on their way. *Oeste.* Up. Voltage."

Stark watched the gun for a moment, wondering if she could really kill twice in as many hours. "Rosangelica," he warned.

She lifted her face as if startled. "I know. We need him alive now."

"Doctor?" Domenica said. "Get Pedro. Where's Pedro?"

"No. Pedro is—no," Stark said. He refused to look at the body, its head injuries. They were too much.

"Oh. Oh," she mewed. Then Domenica said, "But we did it. Pedro and I fooled Joaquin Delgado." She tried to open her eyes but the blood made her squint. "I have it. I kissed him to make sure. I have it."

"Holy Mother of God," Rosangelica said, coming to stand next to Domenica.

"You have it? No." Stark couldn't make sense of what she'd said. They had Joaquin. They had his blood. They didn't need a human host now. "Why? Why did you do this?"

She put a hand on her chest, and said, smiling, "I volunteered."

Stark stood there feeling like Carlos IV, stiff and unmoving, expected to stand here with a bronze face while a pyre made of his friends blew oily smoke straight at him. "No, Domenica."

"Contact Dr. Ahwaz, Rosangelica," Domenica said. "I'm ready."

Inside her helmet, Rosangelica muttered, "Paprika. *Primavera.* Epilepsy. Get him back to the hot lab. *Pepenar."*

"Oh, you sad, sad, little—" Stark shook his head in disbelief and opened the push pack he'd originally grabbed from Muñoz's Joint office and swabbed the syringe filled with omnivalent vaccine. Then he injected her. People had died of Generation One in minutes at Zapata Hospital. Such a risk. She might have died needlessly if they hadn't arrived in time to vaccinate her. The omnivalent would only delay the inevitable, but even a delay of mere hours was crucial. He withdrew the needle from Domenica's arm. Stark's cruel, clever plan to lure Joaquin into the open had worked all too well and now that it was finished, Stark felt flayed open by it, his bones and blood exposed.

"Ginger. *Gingibre*. Handkerchief," said Rosangelica.

Stark turned away and found Joaquin's medical kit, jerking it open and shutting out Domenica, Rosangelica, and this bloody scene as he removed gloves and an empty syringe. The coldness that Stark had felt only a few hours ago had melted and now reined in a passionate anger. He knew which way this was headed. The worst jobs in humanity's most wretched moments always fell to Henry David Stark, after all. He swiftly knelt at Joaquin's side and took his teacher's hand. They didn't need his blood, now that Domenica had contracted the virus, but in case the recoding experiment failed, they would need a sample from Patient Minus One. Now more than ever, Stark didn't want to be trapped without options.

Joaquin couldn't move. Something was wrong with his back, but he opened his heavy-lidded eyes extra wide, as if afraid of falling asleep, and watched the needle. "Vaccine from unmutated virus?" he said in English.

Stark thumped a vein on Joaquin's arm with his thumb and growled in English, "You just so damn smart, ain't you?" Then in contempt for both himself and Joaquin, muttered, "Ghana."

Joaquin shook his head, and said regretfully, "I win either way now, Enrique."

It was what Joaquin said after Stark forever failed to defeat Joaquin at chess. Stark stuck Joaquin hard and drew a plunger full of blood, then sealed the syringe in a cryopack from the kit. The impending resurrection of the epidemic was upon them, but the Task Force's chances of stopping it had just quadrupled. "We just gonna see about that."

"You can't stop what I started." Joaquin kept shaking his head as if disappointed. "You should thank me."

Stark couldn't stomach hearing that voice anymore. The sounds of clambering made Stark turn as Carriego waved a team of suited *medicos* into the room and over the ALHEPA filter's wreckage.

"Why don't you have a suit on?" one of the doctors shouted at Stark, Racal speaker cranked.

"You brought up two suits, right?" Stark said, standing. "Give me one. And two of you get Sister Domenica to the Immune Complex *ahorita!*" Stark began tugging on his suit, trapping any stray viruses he might have contracted inside the Racal-plus with him. He pointed to Joaquin. "And get that man suited, too. Hurry!"

"But you can't leave this room," the doctor who had handed Stark the new suit said, "not with all this blood. Not without having an assay yourself. We have to quarantine this whole facility before—"

"This man has been injured. He's been shot," said a doctor, taking a closer look at Joaquin. "We can't put a suit on him!"

"That man is the source of the outbreak," Stark said. "Suit him. It's the best way to quarantine him or he'll spread it all over La Alta."

An awed silence filled the room and the only sound was Stark stuffing himself into his suit. The team of doctors moved slowly through the horizontal sunset light, cutting long black shadows behind them. Two crept toward Domenica, and the others stepped in a deliberate circle around Joaquin Delgado where he lay in the center of the cell, as if they did not want to disturb the elements of the prophecy as it had been told to Mexico for weeks.

The nun.

The Spaniard.

Pools of infected blood.

When the team had Joaquin suited, they sprayed his clean suit with bleach and did the same for Stark's and Rosangelica's suits. Then they moved all four of them—Domenica, Joaquin, Rosangelica, and Stark—into the cloister's quarantine room, standing them in the particle arresters and spraying them down again. Rosangelica kept linking to her satellites as they moved from stage to stage in the antiseptic operation.

"*Besame*. Sesame. *Caje*. Kismet."

Carriego and a doctor carried Joaquin, his arms draped over their shoulders as he limped, his helmet sagging forward. Two other doctors all but carried Domenica, urging her to keep her head up. The cloister outside the quarantine was empty. So were the hallways outside the Cloister of the Virgin of Guadalupe. Ascensión was never this quiet.

"Someone spilled the beans," said Rosangelica.

"Just as well. We're taking chances by moving Joaquin," Stark said. "Better if the corridors of Cuauhtémoc are empty." He looked at Joaquin hard, hoping for an acknowledgment of guilt or an apology.

Rosangelica was watching Stark. Finally, she said, "You don't need him anymore?"

The question chilled Stark. She was going to kill him. If she could shoot an innocent infected doctor, then killing Joaquin Delgado would be a lark. Stark held the black case of the medical kit to his chest. "I have what I need."

"Are you absolutely positive? I don't want you saying afterward—"

Stark turned away. It was like looking at a vicious caricature of a dear friend. "No. We don't need him anymore."

"Estarque," Rosangelica said. "Beyond my wildest fantasies, I never considered taking Joaquin Delgado alive to stand trial." Already the name had a sneer to it, a luscious, coveted hatred. He would never be Joaquin or Dr. Delgado again. Forever would he be remembered in Mexico as *Joaquin Delgado,* and all that the odious name implied. Rosangelica said, "Carriego, let's take him to the Majority Holding Cell. They have the cleanest cells in town."

"Hear that?" Carriego said to Joaquin. "Emil the Damned wants only the best for you."

Rosangelica and the two carrying Joaquin walked out of the cloister and made their way across the esplanade of swaying date palms and crimson bromeliads. Creamy sunlight fell on their white suits, and the vast, empty space around them seemed claustrophobic to Stark, the enormity of the tower itself constricting around them.

"How are you, Domenica?" asked Stark, turning to her.

"I must be heavy."

By the looks on their faces, the doctors didn't mind helping the most famous woman in Mexico.

Stark looked back at Rosangelica and her quarry, noted a few people in white Racal suits skirting the palm-tree-lined margins of the esplanade. "We have to get to Dr. Ahwaz's office, and then you can rest, Sister."

—... *the last of three troop movements, these from Arizona into New Mexico [data to follow], doubling the supply line into San Antonio [sat link codes sent 0300] in case things got dicey and a line of war drones [packet the sabihonda for codes] angled for an expected attack from the strategically superior Blue units in the hill country north of Austin [31 long by 98 lat] that way when the ground war starts our boots are covered all the way up the Guadalupe [but they will need security codes so that—*

Rosangelica walked behind Joaquin Delgado, Carriego, and the doctor. Carriego's black-leather coat was a hard contrast to Joaquin's white Racal suit. Her eyes drifted lazily away, to another set of white suits in the distance, shadowing along the northern edge of the esplanade.

—highest military clearance authority to Rosangelica [node: 4x4x4x4x4x] and there can be no further discussion. She brought to us the Holy Grail of the Cassini satellite codes from Houston. Listen to her, Ministers. She is as my own mind in the Austin and Almaty shipment matters. >Agenda Point 205.605 Outbreak Task Force Coordinator< I am awaiting an explanation from Rosangelica, Chief of State. I concur. Her actions were rash. I will inform you of my judgment in this matter when—

On the south side of the square, three more people walked parallel to Rosangelica, the *medicos*, and Joaquin Delgado. That made seven altogether.

—reports an Almaty shipment [800 million pesos Iranian-Siberian crude] aweigh off coast of Maine. Pemex seeking reprisal against Kazakh-Ethiopian Consolidated. Old US corporate chauvinism at work. KEC in violation of embargo Chapter Two. Contact oil ministers at Tenghiz, Kazakhstan, Pan-Islam re isolation of USA as Mexican vital interest. Federal sabihondos should be prepared to attack KEC central net—

More people emerged from the shadows of the far corridors and edged forward into the sunlight. Ten or fifteen of them. Strolling along.

"You paying attention to that?" Carriego asked.

The people were still too far away, walking too slowly, for Rosangelica to consider them a threat. When she could discern facial features, she would decide what to do.

Adjusting the holster under her armpit, she said, "They're just gawking. That's all. Keep moving."

—citing the work of noted futurist and economist, Dr. Isuzu Ibrehim. (12) "The technology has been in place for decades but there have been too many small players on the international geopolitical arena for any single free agent to take advantage. The United States was the last, strongest candidate to create an established orbit economy. If it weren't for woeful agriculture problems in the US, that country would still be a candidate. This leaves China, India, Mexico, Brazil, and Kazakhstan as countries with the populations and oil reserves capable of maintaining a double economy: a megalithic oil-based financial system on earth supporting the info and tech commodities of an orbit-based research and development system in outer—"—

Rosangelica was still a little drunk from the tequila, which caused her wetware to race. She could have controlled it if she wanted to but it was fun to let her alcohol-suffused connections run where they willed. She could watch the surge of information, react to it if need be—recommend that the supply line into San Antonio not be doubled, for example—or she could watch reality, the world, the thirty or so people slowly closing off the angle she would need to leave the esplanade and enter the Majority Cloister. She could contact the civil militia node with a blink of her eye. Or she could un-zip her suit and draw her gun before any of them could react. Plus, there was Carriego.

Total control of the situation.

>PEMEX< *Belay reprisals against Kazakh-Ethiopian Consolidated. We can't afford to upset Almaty commersants [Russ trans: businessmen] or Pan-Islam oil imams.* Sabihondos *otherwise engaged, unable to commit to node warfare. I rec-ommend swamping US offer on cargo and purchasing Almaty shipment Iranian-Siberian crude for 1 billion Mexican. If KEC will not transfer title, node me at once.* >Minister of Defense< *Strategy for Austin offensive is too conservative. We don't have the resources for two supply lines. As soon as outbreak is under control I will release the Cassini codes to you. Draft attack accordingly.* >President for Life< *I have Joaquin Delgado.—*

Rosangelica let her hands swing at her sides, unconcerned by the figures in white. They followed as if being towed by subtle forces of magnetism or gravity.

Curious, Rosangelica tapped into their discussion.

—*that it's him.< >It's him.< >That's him.< >The Spaniard. From the prophecy. I know it's him.< >That's him.< >He's right there.<*

"What's happening?" Stark asked, anxious as an expectant father.

Jarum worked his palms together as if he were crushing something in his hands. "She's dying now."

"But is it working?"

"We won't save her," Jarum said. "But she just has to live long enough to let the new immune system create the T cell." Jarum sat quietly for a long time, swiveling his chair back and forth and listening to it squeak. "Genera-tion One. You are a lucky son of a bitch, Henry David Stark."

Jarum never swore, but that was the third time he'd said that since start-ing the tests on Domenica.

"Now what's happening?" Stark asked. "Is she developing the fever?"

"Yes, a very bad one," Jarum said. "That's good. It means one of the immune systems is winning."

"Let's hope it's the visiting team," Stark said.

Numbers scrolled up the silver screens, but Jarum ignored them. He read the interface on his desktop memboard. Finally, the numbers stopped running, the gel screens cleared, and the three *i.a.*'s chattered at Jarum. "There. She's dead."

"Finally," Stark said.

"Well?" Domenica asked from the other chamber, her voice twee in Jarum's memboard. "How did I do?"

Jarum shifted in his chair so that he was facing the window between the chambers, speaking to Domenica as well as Stark. "Domenica1 offers the same results as the three Debora sims," he said, eyes on Stark. "Her natural immune system killed the wetcoded one, but the matrix got a good look at it before it collapsed. We're very close."

"Chance of success for the matrix?" asked Stark. "Despite killing Domenica in the process?"

Jarum pulled up the number with a grudging flick of his hand. He raised his eyebrows. "Fifty-four percent of creating the T cell we need."

"Generation One almost quadrupled our chances."

Jarum pushed the memboard away in fatigue and irritation. Certainly in his research clinic back in Bethlehem, it wouldn't be good enough. But in this situation the number was promising. He put his hands behind his head and stared at the screens. "I near my limit."

Stark wanted to say the number was good enough but he knew they had to squeeze every percentage point they could get out of these simulations, or Domenica would die without the matrix they needed to wetcode a proper T cell.

"Fifty-four percent?" Domenica said. "That's excellent, Dr. Ahwaz."

Stark turned away as if the sound of Domenica's voice were a slap. He checked the timepiece on his suit's twenty-four-hour air tanks. Because Stark had dosed her with omnivalent vaccine right away, Domenica had eight hours before her Generation One virus mutated.

The door buzzer sounded. Someone wanted into the level-six hot lab.

Stark checked the security screens and saw a figure in Holy Renaissance red-and-black Racal-plus suit. He couldn't see the face, but one red glove was raised, giving the camera the finger.

"I wonder where she's been," Jarum said, glancing at the security screen and buzzing the door unlocked. "I haven't seen her since this morning."

A moment later, Isabel joined them, smiling wanly at Stark, the same sort of smile she'd given him a week ago, when he first arrived in Ascensión. He could read her haggard face plainly. Muñoz's death had cracked her in two. Domenica's infection, a kick in the head afterward.

Jarum filled the awkward pause, saying, "Is everything all right, Doctor?"

Isabel shrugged. "I went to Cazador to see about an exit pass back home." Isabel sat next to Jarum, where she could see his gel screens and Stark, too. Her back was to Domenica in the lab. "He said no."

Stark said, "You were going to leave us?"

She nodded, her gaunt face looking almost skull-like, even worse than this morning in her bedroom. "Cazador won't let me go. He says I'm needed here."

Isabel had never abandoned ship before, never in their many outbreaks together had she even offered a slim hint that she was finished—quite the opposite. She normally stayed until an outbreak was officially declared over by Stark or WHO. Rare for a pathologist or wetcoder. "You *are* needed here, Bela," Stark said.

"Cazador also told me he's coming to oversee this project. But he wanted you to know, Henry David, that Orbegón has reinstated you as Outbreak Coordinator." Isabel sounded like she was forcing breath and words out of her body. "So where is the project now?"

Stark was relieved to hear her ask, but it was a hollow victory. No sassiness. No cursing. She was a ghost, half-here, only. "We were just discussing our bright sunny options," Stark said, nodding to the bank of i.a.'s and memboards.

Isabel said, "What's your success rate up to?"

"Fifty-four percent. But we still can't save the subject, Isabel," Jarum said.

"Is fifty-four percent good enough?" Stark asked Isabel. Clonufacturing was ready. If they could get them a viable matrix and augmented T cell, a vaccine would be finished hours later. "Can we proceed on a coin flip?"

"It's an impressive figure." She leaned toward the nearest gel screen, scanning it. "But the wetcoded immune system still gets strangled in birth."

"Now I understand your contempt for this project, Isabel. It's maddening!" Jarum gesticulated at his screens. His daughters' faces in their photos smiled at him as if bemused by Father's outburst. "We can recode eye color and skin tone, but not one little immunocyte?"

"Explain it to me, Bela. Why is it so difficult?" Stark said. "If Joaquin Delgado can recode a virus that slips past every Mexican immune system's histocompatability exam, why—?"

"It's not every Mexican," Jarum said.

"I *know* it's not every Mexican, Jarum," Stark said, irritated, but Jarum had turned away with an abrupt swivel of his chair. "It's Native Mexicans and people who've received the wetware therapy. But what I want to know is—"

"*Cálmate*, Doctor. Shh shh," Isabel said. "Listen, it's like this." She looked at Jarum, who began nervously tapping numbers into his memboard. "A virus is simple, Henry David. One cell, that's it. But an immune system? I personally don't think we can account for all the nuances, all the variables, all the complexities of an immune system. A number of systems working simultaneously within the body are responsible for creating a T cell, so creating a matrix of viruses and nanocoders that will rewrite them simultaneously is a very ambitious task."

Stark stood with his hands on his hips. She wasn't making this any clearer. He watched Jarum typing furiously and pretended to listen to Isabel.

"It's like a digital drawing of sunlight," Isabel tried again. "An artist can't predict the natural nuances of how light will fall on every fluttering leaf. The shadows. The shades of green. It will always look wrong to the human eye."

Isabel rarely spoke this way, usually never had patience for the poetry of her work. Stark imagined it was a reflection of her despair.

"It's the same with recoding a whole immune system to recognize even two simple viruses. We can't account for all the subtle processes at work in an immunity response. We can try, but the first immune system will always see the second for what it truly is—an invader. A foreign body," Isabel said. "Simple wetcodes, like recoding eye color or Jarum's rewriting a tropism code, work better. Easy. One sequence, and you can turn any human being into a *mestizo*. One sequence and the virus can attack the *pilone* wetware *and* the immune system—"

Isabel paused.

Her pupils dilated as if something had caught her eye, then she let out a little sigh of a laugh, astounded.

"What?" asked Stark.

Jarum's chair squeaked slowly as he turned to Isabel.

The two doctors stared at one another in a frieze of marvel.

"How could we not have seen it?" Jarum breathed.

"Seen what?" Stark asked.

Isabel closed her eyes, shook her head. "Oh my God."

"What? What?" shouted Stark.

"The *pilone*," Jarum and Isabel said together.

Silence bloated in the room as Stark waited for an explanation.

Jarum turned to Stark and his face seemed to spread apart in a horrified expression. "The matrix will destroy *pilone* wetware. We're differentiating a T cell that will be tropic for the same sequences the virus is."

"But the matrix," Stark said, "won't it—?"

"*Any* successful matrix we create will destroy the virus and the *pilone* wetware," Isabel said, "because they share the same DNA."

"If we want the matrix, we have to forfeit the *pilone* network?" Stark asked.

Isabel nodded.

Panicking, Stark recalled how quickly omnivalent vaccine had been put into production during his phone call with El Mono. "What about a vaccine?"

Jarum shook his head, frowning in dismissal. "Same thing. Vaccine? Recoding matrix? Same thing."

"Joaquin must have known from the beginning," Isabel said. "We've been playing right into his initial strategy with the recoding project."

Stark shook his head in reluctant appreciation. Even shot, captured, and jailed, the man still controlled the battlefield. Would Mexico ever agree to such a drastic measure to stop the outbreak? Stark's mind was filled with the image of Joaquin, lying on his back in a spotlight of his own blood, and he suddenly understood what Joaquin had said in Domenica's cell.

I win either way.

"We have to tell the Holy Renaissance what's at stake," Jarum said. "Cazador will be here soon."

"We can't do that, Jarum," Isabel said.

Stark looked at Isabel, surprised. "We can't?"

Isabel's voice was flat and her eyes were hard, half-closed. "How much time do we have?"

"Less than eight hours," said Stark, checking his tanks again.

"Then we absolutely cannot tell anyone," Isabel said with a derisive shake of her head. "This is our one and only shot."

"But it would be unethical to spring this on them," Jarum said. "All the people who will die as a result of this—?"

"No, no," Isabel said, "*pilone* users won't die. Dengue-6 destroys the Self status of the wetware, and that's what causes immediate death in *pilonistas*. The recoded immune system will simply disable the wetware. It won't try to expel it from the body. When we run the sim, we'll see if I'm right. But Jarum," Isabel said, grabbing the arm of his chair and turning him to face her. She raised an index finger. "Before Cazador arrives, we must agree to say nothing."

"But the chaos and social upheaval? All over again?"

Isabel shook her head. "Compared to a cure for Big Bonebreaker, the *pilone* is an expendable toy."

Jarum said, "But who are we to decide that for a country?"

Stark watched Domenica lie back against her pillows, with Sister Evangelista offering her juice from a cup. He said, "Jarum?"

He looked over at Stark.

"Four words," Stark said. "Grandmother Muñoz's Tripe Soup."

Jarum nodded once, understanding. Then closed his eyes and nodded vigorously, with enthusiasm. "Absolutely. Absolutely right, Henry David." He turned back to his computer and began creating a new sim, titling it *Domenica2*. "I suppose it's the nature of this epidemic that we should have to perform an evil to undo a greater evil," Jarum said.

Isabel lifted her head and looked into Domenica's room. Someone was entering. Someone with an entourage. "Look. It's Cazador."

Stark turned to the window again. The Chief of State's ponderous belly was unmistakable, even in a Racal suit, as he crossed himself, approached Domenica's bed, and crossed himself again.

"Well, well," Stark said. "Someone's had a change of heart about *La Patrona de los Plagos*."

"Cazador's no idiot," Isabel said. "He knows an opportunity when he sees one. He told me so himself."

"What do you mean?" Stark asked.

Cazador knelt and prayed as Domenica put one hand on his shoulder, praying with him.

"He's about to create a Mexican icon out of Domenica—and the Holy Renaissance will take all the credit for it," Isabel said. "He's already scheming for power in a postplague Mexico."

The Majority Holding Cell was filled to suffocation levels. No windows. One door. People in white Racal suits stood on chairs, on waiting benches, on plastic-covered couches, and on any piece of furniture or object that might give a foothold.

At the center of the crush was an *ojo*, feeding live to Rosangelica, who fed the signal straight to her media satellites.

All of Mexico was watching.

Rosangelica sat outside the crowded room. Three soldiers armed with *Sangre de Cristo* class rifles stood beside her and Carriego. They were waiting for her to give the order to clear the room. Rosangelica was watching the *ojo*'s feed as it flickered across her optic nerve's screen, waiting for just the right moment.

She cued the *ojo* inside the holding facility.

>*ojo*< Get in close. Interview him. Get him to talk.< She told him.

The *ojo* pressed between people packed into the little room, inching toward the bars. "Hello? Dr. Delgado? Hello?"

Joaquin sat stiff-backed in the one occupied cell, right leg stretched out in front of him. He looked out at the crowd through vertical bars that hummed with a charge. The room was so quiet that the *ojo* was picking up the sound of electricity coursing through the bars. Rosangelica waited for the tension to mount.

The gathering was silent in its fury. Would Joaquin address them? Attempt to explain himself? Hurl vituperative insults through the bars at his captors?

Rosangelica hoped so.

From her node, she fed a series of reports through the Holy Renaissance propaganda engine. She began with historical documents from twenty-five years ago, spewing them across the *pilone* network:

Student Joaquin Delgado Defies Mayor Emil Orbegón of Monterrey.

Joaquin Delgado Casts Aspersions on Rising Holy Renaissance.

Joaquin Delgado Joins US Centers for Disease Control.

Then she moved on to more current events. *All Signs Point to Joaquin*

Delgado as Big Bonebreaker Terrorist. Joaquin Delgado Murders Three Mexican Sabihondos. *Joaquin Delgado Captured Attempting to Murder Santa Domenica.*

That last report was from the Chief of State's office and had Roberto's air about it. He was making a play for Domenica, taking her into his fold and creating a Holy Renaissance saint out of her. Let him. Let Roberto Cazador reinstate Stark, too, and let him take credit for a cure. It was ultimately too abstract. *Humans are fearful beasts,* Rosangelica thought. *They need security more than they want hope.* And they wanted to see villains slain more than they wanted heroes exalted.

"Besides, the nun's an insurgent," Carriego had said to Rosangelica. "That one will blow up in Cazador's face."

Outside the holding facility, beyond the *plasceron*-glass barrier that the three guards had locked in place, was another wall of white moon suits. Three hundred people, Carriego had warned her, were spilling out into the esplanade outside.

"Dr. Delgado," the *ojo* was saying. "Dr. Delgado, were you trying to kill Emil Orbegón? Is that why you did it? Did you want to kill Cardinal de Veras, too?"

The feeds streaming through her wetware fell away as Rosangelica's full attention bored in on Joaquin Delgado.

"Are you a racist, Doctor? Do you hate Mexicans?"

Joaquin said nothing. He sat with his palms flat on his thighs, staring at the floor in front of him.

Rosangelica feared the lack of response would kill the moment. But no, it fueled it. The people in the holding facility wanted answers. The three hundred people outside wanted inside, wanted answers. Aggregate figures comprised of *pilone*-user ratio, reaction/approval ratings, and *pilone* market shares were scaling toward 85 percent, Rosangelica noted, tapping her marketing sats.

All of Mexico was watching, listening, and hating.

The guards looked back and forth between the two groups on either side of them and gripped the barrels of their rifles. Their one exit was a door behind Rosangelica, guarded by Carriego. She'd made certain it was open after allowing that crowd into the holding facility.

The *ojo* edged ever closer to the bars. He still had a couple helmets blocking his view of Joaquin. "Can't you tell us why?" The *ojo* was getting frustrated with Joaquin's silence. "Tell us why, Doctor!"

Rosangelica urged him on. >*ojo*< You've got him now. Now's your chance! He can't ignore you!<

"You used to live in Ascensión!" the *ojo* shouted. "You spent your childhood here! How could you do this to your *pueblo*?"

Good, Rosangelica thought, watching the aggregates—*87%. Good.*

"You invented the *pilone*!" someone near the *ojo* shouted. "You invented wetware!"

"You gave Mexico our prosperity and place in the world!" someone else shouted.

"Why would you betray Emil the Damned after he fed you in Monterrey?"

Eighty-nine percent. A saturated market with barely a single passive viewer in the audience. Rosangelica crossed herself.

Someone outside the holding facility's *plasceron* barrier shouted, "You gave birth to the Holy Renaissance! Why would you turn around and destroy us?"

Inside the holding facility, the room had built to a roar of Racal-suit speakers, crackling with invectives.

"*¡Hijo de puta!*"

"*¡Diablo! ¡Cabrón!*"

"*¡Diablo!*"

The *ojo* reached the bars.

The aggregate number in the corner of Rosangelica's eye reached 92 percent.

Joaquin looked up, right at the *ojo*.

Right at Mexico.

"There it is. Come on. Follow me," Carriego said.

Rosangelica led the three guards after Carriego, out through the side door. In her optic nerve she saw Joaquin shake his head in magnificent sadness.

When they were safely in the director's office, Carriego locked the door, then Rosangelica fed the code into the holding facility security node, causing the *plasceron* barrier to slide aside.

The room Rosangelica had just vacated filled immediately with shouting and shoving as three hundred people pushed their way in.

Ninety-six percent.

Joaquin's eyes were full of hatred for the list of accomplishments and epithets being shouted at him, Rosangelica imagined. But staring into the eyes of the *ojo* as Joaquin was, it looked like hatred for Mexico.

Allí está, Rosangelica thought.

Then she popped the bolts on the door of his cell, and the crowd poured in, past the *ojo,* and Joaquin disappeared in a swarm of Racal suits.

CHAPTER

35

THE CATHEDRAL DE SAN CUAUHTÉMOC had chambers above, built right into the crimson and gold ceiling, not for balconies or choirs, but for light. Alabaster statues gazed over the giant space below, like angels peering down from the vaults of heaven, shafts of milky sunlight fell on their faces, on the human beings below. These weren't statues of white-gowned angels, Stark realized, looking more closely from beside the altar. They were bloody saints, wounded in their martyrdom. San Felipe by spears. San Esteban by arrows. San Bartolome and San Xipe, flayed. They hovered above in their chambers of light as the Cathedral of La Alta filled beyond its two-thousand-person capacity with the political court of Ascensión, and seemed to watch with the resignation of the mortally wounded.

Hope you folks up there got some sway, Stark thought. A cordon of soldiers, wearing gloves and masks, marched suited members of the Orbegón presidential family into the cathedral, and all those present stood. *We about to let loose some more chaos down here.*

Infrared cameras flashed from the meager international media corps, as Lady Stephanie Orbegón, the president's wife, walked in front, leading her grown children and toddling grandchildren, all in Racal suits of red and black. Behind them strode Emil the Damned, an imposing *ranchero* of a man, wearing the simple clear plastic clamp mask and rubber gloves of a hot-zone relief worker. He walked in slow meditative steps, his folded hands leading the way.

Stark stepped aside as the president approached the altar. Orbegón crossed himself, kissed his fingertips, crossed himself again, then one last time. He ascended the altar steps and walked toward Stark with his hand out. Stark felt like a teenage boy next to the towering Orbegón. "Thanks to God for making this possible, Dr. Stark," said Emil Orbegón.

Stark shook his hand, looking up into the famous face with its moustache and chevron eyebrows, unable to decide if Orbegón were thanking him or God. Stark kept quiet.

A squad of septic troops in full Racal suits took up position between the Orbegóns and the crowd, and next came a parade of men in red capes and red skullcaps. *The Holy Renaissance,* Stark figured, the *real* Holy Renaissance—not the political party, but Cardinal de Veras and his band of rebel bishops and cardinals who had split from the Vatican. Preceded by lit incense, their capes swirled through the smoke as they walked to the altar.

Stark looked down at his air-tank timepiece. *Quite a show the nun and the Jefe put together on such short notice.*

"You name it," Roberto Cazador had said, after the Task Force had confirmed that the matrix was ready with a 78 percent chance of success. "You tell me how you want it done, Sor Domenica, and I will make it happen."

Domenica, mouth pustules cracking around the margins of her lips, smiled. Her fever made her eyes bloodshot, but they gleamed with desire. "I want it with the Holy Renaissance there to watch me go. I want the Orbegóns there. I want every *ojo* and camera in the city there."

"Of course," Cazador said. Such trifles were obvious, and under way.

Stark watched the actress buried in the nun reemerge. "Mexico needs this ritual, and we want it to be fabulous."

The cathedral doors opened a third time, and a procession of flickering red candles in silver candlesticks entered. "The train of the Mexican saint," Domenica had called it, describing the details to Cazador. Thirty girls in white coveralls, carrying votive candles. "Not one over the age of thirteen. The essence of virginity. Mexico expects purity now."

Stark was disgusted by Domenica and Cazador, feeding on each other's enthusiasm in the sim lab, devising this spectacular sacrifice. Domenica had wanted the Basilica for the site of her death. Cazador did one better and gave her the La Alta Cathedral San Cuauhtémoc. Domenica asked for the political elite to attend; Cazador gave her the very nucleus of the Holy Renaissance. Domenica had wanted a display that would resonate for her insurgent allies, Stark figured, and Cazador obviously wanted Orbegón to seize control of this symbolism after she was dead. So they used one another, each to their own extravagant, Machiavellian ends. From the altar, Stark could see by the expectant faces of those in attendance that the symbolism of the event was working on everyone in the cathedral.

After the thirty girls took their places along the steps of the altar, Sister Domenica finally appeared. The crowd, which had swelled to perhaps three thousand, surged toward the central aisle to see her entrance. The nun lay in a crystal coffin bordered by gold, wearing a black mantle embroidered with a red cross. Eight men in red-and-black antiviral suits carried the coffin on a bier.

"Is she dead?" a woman shouted, and people throughout the crowd repeated the question.

As Domenica passed into the cathedral, Stark could see that a white veil and wimple adorned the nun's head. Holding the cross of a rosary, her hands were folded on her chest. Lilies and roses covered the glass case, and a small cross of red paper lay close to her head. Sitting up against red-and-black pillows, Domenica stared straight at Orbegón as she approached him. She didn't look like an insurgent nun or a radical street actress. She was now a sixteenth-century Madonna straight out of the Black Plague.

The soldiers pushed the crowd back and the Orbegóns separated to allow the processional to ascend the altar. Behind her bier, two men carried a great crucifix, the wooden Christ sprawled across it in cruel detail. Thorns bit into His brow. Fingers clutched the nails in His palms. His side spilled painted blood like an open faucet and His legs were mangled. *What Mexico does to their saviors,* Stark thought.

As coffin and cross were positioned on the altar, the cathedral fell silent. Three priests stepped forward and lifted the lid from the glass coffin, dumping the flowers aside. Sister Domenica struggled to sit up and a great cheer exploded in the square. The thirty girls set down their small candles and stepped forward with large spools of red ribbon. They handed the ends to Sister Domenica and the girls unreeled the ribbons out into the crowd. The crowd took the spools and passed them to the back of the cathedral, connecting crowd to nun.

"Santa Domenica!" People struggled and fought to grasp ribbons. "Santa Domenica!"

When the spools had been unwound, Sister Domenica cried out,

"*¡Mexicanistas!*" Her voice was strained but clear. She repeated the call until her voice sounded lonely in the vast cavern of the church. "This morning, Lord Jesus Christ suffered the disease unto me! He brought it to me and I accepted it."

Penitents at the back of the church cried out before she'd finished her sentence and the crowd wailed its disbelief.

"The disease was a puzzle but it has been solved. It was a mystery, but no more," Sister Domenica's clear soprano voice rang out. "Tonight, the first vaccine will be released to you. But I am the price you pay for the cure."

A priest motioned to Stark and he stepped forward carrying racks of liter bottles attached to hospital tubing. While the priest bent low to Sister Domenica's ear, reading to her from a small black book, Stark rolled up the sleeves of her mantle. He then arranged the bottles nearby and there was a long pause as the nun nodded and answered the priest quietly.

Domenica and the priest crossed themselves, and Stark came forward with the recoding solution that would either design potent T cells or pass uselessly from her body—either way, in terrible hemorrhages.

Seventy-eight percent success ratio, Stark reminded himself as fear and doubt passed over him.

Domenica raised her hand, holding him in place for a moment. She turned to the congregation, and said, "By tomorrow night, we will know how successful the cure is," she said. "You can put your babies to bed without fear that they will not wake up. You can read that book you were meaning to read a month ago, take that long walk in the park without wearing plastic gloves." The crowd prayed, sighed, and some laughed with hope that her words would come true, crossing themselves, all three thousand of them. "Tomorrow night," Domenica continued, "after you've received the vaccine, you can take off your masks and light that cigarette you've been waiting to smoke."

The crowd laughed quietly, caught in the light anxiety of contradiction, perhaps, of virtue advising vice.

But Stark didn't laugh. He knew what she was advising.

Tomorrow night, after the vaccination program was well under way, the *pilone* network would crash again.

The long line of M32s in the club-cum-church.

Old Antonio.

The unsmoked cigarette.

How could she know?

Domenica looked up into his face, a challenge in her bloodshot eyes, and nodded to Stark. *Go ahead.*

Stark looked over at the rangy Emil Orbegón, who closed his eyes behind his spectacles when Stark turned toward him. Right under the Holy Renaissance's nose, she had just signaled to Old Antonio and Pirate that the revolution should begin tomorrow night.

Stark whispered in his lowest, kneeling beside her glass coffin, "How do you know what the vaccine will do?"

"Pedro," she whispered to Stark, leaning back against the pillows. "He told me that if you came up with a vaccine," Domenica motioned him closer so that she could whisper right in his ear, "the *pilone* would fall, that the Holy Renaissance would be helpless against us."

"Sister, I can't," Stark whispered, holding the syringe that carried the recoding matrix. "I told you this morning, I'm not Mexican. This isn't my fight. I can't be the one to do this."

Domenica laid a hand on his wrist and gave him her eyes again, but it was a new expression, devilish and playful, a face he had only seen in the old images of Chana Chenalho. "I say," she whispered, "that you are Mexican."

Stark was ready to step away from the glass coffin, call Rosangelica to him, and end this fabulous show.

"'You are indigenous even though you are not indigenous,'" hissed Domenica. "The Purépecha elders told that to another white named Marcos, many, many, years ago." She tightened her grip on his wrist when he tried to step away. "I told you when we first met that I know you. And I do. I saw your land in you, the way you stood, and the way you spoke. You're never just a doctor." Domenica lifted her hand from Stark's arm, freeing him. "You're never not a farmer. You are always of the land, and so you are us."

Stark closed his eyes. Her words were like a release, a flame of relief.

"Now. Take my blood." Domenica touched Stark's chest and gently pushed him away. "Do what you have to do."

Stark turned and scanned the crowd with furtive eyes, saw Isabel, and held her gaze for a long moment until finally she nodded, crossing herself.

Stark knelt and pressed the tip of the needle into the crook of Domenica's arm. She shut her eyes. Then he injected her, the needle penetrating her skin, entering her vein. He was bonded to Domenica in the moment, fingers on syringe, needle in skin. He was connected to her land, as though his heart were beating blood into these people through the needle, through the red ribbons, down into the veins of Mexico, beating in his own self, into HD, his grandfather's farm, his land, and this land back into his own body. He wasn't just giving them a cure. He was giving Mexico a new future, a new land, and taking back for himself, he realized, the same thing.

Almost immediately Domenica pressed herself backwards into the glass coffin, sucking in a great, gasping lungful of air and clutching the fabric of her dress.

Stark backed away. The feeling of interconnection fled as he looked down at Domenica in her agony. His instinct was to help her, but Domenica had said Mexico would want to see her death, however bloody it might be, so he retreated to the far side of the altar, by Orbegón. Stark felt as though something had been severed from his body as he turned away, his head bent, and hands covering his face.

But Mexico watched. They had seen this scene too many times in the last week, in death and destruction, not to want to see it now in healing. Blood gushed from Domenica's nostrils first. Then her mouth. Blood smeared along the glass walls of the coffin and three thousand people screamed at once. A startled flock of doves took flight from inside one of the ceiling chambers and their wings glittered through spot lighting aimed at the saints. The crowd pushed forward, but the cordon of guards kept them back.

Next to Sister Domenica's dying body, one bottle filled red. Then another, filling each until all three sat like red cylinders on the altar. The pheresis began spinning in the cylinders, plasma separating from the red blood cells. Arresters in the bases of the cylinders began counting platelets and immunocytes, isolating them for the matrix of wetcoded viral engines to come.

Touching his tongue to his healed lip, Stark lowered his hands when he heard the whir of the phereses and watched Orbegón descend the steps to pray with his family. Jarum Ahwaz ascended the steps to examine the results. Stark could see the future from the altar, as sure as he was watching it on a monitor. If the recoding was successful, a thousand pallets of vaccine would be cloned by midnight. And another thousand by morning. Vaccination teams would circle the hot zones, and by nightfall tomorrow, after another two thousand more pallets of vaccine had been distributed, the vaccine would disable enough wetware that the *pilone* network would crash for the second time. Old Antonio would give the order, and *Los Hijos de Marcos* would engage confused, disConnected Holy Renaissance troops in Ascensión. A similar thing would happen in Texas and the Mexican government would find itself pinched between reinvigorated civil unrest and hungry US Federal troops, eager for revenge. There wouldn't be time for Cazador, Ofelio Xultan, or even Rosangelica to analyze why the *pilone* network had fallen. The revolt would be swift, Stark prophesied, and the murderers would be cleansed from Mexico's halls of power.

Jarum straightened and looked at Stark until Stark turned and met his eye. "Done. We have it isolated."

"And?" said Stark.

Jarum had a hitch in his voice. "I'll take this back to the lab and begin cloning at once."

From his pew, Emil the Damned heard Jarum and smiled. The president kissed his wife, then faced the two doctors, standing and raising his hand in a salute of thanks.

CHAPTER

I AM SELF, said the twin viruses, week after week, whispering into the ear of the immune system. *I am you,* they lied, speaking the body's own language. They held up mirrors to the collective immune system, whispering, *Look, I am you, I am you,* as they bred with the body's own cells, leaping from skin to skin via handshakes, kisses, family dinners, laughter—infecting, breeding, killing. Infecting, breeding, killing.

The collective immunity had never seen these viruses before. T cells searched their inherited memories, the immunological archives from the mothers of every previous generation, but wrongly called these viruses *dengue.*

Then tidings came from outside the body. A barrage of wetcoded viruses and nanorecorders appeared, carrying information about the twin viruses and how to fight them. Immediately, a new T cell entered the bloodstream.

I am you, the augmented cell said. *The viruses are not.*

Like a vision, the body could now see what had to be done to protect itself. Integrating and imitating the new information, the immune system created an army of defenders, mimicking the genetic structure of the augmented immunocyte.

I am Self, said the vaccinated body, and its colonies of killer T cells agreed, *We are Self.*

When the viruses leapt into the vaccinated body, this phalanx immediately inspected, arraigned, and killed the viruses before they could find purchase.

We are Self, said the phalanx, as it identified cells in the brain that did not belong in the body. *You are not Self,* they told the *pilone* wetware. The defenders lysed these cells, rendering them ineffective. *Now you are Self, too.*

The collective immunity transformed into an ever-constricting maze in the population, and the viruses found fewer and fewer bodies in which to breed. Those that received vaccinations imparted a kind of immunity on those that didn't, a statistical barrier between the viruses and the unvaccinated. Working in tandem with nanophages that entered the bloodstream and devoured the viruses, the body of Mexico, week by week, quelled the epidemic.

You are gone. We remain. We remember. We are Self.

Afterward, the immune systems of vaccinated women wrote the names of the viruses into the archives of their immunological memories—a benefit unforeseen by the designers of the augmented T cell. If they became mothers, these women imparted to their babies the names of the two viruses, so the bodies of their children would always remember.

We are Self.

ABOUT THE AUTHOR

Barth Anderson's short stories have appeared in *Asimov's*, *Strange Horizons*, *Polyphony*, *Alchemy*, *Talebones*, *The Journal of Mythic Arts*, and a variety of other quality venues. Barth received the Spectrum Award for Best Short Fiction in 2004, and he writes regularly for *Utne Reader*'s Best of Indie Press–nominated *Wedge Newsletter*. He lives in Minneapolis with his wife and son. *The Patron Saint of Plagues* is his first novel.